MISTLETOE & MR. RIGHT

SARAH MORGENTHALER

 sourcebooks casablanca

Published by Sourcebooks Casablanca, an imprint of Sourcebooks
P.O. Box 4410, Naperville, Illinois 60567-4410
(630) 961-3900
sourcebooks.com

Library of Congress Cataloging-in-Publication Data

Names: Morgenthaler, Sarah, author.
Title: Mistletoe and Mr. Right / Sarah Morgenthaler.
Other titles: Mistletoe and Mister Right
Description: Naperville, Illinois : Sourcebooks Casablanca, an imprint of
    Sourcebooks, [2020]
Identifiers: LCCN 2020020039 (print) | LCCN 2020020040
(ebook) Subjects: GSAFD: Love stories.
Classification: LCC PS3613.O74878 M57
2020 (print) | LCC PS3613.O74878
    (ebook) | DDC 813/.6--dc23
LC record available at https://lccn.loc.gov/2020020039
LC ebook record available at https://lccn.loc.gov/2020020040

Printed and bound in the United States of America.
SB 10 9 8 7 6 5 4 3 2 1

For the best parents ever. Thanks for always believing in me.

CHAPTER 1

SOMEONE HAD DRAWN A GIANT penis in the snow.

"At least it's anatomically correct." Newly minted Moose Springs, Alaska, property mogul Lana Montgomery tilted her head, considering the artwork carved so precisely into the mountainside.

"A snow angel might have been more appropriate." Ben, her construction manager, scratched the back of his neck, trying and failing to keep a professional tone. "It is two weeks until Christmas."

"Yes, but then the message might have been lost. At least the mistletoe is a nice touch."

Nothing said *screw you* like an acre-wide penis pointed at your future construction site.

Ben exhaled a breath into the cold winter air as if trying to cover a snort. "The locals are consistent, I'll give them that."

The penis was causing problems, as penises tended to do. The artwork was the most recent in a long list of attempts by the Moose Springs locals to halt Lana's luxury condominium project. At least the snow art was refreshingly different from her normal issues: an accountant stealing from the family company here, insufficient returns from an ill-advised investment there, and bad PR from someone in the family playing too hard with the Montgomery money just about everywhere.

A cheerful approach to life meant Lana was good at smoothing things over, but cheerfulness didn't help the slight crow's-feet at the corners of her eyes or the permanent stress line trying to carve itself into her forehead.

Thirty-two was too young to feel the weight of her responsibilities this heavily.

"I can get a snowcat out here to level this out," Ben offered.

"Let's leave it for a while." Lana smiled congenially at her contractor. "Let them have their fun. Someone went to an awful lot of effort to put this here without being seen, and I'd hate to disappoint them. Plus, who knows what they might choose for the follow-up pièce de résistance?"

"They don't get to you at all, do they?"

"I'm not *completely* immune to the attention." Lana scooped a handful of snow into her gloved palm. "I'm also hoping it won't take too much time before they stop being angry with me."

"You did buy up the entire town," Ben said with an amused look. "Folks in a place this small don't take that sort of thing lightly."

"Property owners hold a lot of political sway in Moose Springs. We can't build a condominium on a mountainside without the town council's approval."

"And you wonder why they don't like you." Ben softened his teasing with a good-natured chuckle. "Don't worry. As soon as the place gets built, they'll get used to it…in a couple dozen generations or so."

Montgomerys didn't snort. At least they didn't in public, but what happened on a penis-carved mountainside stayed on a penis-carved mountainside. "Be careful, Ben. Your optimism is showing."

Ben barked out a laugh, then waved his hand for her to follow him. She lobbed the snowball toward the closest mistletoe leaf before heading back to her snowmobile. It slipped and slid on the loose powdery snow until she maneuvered into Ben's tracks. They circled the mountainside property the Montgomery Group had purchased from Moose Springs Resort and then tightened the circle to where her eventual luxury condominiums would be built.

Key word: eventual.

At the top of today's to-do list was checking on the construction site progress. As sites went, this one was sorely lacking. So far, they'd only driven tall stakes with bright orange plastic flags on the tops to mark the boundaries of what would soon become the riskiest venture Lana had ever started.

The condominiums were meant to lure the rich and powerful from all over the world into permanently sinking their wealth into the town of Moose Springs instead of simply arriving for a two-week ski vacation every other year. New residents would enjoy all the amenities of the resort with the permanence of a personal vacation home.

If Lana could get the darn place built.

As they reached the top of the site, highest on the mountainside, the town was at its best view. The lake below Moose Springs Resort had frozen over, now crisscrossed with tracks from snowmobiles and sledding children. Nestled in the bottom of the valley were tiny buildings set among thick stands of evergreen: the homes and businesses and people of Moose Springs. The lifeblood of this town.

Lana loved Moose Springs in a way she'd never loved anything before. It had stolen her heart and soul since her first visit as a young child, and she was determined to drive a stabilizing steel bar through the picturesque Alaskan town's shaky, tourism-driven economy no matter what. But just because she believed in what she was doing didn't mean the town did too.

Lana hadn't given up hope she could get them on board with her plans, but as of yet, she had very little support in either the community or her holding company.

"Ask for forgiveness, not permission," she said to herself as they slowed. Calling forward over the rumble of the engines, she asked Ben, "Are you sure we can't break ground sooner?"

"Not unless we want to be digging through eight feet of snow."

Lana's work schedule limited her time in Moose Springs, but she was invested in doing this project right. For months, she and Ben had been up to their elbows in architect plans, zoning requirements, and a sleigh full of red tape. She'd hoped their progress would have been further by now.

"I thought construction during winter was common in Alaska," Lana said.

"Yeah, if you need a roof replaced or a kitchen remodeled. Not this behemoth. Listen," Ben said, "it's not impossible, but the costs for site prep are going to skyrocket, and there's not much we can do about getting material in until the access road gets widened and the gravel down. Ever tried to off-road a semi loaded with heavy equipment?"

"Point made. We wait until spring." When Ben opened his mouth, Lana added, "*Early* spring. I'm getting this done as fast as humanly possible. And, Ben? When you start hiring day labor, supplement your crew with as many local hires as you can, please. It'll save us on per diem."

He gave her a knowing look but didn't call Lana out on her decision. Her construction manager knew exactly why she wanted the locals to benefit from the jobs this project would provide.

She really did love Moose Springs. Which only made it worse knowing how much they hated her.

In the distance, a heavy cloud clung to the top of the highest peak, one usually obscured by the weather on less clear days than this.

"Mount Veil is looking particularly ominous today," she mentioned, stalling because she would much rather stay outside with Ben then go back to her suite. Moose Springs Resort was a world-class luxury hotel offering absolutely anything she could possibly want, but an empty room got lonely. Besides, the snow-covered Alaskan mountains were always worth taking a moment to appreciate.

Ben glanced at the giant hovering in the distance. "Veil's not Denali, but it's one badass monster. You ever try to climb it?"

"I'm more of a snowmobile girl." Lana patted the handle of her ride.

"If you're going to be a resident of Moose Springs, you're going to need to use the right lingo. This is a snow machine."

"I'm not a resident," she informed him. "I stay in the resort."

"You own property, don't you?"

"The company owns property, not me."

Chicago, London, Singapore, the Virgin Islands...the Montgomery Group had their hands everywhere. But just because it was easier to stay at her family's holdings didn't mean she belonged in any of them. In the first thirty some years of her life, Lana had learned a lot from the company. Negotiating a million-dollar deal over cocktails was a normal Thursday for her. She could outmaneuver veteran CEOs while making a single martini double twist to perfection. But she'd never learned how to feel at home.

"Buying land doesn't make you part of a town, Ben. I wish it were that easy."

"Well, ma'am, either way, you had better get down to the town hall meeting."

"Why is that?"

Ben grinned at her. "Because they're still trying to figure out how to get rid of you."

Most town hall meetings were held in, well, a town hall. But not Moose Springs.

In Moose Springs, town hall meetings were held in an abandoned barn on the far side of town, complete with snow piled up around the building to near impassability. If one wanted to get to the barn door closest to a parking spot, they better have some gumption and a sturdy pair of shoes.

Wading through knee-deep snow in high heels was never fun, so Lana changed into a cute but sturdy pair of boots she kept in the backseat for this very purpose.

When she reached the door, it stuck, so Lana put her weight behind her pull. Apparently, the barn had not only been decorated for the holidays on the outside, but it was also being used to store the town's Christmas decorations. Someone had stacked a pile of three-foot-tall plastic Christmas elves against the other side of the door, because when it finally swung open, the elves saw their chance to make their escape. She jumped back to avoid the avalanche, ending up in a snowbank halfway to her now very cold knees. The closest elf was facedown in a boot hole, looking like it had officially given up on making it through the holidays with a semblance of dignity.

Through the open doorway, Lana could see that the inside of the barn had been turned into a makeshift town hall. Folding chairs filled what once had been a large area to store hay.

As everyone in the back few rows turned in their seats to stare at her out in the snow, Lana gave them an awkward wave.

"That was unexpected," she said, trying to cover her embarrassment with cheerfulness.

"There's another entrance on the other side," someone muttered.

Well. That certainly would have been informative.

Rescuing half a dozen cheap plastic elves from a snowy death wasn't the worst thing she'd ever done, although she would have appreciated a few less smirks aimed her way. Lana never had liked it when everyone looked at her when she stepped into a room. She was used to it, but she didn't like it.

She'd learned a long time ago to compensate for that discomfort by throwing her best and brightest smile to the room. Usually it worked to lessen the tension, but not this time. The gathered townsfolk most definitely didn't smile back.

The smiles had been fewer and farther between since her condominium project had been announced.

"Tough crowd," she told the plastic elves in her arms.

If Ben hadn't told her where they held town hall meetings, she never would have been able to find it. By the looks she received when she headed toward the front of the barn, more than a few people wouldn't have minded her absence. But as meeting halls went, the barn worked well. A wooden stage had been built on the end farthest from where Lana had made her less-than-grand entrance, and at least most of the people present hadn't witnessed her faux pas. They'd scooted the chairs around to form rows facing the makeshift stage up front.

They'd tried to make the barn seasonally appropriate, filling it with a cheerful if haphazard assortment of holiday decor. Most was fairly innocuous, but liberties had been taken with Rudolph's antlers, and something seemed to be going on between Mrs. Claus and Frosty the Snowman if the twinkle in her eye was to be believed. The pile of elves had been hanging out near the rear escape exit, the one Lana had unwittingly entered. They'd probably had the right idea.

The combination of strings of blinking Christmas lights, red and green plastic ornaments, blue and white papier-mâché snowflakes, and gold sparkles painted on popcorn balls was somewhat jarring. Someone had mounted a star on the top of a cardboard cutout of a lamp made out of a woman's stockinged leg, with several presents stuck underneath.

Drawing her coat close to chase away the chill, Lana scanned the room, searching for a friendly face among the familiar ones. She breathed a sigh of relief when she spotted a short, slender brunette in glasses seated off to the side, across the room from a folding table loaded with coffee urns and holiday treats. Zoey Caldwell glanced up from the book in her lap as Lana approached, brightening when Lana waved at her in greeting.

"I saved Graham a seat, but you can have his," Zoey said. "He's been a brat all day."

"Is he ever not a brat?" Lana replied, sitting next to her best friend.

"Hmm, good point." Zoey's boyfriend was many things, and a brat was definitely one of them.

The constant good mood Zoey had been in since meeting Graham and moving to Moose Springs the previous summer still hadn't faded, and she gave Lana an enthusiastic hug. A hug Lana happily returned. It was embarrassing to admit how much Lana wanted those hugs…and needed them. They had met years ago at a truck stop diner outside Chicago. Zoey had been Lana's waitress, and something between them had simply clicked. If Lana had to be honest with herself—which was more of a pain than she wanted to think about at the moment—her relationship with Zoey was the healthiest human interaction she'd experienced in her entire life. And it meant more to Lana than Zoey realized that they would be spending the holidays together.

Lana glanced around. "I was hoping Jake would be here."

Jake was originally Graham's dog, but all three of them worked equally hard at securing the blind border collie's affection. So far, Zoey was winning.

"We asked him if he wanted to come, but he preferred to sleep by the fireplace." Adjusting her glasses, Zoey said, "I think he was done being dressed for the day. Graham changed his outfit four times."

"Jake's wearing pajamas right now, isn't he?"

"His Christmas Ninja Turtle pj's," Zoey said. "They're his *favorite*." They both knew whose favorite those pj's actually were. "How did the meeting go?"

"Festively phallic," Lana said. "How did it go meeting Graham's parents?"

"They're like him. Loving, wonderful, excessively loquacious. Their place in Anchorage is right off the inlet, and it's very cute."

"But?"

"But that's a lot of Barnett humor in one room." Zoey shuddered. "I might need to crash with you tonight so I don't murder him."

"My couch is always yours." Lana squeezed Zoey's hand, briefly leaning into her friend's shoulder companionably. "I don't think the heater is doing much to help."

"Graham is bringing another one and some more chairs. I guess people always show up when his cousin's wife, Leah, makes her holiday mix."

As Zoey expounded on the deliciousness of holiday mixes, Lana made a mental note. Leah, Graham's cousin's wife, owner of a local car rental business and one of Lana's recent acquisitions. These days, it seemed like everyone was either directly or indirectly affected by her company's mass purchase.

"You have your work face on." Zoey nudged Lana with her elbow. "You've been running a hundred miles an hour since this summer. You need a day off."

"If I took a day off, I wouldn't know what to do with myself," Lana replied. Zoey wasn't wrong though. Lana was dying for a day of no phone calls, no emails, and no penises.

"Have you ever been to one of these things?" Zoey asked.

Lana started to answer, but Zoey was immediately distracted as her boyfriend arrived, his muscled arms full of space heaters.

Graham Barnett, a cheerful Alaskan local in his late twenties, was about as handsome as a man could get. Tall and broad shouldered, Graham tried his best to be lazy as often as life would let him, which wasn't very often these days. Despite his best efforts to the contrary, Graham's small one-man diner, the Tourist Trap, had become a foodie sensation for the thousands of guests who passed through Moose Springs every year.

Despite trying to run his customers off with grumpiness and bad service, they just kept coming back in droves…Lana included. His specialty cocktail, the Growly Bear, had become world-renowned, in spite of Graham thinking they were disgusting. Considering Graham had wanted to be a professional chainsaw artist and live a life of solitude in the woods, he found the entire successful entrepreneur thing to be very disappointing.

Pausing just inside the doorway, Graham searched for Zoey in the crowd. Beside her, Lana could hear Zoey's breath catch. The pair met the previous summer over one of those Growly Bears, when Zoey had joined Lana on a two-week vacation over the Fourth of July. Since the moment they first locked eyes, the diner owner had been smitten. And since Zoey had chosen to stay in Moose Springs permanently, the pair had been inseparable.

Happy was a good look on both her friends.

"Hey, Romeo, move it," a muffled female voice spoke up from behind Graham. "My arms are getting tired."

Chuckling, he moved into the barn, looking for a place to set his heaters. Graham's best friends—the very tall, very man-bunned Easton, and Easton's heavily tattooed twin sister, Ashtyn—followed him, their arms full of extra folding chairs. Where one found a Graham, one usually would find the Lockett twins, although it was impossible to identify the leader in their little trio. Easton's expression was hidden behind his reddish-brown beard, but Ashtyn's super short, multicolored spiky hair was both visible and fabulous.

"I wish I could pull off that style," Lana said as she watched Ash, fingers absently touching her shoulder-length auburn locks. The closest she'd come to exciting was freshly redone lowlights for the winter.

"I wish I were brave enough to." Zoey quirked a grin at Lana. "Brace yourself. A Moose Springs town hall is nothing like what you'd expect. They get a little weird."

"Quirky weird or get-out-of-the-room weird?"

"It's more like...do you remember that guy who always came in at the end of my shifts on Friday nights?"

"The one with the underwear or the one without?"

"The one without." Zoey rubbed her hands together to warm them. "This will be worse."

In a place where Lana was an outsider, being reminded of her and Zoey's shared history caused a rush of affection to wash over her. And she wasn't the only one overwhelmed with affection for Zoey Caldwell. Graham's face split into a broad, almost silly grin as he strode across the room, ignoring the leg lamp and heading straight for them. He dropped into the seat Zoey had saved on her other side and kissed her.

"Hey there, Zoey Bear." He wrapped his arm around her shoulders, giving her the perfect place to snuggle for warmth at his side. Over Zoey's head, Graham offered Lana an amused look. "Greetings, supreme overtaker."

"Graham, stop." Zoey frowned at him, poking his stomach with a finger. "You're going to make her feel bad."

"He's only teasing me," Lana said. "Graham teases the people he likes."

"See?" Graham flashed her that charming look of his, the one that always got him out of trouble. "L knows me."

That was true enough. Most importantly, Lana knew that of all the locals, Graham hated her plans for Moose Springs the most. He'd spearheaded most of the attempts to delay her condominiums, and he wouldn't mind one bit if her project failed. But that didn't mean he wasn't her friend. He'd still hug her when he saw her and get mad if someone called her a rude name. He'd let her throw rambunctious parties at his diner if she needed a distraction for the evening, and he'd break pretty much every "no tourist" rule he had for her in the name of a friendship they'd been cultivating for several years now.

They just didn't always agree on the tourism thing.

"I'm going to get myself a treat." Lana stood up, smiling warmly at her friends. "Would you like anything?"

"Usually I'm the one tossing food your way. I'm happy to sit back and let you be the bearer of delicious things."

"I'd like a coffee, please," Zoey said.

"A complicated, no-one-can-get-it-right, super coffee with the exact right amount of everything, or she'll give you hell for it."

"Lana will get it right."

"Einstein couldn't get it right." Graham winked at Zoey.

"Lana's much smarter than you, and even if she did get it wrong, I wouldn't say anything. Unlike you, who has deliberately screwed up my coffee every day this week because you think it's funny."

"You get the cutest little scrunchy face when it's too sweet—"

"Graham."

"Or not sweet enough."

"*Graham.*"

"Or if there's *regular* dairy instead of nondairy creamer—"

Lana left them to their conversation, having been exposed to their antics enough to know how this would progress. Graham's particular brand of affection was exactly what Zoey needed in her life. And if Graham following her around like a lovesick puppy was any indicator, she was exactly what he needed too.

Lana didn't know what she needed, but some eggnog would be a pleasant start.

A table had been set up along the wall, complete with coffee urn and cookies, the little hard ones from a Christmas-themed tin. So far, no one was eating the cookies, preferring a large Tupperware container full of homemade party mix. Sadly, there was no eggnog and not enough hands, so Lana fixed coffees for three instead. Taking a small portion of party mix and two cookies out of politeness instead of any real desire to consume either, Lana turned and bumped cookie plate to cookie plate into the man behind her.

"Oops, sorry. *Oh*. Hello, Rick." Lana glanced up at the only person in town who made her heart skip an extra beat.

"Hey." The quiet, rumbled word was nice, especially from a man more known for nodding than talking.

Hazel eyes a shade greener than she remembered gazed down at her over his own coffee. Normally clean-shaven, Rick Harding must have slept in late that morning, because the light stubble on his face was as unusual for the pool hall owner as it was attractive.

There had been a time when Lana had considered Rick somewhat average. Average height, somewhat larger-than-average muscular build, with a strong jaw on a pleasantly attractive face.

Then he'd come to her rescue the previous summer after some disgruntled and inebriated townsfolk had taken her to task for announcing the condominium project. Someone had caused her to deliberately fall, hurting her arm. After helping her off the ground, Rick had promptly punched the lights out of the man who tripped her.

There were many people in Lana's life but very few heroes.

"It's really good to see you again," Lana told him sincerely.

"I didn't realize you were back in town," Rick said in his low, rich voice.

She'd never been able to decide if he was quiet or shy or maybe both. But the fact that he'd noticed she was gone somehow warmed her far more than the coffee cups she was balancing.

Considering how much Lana traveled for the family business, she wasn't used to people missing her.

"I had to meet with my general contractor. We start construction on the condos soon."

Rick nodded, glancing at the coffee in his hands.

Lana liked how his hands were strong and how his fingers—callused from work—wrapped around his coffee cup. She liked his broad shoulders and the way his jeans were worn from use, not styled to look that way. The flannel-lined hoodie he wore reminded her of the woods and being warm and Christmastime. Back when she was young enough to believe Christmas was reindeers and mistletoe and lists to Santa, not emotionally charged dinners with an extended family more interested in profit margins and expensive cocktails than truly enjoying one another's company.

They hesitated, an awkward moment when Lana wasn't sure what to say and Rick stood there saying nothing. Then of course they spoke at the exact same time.

"Are you—?"

"Do you—?"

A flush reddened his face beneath the scruffy beard. "Sorry. You first."

He looked so cute, shifting on his feet.

"I was going to ask if you're ready for Christmas. The presents, the tree, all that stuff."

A soft snort was his answer. "It's not really my holiday," Rick said. "Are you staying around?"

He sounded almost hopeful. Lana wasn't a blusher, but something about the way he was looking at her made her cheeks heat. "I was hoping to."

A group of small children singing Christmas carols in their best Chipmunks impersonations came past, and Lana couldn't help smiling at their cheerfulness. She looked up and saw Rick smiling too.

"Not your holiday?" she asked teasingly.

"I like seeing the kids enjoying themselves." Rick shrugged, then he said, "I suppose this is all for them anyway."

"No fun for the adults?"

Hmm. That hadn't come out the way she meant it.

Rick ran a hand over the back of his neck, then he muttered under his breath, "Not this one."

A loud clearing of a throat pulled their attention to the stage and the tired-looking officer standing on it. Jonah wasn't the mayor—as far as Lana was aware, there was no mayor—and the members of the town council all collectively slouched in their seats, refusing to meet Jonah's eye. Which left their poor overworked police officer to deal with running the meeting alone, like he dealt with protecting the town alone. Jonah was going to need some backup if her condominiums brought more residents permanently to Moose Springs.

Rick followed her line of sight as she frowned at the police officer.

"Not a fan of Jonah?" Rick asked. The man was perceptive.

"Actually, I like him a lot," Lana said. "I'd like him even more if he weren't stretched thin enough to see through. I'm hoping to talk the new mayor into giving him a little help."

"We don't have a mayor." Rick's eyebrows knitted together in confusion.

"I suppose I could always run."

She'd meant it as a joke, but the look of horror on his face almost managed to hurt her feelings. Then abruptly, he chuckled.

"You'd be good at it." Those greener-than-normal hazel eyes crinkled with amusement. "Better than I was."

A compliment from him felt like a warm brownie and a mug of hot tea in front of a fireplace. She basked shamelessly in the pleasure of it. Then suddenly, what Rick had said registered.

"Wait, you were mayor?" Too bad Rick wasn't the mayor now. Lana could only imagine how much easier her life would be.

"Only for a month, a few years back. We all took a turn, and none of us wanted anything to do with it. This town is a pain in the ass."

Lana couldn't help her laugh.

"L, you can flirt later," Graham called from their seats on the other side of the barn. "Rick, be careful, buddy—she's a piranha in sheep's clothing."

"Pariah, dearest," Lana replied.

She turned back to Rick and saw a deeper flush had reddened his face. Rick opened his mouth as if to continue the conversation like a normal human being, then promptly shut it again. He glanced down at his coffee cup, clearing his throat.

Lana knew she made him nervous, and while it wasn't a first for her, she wished that Rick found her more approachable. It was nice having someone to talk to. Feeling as if perhaps she'd overstayed her welcome, Lana took an awkward step back. Rick's gaze flickered upward, and he froze, going an odd sort of pale. Lana followed his eyes to the sprig of mistletoe above her head. "Oh dear. That makes things awkward, doesn't it?"

The poor man looked like a deer caught in headlights, so Lana helped the situation by scooting sideways, out from under the mistletoe.

"Well, I better take my seat," she said.

"Do you need help?" Rick started to ask as she turned, juggling her off-balance coffees, but his helping hands only jostled them more. "Oh, sorry."

He cursed when the closest coffee spilled on the sleeve of her coat. The poor man was so unsettled that when he grabbed some napkins from the table, dabbing them at her arm, he managed to pour coffee all over his own hand in the process.

"Are you okay?" Lana tried to check his hand, but Rick seemed more worried about her jacket.

"Shit, I'll pay for cleaning that," he said, mumbling as he kept dabbing at her coat.

"It's nothing, Rick. Please don't worry." She waved off his attempts to de-coffee her clothing. "Did you hurt yourself?"

"Naw." Rick gripped his handful of coffee-soaked napkins. "I have thick arms. Skin. Arm skin. Damn, I don't even know what I'm saying. Are you sure I didn't burn you?"

"I promise."

A teenager made the same mistake as Lana, opening the wrong door to come inside, and the plastic elves once again made a clatteringly loud break for freedom. Lana looked over at the noise, wincing in sympathy. Then she turned back to Rick.

He looked like he wanted to be anywhere else at that moment. Since Rick had saved her once, Lana was happy to save him in return, even if it meant denying herself his company.

Still, she couldn't help giving him a flirty wink. "I'll see you later, Rick. Watch out for that mistletoe."

Lana returned to her seat before she could see his response, unloading her treats into her friends' arms. As she settled back in her chair, Lana caught Rick glancing her way from his own seat, and she offered him a wave of her fingers. He nodded with a shadow of a smile before turning his attention to his cookie plate.

Graham draped his arm over Zoey's shoulders, kicking one booted foot up on the chair in front of him. Ash had joined them, stretching her long legs out in front of her, ankles crossed and boot tapping against the leg of another chair. If the man sitting in front of her minded, he was smart enough not to say anything. Easton at least tried to contain his broad shoulders and long limbs, but it was an effort. The man climbed mountains for a living, and he was as tall and strong as a boulder himself.

"Were you talking to Rick?" Zoey looked up from her phone. "He's the sweetest guy. We invited him over on Christmas Eve. He always spends it alone."

"Which was a bad idea." Graham glanced at her with an indulgent look.

"Why? He's alone on Christmas. How is that okay?"

"Rick's alone on Christmas because he wants to be alone on Christmas," Ash added. "And he's not alone. He's with his nephew, Diego."

"Which is basically the same as being alone," Graham joked.

Lana knew who Diego was but only in the context of the Moose Springs Resort employee who grimaced when he forced pamphlets and granola bars on unsuspecting guests.

Zoey's chin lifted a little, a signal she was digging her prover-bial heels in. "No one wants to be alone on Christmas."

"Unless they've attended a Montgomery holiday party, in

which case they absolutely want to be alone on Christmas." Lana shared a knowing look with her friend, who had suffered through more than one of said parties at Lana's side.

Zoey shuddered. "Yes. Unless that."

"All right, people. I have an announcement," Officer Jonah said, his words barely denting the chatter in the room. "I know we were hoping to be free of—"

A group in the back row started snickering, oblivious to the meeting starting. Someone had procured a beach ball–sized plastic inflatable snow globe, and it was hard for anyone to focus on Jonah with the snow globe bouncing back and forth from one side of the seats to the other.

Finally, Easton stood up. At almost seven feet tall, he didn't need to glare at the collected locals, and he didn't need to yell to make everyone quiet down. Instead, he simply stood there, meeting people's eyes until they naturally fell quiet and into order.

Lana raised an eyebrow. "I need to package that and sell it to a few of my colleagues."

"Easton comes from Sasquatch stock," Graham said under his breath to Zoey. She bit her lip to cover her giggle as Easton dropped back into his seat.

The folding chair creaked beneath his weight, which made Lana nervous. Technically, this building was hers too, which meant if Easton was injured by way of collapsing folding chair, Lana's company was liable for a lawsuit. The standard-size folding chair simply didn't accommodate a Lockett-sized person.

On the stage, Jonah sighed. "Before we begin, does anyone have any announcements?"

"Oh, that's me." Lana stood, juggling her coffee, her phone, and her plate. "Sorry, I need...oops. Well, I suppose that cookie had better places to be than with me."

Zoey smiled at her encouragingly. In a room full of people, hers was the only friendly face in the crowd. Lana had spent enough time in front of a boardroom not to shift uncomfortably, but she couldn't keep her fingernails from drumming her coffee cup, a nervous tic she'd never been able to break.

"I've posted the information on social media and passed out flyers, but I wanted to remind everyone that the Montgomery Group is hosting a Christmas party for the town on the twenty-first, with cookie decorating, Santa, and lots of fun activities for kids of all ages. It starts at noon and lasts until the fun runs out."

Silence. Complete silence.

"Special gifts for any children who come and free treats for all."

A cookie could be heard dropping across the room. Lana added cheerfully, "And this party mix is delicious, in case anyone missed out."

No one so much as blinked.

Okeydokey.

"That went well," Zoey said with more optimism than Lana felt. Lana sank down in her seat. Love must have damaged Zoey's eyesight along with her ability to read a room.

"They think I'm the Grinch about to steal their Christmas," Lana replied.

Graham shot her a sympathetic look, reaching over Zoey to squeeze Lana's hand. "Don't worry, L. They'll get used to it eventually."

"That's right," Zoey said firmly. "And if they don't, they'll have us to deal with. We've got your back. Right, Graham?"

His expression melted. "Always, darlin'."

It was hard to watch them and not feel a little hope about the status of the world. Too bad this group of people was convinced Lana was going to bring ruin to them all.

"As I was saying," Jonah continued, "I know we were all hoping for a year free of trouble, but I regret to inform you, there's been an...incident."

"What kind of incident?" Easton asked.

"Out at John and Cheryl Price's place." Jonah hesitated long enough that Lana's curiosity rose. Then he sighed as if exhausted. "All signs point to the Santa Moose having returned to town."

A complete hush came over the town hall. Graham straightened from his customary slouch, shoulders tensed.

"What's a Santa Moose?" Lana asked in a whisper.

"Scourge of our existence," Graham replied. "Like an ROUS, but no flame spurts to save ourselves in."

Jonah cleared his throat louder. "Last year, we almost managed to track him down, but unfortunately to no success. The Moose Springs police department—"

"That's just him," Ashtyn said.

"—and volunteers from the town—"

"That's just me," Easton added.

"—found that the closer to Christmas, the worse the pattern of destruction got. While in past years, we've been hesitant to get Fish and Game involved, after the seeing the Christmas decoration destruction out at the Prices', I think it needs to go to a vote."

"Are we talking about killing a moose?" Zoey shoved her glasses higher on her nose. "Why wouldn't they move him, like Ulysses?"

Last summer, an accident had happened with a moose very close to Graham's heart. Ulysses had been successfully relocated away from town after injuring a tourist, but Lana knew Graham still missed the massive animal.

"Move him?" Graham shook his head. "Zo, no one's ever *seen* him."

"You're kidding."

"Nope. For three years now, he's been the Ghost and the Darkness. It drives East nuts. First thing on four feet he couldn't track."

Easton shrugged a single broad shoulder as if accepting this as truth.

"Graham, would you like to take over the meeting?" The officer's face was a study in pleasant detachment, but his right eyelid had started to twitch.

"Naw, you're doing great, Jonah."

"Do we have volunteers to try to locate the Santa Moose?"

Another silence fell across the room—an atypical silence for a town normally happy to help one another. Especially when it involved sneaking about in camouflage and drinking beer.

"You're not actually afraid of this thing." Zoey looked between Easton and Ashtyn, both of whom would—and had—braved storms and flooding and everything else the brutal Alaskan weather could throw at them.

"You poor innocent woman," Graham said. "We're terrified of it."

"Maybe I can catch it." The words had left Lana's mouth before she realized what she was saying.

"*You're* going to locate an unhinged and possibly nonexistent moose?" Zoey looked at Lana as if she had lost her mind.

She hadn't meant to volunteer, but so many people were looking at her that she felt compelled to say, "If it's a threat to the town? Well, I suppose I should at least try."

Graham's eyes flickered over Zoey's head to meet Lana's. "L, the last thing anyone wants is for you to get hurt."

"Has this moose hurt anyone yet? Besides Christmas decorations?"

"Well...no." He flashed her a grin. "All right, if you want to take on the trouble of tracking an untrackable moose, be my guest. And we'll do you one better: if you personally save us from the Santa Moose, the town of Moose Springs will consider your trespasses forgiven."

"Promise?"

"I'll even pinkie swear."

Graham was a big guy to pinkie swear, but he did so with the seriousness she expected from a man who had never taken a thing seriously in his life.

"Let me know if you need some backup." He gave their tangled pinkies an extra squeeze. "For real, this moose is dangerous."

"Don't worry. I'm all the backup she needs." Zoey waited until Lana was free of Graham's pinkie, then bumped her fist.

And okay, Lana knew nothing about catching wildlife. If she failed, she would only reinforce the assumption she didn't belong in Moose Springs. Her position could weaken, and maybe negotiations with the town council would become more difficult. If Easton couldn't track this moose, no one would ever believe she could do it. Still, Lana knew her limitations, but she also knew her strengths. This wasn't the first challenge she'd taken upon herself. If anyone could think outside the box, it was her. And if she didn't fail...

She wanted a home. Moose Springs was worth the risk.

Jonah—having waited with the patience of a man with a newborn at home—continued his tired drone.

"Well, it seems Ms. Montgomery will be apprehending the Santa Moose. Are there any more announcements anyone wants to make?"

Nope. Just that she was officially in over her head. Completely, utterly screwed. Stuffing the rest of a hard, moisture-stealing cookie in her mouth, Lana swallowed, determined to ignore the eyes still watching her with thinly veiled curiosity.

She was going to make it through her first Christmas in Moose Springs, even if it killed her.

CHAPTER 2

SOMETIMES IT WAS HARD FOR Rick to watch his beloved town—his friends and family—be complete asses.

The poor woman had announced a Christmas party, not the bulldozing of their homes. And as someone who'd personally tried to catch the Santa Moose, Rick knew Lana had set herself up to fall spectacularly. The only difference was that too many in this room would love to see her fail. Someone should warn her the moose was dangerous—someone closer to her than Rick. Zoey might not know better, but Graham shouldn't keep giving her pinkie swears and promises that catching the Santa Moose would change anyone's mind.

Lana wasn't going to win over the town. Not when she owned most of it.

"Last chance, is there anyone else who has an announcement?" Jonah asked, trying to draw everyone's attention back to him. It wasn't working.

Rick glanced at Lana, and for a brief moment, she let her breezy smile fall, her shoulders slumping as she nibbled on a bit of cookie. He hated being the center of attention, and everyone already knew he held a pool tournament every year right before Christmas. But too many people were staring at her, and not in the good way. Without realizing what he was doing, Rick shoved to his feet.

Standing there self-consciously, Rick said, "I'm doing the holiday pool tournament thing again this year. Same day as Lana's thing, later that night. So...yeah."

So far, the tournaments he held at the pool hall were still lucrative enough to keep running them. They were a pain in the ass, but they got people in the door. And lately, his door hadn't been swinging open nearly as often as he needed it to.

"There's a bigger prize this year," he added. "A thousand dollars to the winner."

Ash flashed the room a smirk. "What Rick means is I'm going to be a grand richer. If you're smart, you'll stay home."

"Please, Zoey's gonna crush you," Graham bragged.

"You two never stop." Zoey sighed good-naturedly. "Are you sure you aren't all related?"

As they argued about whether or not Graham's mother and the Lockett twins' father could have been secretly involved in a romantic tryst, Rick stood there feeling stupid. There had been more, but he wasn't all that interested in continuing. The only one still paying attention to him was Lana. Rick gratefully dropped back into his seat. Lana shot him an appreciative look from across the chilly room, warming him far better than the space heaters working overtime.

Man, that woman was pretty.

The first time Rick had seen Lana Montgomery on one of her

many visits to Moose Springs over the last several years, his eyes had nearly fallen out of his head. That look had been by accident, and as a then happily married man, Rick had kept his eyes firmly anywhere else when the bombshell was in his vicinity.

Now that he was allowed to look, Rick tried not to. Curves like hers were dangerously fast, and Rick's life had slowed to a crawl. Not only was he not interested in dangerous curves, he was seriously considering getting off the road permanently. Rick wasn't a loner, but he was a private guy. And when you're brutally, humiliatingly left in front of the entire town, it does more than make you a source of local gossip.

It makes you the most pathetic schmuck in the entire village.

Normally, Rick was not the kind of man who women like Lana noticed, so he didn't understand why she flashed him a sweet smile across the room. He tried to return that smile, but it was awkwardly done at best, probably coming off as a grimace. The last few years hadn't been the easiest, and Rick was out of practice. Her positivity never failed to impress him though, especially when she had her hands full with a town that hated her.

They all heard Graham's joke that she was the evil overlord, but it was true that nearly every business owner in the town hall was waiting for the proverbial axe to fall on them. When the Montgomery Group bought out most of the commercial property in Moose Springs, it left the bulk of them at her mercy. If she felt like it, she could take down the entire town.

He was very aware of how behind he was on his business's rent and that he owed the gorgeous woman across the row more than he could hope to regain before rent came due again.

Like everyone else, Rick was worried about keeping a roof over his and his nephew's heads. Then again, powerful women had always been a turn-on.

Rick had zoned out, missing whatever Jonah had left to say. Apparently, the meeting was over. Jonah had places to be and things to do, even if their overworked police officer didn't want to go there or do those things. Rick lingered in his seat, letting everyone else mill about and move toward the exit, then he rose to his feet and started to put up the folding chairs left on the barn floor.

Out of the corner of his eye, he watched Lana and Zoey in a spirited discussion as they folded chairs on the other side of the barn, but their voices were hushed. Only the words "moose" and "proper attire" were audible. Graham, who was within hearing distance of the pair as he turned off and gathered the space heaters, kept chuckling.

Ash normally would have helped, but tonight she sat on the top of the snacks table, finishing the last of the cookies instead. A cigarette was in her hand. Ash didn't need another brother figure in her life, but Rick had been playing that role with both of them since they were kids. Besides, Christmas had been tough on all the Locketts since Ash's and Easton's mother had died, so he tried to pay more attention to both the twins this time of year.

"Didn't anyone tell you it's dangerous to smoke in a barn? And illegal?"

Not that Ash had ever let a little thing like breaking the law stop her from what she wanted to do on any given day. She snorted, waggling the travel mug she was using to flick her cigarette into.

"I live on the wild side," she said. "Plus, no hay or Jonahs in here. I'm pretty sure it'll be okay."

"The elves might not like it."

"They're sugar addicts, all of them."

One of the plastic elves had survived being played with by a group of children, only to be abandoned on the floor. Retrieving it, Rick stood the elf on the table next to Ash's hip.

At her raised eyebrow, he shrugged. "You looked lonely."

"I'm not lonely." Except Ash spent a lot of time by herself, flying supplies up and down the state. Years of knowing her had taught Rick that the lonelier she felt, the more she smoked.

"You're not *not* lonely."

"I suppose I'll have to go to Lana's stupid party." Sighing, she finished her cigarette. "Zoey will make sad eyes at all of us if we don't."

"It's free cookies," Rick said. "Who's going to pass on those?"

Ash's lips curved. "I don't know, but the more that pass, the more leftovers for me."

They'd known each other all their lives, so Rick wasn't buying the tough routine.

"You'd go even if Zoey didn't say anything," he said. "You're much nicer than you pretend to be." Rick unplugged the coffee urn and handed it to her. "And more useful."

"Yeah, yeah." She slid off the table, coffee urn in one arm, and managed to light up a second cigarette one-handed.

Two cigarettes in a row was a definite sign this holiday season wasn't going any easier on Ash than it was on Rick.

Everyone else had finished clearing up after the meeting. Since the Lockett twins were both on the town council, Easton had keys to lock up. Rick tried not to focus on Lana saying her goodbyes and heading for her Mercedes SUV. Ash and Easton went straight to Ash's Jeep while Graham wrapped an arm around Zoey's shoulders, the pair lingering on their way to his truck. Lana had parked right next to Rick, on the far side of the lot. Meaning he had to trail her across an empty parking lot after dark.

Well, that wasn't creepy at all.

Stuffing his hands in his jacket pockets, Rick hoped it didn't seem like he was following her, even though technically, he was. He had no idea if she even knew he was there...her head was down as she rapidly scrolled through a message on her phone. Rick hadn't spent much time around Lana, but over the last several years, the socialite had visited Moose Springs enough that she was a familiar fixture in Graham's diner, the Tourist Trap, a drink in her hand and a grin on her face. She and the bartender had been friends for a while now.

Lately, Lana's bright smile had been replaced with a focused expression and a frown more often than not. She'd been in "work mode" ever since this summer, when the town had learned of her condominium project. It was as if Moose Springs consumed her every waking moment.

It didn't escape Rick's notice that he was overly aware of her facial expressions for a man who could barely get a word out when she said hi. Yep, definitely not creepy at all.

Slowing his pace so Lana reached her SUV well before he reached his car, Rick waited for her to unlock her door. She had parked facing away from the barn while he had backed in, and there wasn't much room in between the two vehicles.

"I promise I don't bite," Lana told him sweetly.

Her voice was this combination of smooth and husky that made him think of blankets in front of a fireplace, warm red wine, and slow kisses beneath the firelight.

"I didn't want to crowd you," Rick explained, allowing himself to scoot an inch closer. He watched her unlock her SUV and set her purse on the passenger seat.

"My personal bubble is less inflated than most." Lana offered him a warm smile as she took a step toward him. "I think I was born with it leaking."

Rick had the sheer brain-destroying pleasure of the scent of her perfume lingering in the cold winter air.

"Mine is made of duct tape and plastic pipe," he said randomly. "It's indestructible."

Lana laughed softly. "Why does that not surprise me at all?"

He shouldn't be this focused on her eyes or how long her lashes were. Rick really shouldn't be wondering if his own personal bubble could stand to be deflated a bit. He didn't try to keep people at arm's length, but he still managed to do so.

Rick probably should have said something clever, but he was saved by Graham's truck pulling up and the window rolling down.

"Hey, Lana," Graham called through the window. "Hold up a second. I forgot to give you something my ma made for you."

Graham hopped out. Unlike Rick, he had no problem squeezing in between the cars to hand Lana a reusable shopping bag while Zoey waved enthusiastically from the car. Blinking in surprise, Lana looked down into the bag, her face brightening.

"I get a sweater?" Lana asked.

"An ugly Christmas sweater," Graham corrected her with a

chuckle. "Except she doesn't realize it's ugly. I told Ma that you wanted to match Jake the next time you watch him. He has his own. Sorry there are so many balls on it."

"Too many balls has been the theme of the day." She clutched the sweater to her chest as if it were a precious gift. "I *love* this. Please tell your mother thank you for me."

"Already done, darlin'. Happy holidays from the Barnetts." He gave her a huge hug, which Lana enthusiastically returned. Rick tried not to feel awkward as he stood there, unable to get into his car and not a part of this moment of holiday joy.

"Want to see?" she asked Rick as Graham loped back to the truck, swinging inside. Turning the sweater around, she held it up proudly.

Rick scratched his head, trying to think of something polite to say, unwilling to dash her enthusiasm. "It's festive."

Yes, festive was safe.

Lana's grin widened. "And?"

"And obviously designed by a woman with a completely innocent mind."

"Isn't it?" Lana exhaled a soft laugh. "I love this. My day has been far more sexually explicit than I possibly imagined when I woke up this morning."

Rick felt his face heat up, and he directed his eyes anywhere but the sweater. Nope, he wasn't thinking anything at all beyond this was his car, and at some point, she would let him in.

"Headed home?" Lana asked as she tucked her gift back in the bag.

"Figured I might reopen the pool hall. It's still early."

Lana waited, and when it became clear that Rick didn't have anything particularly brilliant to add to his statement, she gave him a pretty smile. "Well...good night."

He could have stood there in the awkwardness, inhaling her perfume like a drowning fish, all night long. But that would be weird. And Rick was many things, but he tried really hard not to be weird. Instead, he nodded and put his hand on her car door, waiting until she got in before lightly closing it for her. He liked that she mouthed "thank you" through the window.

As he got in his own car, Rick tried to ignore the fact that her smile was the best part of his day.

———

No one would have blamed Rick if he'd headed home for the night instead of reopening the pool hall until regular closing time. Most of the other business owners wouldn't bother to go back to work after the town meeting. But the drive back to his pool hall wasn't long, and Rick didn't have anything better to do.

The town of Moose Springs had gone all out for the holidays this year. Telephone poles lining the roads were decorated like giant candy canes, with signs wishing everyone happy holidays. Giant plastic snowflakes hung below streetlamps, glittering in the passing headlights. Everywhere he looked were strings of multicolored lights, tinsel-draped evergreens, and giant inflatable reindeer.

If the reclusive Santa Moose ever made it downtown, the animal would have an absolute field day.

As he drove, Rick did his best to ignore the decorations. Christmas used to be his favorite time of year. Since Jen had left, it pretty much sucked. Hard. Rick still liked Christmas…but damn if it didn't seem to cut him up a little more each year.

When Rick and his ex opened their pool hall, they made a promise to themselves: no tourists. At least not if they could help it. Rick had grown up in a small town overrun with tourism, hating the constant stream of strangers just as much as anyone. And after a drunken tourist in a sports car had T-boned Jen's sister's car, killing his ex-wife's sister, brother-in-law, and niece, the choice to operate for locals only hadn't just been a preference…it had been necessary for Jen's sanity. But Jen was gone, and it was just Rick now.

If he had to pick money or peace of mind, it had always felt like a no-brainer. These days though…these days, it was hard to justify the decision to stay loyal to his town and his and Jen's dream when he could barely keep the lights on.

At some point in his life, Rick wanted to eat red meat that wasn't in the discount bin and maybe drink brand-name soda again.

His nephew, Diego, was working an evening shift at Moose Springs resort tonight, so there was no one waiting for him. The holiday season had left the always busy resort absolutely overrun with tourists ready to hit the ski slopes. All it would take was sticking an open sign in his window and throwing a flyer up on the resort wall, and all his troubles would fade away.

Of course, those problems would promptly be replaced with new ones. Like his wine selection being subpar or his bathrooms not having the properly scented soap. He'd be hit with the thousands of complaints the business owners who were open to tourists had to deal with on a daily basis, leaving them desperate for a place to escape. The tourists were a constant presence. On the streets, in the grocery store, clogging up the gas station lines, and having accidents on the icy Alaskan roads.

They were *everywhere*.

Moose Springs was a small town, and it didn't take much to get from one end of Main Street to the other. There wasn't a "bad side" of town, but the side street he turned off of was less appealing to someone searching for the quaint Alaskan appeal Moose Springs was renowned for.

Gone were the brightly painted reds, sky blues, and cheerful oranges of the tourist attractions, replaced by muted and faded paint, weathered wood siding, and buildings constructed of plain concrete block walls. Here, weathered sheet metal roofing protected businesses instead of new shingles, and some of their walks hadn't been cleared. Most storefronts seemed unoccupied to the outside eye, with parking lots discreetly set in the back of the buildings so the tourists wouldn't be tempted to stop in. Anything to give the appearance of being uninteresting to the outside world.

The town was split evenly these days. Half of the businesses welcoming tourists and half of them doing everything in their power to go unnoticed.

From the outside, the pool hall blended in with the rest of the town's buildings, but Rick was rather proud of the inside. He'd replaced the flooring himself with rich wooden planking when he'd first opened the business. The fireplace in the corner was cozy and often the preferred spot for his customers to gather. The pool tables themselves were in good condition, and the barstool tables lining the walls were level, the seats worn but immaculately clean.

The short, modest bar in the corner might only serve a few customers a day, but the wood was carefully stained and polished until it gleamed.

Rick's pool hall had started as only a pool hall. But the winters were cold, and the nights were long. Plus, there was only so much he could charge for a game. Serving pizza and beer filled in the gap but never quite enough to make more than ends meet...if that. More than once, Rick had wondered if a more successful business would have made a difference in his failed marriage. High school sweethearts turned just one more statistic. Jen had stuck it out for eight years, two months, and fifteen days. Then she'd packed her bags and moved on. She hadn't wanted anything in the divorce. Not half the bar, not the house, not alimony. Jen only wanted to be free.

Funny. Up until then, Rick hadn't realized being with him was a prison. Even now, three years after the ink had dried on their divorce papers, the shame still burned hot in his veins.

The reindeer bells he'd hung on the door handle jingled as a lone customer came in, the first in an hour. Truly, Rick tried not to look, but when it came to Lana, not looking was awfully difficult. Especially when she was walking into his pool hall with nothing but ten empty pool tables between them.

"I'm sorry," she said, glancing around with a quizzical expression on her face. "I didn't realize you were closing already."

"Not closed," Rick replied, feeling the back of his neck heat up at the lack of customers. "Some weeknights are slow."

Slow. Dying. Currently death rattling as they spoke. It was mortifying, considering she was his landlady. If the emptiness bothered her, Lana covered it well, choosing to meet him at the bar and slide into one of the seats.

"I figured you were headed home like everyone else."

"I guess we have preferring a pool hall in common." Lana crossed her mile-long legs as she leaned an elbow on the bar top. Offering him a quirked curve of her lips, she added, "A hotel isn't as homey as one might wish, even if it is a pleasant place to stay."

Pleasant. That monstrosity on the hill pretty much summed up all the things he—and most of the town—would never be able to afford. For her, it was merely pleasant.

Why was she there? Rick's heart hammered in his chest, which was more than inconvenient considering his stomach was twisting into knots. She must know about the back rent. Someone had let it slip over the summer that Rick's place existed, bringing Lana and Zoey in for the first time. Since then, Lana had never come there unless she was with Zoey or Graham, so showing up alone must mean she was there for business.

Damn, damn, *damn.*

"Is there something I can help you with?" he asked, trying to cover his distress with a relaxed tone.

"A glass of wine would be nice."

Most people didn't have a glass of wine while evicting their tenants. At least Rick didn't think they did. Honestly, he had no idea what it was like on the other side of this arrangement.

"I have red or white." Rick shifted on his feet, glancing at the door. Was it too much to ask for another customer to walk in and save him from the financial conversation he knew was coming?

"Or I could mix the two, make some rosé for you." Even as he said it, Rick cringed.

"I'll take the rosé."

Of course she would. So Rick went about adding cheap red wine to cheap white wine, feeling her eyes watching him as he did so. He handed her the glass. She took a sip without missing a beat, so either his concoction was successful, or she had one heck of a poker face. He'd tried tasting it before, but Rick wasn't much of a wine drinker, so he didn't know the difference between good wine and bad.

Since most people didn't order the house blush, he'd always assumed it was bad.

Settling into her seat more comfortably, Lana leaned on the counter. "Christmas in Moose Springs. This is a first for me." Swirling his terrible excuse for a rosé in her glass, she glanced out the window. "Anything I should know?"

"About the holiday or about what toes not to step on?"

A pretty smile curved her lips. "Both."

"The hotel you're staying in is about to be stuffed to bursting. When the Christmas crowd flocks in, it's standing room only up there."

"It's been a little crowded for my taste," Lana said. "Although it's always nice seeing everyone full of the holiday cheer. The decorations are fabulous."

Rick glanced at his pitiful attempts to spruce the place up. A fake Charlie Brown Christmas tree on the end of the bar with beer cap ornaments wasn't exactly high-end design. His ex had put it up the first year they'd opened, and Rick hadn't been able to throw out that sparse excuse of a tree, no matter how many extra needles it lost every time he pulled it out.

Lana followed his glance toward the tree, then she smiled at him. "But I always did prefer holiday decor with meaning."

An awkward silence fell between them, in which he tried and failed to think of something to say and she sat there, sipping her wine and not rescuing him.

"I make you very uncomfortable, don't I?" Lana finally sighed. "Don't worry. I won't be long. I wasn't ready to go back to the resort and face the pile of paperwork waiting for me. There's too much to do back there and never enough hours in the day."

"We probably should talk about the rent," he said tightly. It was best, he supposed, to get it all out in the open. "I know the check I wrote this month isn't enough, but the list of crap that keeps breaking down is ridiculous."

"We don't have to talk about that unless you want to. I actually came for a drink. I'd normally go to the Tourist Trap, but…"

"But Graham fell in love, and who knows where he'll be?"

"Oh, I know *exactly* where he is." Lana's lips curved before she took another sip. "And I know they're not interested in having any company right now."

"There's a nice bar at the resort." Nicer than his anyway.

"Is that your way of asking me to leave?" She flashed that playful look of hers his way, and suddenly Rick realized something very important about Lana Montgomery. That breezy smile of hers, the one she used no matter what the situation? It was total bullshit.

There was a bottle of bourbon beneath the bar that was Rick's private stash. He'd never opened it before because…well…it was pricy, and he hadn't had any reason to.

The top was sealed in wax, dripped artfully down the neck. Instead of trying to pretend to be someone he wasn't—someone used to bottles like these—Rick pulled his knife out of the leather case he kept clipped to his belt. It had been his father's knife and his grandfather's knife, passed down in the family since his grandfather had gotten it after coming home from World War II.

Once, Rick had assumed it would be his son's knife. Then life had taught him a few lessons, and he'd set those assumptions aside. Today, it was the knife that scored a circle around a bottle of bourbon he hadn't planned on opening. After popping the top off, Rick poured her a glass first, then a second for him.

"Thank you." Manicured fingers lifted the drink. Lana sniffed delicately, as one was probably taught to do with alcohol. Rick didn't know. He was more of a Bud Light kind of guy.

Rick took a drink and then started choking. This time, her breezy laugh was softer, throatier. Real.

"Some people cut this with water or add ice," she told him before taking a sip. "It's more of a slow drink than a…"

"Chug?"

"Yeah, you totally chugged it."

Rick added a couple of ice cubes to his drink. He offered her the same, but Lana shook her head. It shouldn't turn him on knowing she was sipping an alcohol that had made him choke, but there he was, trying his darnedest not to look at her lips touching the rim of the glass.

"I figured it's better than the rosé. Still, probably not like what you're used to."

She hummed in a noncommittal fashion.

It took him a while to look up at her, and by then, she'd gone back to staring out the window.

"I promise I'm not half as bad as they think I am," Lana told him, that bright, teasing smile back on her face as she absently played with the single string of miniature multicolor lights he'd taped along the bar. "Only a third as bad, sometimes a quarter."

Such total bullshit. He'd hurt her feelings.

"Never thought you were."

Four words that wouldn't fix what he'd broke, but the sweet look she gave him almost made him think he'd been forgiven.

"Besides, I kept expecting you to come in here," Rick said, giving her another opening to talk about the back rent. Another opening she didn't take. Instead, she sipped her bourbon.

"This is really quite lovely." Lana ran a thumb along the rim of the glass, her finger trembling lightly. Maybe she was cold?

Of course she was cold. The furnace in the place sucked.

"Any advice for me? Rumor has it that you're no stranger to moose catching."

Rick shook his head. "With that moose? Not a one. We've tried and failed to catch it every year."

"Well, I've already started brainstorming. I think the key is to find the right lure. Just like with fishing, if you know what attracts it the most, even a Santa Moose can be snagged."

"Just be careful out there. Fish aren't over six feet tall, and they can't kick your head off," Rick said with a chuckle.

"I'm tougher than I look," Lana promised with a little curve of her lips. "I'm betting I can pull this off."

"If anyone could, my money's on you," Rick told her, leaning on the bar between them. She flushed in pleasure, which hadn't been his intention, but Rick sure didn't mind. "So what's it like owning the town?"

Lana shook her head. "I don't own the town. I'm simply a caretaker of some of the buildings for now. Speaking of which, you mentioned things are breaking."

"Is this where you ask for the tour?"

"Are you offering?"

The last thing he wanted to do was take Lana around in the back, but Rick knew he didn't have a choice.

So he showed her the modest kitchen, where he made and froze pizzas to cook for later. Everything was spotlessly clean... Rick had learned early that a clean kitchen was incredibly important in a business, but what he had was either run-down, breaking, or broken. Rick had stuck Post-it notes to everything based on priority of fixing. The freezer door that kept sticking was low priority. He could muscle it open as necessary.

The heater was shot, leaving a cold kitchen with space heaters positioned under sinks to keep the pipes from freezing. That was a little higher up the list but still not the worst of his troubles by a long shot.

"It's not half this cold in the other room," Lana said, shivering.

"The ducting is jacked up somewhere, but I'm too large to access it. I think an animal ripped it up. It stays cool enough not to need an air conditioner in the summer, or I grab a fan. It's a waste of money to dump heat in here in the winters, so I use space heaters under the pipes. I shoved some insulating foam in the vents I could access to keep the air in the front room as much as possible. The fireplace out there helps a lot."

"Foam in the ducting? Isn't that a fire hazard?" She sounded concerned.

"I used the rubber kind, and I check it to make sure it doesn't get too hot."

"Didn't you tell the previous owners?" When Rick shifted uncomfortably, Lana's frown deepened. "Let me guess—they said any internal building issues were the tenant's responsibility. The contracts they made you sign were ridiculous."

Since Lana's company had bought out those contracts, it was the same deal Rick had with her. And he would have stuffed his head in a snowbank before telling her he couldn't afford to call a ducting company.

There was more. Windows that were old, leaking in water and leaking out heat, no matter how much caulk he used. A delivery ramp with a dangerously wobbly railing. Wiring for both indoor and outdoor lighting that he was slowly fixing as he had the time.

"Why didn't you tell me?" Lana frowned, turning a circle as she took in the damage.

His silence must have spoken volumes, because this time, Lana failed to keep a professional expression. "I'm aware I'm not the most popular person in this town, but I'd be remiss to let one of my properties go into disrepair. Didn't you get the memo?"

"We all got the memo." Rick didn't meet her eyes. "I guess I was hoping if I didn't make waves, I might be able to catch up on rent before someone said anything."

Rick knew he wasn't the first person to admit they were struggling to make ends meet. However, it was humiliating to stand in front of her, jaw tight and gaze on the wall over her shoulder.

"I know."

Rick's eyes found hers. "You knew?"

"The Montgomery Group holds the leases, but I'm personally invested in what's happening in this town. I know as much as I can about the businesses here, including the owners of those businesses." Lana added, "Don't worry. I'm not trying to unearth everyone's deepest, darkest secrets."

"You wouldn't find much." With a rueful look, Rick shook his head as he led her back to the front room. "In Moose Springs, we can't keep anything secret if we wanted to. I'm guessing they all know what I had for breakfast this morning."

Lana slid back onto her stool. "The first of the month is coming fast."

"Yeah, the Christmas decorations keep reminding me." If she knew he was behind on his rent, she'd know how much. And she'd know it wasn't going to get any better in the next two weeks.

"Play me for it."

Rick's eyes stayed on the wall as he tried not to let his flaring pride show. "For the back rent?"

He would rather be punched in the face than accept that kind of charity.

"No, for an extension. You're good for the rent, Rick. It never occurred to me otherwise. But if I start giving extensions, everyone will want them. Then it'll become a nightmare for the manage-ment team. You'll have to play me for it."

His mouth twitched slightly as he finally looked at her. "You sure? I'm going to win."

"Don't underestimate me. Men have a bad habit of underes-timating women in business affairs. It never goes well for them when they do." Her eyes flickered over to the pool tables as if considering the challenge she'd offered him.

Agreeing would have been so easy. Instead, Rick reached out and touched Lana's hand to draw her attention back to him. The action had been instinctive, but in hindsight, feeling her smooth skin beneath his rougher fingertips was dangerous. An unexpected attraction was one thing. Having her this close, the subtle scent of her perfume scrambling his wits and clawing at his defenses, was another.

"I'm a decent player." Rick felt obligated to warn her. "It's kind of a hazard of the profession."

Lana gave him an arch look, one that made him lean in closer. "Well, then I won't feel too bad when I beat you."

"You're welcome to try," he replied, taking his favorite cue from its spot leaning behind the bar. "I'm game if you are."

Her soft, rich laugh matched the bourbon perfectly.

Lana brought her rosé and her bourbon to the table closest to the fireplace. "I'm a little chilly." She shrugged her jacket off once they were in the vicinity of the space heater he'd set next to that side of the wall. "You'd think I'd be used to the weather after so many Chicago winters."

Rick grabbed a second space heater from near the door and

plugged it in, aiming it her way. Then he glanced at the cold fireplace. "Want me to get a fire going?"

"Maybe next time." Her eyes sparkled as she chalked her cue stick. "This won't take very long. Best out of three?"

Unable to resist the challenge in her eyes, Rick found himself dangerously close to smiling. "Your break."

The sweater Lana wore was long enough that it stayed snug around her hips when she bent over to break, but the loose cowl neck slipped down her shoulder. Rick was learning a lot today about Lana and himself. Apparently, he was a shoulder guy. Who knew?

"You're staring at me." Lana looked up, and when she flashed him a heart-stopping grin, Rick was tempted to throw the game for the sheer hell of it.

"You're gorgeous," he said quietly, since all sense had already abandoned him.

Lana missed her break. The cue slipped right off her knuckles, sending the white cue ball spinning sideways, nowhere close to the triangle of billiard balls she was trying to hit.

Rick took the ball and ignored her protestation, placing it back in her hand. "I'm sorry. I wasn't trying to make you uncomfortable."

"I never said I was uncomfortable," Lana replied, glancing at him out of the corner of her eye as she offered him a flirtatious look. "I also never said thank you. That day down by the lake when you ran off those jerks."

"You said thank you. You sent me a letter."

That letter was the oddest thing in his home. Lana's handwriting had been smooth and polished, as if she'd learned how to write a letter professionally. Whereas her words had been chopped, difficult to follow, as if she herself hadn't really understood what she was trying to say.

The thick, silky paper had been folded into a lined envelope actually embossed with his name. But the stamp on the front had been slapped on partially askew. The combination of polish and haphazardness confused him. Rick probably had paid too much attention to the thing.

She could have sent him an email.

"You're the only person in town who doesn't make me uncomfortable," Lana told him.

"You're the only person in town who makes me feel like I'm thirteen again." That hadn't come out the way he wanted. Rick cast around, once again hoping someone would save him from himself. No one did. "It's the whole head cheerleader thing. You don't go sit at her table unless you want the whole school to watch you get milk thrown in your face."

"Mathletes."

"What?"

"I was in the mathletes. It's like debate club, only we tried to solve math problems faster than our opponents."

Suddenly, he laughed. Not at her but because he never in a million years would have pictured this woman scrambling to out-math anyone. And damn, it felt good to laugh.

"You're making fun of me." Lana's cheeks had turned rosy, but her eyes were sparkling with self-deprecating humor. "It's okay. My cousin Killian teased me about it mercilessly. Race car Killian, not polo Killian. Polo Killian was in mathletes too."

Rick raised an eyebrow. "You have two cousins named Killian?"

"Ridiculous, isn't it? You'd think one would be enough. I promise race car Killian is the far superior Killian, no matter what I tell him to his face. When dealing with Killians, one must keep their egos in check."

Her description of her family caused his mouth to twitch upward. "Isn't Killian the one Graham beat up?"

"Race car Killian. And Graham didn't *beat* him up," she said, defending her cousin's honor. "There were simply words exchanged in a more physical form than normal."

"Graham was pretty upset," Rick reminded her. "Zoey nearly got killed in that rainstorm Killian took her four-wheeling in."

"I'm fairly sure that was equal opportunity near death. Zoey wasn't exactly making her best choices. Getting dumped by her dream guy can do that to a girl." Lana took her time lining up her next shot. "Killian didn't deserve it. Speaking of which, I'm about to run the table, which you don't deserve either. Sorry, dearest."

Sure enough, Lana ran the table on him, earning herself the first win of three.

Since she'd won, it was Rick's turn to break. No one had come in, and he doubted that would change much in the next hour. Still, the night wasn't a bust at all. This was the most alone time he'd had with a woman in ages, and he had to admit he was enjoying himself. Maybe a little too much.

Lana watched him break, her hip distracting him as she leaned against the table. "If I did an internet search, what would I find about you?"

"Probably far less than you'd find about most people." *Don't bring up the divorce.* It was weird to bring up the divorce. *Don't say the d-word.* "I'm divorced."

Yep. Because why not ruin the last pleasant fifteen minutes with something awkward and uncomfortable?

"I'm sorry. That must have been hard."

Hard. Humiliating. Hurtful. Hell. Something that started with an *h*.

"It was a while ago," Rick grunted, taking his first shot.

He didn't even know why he'd brought it up, except the divorce felt like the defining moment of his adult life. A massive, soul-crushing defining moment that the thousands of strangers passing through Moose Springs never knew or cared about.

"I think I saw you with her once when I first came to town. I'm sorry I never got to meet her."

It was a simple observation, probably thoughtlessly—if politely—spoken. But it meant something to Rick that she had noticed.

"It's fine. We run in different crowds." Rick glanced at her, finding those glorious eyes watching him.

"You'd think that wouldn't be the case when I've been running away to Moose Springs every chance I got for years now." Lana brushed her hair out of her eyes as she waited for him to take his next shot. "Anything else? No runs as a bull rider down in the lower forty-eight? A sordid past as a grifter? Secret card shark?"

"I was semipro at pool." Rick almost felt guilty as he sunk his next ball. "I won some money touring around, but it never panned out into anything bigger."

"So I'm playing a professional."

"Semiprofessional." When he promptly missed his third shot, Rick added ruefully, "That was a while ago."

Frankly, he'd be lucky if he made any shots, as distracted as he was by Lana's presence.

"You don't have to undersell your skills, Rick." She leaned over the table, solidly sinking her first ball. "I don't make a habit of being intimidated by the well-earned prowess of my companions. Don't take it too hard when I really do beat you."

"If you do, you'll earn it fair and square."

They shared a grin over the table. He had watched her play long enough to intuitively know he was better than her. But Rick liked how there was a small part of him that wondered how much better. Pool had always been his thing, but that didn't mean she wasn't good enough to take advantage of a misstep on his part.

And man, did she have him off his game.

"By the way, I'm not your landlady," Lana informed him as she circled the table, choosing her next shot. "I work for a conglomerate that owns this building. You don't answer to me. We both answer to them."

Maybe. Or maybe she was trying to reassure him of their equal footing when he knew damn well the footing wasn't equal at all. At least she was smiling at him for real. How had he never known the difference until tonight?

Lana barely missed her shot, leaving the cue ball in a near impossible place for him to play. She'd snookered him.

"Sorry," she said impishly.

"Sorry for what?" Rick replied, unable to help himself from

showing off a little. Most players couldn't pull off a kick shot from that angle, but he'd grown up on the game. There were very few shots he couldn't make. At her low whistle of appreciation, Rick decided that it wouldn't be too terrible to show off a little more.

He ran the table in under a minute, then sank the eight ball with a satisfying thump.

"Your break," Rick said.

"I'm surprised you only went semipro." Lana set the billiards for the last game.

"Wasn't the right scene for me." Rick tried to cover how much he enjoyed impressing her by taking a sip of his bourbon. "Living in hotel rooms leaves a lot to be desired."

He realized what he said, but before he could backtrack, Lana gave him a wry look. "I learned that particular lesson when I was a child. My closest companions were always the housekeeping staff and the concierge attendants. They were always the best at hide-and-seek."

"Sounds lonely."

"I had friends, but most of them fit in my back pocket and had to be replaced when their bindings gave way."

Rick chuckled. "They were probably more loyal than most."

The last game was tougher because her break was excellent. Lana sank her first three balls, then she barely missed her fourth. Rick needed that extension, so even though he would have loved to draw the game out—if just for a few extra moments of her time—he didn't have the luxury. He ran the table with the quick, clean shots that had earned him enough money to open the pool hall in the first place.

"Your win, Rick." She offered him the cue ball. Lana's voice was softer, richer, and so sexy the sound of it was already seared into his brain. "The extension is all yours."

Staying where he was, Rick held her eyes. "What do you get out of it?"

"The knowledge that one more thing is right with the world tonight. A good man catches a break."

His hand brushed against hers as he accepted the cue ball. Every week, people handed him back sets of billiards without it being a problem. But when her fingertips lingered against his, neither of them pulled away. She was tall enough that he wasn't looming over her but near enough that the scent of her filled his nostrils. He'd never met a woman who could steal his breath away by shifting forward a critical inch. And suddenly, her head was tilted back to hold his eyes, and Rick was fairly sure he wanted to kiss her.

If she closed one more inch between them, he might even be convinced she wanted him to kiss her too.

He shouldn't. There was more than unpaid back rent standing between them. Lana was used to a whole hell of a lot more than Rick could ever give anyone. He'd learned the hard way his life wasn't enough to make a woman happy. So Rick stepped back... even though he would have much rather stepped much closer. Lana blinked as if coming out of a daze, then she stepped back too, reaching for her coat. She shrugged it on, belting the soft leather at her waist.

"Sometimes people deserve a break," Lana said. "And maybe I wanted the fun of almost beating a handsome semiprofessional at his game of choice." The playful tone in her voice gave her away.

"You did Google me, didn't you?"

"I'll admit to doing my research," she said. "You're welcome to return the favor."

As she walked toward the door, her jacket hugging her hips, Rick had to admit that he might take her up on that.

"Oh, and, Rick?" Lana paused at the door, smiling at him over her shoulder. "If I don't see you before then, have a merry Christmas."

It was looking better already.

After Lana left, only one customer came in to play a round. One. Between that and the meager daytime business, today wouldn't even cover keeping the lights on. Rick stayed until he knew there wasn't a point anymore, then he locked up and headed home.

Home was a modest ranch on a few acres of land, butted up against the far side of the Lockett property. Even though the bulk of the landscape didn't belong to Rick, there was a feeling of solitude and privacy to the property he loved. Since he worked a lot of hours, often until late in the evenings, he'd installed solar-powered flood lamps outside the house.

With the days shortening to fewer hours of sunlight, those solar-powered lamps wouldn't get the power they needed much longer. He'd have to double-check the backup batteries. Mentally adding that to his to-do list, Rick parked under the empty metal carport next to the house, even though Diego's car was already in the drive. Diego had the run of the place—and had since he'd come to live with them as a teenager—but he'd never truly settled in. And he never took the place under the carport, no matter how many times Rick reminded him that he was welcome to it.

Life hadn't been easy on the kid. He'd survived a car accident that had killed his whole immediate family. Jen had promised Diego that he had a place with them, but then Jen had left too. Since then, Diego had been stuck with Rick, who didn't know a thing about raising a teenager.

The least he deserved was a windshield free of snow every once in a while.

The path to the house was scraped clear, leaving one less thing Rick would have to do himself. Not for the first time, he was grateful for the extra pair of helping hands...even if those hands were connected to the surliest twenty-year-old he'd ever met.

When Rick opened the door, a cat was waiting for him beyond the foyer rug, eyeing Rick with disapproval.

"Evening, Roger," Rick said.

Roger's tawny eyes were flat. As far as he could remember, Roger had never liked anyone, not even when they'd brought him home as a kitten from the shelter in Anchorage. In the years that followed, Roger had grown as heavy and as long as a small bobcat. And his distrust of Rick had grown proportionately.

"I got home as soon as I could," he told his ex's pet.

Roger mewed, a dismissive sound if he'd ever heard one. The orange tabby's tail twitched, a sure sign he was displeased.

"Okay, fine. But Diego's here. I'm not sure why it always has to be me."

Rick leaned over and picked up the massive house cat, adjusting his hold so Roger was in his favorite spot, cradled along the length of Rick's forearm, belly up and head flopped back.

For some reason, Roger preferred to look at life upside down, dangling from Rick's arms. Flipping a switch to turn on the Christmas lights they'd strung up along the hallway, Rick frowned at a three-foot section that had been pulled down. Some of the lights were out.

"Roger, are you eating my decorations again?"

The tabby mewed his innocence...not that Rick believed him.

"Hey, crazy cat guy," Diego called from the living room. "Did you pick up milk?"

Dammit. Rick knew he'd forgotten something.

Draped across the same side of the same living room couch he'd been sitting on for years, Diego still managed not to look sure of his place there. Like Roger, Diego had tawny eyes and a bad attitude. But since they were the only family Rick had, he figured he was lucky. Sure beat coming home to an empty room.

"You didn't get the milk." Diego rolled his eyes.

Knowing he was busted, Rick countered, "When did I become the crazy cat guy?"

"When you decided to stop dating and showering and started talking to the cat instead." Diego didn't smile very much, but he was really good at smirking. And that was definitely a smirk on the kid's face.

"I still shower." Rick raised an arm to give himself a sniff. Did he smell? If he did, had Lana noticed? They'd been standing awfully close...

"I fed Darla." Diego managed to sound like that was somehow Rick's problem. "She's mad at you."

"She's not mad at me. She loves me."

"Go ask her about it. She seems mad."

Well, that was never good. So off to the "study" Rick went to apologize to a hedgehog. The study was actually a third bedroom that Rick had arranged with bookshelves and an old desk. And also Darla.

Tucked in the Roger-proof cage he'd built her, the tiny hedgehog was sleeping deeply. Complete with a little house, furniture, and even a hedgehog-sized potted plant, Darla had the good life. When Rick adjusted Roger on his arm, visually checking Darla's water bottle—because opening the cage with Roger present was a bad idea—the movement woke her up, earning him a sniff and then her quills fluffing up as she turned her head.

Yep. That was a disgruntled hedgehog.

"Sorry, Darla. I had to work late."

She refused to look at him.

"It's how we eat, honey," he reminded her. Darla was not willing to be convinced.

When he returned from the study, Diego followed Rick into the kitchen. While Rick rubbed an upside-down tabby belly, Diego pulled two large bowls out of the dishwasher, still steaming and beaded with moisture from a freshly run load.

"All you had to do was buy the milk." Holding up a nearly empty gallon of milk, Diego shook it pointedly.

Amused at the younger man's grumbling, Rick grabbed two boxes of cereal from the cabinet with his right hand, knowing better than to set Roger down to use his left. Roger required a solid ten minutes of upside-down reflection before consenting to be uprighted. Any less than ten minutes would result in a meow, flattened ears, and a scratch. Any more than fifteen minutes would bring a bite and some fairly dramatic hissing.

Roger's needs were complex and many.

This week, dinner was Raisin Bran and Cheerios. Next week, it would be Apple Jacks and Frosted Flakes. Really, it depended on who did the shopping. There was a kitchen table, but they hadn't eaten there since Jen had left. It had become Roger's domain, where he draped himself, tail twitching, judging whatever Rick was up to that day.

"I went to the town hall. Jonah said the Santa Moose is back."

"No shit. I'll tell Quinn. She loves crap like that."

And Diego loved Quinn, the curly-haired young woman he worked with up at the resort. Not that he'd ever told her. Rick supposed opposites could attract. Quinn was bright and sunny and happy, and Diego was...well...Diego.

But still...he'd waited dinner on Rick. And that was progress.

They'd been doing this for three years now. Cereal. Roger. Sitting on the couch to watch TV and eat in silence. Pissed-off cat on one side, pissed-off twenty-year-old on the other, Rick picked up his cereal bowl and took a bite.

Unbelievably grateful for them both.

CHAPTER 3

EVERY MORNING, LANA TRIED TO put her own makeup on. Every morning, she failed.

This morning was like all the rest, but still, she was determined to try. As she stood in front of her bathroom mirror, makeup laid out on her vanity in front of her, Lana didn't want someone else to take care of this for her. She wanted to pick up the eyeliner and put it on herself. She wanted to feel normal. She wanted to feel competent.

Except...when Lana lifted her hands, they would always shake.

Her hands had been this way for as long as Lana could remember. The best her doctors had come up with was that it was a low-grade stress reaction, starting in her childhood and settling into permanency by the time she had grown. Stressful situations made it worse. Yoga, meditation, and a lot of time in therapy made it better. The result was Lana could control the shaking... to a point. But it was her tell. And when one stepped into boardrooms for a living, it was never good to have a tell.

The hardest part to stomach was the fact that no one ever

blinked an eye at her requests to have her makeup done at whatever hotel was home for the week or month. As if she were shallow—or spoiled—enough to insist on having even the smallest lines of liquid liner painted on her lids for her.

But the opposite was worse. When one was a Montgomery, eyes were always watching. And shaky hands didn't let her achieve the required facade of having herself completely together at all times.

Maintaining the family reputation went hand in hand with maintaining the company's reputation. Whether it was commercial, industrial, or residential real estate, the Montgomery Group had their hands in it. Hundreds of transactions, thousands of properties. From tiny studio apartments to skyscrapers. Lana had facilitated those acquisitions ever since taking her place at the head table of the family business. Working for her family might have given her premature stress lines, but it had also given her an important position at the top of a powerful company, with all the challenges and personal gratification that came in meeting those challenges. Her job had made her stronger, tougher, and more business savvy. She had seen the world one boardroom at a time, experiencing things most people only dreamed of.

But never once had the Montgomery Group given Lana the one thing she'd always wanted: a home.

Abandoning her makeup, Lana made herself a cup of tea. She liked to start her mornings this way, standing in front of the window, her robe wrapped around her, and her shaky fingers cradling a warm drink. She gazed out at the thick blanket of snow covering the mountainside, evergreens thrusting vertically into the sky, strong and straight trunked even in the harshest of Alaska's weather.

No matter what was thrown at them, those trees stayed tall and true, refusing to bend and break.

On every city street, on every beach, in every desert estate... no matter where Lana went, she always thought of these trees. Taking her strength from the lifeblood of the place where she one day wanted to stay forever.

A knock on the door of her suite pulled Lana's attention.

"Ms. Montgomery?" Quinn, her favorite employee at the resort, stuck her curly blond head in through a small opening in the door. "You asked to be woken at seven."

"You can call me Lana," she gently reminded the young woman—not that any of her overtures for real friendship had stuck with the employees at the resort. "And thank you, Quinn. A wake-up call would have been sufficient though. No need to come all the way up here."

The last time she had seen Quinn's name badge, it had read "Hospitality Specialist." Now, her title had a "Head" in front of the other two words.

"Did you get a promotion?"

A rosy blush filled Quinn's cheeks. "Hannah promoted me when she took over as general manager."

"Good." Lana nodded. "It won't be long until you get more. You're very skilled at your job."

The young woman beamed at the compliment, but it wasn't unduly given. Hannah had been smart to advance the best inside her company. Jackson Shaw—the playboy son of the resort owners—wouldn't know a good employee if he tripped over them. Working with Hannah was far easier than dealing with Jackson, and not only because Hannah took her job seriously. Jax would rather hide in town with Graham and Ash than answer her calls or actually show up for any of their scheduled meetings.

No stranger to diversionary tactics, Lana was now no stranger to the pool hall Jax kept hiding out in.

She liked it there too.

"I heard you're trying to catch the Santa Moose," Quinn said, her large eyes widening. "Do you really think you can? It causes so much trouble."

"I'm certainly going to try," Lana promised. "I spent half the night researching how they usually go about relocating a moose. We'll probably have to think outside the box on this one. At the risk of sounding judgmental, it does seem to be quirkier than most."

Quinn looked suitably impressed.

"Come sit with me a moment," Lana invited the younger woman. "Tell me all about this new promotion of yours."

Quinn never needed to be asked twice to talk, which was something Lana loved about her. Lana had positioned a chair at her favorite spot to look out the window. Patting the arm of the chair for Quinn to sit, Lana leaned against the windowsill, shoulders pressed to the cold glass.

"Would you like a cup of tea or some coffee?"

"You? Getting something for me?" Quinn looked horrified at the idea of Lana serving her.

"I promise I won't keel over dead at having to lift a finger." She abandoned her window and the trees for the kitchenette.

"Coffee, please. Black."

"You take it strong." Lana raised an eyebrow.

Quinn radiated a sort of bright energy that was both positive and addicting to be around. She was also the most likely person in Moose Springs to have a house decorated roof to floor in unicorn plushies and puppy dogs with bow ties. The idea of Quinn taking anything strong warred with Lana's previously held assumptions about her. Quinn seemed more the sprinkles and whipped cream type.

"Diego always says if I stopped drinking so much caffeine, my hair wouldn't stick out in every direction." Quinn snickered. "I think if he drank a little more, he wouldn't be such a grump."

The single-serve coffeemaker never took long, although longer than one with pods might have. Quinn wasn't the only one who drank a lot of caffeine to keep going, and Lana preferred to avoid creating a small mountain of plastic pods in a landfill simply because she worked too many hours. Returning with Quinn's coffee, Lana settled into the couch, tucking her legs beneath her. It wasn't the Montgomery way of sitting, but she couldn't have cared less about propriety at the moment. Her toes were cold.

"How's everyone handling the ski season?" she asked. Having never spent an actual Christmas at Moose Springs, she hadn't known how busy the resort would actually be. She'd always returned for the best skiing in late January. Rick wasn't wrong— the resort was filling with more visitors every day.

Quinn slurped her coffee as if it weren't piping hot. The young woman must have a tongue devoid of nerve endings. "Christmas weekend is *so* busy. But I like it. I love staying busy, plus there's all the different parties everyone is throwing, although nothing like your gala this summer. That was the absolute best party I've ever seen here, and everyone was wearing such gorgeous gowns, and oh my gosh, can you imagine if it had been *holiday* themed?"

Quinn sucked in a breath, merrily plunging into a fifteen-minute description of how much she loved holiday parties and how much she wished she could attend the ones in town, but she was always so busy, not that she minded. She'd started taking classes in hotel management online, so one day she might be able to be a manager too, not that Hannah needed any help, but there was an assistant manager position open.

Another breath and a slurp of coffee. "Oh, and then I was telling Grass—"

"From the front desk?"

"He's been promoted too. He's a temporary night manager until they can hire someone with enough experience. So many people have applied, but for some reason, Mr. Shaw hasn't hired anyone yet. It's driving Hannah up the wall."

Lana frowned to herself. No, he wouldn't want to hire a night manager because Jax didn't want to admit the hotel was stretched too thin financially. Instead, he'd stretch his current manager too thin to make up the difference.

"—how Hannah's trying hard to promote as many of us as possible," Quinn continued on, blissfully unaware of Lana's train of thought. "At least the ones who live in town. I think Grass is going to stay permanently now, when he used to be seasonal. I told Diego that Grass got the promotion, and you should have seen how annoyed he was."

Quinn made a face, imitating Diego's surliness. "He looked like he was sucking on a lemon, but you can't blame Hannah. Diego is so nice, but he hates being here, and he doesn't try to hide it. Why would she promote someone who can't stand the guests?"

Realizing what she said, Quinn's large, expressive eyes went wide. "Oh, I mean...I didn't mean..."

Patting Quinn's hand, Lana laughed softly. "Trust me, I'm well aware of the inherent biases of the locals. Graham loves to remind me every chance he gets."

"Oh, he's the *worst* about meeting new people. Me, I love it. His girlfriend works here now. He didn't mind meeting Zoey, did he? See, he's just too stubborn about the tourism in town."

Quinn promptly launched into a description of how amazing Zoey was, which Lana could only agree with. Unable to get a word in edgewise, Lana settled in, finishing her tea as Quinn continued her one-person conversation.

"And then I told Mr. Shaw that Zoey—Oh! I almost forgot why I came here instead of calling." Quinn riffled through her pockets, finally withdrawing a bright orange sticky note. "Mr. Shaw left this note last night. He said to tell you he needs to reschedule your meeting. He has pressing business in town."

Did he now? Pressing business like snowmobiling out on the lake all day or darting off to New York and not telling anybody.

Lana barely kept from sighing, only because Quinn wouldn't have understood the reasoning behind it. "Would you be willing to give Jax a message for me?"

When Quinn nodded earnestly, Lana decided on the more pleasant of the two messages she was considering. "Please tell him that I'm happy to meet him in town whenever his *pressing* business is completed" was far nicer than what she was tempted to say.

Which was: he'd better get his ass in a chair, or she was getting lawyers involved.

This wasn't the first time he'd ducked her. Lana was far too busy to keep playing his game, which Jax knew and used shamelessly to avoid growing up and actually being a productive member of society. It was his job to work with her on coordinating the condominium construction, to negotiate terms for amenity sharing, and a hundred other details that popped up every day. So far, every time he dodged, Lana had been able to shift and stand in his way. Every time he ducked, she simply aimed lower. Jax was good at running away from his responsibilities, but Lana was much better at sticking her foot out and making him trip.

Hiding out in town was his most recent trick to avoid her.

"Well, I better get back to work," Quinn said cheerfully. "Hannah won't like it if she catches me sitting."

When she reached the door, Quinn hesitated. "Ms. Montgomery? The next time Mr. Shaw is having a late breakfast in the VIP lounge, I can call you. He usually times breakfast for when he knows you're in a morning meeting."

That sneaky son of a bitch. Lana wasn't surprised one bit.

"You're a treasure, Quinn," she told the younger woman. "I'll make sure to mention it to Hannah."

Quinn blushed beet red at the compliment, then hurried out the door. The young woman was sweet and never seemed to lose her wide-eyed startlement at the guests in her care. Lana didn't have the heart to tell her that ninety-nine percent of the "special" guests Quinn catered to were selfish, spoiled brats.

"I probably resemble that," Lana murmured to herself as she made a fresh cup of tea and took it into her bathroom. This mug was made to retain heat for a long time. Better for slowly sipping a drink and for keeping one's fingers warm. She sat in front of the mirror, opening her makeup kit.

Maybe today, if she focused hard enough, her hands wouldn't shake. Maybe today, she could be what she wanted to be...a woman with some mascara and without a reputation to maintain. A woman who would face the world with her head held high, who would make good choices for her company, for her family, for her friends, and for the town she loved. A woman who wouldn't be sitting alone at a bar at the end of the night, trying to shed the stress of her workday, because at least the bartender was someone to talk to. A woman who could catch an uncatchable moose and earn the approval of the people she desperately wanted to accept her.

Three dark smudges on her eyelids later, Lana quietly put her mascara away.

It had been a horrible death.

Arms crossed over his chest, Rick took a step back from the carnage in front of him. Jonah was made of stern stuff, but even he shifted uncomfortably. They'd been standing there in the snow for a while, taking it all in.

Some things...some things you couldn't unsee.

"Takes a lot of rage to do something like this," the officer finally said.

"Or premeditation." Rick jerked his chin toward the pile of nearly unrecognizable crushed plastic, a red nose still blinking its final death blinks. "Rudolph never stood a chance, did he?"

The destruction was disturbingly familiar. One Christmas display trampled, the sleigh battered and overturned, Santa's bag of toys launched to the rooftop of the singlewide trailer they stood in front of.

Babbling Brook was a nice name for an empty lot of land down the road from Rick's place. Highly sought-after rental trailers sat at regular intervals, backed up to the small creek giving the RV park its name. Generally, the trailers housed seasonal workers, but there were a handful of familiar faces who made Babbling Brook their permanent home.

Babbling Brook was just one of the places that now had a new owner.

Rick passed by every day, twice a day, so he was used to the cars regularly parked in front of the trailers. The squad car was an irregular visitor, so Rick had pulled over to see if Jonah needed any help. Sadly, they'd all been too late to help the poor decorations in the RV park's front yards. The Santa Moose had struck again.

"You think we should call Lana?" Rick asked Jonah, glancing up at the curious faces peering at them through RV windows. The police officer had already taken everyone's statements, then asked for them to stay in their homes as he surveyed the moose's crime scene.

"You think she knows this place is hers?" Jonah asked,

scratching beneath his chin. "Not sure she'll care about a few acts of vandalism."

Vandalism. Such a mild term for the destruction of an entire community's Christmas displays. Lights ripped off porches. Elves trampled in the middle of present building. One poor inflatable snowman dragged nearly a hundred feet and torn to pieces.

But the real damage...

"Seems the reindeer were the moose's primary targets." Jonah pulled a pad of paper from his inside jacket pocket, then made a few notes. "Can you think of any reason why?"

If someone hadn't known any better, they would think Jonah took these kinds of reports every day. As for Rick, getting called to help out with an animal relocation was one thing. But identifying the inner psyche of a psychotic moose was beyond his scope of expertise.

"This is out of my wheelhouse. I'm not an animal behavioral expert, Jonah. You'd be better to call Fish and Game on that one."

"No, but you and yours have been around these parts for a long time. Your daddy was so smart about these animals, he was half moose himself."

"With the bullheadedness to prove it," Rick joked. "Drove my momma nuts. Guess that was something we had in common."

"How are they doing?"

"Florida is working out better for Dad than the cold up here."

"Yeah, that sounds better and better these days."

Rick had been an unplanned child, and his parents had been well past the point of thinking they'd have kids when he'd come along. With a father in his late seventies and a mother not far behind, the move to a warmer state had been the right call. Still, Rick wished he had a chance to visit them more or at least help them out a little beyond sending what spare money he could.

"All right, I'll make up a report and add it to the file." Jonah scratched the back of his neck. "Do you think there's any chance the moose will come back to this location? Or will it move on to another target?"

"I've never heard of him hitting the same place twice. This guy's MO is pretty clear. He gets in, does his thing, and gets out without anyone the wiser. You may want to tell everyone to put a curfew on their reindeer until the season is over."

Jonah raised an eyebrow. "You're asking me to cancel Christmas?"

"I'm saying that one of these days, some kid is going to be playing in the yard when this animal comes in looking to do some damage. Better to be safe than sorry." Rick picked up a plastic cartoon duck dressed as Tiny Tim, which somehow managed to escape the slaughter by hiding beneath Ebenezer Scrooge. "All joking aside, this has been going on too long. We need to catch the Santa Moose and be done with it."

A spark of humor reached Jonah's eyes. "Well, I suppose we'll have to wait on Ms. Montgomery to catch it, won't we?"

Rick liked Jonah, but he didn't love the way the cop's lazy drawl turned toward amusement.

"You think she won't?"

"I think there's a whole lot of us that have tried and failed. If Easton can't track him, what's she going to be able to do?"

"I don't know, but I wouldn't count her out just yet."

Jonah chuckled, but Rick deliberately ignored him. He set Tiny Tim back on his feet before brushing the snow off his hands.

"I'll call you if I think of something."

Cartoon moose always looked shiftier in Santa hats.

"Okay. Let's talk strategy," Zoey said as she finished drawing arrows pointing at the moose.

Zoey was a tiny thing, and in front of the conference room's oversize dry erase board, she looked even smaller. But pound for pound, Lana's best friend had more guts packed in her than any of them.

"I feel like I've been talking strategy all year." Lana leaned back against the conference table behind her as she checked her phone. "I'm sorry my morning ran long. I had to get spiffed up in the salon. I've ordered us breakfast."

Zoey wrinkled her nose. "Is it—?"

"It's all Zoey friendly, I promise. No trout on toast."

Which was silly because the resort was world-renowned for their trout on toast. The things one did for their friends.

Lana glanced at her watch. "Okay, we have thirty-five minutes before your shift starts, and I need to go hunt down Jackson Shaw in town, then pick up the cookie decorations for my Christmas party."

"Isn't the resort taking care of that?"

"I thought it would be nice to buy the supplies locally." Lana sat in her chair, crossing her legs at the ankles, knees tilted off to the side. Like a Montgomery.

One day, she would sprawl. She'd walk into her family's sitting room in a pair of crushed velvet track pants, and she would sprawl like no one had ever sprawled before. Perhaps she'd do it on New Year's, just to see their reactions. For now, she sat at her conference table, eyeing the cartoon moose on the board.

"Are we taking this seriously?" Lana asked. "Because between us, I have a feeling we're being set up as the butt of the joke. If there's no Santa Moose, we're just two people running around in the woods."

"I don't think so," Zoey said. "I think this moose is a real thing. Graham was in a rush to get home after the meeting last night, and he was up really late Santa Moose–proofing the property. He dragged all his carvings inside the workshop and locked it up tight. He won't let Jake out of the house without us there."

Lana pursed her lips. "The local newspaper this morning said to be careful around decorations. I thought the reporter was joking."

"Oh no. Apparently anything that blinks red and green and white sets the moose off." Zoey set a hip to the conference table, her expression stubborn. "Lana, you're my friend. Everyone else here, they're nice, but they're still Graham's friends. You're mine. And *my* friend has decided to catch this moose, which means I'm going to help her succeed. Even if we only end up as a couple weirdos running around the woods."

Lana stood and went to Zoey, hugging her tightly. Montgomerys rarely hugged outside the family, but Lana had been breaking that rule most of her life.

"Thank you."

After hugging her in return, Zoey pulled over the mobile dry erase board, angling it toward their seats.

"Okay." Lana put her hands on her hips. "We're going to need some MCE."

"MCE?"

"Moose chasing equipment." Lana wrote the letters on the board and underlined them. "And the most important MCE is a good plan of attack."

As Lana and Zoey sketched out their plan, Lana considered how much was riding on this. The town depended on them, and she was going to prove herself worthy to be there...even if she had to break a couple of local holiday decoration ordinances to accomplish their goal.

If one was going to catch a Santa Moose, one *must* do it right.

───────────

The holidays were a good time to be in Moose Springs, even if it was impossible to find parking. Maybe a truck would have been better in the snow, but Rick could appreciate being able to squeeze his car in the tiny spaces left on the side of the street where rental vehicles were parked too close to one another

One couldn't live in this town without being an excellent parallel parker.

Since money was tight, Rick didn't order one of the famous cinnamon rolls at Frankie's, but he did get a cup of tea, nodding in greeting to a sleepy-looking Graham as he came inside. Standing outside on the staircase leading down to the parking lot, Rick let the mingling scents of bread and crisp, fresh winter air play about his nostrils.

High up on the mountain, he could see the ever-present resort looming above their heads, a relentless reminder that this peace and quiet would only last for so long. And off to the left, the beginning outline of what would be Lana's condominiums was starting to take—

Wait. Was that a penis?

"Morning, Rick." A far more awake Graham returned, a box of cinnamon rolls tucked under his arm and two coffees juggled in his hands. He grinned up at the mountainside. "Enjoying the view?"

Rick raised an eyebrow. "You know anything about that?"

"Must have taken some effort." He chuckled, continuing on down the stairs.

Rick sipped his tea, enjoying the heated drink on his throat. With one last look at the mountainside, Rick resisted the urge to go back for something at Frankie's and headed down the staircase instead. He knew he wouldn't remember Diego's milk if he waited until tonight to pick it up, so he angled across the street to the town's tiny grocery store.

Crossing the street downtown was dangerous business, especially with tourists unused to the snowy conditions. No amount of salt on the roads or snowplows clearing the streets could keep them from skating around and nearly running over the locals. At least it was early enough that Rick only had to dodge one shiny new rental car as it whipped out of the grocery store parking lot far too quickly.

A familiar figure backed out of the door, her arms filled with three very full reusable grocery bags, trying to pull her keys out of her purse as she hustled across the parking lot. Rick saw it coming, being no stranger to black ice around there. Despite her boots, Lana took a wrong step, and her feet slipped right out from beneath her.

Just because he saw it coming didn't meant Rick was fast enough to stop Lana from skating across the asphalt, yelping as her legs went one way and her grocery bags the other. How she managed to save them from spilling was a feat of near super-power-type coordination, although she did land on her knee hard enough that Rick winced.

Jogging over to her side—ignoring the still hot tea splashing onto his hands as he did so—Rick nearly ate it himself in his rush.

"That looked like it hurt," he told her gruffly, taking two of her bags with one arm and wrapping his other around her waist. "Are you okay?"

"Nothing damaged but my pride. That could have been a lot worse."

"I can't believe you kept ahold of everything without twisting your back out."

"Yoga is good for flexibility. I can become a pretzel if need be."

Which was something Rick shouldn't have allowed himself to think about. Feeling his face heat despite the cold, Rick cleared his throat. "Well, let's get you up off the ice."

In theory, Rick was more than strong enough to help a woman and her groceries off the ground. But when he planted his boot and pushed himself up, Rick only reached about a foot off the ground when he realized that foot wasn't quite as sturdily planted as he'd thought.

For the second time that day, Lana Montgomery ate it in a parking lot, and Rick was right there along with her. He cracked his head on the asphalt hard enough to see stars, and he was fairly certain his elbow was wedged in his landlady's cleavage.

Son of a bitch.

"That didn't go the way I expected," he told the sky above him, feeling something round and plastic rolling off his abdomen.

Looking down, he saw one of many containers of sprinkles making a getaway. Several more were scattered from the overturned grocery bags, along with...yep. Tampons and gummy bears.

A feminine giggle was about as shaming as being covered in sprinkles. Mentally cursing his own lack of coordination, Rick sat up, rubbing a rough hand over the back of his head to check for blood.

Coming up to her knees, Lana had the grace not to tease him about the gummy bears pooled on his lap. "Are you all right?"

"My pride may have taken a hit there, but the rest of me is fine."

"It was my own fault," Lana said. "I was distracted by the artwork on the mountain, and I stepped on the wrong spot."

"I'm sorry some idiot drew a penis on the mountain," he told her. "If you want, I can help you get rid of it."

"Thank you, Rick. You're a dear, but I'll manage. This isn't the first unexpected and unwelcome penis to point my way. I plowed over the rest, and I'll scrape this one from existence too."

Wincing at the imagery, he said ruefully, "I keep finding myself in the oddest conversations with you."

"It's the magic of being around me. Life is never boring."

She looked great as always in a snug winter dress only she could pull off, paired with a fitted jacket and sleek calf-high boots.

"Are you going on a date?" At nine in the morning? He couldn't imagine why else she would be dressed up so much.

"Goodness, no. Since I've become the scourge of the town, my romantic prospects have taken a turn for the worse. I have an important video conference later, and I wasn't sure I'd have time to change."

"Oh." Clearly, Rick was not at his smoothest this morning, but Lana didn't seem to notice.

"I'm also supposed to have a meeting with Jackson Shaw," she continued. "We're discussing the groundbreaking. Among other things. I need to get him pinned down somewhere. That man is slippery as an eel when he's avoiding work."

"Yeah, he's been like that since we were kids." As he helped her repack her bags, Rick noticed all the shakers of brightly colored sugar sprinkles that hadn't spilled. "You must like decorating cookies."

"I adore it," she said warmly. "These are for the Christmas party. I prefer to buy local. Don't worry. I put the order in ahead of time, so the store wasn't bought out."

As he followed her to her car with the bags, Rick tried to keep his focus on her shoulders and not the subtle sway of her hips. Lusting after one's landlady was not a good idea. Especially when she was cutting him a break. Still, she had curves for miles and shiny hair.

So shiny...it was probably soft too.

"Hey, Rick?"

Pulled out of his thoughts, Rick's knee-jerk guilt made him blurt out, "I wasn't."

"You weren't what?"

"Umm...never mind." Rick bent over and set the bags in the already full back seat of her car, carefully rearranging them so a quick tap of the brakes wouldn't result in them toppling over. "Well, there you go."

Rick watched in detached horror as he patted the top of the bag. Yes. Because sounding like a fool in front of the gorgeous woman wasn't enough, he had to keep looking like one too.

Somehow, Lana seemed to have missed it. She set a hip to the side of her car and smiled up at him.

"I had fun the other night," she said. "Anytime you want a rematch, let me know."

Was she flirting with him? Because embarrassment aside, Rick was tempted to brush the dust off his rusty skills and give it a try.

"Are we betting again?" he asked.

"Depends if there's something good on the table."

Yep. That was definitely flirting. She waited for him to reply, and Rick opened his mouth. Nothing. He had *nothing*. Was it possible to be any worse at this?

"I should probably go track down Jax," Lana mentioned when Rick's mouth refused to help him one bit.

"Good luck with your meeting." Rick jutted his head toward the brand new pickup barely visible as it headed down the mountainside, parallel to the snow art. "That'll be Jax. If he's being too difficult, make him meet you at Dirty Joe's one morning. Jax usually doesn't go there unless someone forces him."

Dirty Joe's was the most popular hole-in-the-wall coffee shop in town, guaranteed to be claustrophobically busy at all times. If the drinks weren't so good, no one would even try to step inside.

"You're an amazingly helpful person, Rick," Lana told him.

"Just trying to be a good friend."

Wait. No. *Noooooo.* He'd used the f-word. The *friend* word. Why? Not that he had a chance with this woman, but why would he do that?

They stood there, the distance between them only a couple of feet apart but far too much. Rick wasn't sure when thinking Lana was beautiful had shifted into trying and failing not to stand too close to her. The fact that she was stuffing her hands in her jacket pockets, standing too close to him too, made it all the more confusing.

He almost did it. He almost opened his mouth and told her she was amazing.

Instead, Rick ducked his head, and he walked away.

Her cousin Silas Thomas was a man sigher.

Now, in her life, Lana had met many a man sigher. The one man in a room full of others hell-bent on making his feelings perfectly clear with a loud, heavy sigh every time he shifted position. A dramatic hand over the back of his neck. Feet kicked out in front of him because the only way for a man sigher to function through his distress at his current situation was to spread and spread some more.

More times than she could count, Lana had sat at in a conference room, recrossing her legs so the pointy end of her high heel could jab into the offending leg of a man sigher getting his spread on. But when stuck on the far side of the table, or worse, on a video call that spanned multiple cities across three continents, a toe nudge and an unimpressed look couldn't cut it.

And boy, were there a lot of men sighing now. Just none as emphatically as Silas.

"Ms. Montgomery..." their chief financial officer, Travis, started to say.

"Just Lana, Travis." She waved off Travis's phrasing with a little flap of her hand. "We've known each other forever."

"Since you were in diapers." The old man's lips curved.

"Nonsense. I came out in Gucci or not at all." Her comment earned a look of annoyance from her cousin Silas. Silas, who had been annoyed since the call started. Silas, who *wouldn't. Stop. Sighing.*

Travis scrolled through a document on his phone—the same document they all had access to. "I've been looking at the budget for the Moose Springs project, and I'll admit to having some concerns."

"This is ridiculous, Travis." Silas's tone was sour. "Forget the numbers. Lana's pet project is already making more work for the rest of us. I already had to cover for her at the investor meeting in Brisbane."

"You weren't covering for me," Lana said firmly. "You were at a party on a yacht, holding a glass of champagne. All you had to do was represent the company and keep your mouth shut."

"I'm fairly sure that's why there were so many models on the boat," race car Killian said, hiding a smirk behind his fist. "To keep you distracted from ruining Lana's hard work."

The man sigher turned into a man sputtering in indignation.

"I'm in charge of acquisitions, Silas," Lana said. "If you're going to step on toes, I'd prefer it to be ones that turn less of an eye toward foot care."

"Meaning stay off her Jimmy Choos, cousin," polo Killian added.

The problem with a family business was that everyone was family. And family gave a certain level of familiarity that could quickly derail these sorts of meetings. Lana pushed ahead, refocusing the conversation.

"I'm not asking for the Moose Springs account to be made a priority, only that the cash inflow be adjusted for some unforeseen conditions."

"Lana, what exactly are these *unforeseen* conditions?" This strong female voice could cut through any sigh, even those offered so expressively and generously.

Lana focused on the screen where her mother was sitting.

While both her parents had made a very positive and very lasting impression on Lana's life, Jessica had been the most influential. Theirs was a family that cared about one another, but they always—*always*—put the business first. They might hug at family gatherings, but they had no problem cutting one another off at the knees if it was for the good of the Montgomery Group. No one's job was secured; it was earned by hard work, dedication, and loyalty. Like a honeybee's nest, each of the worker bees had a part to play.

And working hardest was the queen bee herself, Jessica Madison-Montgomery.

In a world where self-made millionaires and billionaires could be found every time one turned and sneezed, Langston Montgomery was old money. Much older than the Madisons, who had practically built half the city of Chicago after branching beyond their European estates.

Lana had never known if her parents had married for love—although she knew they loved each other now—or if they were part of a subtly arranged marriage in a time when such things were going out of style in their social circles. Maybe it was a mutual appreciation of each other's shrewd intelligence and extreme business savvy. Either way, when the Montgomery and Madison money came together, under the watchful eye of Lana's mother, the Montgomery Group exploded overnight.

Theoretically, with the wealth gathered by the Montgomery Group's holdings, no one in the family should have ever needed to work a day in their lives. But that was not the way they operated. The group's money wasn't *hers*. A bee's hive was where the hardest work happened, not a place to sit and let squander.

Lana would still be negotiating a deal the day they put her in the ground.

"I need to tread lightly," Lana informed her mother. "The town hasn't taken well to the project, and I need to bring them on board. Or somewhere in the vicinity of the ship at least."

"Who cares?" Adrianna—polo Killian's new wife—asked with a derisive snort. "Moose Springs is small potatoes."

"Neglecting small investments in favor of the larger ones is a mistake," polo Killian disagreed, not unkindly. Adrianna's background in marketing was strong, but she had a habit of coming into these meetings trying to flex her muscle. As much as polo Killian adored her, he was a Montgomery through and through. Business always came before emotional attachments.

"Your inexperience is showing, Adrianna," Lana told her, causing a frustrated expression to flash across her features.

"And so is your hangover," Adrianna shot back.

"Lana doesn't get hangovers; it would require her to stop drinking long enough to feel bad," Silas said with a smirk.

Okay, so that comment might have been somewhat unfair. Just because she had developed a bit of a party girl reputation by throwing parties at the Tourist Trap in her downtime didn't mean Lana drank to excess. The constant low-level jockeying for position in the company always upped itself when Jessica or Langston was present.

Maybe they weren't bees. Maybe they were scorpions…willing to turn and sting one another to death.

Lana opened her mouth to tell Silas where to stick that particular comment, but Jessica spoke first.

"Enough, children." Lana's mother sighed. "If my daughter was overimbibing, I'd be the first to know. I know everything that happens in this family. Besides, she wasn't the one making a fool of herself in Australia last week, Silas. Really, dear, try to be a little more professional when there are attractive people around. We do have a reputation to maintain."

The man sigher turned a bright shade of red. Race car Killian snickered, earning an amused look from polo Killian and a nasty one from Silas.

Polo Killian had been sitting in on these meets for his parents for years now, while Lana's aunt and uncle spent most of their time in Beijing and Singapore, facilitating Chinese investment opportunities for the Montgomery Group. Her aunt and uncle always had thrown a fabulous party, and for as much time as polo Killian spent on his Argentinian estates, indulging in his favorite pastime, he was the first to jump on a plane and join them.

The entire family's heart was in the region.

Lana knew the feeling. Her heart was in a region too. Only her region was much smaller, much less wealthy, and could do very little to increase the wealth of a conglomerate used to massively complex, billion-dollar business deals.

Moose Springs didn't matter to the Montgomerys, which made Lana nervous for the town.

"Hold on. Langston is joining the call," her mother said. "My aide has been sending him the meeting minutes, so he's abreast of the topic."

"I'm not sure Father is going to be interested in our extracurricular activities," Lana murmured.

"And yet I get informed of them constantly," a male voice said drolly, the audio feed patching through before the video of Lana's father became visible on the conference chat screen. He was seated in a leather bucket chair on the company's private jet, sipping a cup of coffee despite the low-level turbulence shaking his image.

Lana's father, Langston, was almost—*almost*—the powerhouse his wife was. The fact that both were on this call had everyone sitting up straighter.

"I might be on a delay." Her father's voice was the same calm, authoritative baritone that commanded the attention of those around him. "We're flying near the Andes."

Of course he was. Because it only made sense for her mother to be in Chicago while her father was somewhere in between Buenos Aires and Lima. Next week, he'd be in New York, and she'd be in Paris. The following week? No one knew except their assistants.

Even though her parents loved each other, Lana never understood a life where the person you were supposed to come home to was always thousands of miles away.

"We're discussing Lana's pet project and how much her current level of distraction is costing the company in man-hours," race car Killian informed her father in a lazy drawl.

"Woman-hours, dearest." Lana knew he was teasing her but was unable to keep from rising to his bait. "And I'm handling my business fine. Good morning, Father."

He was a man who rarely showed his feelings, but she knew him well enough to know the watch on his wrist was a birthday present from her when she was seven. The tie was from her mother last Christmas. The affection was there. They just struggled to show it to one another.

"Lana, Jessica." Langston nodded, his sharp mind focusing instantly on the heart of the problem even from half a world away. "Lana, tell me why you're physically in Moose Springs. All this could be handled remotely."

Rattling off her many responsibilities was easy. Convincing her parents someone else wasn't equally fit to cover those responsibilities was harder. By the time her father's plane began to descend in altitude on approach to Lima, she was ready to throw her hands up in disgust.

"It's the holidays," Lana said, her tone indicating she wasn't willing to discuss this anymore. "No one is doing much until the start of the fiscal year. I'm going to stay and attend to affairs in Moose Springs until Christmas, then I'll reevaluate where I'm needed by the first."

"They must really like you in this place," Travis said, tapping his pen against the side of his laptop.

Race car Killian almost managed to cover his laugh. "Something like that," he said.

He'd spent time in Moose Springs too, and he was more than aware of Lana's lack of supporters in town.

As soon as the video call ended, Lana's laptop immediately pinged with a second—entirely expected—call. "Yes, Mother?"

"You look tired," Jessica said. The words weren't meant unkindly and instead were an expression of concern. Still, Lana forced herself to ignore an instinctive reaction to touch her hair in response to the comment.

"Really? I thought I'd paid the beautician enough to make sure I never look tired again," Lana quipped. Free of other eyes, she leaned back in her chair. "Do you agree with them?"

"I agree your Moose Springs project is distracting you, which is a concern in the long run. We need you in the European markets. You know how well you and Killian work together."

"Silas is doing fine."

"Silas is a snot. If he sighed one more time, I was going to have Travis duct-tape his mouth shut."

Lana laughed. "Someone needs to."

"Did you meet someone?"

Lana blinked. "I'm sorry?"

"It would explain some things. I know you've always loved Moose Springs since we were there on vacation when you were a child, but you keep finding reasons to stay around. I don't mind diversification of your portfolio, but these condominiums require very little hands-on attention. Your father and I think you may have met someone."

Of course they did. Because they somehow always knew *everything*.

"I'm here for the town. This place is important to me, and I want to handle things right." Lana drummed her pen against the desk, waited a moment, then admitted softly, "And I think 'met' is a strong word. I may have made a new friend in town, but as much as I travel, there's no point in starting a relationship with anyone right now. It'll just lead to disappointment and hard feelings."

Jessica shrugged. "True. But it isn't healthy to spend all your time alone. Casual dating isn't the end of the world."

"Zoey's here now," Lana added. "If I get lonely, I go bother her."

"It's not quite the same." Intelligent eyes looked right through her, even from thousands of miles away. "This person isn't Jackson Shaw, I'm hoping?"

"Oh goodness, no. He's more overdramatic than Silas and runs through money worse than Killian."

"Which Killian?" Jessica asked.

Groaning, Lana said, "Why? Why do they have to have the same name?"

"Because your father's relatives are insane, darling."

They shared a grin.

"So tell me more about this someone you've haven't quite 'met.'" Jessica leaned in, her interest piqued.

He was sweet. He was kind. He was really good at pool and really bad at meeting her eyes, but when he did...his were the prettiest eyes she'd ever seen. Lana opened her mouth to say it all, but she gave her mother a little smile instead.

"His name is Rick."

CHAPTER 4

JACKSON SHAW WAS NEW MONEY.

As she sat across from him at a little bistro table in Dirty Joe's, Lana hated that the thought had popped into her head. Her opinion of him wasn't affected by his wealth, not in the least. But the reality was new money approached business differently than old money. At most, Jax was third generation and probably the first to have grown up thinking he could live off a trust fund. Unfortunately, business wasn't good, and his parents had made mistakes with their investments. Whether he liked it or not, Jax had to work for a living.

Considering every Montgomery was put to work for the family business from the time they were old enough to stand, Lana didn't have too much sympathy for him.

"Someone needs to take care of the penis," he said. "It's bothering the guests."

Lana wasn't buying that. "I'm surprised you have such little appreciation for snow art, Jax."

She'd heard more than one comment about the penis on the mountainside, and after mulling it over, she said, "Most of the guests are convinced it's a serious piece of art from a local artist."

Jax rolled his eyes. "You're kidding."

Lana took a sip of her drink. "I don't suppose you know how it got up there, do you?"

His smug smile was all the reply she needed.

She could easily believe Jax would be party to snow graffiti next to his own family's business. What was harder to buy was the idea that Jax would invest the effort in creating it. Jax had access to the equipment needed for such endeavors, but he probably hadn't put in a full day's work in his life. Most likely the idea was his, and he'd outsourced the labor.

"Anyway," Lana continued, resting her hand in her lap to hide the fact that it had started to tremor lightly. "I doubt the other guests are so prudish as to care. I've attended enough parties in your hotel to know a little debauchery isn't uncommon."

"The folks want to make a push toward being more family-friendly." Jax shrugged one strong shoulder, his eyes flickering over the room. "I don't make the rules around here, Lana. I only enforce them."

Jax was a smart man and more than a little easy on the eyes. But he would rather be lounging in his flat in New York or drinking in town than sit in a business meeting. Which made keeping his focus on the matter at hand more than a little annoying.

Lana was very appreciative of Rick's tip about Dirty Joe's. They'd managed to procure a table, but the tiny coffee shop was constantly crowded with tourists and locals alike. It was beyond clear that allowing tourists into a business was the key to financial success in town. By the harried expressions of the baristas, it was also deeply stressful.

Apparently, when one was a business owner in Moose Springs, one could either drown in debt or drown in stress. There was no in between.

Every few minutes, someone would bump their arm or purse into Jax's shoulder. Even though the accidental nudges were met with a "sorry, Jax" or a "hey, Jax," she could tell that he was getting annoyed.

"Have you thought about my offer?" she asked, shifting away from snow art and back toward the reason for this meeting.

"The folks want at least four percent more for access to the resort amenities."

"That's five and a half percent higher than the standard."

Jax sat back in his seat, an indulgent look on his face as he crossed his arms behind his head. His elbow was promptly bumped again, and Lana had to hide her amusement behind her drink.

"We're not the ones with something to lose, honey," he told her. "The guests are already coming here."

Lana raised an eyebrow at the endearment but otherwise let it pass. "And when they aren't anymore?"

He tilted his head, the smirk shifting to confusion. "Why would they stop?"

"Because it's overcrowded, and the locals are dead set on keeping everything out. Do you see a fast food restaurant in sight? A gym?"

"There's a gym at the resort."

"In the basement? The one that hasn't been updated in over twenty years, since the resort was built? It doesn't count."

"How do you know about that?"

"Because I stay here all the time, Jax. I have eyes. It was a clever idea, limiting access to indoor sports to encourage money spent on outdoor activities. But it backfired. People want a place to get their CrossFit on." Lana took a sip of her coffee, recrossing her legs. "Trust me. There's very little about this town I don't know."

"Except how to catch a moose." Jax's eyes sparkled in amusement.

It annoyed her when his eyes followed the movement of her legs, although she didn't think the action was conscious. Jax saved his flirting for Ash.

With a sigh, she set her tea down on the table, keeping the mug between her hands to warm her fingers and hide the light tremor. "Yes, well, that particular situation is still under consideration."

Lana had spent the early morning hours scouting the most popular moose sighting locations in Moose Springs, hoping to catch a glimpse of what might be her quarry. And while she'd had the pleasure of seeing lots of the massive, majestic creatures, none were looking particularly shifty.

"You could ask Easton to help you," Jax suggested. "He's a sucker for a damsel in distress."

"To the best of my recollection, I've never been a damsel, no matter how much my distress."

"I don't know. Didn't Rick Harding punch someone for you last summer?"

Lana locked eyes with Jax, knowing what he was attempting to do and almost feeling bad for the man. "That was distress, but I maintain there was very little damseling to be found."

Mentioning Rick was meant to throw her off her game. And it

would have if Jax had asked her if she liked Rick's broad shoulders (she did) or his pleasant voice (that too) or if she was comparing every color of green and brown to his hazel eyes (they were stunning). But Lana refused to feel bad that Rick had come to her rescue that summer.

Jax was going to have to try harder.

"Let's be honest, Lana. You're never going to win them over. You're not catching a moose, you're not increasing tourism, and you're not building those condominiums. Not if we can help it."

In that moment, Lana understood the "we" Jax was referring to, and it wasn't his parents. As many years as he spent in New York, Jax was a Moose Springs man through and through.

Jax might not like Dirty Joe's, but these were his people, not Lana's, and they both knew it.

One point to him.

"I'm willing to agree to three and a half percent but not four. That's nonnegotiable. However, I would like another chai latte. I take it with extra chai."

Jax stared at her. Lana gazed serenely back. And when he grunted and rolled to his feet, Lana knew she'd at least won the battle. Meeting the eyes of onlookers with a friendly nod, Lana stayed in her chair, alone and deep in enemy territory.

It was too soon to know if she had any chance of winning this war.

In the winter, there were always more moose in Moose Springs. Which was why it was perfectly normal to wait at a stop sign while a cow and her two calves crossed the street.

"You can do it. Stay on your feet," Lana said encouragingly to the smaller of the twin calves, watching its long legs sliding on the ice. It slipped, ending up nose down in the middle of the intersection.

"Oh no!" She tried not to giggle at the spindled legs flailing about Bambi-esque as it found its way back to its feet. With the cutest little snort, the calf trotted off after its family.

The driver of a second car waiting patiently in the intersection turned across the four-way stop in Lana's direction. They shared a grin of mutual appreciation of the cuteness...up until the other driver realized who she was smiling at. Concern creased her face as she passed Lana's car.

For a moment, Lana stayed in the four-way stop, wishing for that grin back.

"If wishes were horses," Lana said to herself, choosing instead to turn on some holiday music to play in the background before continuing through the town.

Lana had been a child when they first came to Moose Springs. In fact, the very first moose she had ever seen had been in Moose Springs. Back then, the town was truly a hidden gem, known only to the locals who made the tiny town their home and the few adventurous souls trying to find taller and faster ski slopes.

The Montgomerys had always wintered in the Swiss Alps, the French Riviera, or occasionally in Aspen. Up until that trip, Lana's life had been a blur of metropolitan luxury, Spanish villas, and sprawling countryside estates. Too young to understand who they were, Lana had only understood *what* they were.

The Montgomerys were the ones everyone looked at when

they walked into an office building or construction site. They were the ones who sat at the far ends of the conference tables while others stood and talked. They were a nod, a shake of a head, a tap of a finger on a lacquered wooden surface indicating displeasure.

It took Lana a long time to realize not every family always dined in suits and ties and carefully set tables on private jets weren't the norm. That her earliest education—a string of accomplished tutors—was second only to the education she received at her parents' sides, absorbing boardroom politics as she played with her toys, small quiet things that wouldn't distract.

Then they had taken her to Moose Springs, and Lana's whole view on her life shifted. There was nothing luxurious in town, none of her childish understanding of common amenities. The snow was deep, blanketing this wintery world, and construction on the resort on the hill had only started, so they stayed in a tiny cabin lent to them by a friend of one of her father's colleagues.

As she played quietly with her things, absorbing everything from inside the cabin, she'd listened to her parents' laughter— something so rare that it was cause to take note. In Moose Springs, there were no curt nods. No one tapped an impatient finger or left on a plane for weeks on end.

A hundred thousand dollars in therapy later, Lana had been informed that she had idealized the town in an attempt to process the high level of emotional disconnect she'd always felt from her family. Yes, they loved one another. And yes, their loyalty to one another ran deep. But that loyalty wasn't only to the family as people...it was to the family as a business entity.

Throughout her life, the high pace and higher stress, Lana

never forgot her winter in Moose Springs, her parents cuddling by a fire, the neighbor kids knocking on the door and asking her if she wanted to play.

She did then. She did now too. Unfortunately, no one in Moose Springs wanted to play with a visitor. They were more likely to throw snowballs at her instead.

Despite her many visits to Moose Springs as an adult, Lana hadn't found the courage to ask if Graham, Easton, or Ash remembered her from back then. But she remembered them. She remembered Graham's toothy grin as they made the best snowman ever. How Ash was already tougher than the rest of them. How Easton cried when the snowman fell down and didn't stop crying until he'd "saved" it again. They were part of her reason for coming back here and why the Tourist Trap was her favorite place to eat.

Giving the Tourist Trap a subtle social media nudge had truly been meant as a long overdue thank you from a quiet child without many friends her own age. She hadn't meant to turn Graham's life into a living hell. Really. She hadn't. Which was why she tried to go there so often to talk to him, to help him get through another evening. But Graham had Zoey now, and he didn't need her.

As Lana drove past the Tourist Trap, a slender brunette at the counter proved Lana's theory.

Zoey probably didn't realize she'd taken Lana's seat, the one easiest to talk to Graham from. And Graham, so completely in love with Lana's best friend, would never notice Lana was even gone.

A hundred thousand dollars in therapy allowed her to drive past and truly be happy for them both. Not to stop, giving the couple the space they needed.

Maybe a hundred thousand dollars more would help her figure out how not to feel so damn lonely as she drove back to one more hotel room.

———————————

It had been another slow night. Not dead but close enough that Rick's bank account wouldn't be able to tell the difference. One of these days, no one was going to show up for an entire shift. At which point Rick was going to have to seriously reconsider what he was doing.

Coming inside, he dropped down his wallet on the end table next to the sofa Diego was currently sprawled across.

"I'm thinking about selling out," he told Diego. "At least the tourists actually show up places."

A grunt was all he received from the younger man. Diego must have just gotten home himself because he pulled off his blue shirt of shame—the same blue shirt all the resort employees wore—wadded it up, and lobbed it at the television.

"I already did sell out," Diego said.

"Bad day at work?"

"Is it ever a good day up there?"

"Tell me how you really feel." Rick shrugged. "It pays well. You can get your own place."

"Yeah, but who'd keep your grumpy ass company?" Diego dropped down to the couch.

"Did you see Quinn today?" Rick asked, because like it or not, he was interested in Diego's life. The kid would just have to deal with it.

An instant flush of color filled Diego's face, despite the glare he aimed at his lap.

"You should ask her out."

"You should mind your own business."

Maybe, but since Rick was the closest to family Diego had, he could get away with it. "She's a nice girl, Diego. It's okay to have something nice in your life. Take a girl out, spend some of that money you're such a scrooge about."

"Take your own advice," Diego told him, but Rick could see Diego fiddling with his phone. "I'll go out if you do."

Liquid dark eyes and the best smile he'd ever seen decided to pop into his head. She'd given him enough signs of encouragement that Rick wasn't completely convinced he would get shot down. But finding the courage to ask out the woman of his dreams hadn't exactly been on his to-do list tonight. He'd planned on disappointing his cat and maybe hanging out with Darla for a while. Just because he didn't spend his nights heartsick over his ex anymore didn't mean Rick was ready to move on to being heartsick over someone else. Lana wasn't exactly a permanent fixture in Moose Springs, and Rick had experienced his fill of being left behind.

Except, well…the kid really needed to do something healthier than sitting in the physical remnants of Rick's failed happily ever after, glaring at a blue shirt of shame like it was a copperhead.

"I'll call someone if you call Quinn," Rick conceded. "But it's not my fault if I get told no."

"Way to think positive." Diego snorted, but Rick could see the younger man thumbing his phone nervously.

Rejection preferred solitude, but having a hedgehog never

hurt. They rarely told a secret. Gathering up Darla to keep him company, Rick dressed her in her ugliest Christmas sweater and matching mittens, then put her inside a heated hedgie sock. Rick went to the porch, tucking Darla inside his Carhartt and zipping it up, breath misting in the air in front of his face. It was dangerous to let a domesticated hedgehog get too cold. They could start to hibernate and grow very sick, even die. But Darla loved being outside with him, so a couple of minutes in her warmer would be okay.

Unlike some of the people in his town, Rick had never minded the long, dark Alaskan winters. With the dark came the stars. He'd spent a lot of nights for a lot of years sitting beneath this sky, and it was an old friend.

Some nights, it felt like his best friend.

The kid wasn't wrong. It had been a really long time since he'd taken a woman out. Even longer since he'd called a woman for that purpose.

"What do you think, Darla? Do people even call anymore? Or is it only texting?"

Darla snorted her cute little snout, wiggling in the warmth inside his jacket.

Fiddling with the phone in his hand, Rick knew he wasn't any better than Diego.

"Screw it," Rick finally said, typing a message into his phone to Lana and pressing the Send button. She'd given him her number that summer, not that he'd ever called it. There. He'd texted. Except reception always kind of sucked, and the stupid little bar never finished sending the message. It had tricked him before. Did she get it? Did she not get it? What if it got stuck in the ether and kept sending his message over and over again like he was a weirdo?

Rick had never regretted a "hey" more.

A little text bubble popped up, briefly restoring his faith in technology and the blood flow to his twisting stomach.

"Call me?" he read aloud.

Rick supposed the invitation was better than a few other responses he could have gotten. Yet somehow the idea of calling Lana was far worse than accidentally repeat texting her.

With a sigh, Rick sat on the cold wooden slats of his porch swing, unzipping his jacket a bit so Darla could look out.

The door slammed shut behind him. Diego stomped down the steps, hands shoved in his pockets.

"Where are you going?" he called. Diego ignored him by opening his car door. "Did Quinn say yes?"

Diego answered that with a finger.

"Think that means yes?" Rick asked the hedgehog in his jacket. "You lost your mitten, Darla."

Darla wiggled her little snout, letting Rick tug the protective mitten over her tiny foot before snugging the heated sock around her.

"I think she said yes." Rick rolled Darla over into the crook of his arm. He'd never had children, but he'd wanted them. A surly twenty-year-old, a grumpy cat, and a hedgehog named after a *Buffy the Vampire Slayer* vampire weren't exactly the family he'd planned on, but Rick had learned a long time ago to be grateful for what he had. It could all change in a moment.

He and Diego had that in common.

Since his hedgehog was more important than even this evening's starscape, Rick went back inside and tucked Darla into her heated cage, warming sock and all.

A little squeak met his actions.

"I know, I know, but they come off when you come out of the sock. It's the rules, Darla." She squeaked again. "Baby, it's the rules."

The squeaking hadn't gone unnoticed. After securing her cage, Rick turned to find a pair of tawny eyes blinking at him from the top of his desk, an orange tail twitching.

"Don't eat my hedgehog, Roger. We've talked about this." Roger glared at him balefully.

No one ever listened to him.

When Rick finally had the nerve to call Lana, four hedgie mittens and a bowl of cereal had been attended to, and one cat had been removed from the office, the door safely closed. He returned to the porch, figuring if anyone needed some privacy from a judgmental tabby while making an ass of themselves, it was him.

She answered on the second ring.

"I was starting to wonder if it was me." Lana's voice sounded amused on the other end of the line.

"My hedgehog had a mitten issue. And my cat had a hedgehog issue."

"Your evening sounds far more interesting than mine," Lana said. "The only issue I've had is whether or not to have an olive in my martini."

How could she do that? Jump right into a conversation like

it was nothing when he'd cleared his throat twice in the last two moments, hands sweating in his gloves. Was it hot? It felt hot.

"I'm not a big drinker," Rick told her, going for a third throat clear because apparently, he wasn't capable of better. "Never had a martini."

"So...what are you wearing?"

Rick's jaw loosened, tongue sticking to the roof of his mouth.

"I'm teasing you," Lana said, sounding a bit embarrassed. "Ignore me. I've had one too many olives."

"I'm pretty sure I couldn't ignore you if I tried."

Silence, and then a soft laugh. "Rick Harding, did you flirt with me?"

"Flirted back," Rick said. "You started it."

"Really? I remember a certain 'hey baby' text not that long ago."

"I didn't say 'baby.'" Rick choked on his horror. Yes, it really was hot out there. The twenty-degree weather was much too warm for his clothing choices.

"The 'baby' was implied," Lana assured him.

"Lana, what are you doing right now? Other than the martini olives?"

"I'm trying to figure out how to catch an elusive, violently destructive Santa Moose without the benefit of experience or anything remotely resembling expertise. Why do you ask?"

Rick took a breath, took a chance, and then did the one thing he wasn't ready for...not by a long shot.

"Would you like some company?"

Apparently, Lana would.

It wasn't a date. It wasn't a booty call. Frankly, neither one of them seemed to have any idea of what exactly this was.

But whatever it was, there was a long discussion about ice cream sandwiches and what constituted a dad bod. Lana wasn't sure how the topic had come up, but it probably was the reason Rick had spent the last ten minutes showing her pictures of his fur babies on his phone.

"You have a *hedgehog*. Is that a *Christmas sweater*?"

"Darla is a bit of a fashionista in the winter."

Lana had never been so delighted. Well, she'd once met a baby python snake that preferred top hats and a cummerbund, but Darla had edged out the snake, paws down. Teeny tiny reindeer-themed mitten-covered paws.

She had been close to retiring for the evening, but when a man like Rick "hey baby-ed" her, it was impossible to resist. They'd sat at a little table in the corner of the bar, the trendy plush seating too deep and far too reclined to have a decent conversation in. The seating in her suite was more comfortable, but she didn't want to give off the wrong impression. Besides, the last man who'd been in her room had been there to convince Zoey to fall in love with him.

"Can I buy you another drink?" Rick asked, the words catching a little in his throat, as if he wasn't used to saying them.

She hesitated, playing with the skewer that had once held an olive in her martini. "I'll have a water with you. I'd hate to be the only one tipsy at the end of the evening."

Lana had made a point a long time ago to never let someone else pay for her. She didn't like the way it made her feel, as if she was beholden to them for at least a moment of her company.

Besides, she wasn't sure she wanted to go that many drinks in when he'd been sipping water since he'd joined her.

Still. If she was going to break her rule, Lana was definitely tempted to break it for Rick.

The waiter returned with their waters, and her companion shifted on his purple velvet seat, looking as out of place and as uncomfortable as she was.

"I'm not very good at this," Rick admitted, running a hand over the back of his neck. Lana reached for his other hand, instinctively squeezing it.

"All you have to do is sit there and look good. I promise you're doing fabulously. We're two friends having a drink after what I assume was a long day for you too."

Rick's face flushed a rather adorable shade of red, and he pulled on the neck of his shirt as if trying to loosen a nonexistent tie. Suddenly, he leaned in.

"Thanks for meeting up with me. Diego thinks I need to get out more."

"What do you think?"

"I think he's not wrong. But I'm not sure I could handle more time with Ash and Graham. Easton maybe...he doesn't require me to actively participate in conversations. But I'd have to do more mountain climbing, and he likes the scary ones."

"Like Mount Veil?"

"Veil, Denali. All the big monsters. I'm happier closer to sea level."

Lana smiled. "Me too. At least I'm not a climber. I'm perfectly happy at all elevations. And I'm glad you texted me. I don't have a lot of friends in town. I do my best to be okay with that, but sometimes I wish…" Drifting off, Lana offered, "It is what it is."

"With friends like mine, I can promise you, they're overrated. And intrusive. And constantly bugging me to sign up for every dating app under the sun."

Lana took a sip of her water. "In a town this small, you could pretty much stand along Main Street and shout if anyone wants to see a movie. You'll reach the better part of the town's occupants."

They shared a grin.

"How about you?" he asked. "I'm guessing most of your relationships started in places like Paris or something."

"Trust me, as often as the group runs me across the world, the closest thing to a romantic partner I have is the on-plane snacks," she sighed playfully.

Then in an attempt to be fair to the man offering to buy her a drink, Lana added, "Dating is pretty much a casual thing at this point in my life. I'm never sure where I'll have to be, how long I'll be there, or when I'll be back. Most people prefer a partner who is present and accounted for."

"Most do," Rick agreed. "Sounds lonely."

Most people said exciting. Like her work schedule was one big adventure. But he'd nailed that on the head.

"I'm really close to those on-plane snacks," Lana said, smiling a little. "So what about you? How is a guy as nice as you not taken?"

He cleared his throat, running a hand over the back of his neck, seeming embarrassed. "After Jen left, I wasn't interested. Then I think I accidentally became the reclusive cat lady without realizing it."

Lana tried, but she couldn't help her giggle.

"I only have the one cat, but Diego thinks I'm too involved in Roger's life. And all I do is talk about my ex's nephew, huh?" Groaning at his own words, Rick downed his water like it was a shot of something stronger. "Is this going better on your side than it is mine?"

"It's going perfectly." She could have hugged him, Rick seemed so off his game. "And Diego is your family. If my family was an ounce less scary, I'd talk about them too."

"How's the moose chase going?" he asked.

"Did you know that you can drive around on a snow machine all over this mountainside and not find a single moose in a Santa hat?" Lana sighed. "You'd think it would have the decency to dress appropriately."

On a whim, she reached over and squeezed his hand again. It was a good hand, with strong fingers that squeezed back.

"Rick? Please don't worry. This is a 'hey baby,' not an official date. The rules are much more relaxed. You don't judge me for being a couple drinks along before meeting me, and I promise not to run screaming if you start talking about hedgehog playdates."

Rick barked out a laugh, a warm, pleasant sound that made her feel good for having caused it. "*I* definitely will run screaming. Are you sure you don't want another martini?"

"It's getting late." And late tended to...complicate things. Especially when she was having far too good of a time, and the martini was still warming her veins.

He chuckled. "Afraid I'll turn into a pumpkin?"

"It would be such a shame, with a face like yours."

Rick blinked at the compliment, then this time, he flashed her the handsomest smile. The kind of smile that sent a surge of desire through her, mixed with loneliness and an overwhelming longing to move closer. The kind of smile that kept women who knew better in bars too late at night. No, as much as she wished otherwise, this wasn't a good idea at all. Not when she'd be leaving, and the last thing Lana was going to do was lead him on. Instead, Lana rose to her feet. "Come on. I'll walk you to your car."

Rick quirked an eyebrow. "Shouldn't I be offering to walk you to your room?"

"Yes, but I might get the wrong impression of your intentions," she said, just to make Rick's cheeks flush again.

"How about to the elevator?"

He was such a sweet man. Lana couldn't help but slip her arm through his, hugging his muscled bicep companionably.

Rick had parked in the parking lot off the side of the resort instead of using the valet service, giving them a longer stroll. He offered her his jacket since hers was upstairs in her room, but Lana was used to the cold weather and waved him off. She might not be from Alaska, but she could handle a short walk in the chilly evening air. They reached his vehicle, then he turned.

"Is this where I thank you for the 'hey baby'?" Lana asked.

Groaning, Rick leaned back against the driver's side door. "It really came out that way, huh?"

"I promise I read between the lines."

Impulsively, she started to hug him, then realized halfway into the movement maybe Rick wouldn't want that. Stopping midhug was an awkward business, especially when one's companion had started to return the hug. The result was a tangling of arms and bumping of hands, her hip pressed to his leg and Lana's nose squashing into his jawbone.

"That didn't work, did it?" he said, voice lower and huskier than normal.

One of his hands was on her lower back, warm and strong and very real. Much better than any airline snack.

"It's possible you make me feel like I'm back in middle school, flirting with the cute guy on the school bus."

"You didn't actually ride the school bus to school, did you?"

Lana shook her head, biting her lower lip to keep from giggling. "No. But I have it on good authority there were cute guys to flirt with."

"Well...I *was* a stud in middle school. Best years of my life."

Their mouths were only a few centimeters away from each other. All it would take was turning her head. And then...

And then she would get a call saying she needed to be in Hamburg tomorrow, and she'd just have to walk away. As much as Lana wanted to see where this might go with Rick, he just didn't seem like the one-night stand type. And the idea of hurting him stopped her dead in her tracks. He was divorced and still clearly carrying that hurt with him. He didn't need more from her. So she pressed a quick kiss to his jaw instead.

"Have a lovely night, Rick. Drive home safe."

When she stole a glance at him as she reached the resort doors, the best kind of warmth filled her. He was waiting to make sure she got inside okay. She waved her fingers at him through the window.

It was the best nightcap of all. That dear sweet man got in his car and pulled away, a smile still on his handsome face.

───────────

The phone rang so late, Lana was already in bed, comforter pulled over her shoulders. "I should warn you, I'm half-asleep already."

"I should warn *you*, you're about to get company." Race car Killian sounded as droll as ever.

Lana sighed. "If the warning is coming from you as opposed to official channels, I suppose I should be grateful no one is knocking on my door as we speak."

"Well, not yet anyway. We do have the decency to wait until tomorrow. Silas and I are headed your way."

Hmm. That was interesting.

"Is this for the pleasure of my company," she asked, "or should I reserve the conference room?"

"Aunt Jessica wanted additional eyes on the town. She told Silas to come, but I thought you might appreciate a little backup. Or someone to cheer you on as you give him a wedgie and poke his eyes out. I'm not sure who will be torturing whom."

Killian might be her favorite cousin and one of the family members she trusted the most to be vulnerable in front of, but Lana knew better than to verbalize how nervous it made her that Silas was coming to town.

Silas and she had butted heads for a long time, and it wasn't safe to have Moose Springs caught between them. Instead, Lana looked down at her hand, mentally willing her fingers to stay calm on her bedspread.

"I haven't given anyone a wedgie in a very long time, and my nails are far too nice in this particular shade of mulberry. If anyone is being tortured, it certainly won't be by my own hands."

"Yes, because I'm supposed to believe that you *always* let everyone else get their hands dirty." Killian chuckled. "I grew up with you, Cousin, remember? I know all your secrets."

"This is why I like polo Killian more. He was much too busy being awesome to care about what I was up to." Lana sighed. "Fine, I will see you when you arrive. Anything else I should be warned about?"

Silence, then Killian's voice took a rare turn for the serious. "Be careful on this one. Silas wants to see you fail for his own reasons."

Of course he did. Silas was a snake in the grass, waiting to strike whenever the opportunity arose. The instant he sensed weakness, he would be all over her in an attempt to discredit her in front of the board of directors. Of course he was coming to Moose Springs. He'd probably suggested it to Jessica in the first place.

"Thank you for the warning, Killian. I'll be on my best behavior."

Lana ended her call, then lay back on her bed, staring at the ceiling. Knowing her mother's love of multitasking, this probably wasn't just about the financial investment in Moose Springs. Mentioning Rick had been a mistake. Lana couldn't just date whomever she wanted or hide away in Moose Springs whenever she felt like it without bringing attention to herself or the other person.

When one was a Montgomery, one's position in the company

was tied directly to the fortune behind it. There was a reason she had to work so hard and go where the company needed her. A hundred and fifteen billion reasons. A hundred and fifteen billion ways to make a mistake.

And Lana was positioned to inherit it all.

CHAPTER 5

NOTHING WAS BETTER THAN CAFFEINE in the morning.

Since Lana hadn't gotten much sleep the night before, she was more than happy to sit at Dirty Joe's and get as much of the stuff in her system as she could. Killian's warning phone call had left her too wired to rest, so she'd already had a busy morning, making the most of her insomnia. Driving around town in the earliest morning hours and stalking the brightest of the Christmas displays hadn't yielded a chance to catch the Santa Moose, but it had given Lana a firsthand view of the moose's destruction.

This was the first time she'd gotten to see what it was capable of. The moose had hit the west side of town in the middle of the night, and nothing had been spared. Strands of lights had been ripped from the bushes in front of businesses. Inflatable decorations had been maimed. One poor six-foot-tall plastic candy cane had been dragged into the street and stomped to smithereens. Whoever this moose was, it wasn't afraid to let its feelings known. As she drank her coffee, Lana had to admit that she felt a little envious. Considering Silas was coming to town, she was facing a day of biting her tongue...at least in public.

Thankfully, Lana had asked for backup, in the form of canine moral support. That support was currently heading her way, waiting for a break in the traffic before hurrying across the street.

"Sorry we're late." Zoey hustled over to meet Lana in front of the coffee shop. "Someone was being a total diva about hats this morning."

Okay, Lana was wrong. Caffeine was great, but puppies in sock hats were even better.

The leash in Zoey's hand was clipped to the collar of the most adorable creature in existence. Jake, Graham's floppy-eared border collie, had been blind since birth. The diner owner had found him abandoned as a puppy beside the Tourist Trap dumpster years ago, and an incensed Graham had spent the time in between then and now compensating for that act of human indifference by being the best fur father a guy could be. Never would a day pass where Jake was denied food, attention, designer sweaters in the winter, or sunblock for his wet nose in the summer.

Except for his favorite pajamas, Lana had never seen Jake wearing the same outfit twice.

"He didn't like a hat on his ears? I thought he'd be used to them by now." Lana leaned over, letting Jake sniff her fingers before running them through his silky coat. He wriggled his entire body with happiness, pressing against her legs as his tail thumped the side of her kneecap.

"Oh, Jake's fine no matter what we put on him. It's Graham who's a nightmare. He's convinced that you're going to judge Jake's clothing, and he would not shut up about cummerbunds.

Seriously, who has a cummerbund for their dog? Who has *multiple* cummerbunds for their dog?"

Jake wasn't wearing a cummerbund, but he was wearing a festive green-and-red-plaid sweater with a coordinating knit sock cap.

"A man with discerning taste, love." Lana straightened, giving Zoey an impulsive hug. "Or a serial killer. We're still not sure about him."

"You never should have let him take me home the night we met," Zoey sighed.

"Maybe, but it all worked out for the positive." Lana hooked her arm companionably through Zoey's as they headed into the coffee shop. "Besides, Rick dresses up his hedgehog. A fondness for accessorizing their fur babies might be one of the more adorable local quirks."

"You're in a good mood today."

"I wasn't aware I was ever in a mood other than good," Lana countered. "Perhaps I need to work on being my better self."

"No, they see only good mood Lana. I see real mood Lana, and real mood Lana is in a good mood. Is it a *guy*?" Lana didn't reply, so Zoey elbowed her ribs. "It's totally a guy."

"I have no idea what you're talking about."

"Yep, it's a guy."

They'd started having breakfast or coffee together a couple of times a week before Zoey's shifts at the resort. Seating was never available at Dirty Joe's, but there was a nice bench outside if one was willing to sit in the lightly falling snow.

Lana was more than happy to do so.

Jake was perfectly capable of walking into the coffee shop

with them, but Lana scooped him up as if he were a little dog. She couldn't carry him around one armed like Graham could, but Jake was on the smaller side as border collies went, and Lana was strong. She snuggled Jake as they ordered their coffees.

"I'm amazed he actually has working legs, considering how everyone always babies him." Even as she said it, Zoey was sneaking Jake bits of biscotti.

Lana dropped a kiss to Jake's cute little snout. "I don't baby you at all, do I?"

Nose-to-nose, it was much easier to dodge being licked in the face than dodge the eyes watching them. So Lana did what Lana always did...she met those eyes with as much fearlessness as she had at her shaky fingertips.

"It's a beautiful day, ladies and gentlemen. Is everyone in the holiday spirit?" Nothing, zero, zip. "Say good morning to the nice people, Jake. Good morning!"

Obedient as ever, Jake promptly barked twice, tail wagging so hard, it thumped her back in the best kind of brutal massage a person could ask for. Now *that* broke the icy glares, because no one could resist him.

Lana watched Zoey carefully add her cream and sweeteners just so, and when the drink passed the point of food and reached an artform, they retreated to a bench a little bit away from the coffee shop's entrance.

Grateful for the warmth of her jacket and the fleece lining in her boots—Montgomerys *never* wore fur—Lana sipped her drink, watching Jake sniff around the bench, secure in his position between her and Zoey.

"Thank you for letting me have Jake today."

"Thank you for *watching* Jake today," Zoey said. "There's been another Harold sighting."

Harold was the much-despised Alaskan Food Safety and Sanitation inspector working Moose Springs. Lana had never met the man personally, but from what she'd heard, he was a particularly noxious and petty type of person. The kind to not look the other way when a cute border collie was sleeping next to the grill cook. His reign of terror had started a "Harold watch" through the town, with most businesses choosing to close for the day just to annoy him when they knew he was coming. Oh, Harold would get to them eventually, but the townsfolk made him work for it.

Usually, Graham was the first one to shut down on Harold sighting days.

"Graham has a supply delivery," Zoey continued, "so he can't close up. And Ash has a packed day. She's transporting some people from Anchorage to here, then making a supply run up north. She won't be back until tomorrow, and you know how Graham gets if he goes a night without Jake."

"Adorably overprotective?"

"I was going to say 'pain in the ass,' but yours is nicer." Zoey took the first sip of her coffee. There was a pause as she considered it, then a small sigh. "Close enough, I guess."

"I hate to say it," Lana told her, "but you're going to always be disappointed unless you lower your standards a little. Compromise isn't the worst thing in the world."

"When it comes to coffee, it is," Zoey said serenely, adjusting her glasses on her nose.

Zoey's eyes had dropped to Lana's fingers, where she kept them around her coffee cup.

"The shaking is worse today." Zoey reached over and took Lana's hand in hers. "Are you okay?"

"I've never felt better. It's the cold."

"Why don't you go somewhere warmer for a few days?" Zoey sighed longingly. "I know I wouldn't mind a few weeks on a beach in the Caribbean."

"And miss out on Moose Springs during the holidays? Nonsense." Lana jutted her chin at a pair of teens across the street trying to drive away a moose standing too close to their car, waving their arms and yelling in frustration. "They're practically dripping with the Christmas spirit."

Zoey giggled, then cursed as she spilled her drink. "Ugh, why do I keep doing that?"

"Perhaps you're oversexed, overworked, and far too happy for your own good." Lana was pleased to see the blush spread over Zoey's face.

"I think I might propose."

"To Graham?" This time, Lana was the one to nearly spill her drink.

"Don't tell me you're too old-fashioned to be the one to propose."

"I think if I proposed marriage to someone without a billion-dollar trust fund, the family would be privately horrified. Most of them anyway."

"And publicly?"

Lana exhaled a soft laugh. "Publicly, we would put on our serene faces and refuse to comment. As one does."

"You know what I wish? I wish you could have a serene face that didn't require anything but you being happy."

Yes. Lana would enjoy that too.

Zoey scooted over and leaned her head on Lana's shoulder. "I like having you here. Being around you is the best part of Moose Springs."

It probably wasn't true, not with how utterly happy Zoey was in this new life she'd created so easily for herself. But Lana soaked in her friend's words, thinking this morning, she'd be pleased to pretend otherwise.

They finished their drinks, then Zoey passed over the leash. "I'm supposed to tell you half a dozen things you already know about his daily needs."

"But I already know them, so you won't waste our time."

"Exactly." Adjusting her glasses again, something that had become a habit more than a necessity, Zoey raised an eyebrow. "Are you ready to catch a moose tonight?"

"I was born ready."

With a fist bump of solidarity, Zoey headed off for her car. After she disappeared down the road toward the resort, Lana turned toward her companion.

"What do you think, Jake? Will we catch the moose? Or get trampled to bits?"

Jake was an honest dog, so he whined and stuffed his nose beneath her leg. Patting his head in reassurance, Lana sighed.

"Yeah, that's what I was thinking too."

———

The day Lana turned twelve, she fell in love for the first time. Young love was always fleeting, especially when waiting outside her mother's office while she finished a phone call. The only other person in the waiting area was the assistant's thirteen-year-old son. For those twenty-three minutes between sitting down with her worn copy of *Pride and Prejudice* and trailing her mother out the door, he was the most fascinating creature she'd ever met. Shy and uncomfortable as always, Lana wouldn't have said a word, peering at him from behind her pages with surreptitious glances, but he had been bored and chatty, and he liked to read too.

To Lana, for those twenty-three minutes, that boy was *everything*.

Then, before Lana left with her mother, he'd given her a copy of the book he'd brought along too. Among all the other things Montgomerys didn't do, Montgomerys didn't accept gifts, except from family on Christmas and birthdays. But since it was her birthday—and she'd stuffed the book inside her sweater to hide it from view—Lana kept it. *The Two Towers* hadn't even made sense when she hadn't read the first book in the trilogy, but she'd hugged that book from the boy she'd briefly loved. And every time she picked up a story about adventures in far-off places, she'd felt a warmth of remembrance.

As an adult, whenever she found a spare moment of time, Lana read. And when her time involved puppysitting the most perfect animal in existence, Lana would read to him. After all, the holiday decorations in the resort lobby were exquisite, rustically festive, and utterly on brand with the snowy mountainscape outside. The Christmas songs playing over the radio were relaxing. Her cousins were going to land in the helipad behind the resort anytime now, so it was the perfect moment to steal a chapter or two with Jake.

Jake preferred romance, but he contented himself with Lana's epic fantasies. Stretched out over her lap, he was the perfect place to rest her book, the broken and well-worn spine balanced on his back as Lana waited in the resort's lobby. At some point, Silas and Killian would arrive, and she supposed the least she could do was meet them.

"I see Graham talked you into dogsitting for him."

As soon as he heard Rick's voice, the dozing border collie's ears perked. As Rick approached, Jake's rear end started to wriggle, causing Lana's book to end up in her lap.

"On the contrary," she said fondly. "Graham's *allowing* me some Jake time. Jake's a hot commodity in this town."

Lana patted the seat next to her in welcome. Rick sat, setting a nylon tool bag at his feet.

"Reading during work hours?" His warm baritone was better than her morning coffee.

"I am the product of my environment." She waggled her book at him. "What can I say?"

"An environment that induces escapism. May I?" At his request, Lana handed the book over, wondering why she suddenly felt shy. Maybe because it was her favorite, and these days, Rick was becoming one of her favorites too.

Rick turned the book over, reading the back cover as if he truly wanted to know what she was reading.

"It's something I've read a few times since I was a kid." A hundred. At least a hundred and ten times.

"Looks well loved." Rick tapped a thumb on the spine before handing it back.

"I buy a new copy every couple of years. I try to read the newer stuff, but sometimes you want to open a book and know you'll be happy with what you read. It's like…"

"Like an old friend," Rick said, as if he completely understood the feeling.

"Exactly."

An old friend who had been there, when it felt like "there" was everywhere, and everywhere was pretty much a life of empty hotel rooms. Their eyes met, and Lana felt a rush of warmth flood through her. Had it only been last night that she'd seen him? For some reason, it felt a whole lot longer.

"I have another copy on my phone. Do you want to read this one?"

If she had been a dog in a bib, rolling a meatball toward him with her nose, Lana couldn't have possibly felt more awkward. Rick accepted the book, tucking it into a pocket in his heavy winter jacket.

"Thanks. I get a lot of downtime at work. Reading passes the time. Hey, last night…" Rick cleared his throat, and just like that, Lana was twelve again, and their twenty-three minutes were up. It wasn't safe to let herself too close to him anyway. Last night might have caused a kind of toe curling she hadn't felt in forever, but Lana was a realist. A "hey baby" between two lonely people just before the holidays was not a promised path to happily ever after.

"It's all right," she said. "I understand. No need to explain."

Maybe Rick would have the decency to leave before her smile

slipped and the fact that she was oddly devastated became humiliatingly clear.

"I was going to say last night was the best night I've had in years."

Ah. Well. That was a different story, then.

Lana didn't trust herself to immediately answer. Her heart pounded in her chest, loud enough that she couldn't hear, let alone think. Thankfully, Rick was a patient man. He simply waited, resting a strong hand on Jake's back.

"I had a nice time too," she finally said.

Only a slight relaxing of his shoulders gave him away. Maybe Lana wasn't the only one feeling the whiplash, because he took her hand, squeezing gently before saying, "I was hoping so."

Rick had no idea how little human contact she had in her life or how no one had held her hand in…well…she couldn't remember. Lana tried very hard not to hold on to his too tight in response.

"Did you catch your moose yet?" he asked, as if—like the book—he truly cared about her mission.

"Tonight's the night. Zoey and I are on the hunt. Moose will be relocated, peace will be restored, and Christmas decorations everywhere will feel safer. "

He flashed her a quick grin. "Let me know if you want some backup."

She almost took him up on it. Before Lana could answer, a message chirped on her phone, breaking the moment between them.

Rick let go of her hand so fast she almost thought he was embarrassed. But the way he was looking at her, his hazel eyes locked on her, it was hard to believe his interest wasn't real. Real and welcome and amazingly confusing. Unfortunately, this wasn't something she could take the time to figure out now. Not with a second, more imperious message beeping on her phone.

Taking refuge in a puppy, Lana stood, Jake's leash in her hand.

"I'm sorry, I have to go meet two of my company's board of directors," she said. "I'd invite you, but one of them is fairly annoying."

Rick nodded, rubbing his hands together. "It's fine. I should go too. I promised Hannah I'd fix the pool table in the game room. It keeps eating balls."

"You're daring me to say something off-color, aren't you?"

"The thought crossed my mind." He chuckled, standing.

Lana patted his arm, thinking the muscles beneath his waffle shirt were nice and firm. "It's hard work being competent."

He flashed her the sweetest look, making him far handsomer than every other man in town. He probably didn't even know it. "Have a nice day, sweetheart. I know being our evil overlady is a busy job."

"You too?" When Rick winked at her roguishly, there was absolutely no way she could be offended. As Lana hustled off to the helicopter pad on the far side of the complex, she couldn't help the curving of her lips.

He'd called her sweetheart. Lana was pretty sure she liked it.

―――――――――

This must have been a slow week for Locketts, or else Ash was working outside her comfort zone for some extra Christmas money. The familiar helicopter with its telltale dragon artwork rarely played courier for travelers uninterested in making the drive from Anchorage International Airport to Moose Springs.

Lana waited for her cousins with Jake at her side, standing far enough away that there was no risk of Jake getting accidentally hurt by strong propellers blowing ice and snow around them. Ash landed with a harder thump than usual, at least from what Lana had seen of the pilot's skill.

Silas got out of the helicopter, a telltale sneer on his face as he ignored them all, focus on his phone. A bemused Killian followed, catching Lana's eyes from behind Silas's back and making a face at Silas. She didn't even try to cover her amusement.

"Did you get a dog?" Killian asked.

"I'm puppysitting." Lana took a step back. "He's blind. Let him sniff you first."

Sniffing completed to Jake's satisfaction, he pushed his muzzle into Killian's hands. "Hey, buddy," Killian said, instantly charmed. "I like your hat."

"Only the finest in attire for him." Lana deliberately sounded aloof, making Killian laugh.

"At least you didn't stuff him in a Chanel bag," he said.

Abruptly, Silas looked around, sniffing in distaste at the stunning scenery. "So this is Moose Springs? The pictures online did it more justice than it deserves."

Lana rolled her eyes. Silas was family, but he didn't have the Montgomery name. That shouldn't have been a bad thing, but Silas had always been insecure about his place in the family. Where Lana was privately envious of Silas's anonymity, he was desperate to prove himself to the group. Lana felt compassion for him...but honestly? The man was tiresome.

"So to what do I owe the pleasure of your company?" Lana

asked, even though she already knew. Silas was about as sneaky as a pig in an inspector's cape. "If you're here for the ski slopes, I'm happy to arrange a private lesson."

Lana could practically see Silas's hackles raising. Like all the Montgomery family, her cousin had learned to ski practically as soon as he could walk.

Before Silas could answer, Ash cut the engine and climbed out of the helicopter, grabbing two bags out of the cargo area. Killian moved to help her, but Ash didn't need help dropping Silas's custom-made, hand-stitched crocodile leather suitcase to the snow. She did hand Killian his much more modest, if equally well-made, bag with slightly less contempt.

"I should have guessed these two belonged to you," Ash said to Lana.

"I take it you failed to impress our local helicopter pilot." Lana grinned as she greeted her cousin with a hug. "Killian, you're losing your touch."

"You're lucky the mouthy one didn't get tossed out halfway between here and Anchorage," Ash added. Silas shot her a dirty look, which Ash returned in spades.

"The customer service was as lacking as the amenities," Silas said.

"I offered him a beer." Ash shrugged. "Not my fault he had to get all snooty about the brand. Hey, Jake."

The border collie wagged his tail, wriggling at the sound of Ash's voice. "I can take him," she told Lana as she moved over to scratch Jake's ears. "Graham can suck it up and survive without him until tomorrow."

"No, it's okay. He's making my day far more pleasant than it would be otherwise."

Ash snorted, glancing at Silas. "Yeah, I can see why." Patting Jake one last time, she stood and nodded briefly to Lana. "Later."

"Why do I get the feeling that's her version of a loving hug goodbye?" Killian watched Ash head back to her helicopter, his eyebrow raised in appreciation.

"I wouldn't suggest it," Lana said. "She's liable to make mincemeat out of you before you can blink twice. Not that you've ever listened to a warning to play it safe in your life."

"I'm perfectly capable of being circumspect. Where's your friend Zoey?"

"Point made," she said.

"We're not here for that." Silas sniffed, dismissing Ash and the helicopter as he turned around, taking in the stunning winter scenery. "The Montgomery Group wants to know more about the Moose Springs acquisition."

"Information I've been forwarding regularly. Silas, haven't you been reading my emails? I'm hurt."

She wasn't. Most of the emails he sent, she shoved in a folder to be looked at later. The man had never learned to be brief in his life.

"Your reports are filtered through rose-colored glasses, Cousin."

Lana didn't miss a beat. "And you two boys were sent to check up on me. I'm not sure whether to be embarrassed or offended."

"Offended, knowing you," Silas shot back.

"Oh, Silas, not offended for me," Lana said pleasantly.

"Offended for you. You wouldn't know what to do with a town like Moose Springs—or any town really—even if I tried to teach you. Your lack of bedside manner might be appropriate for other markets, but frankly, you have the likability of a garden slug in a salad bowl. No one wants you around. And in an acquisition like the Moose Springs properties, getting along with the business owners is far more important than flexing your muscle."

Needling him was too easy...and too tempting to resist. Which was why she patted his arm. "What muscle you have, Cousin."

Oh, if looks could kill.

"Do I need to separate you two?" Killian asked, stuffing his hands in his pockets as he looked in between them in amusement.

Before Silas could respond, Lana shut him down.

"Silas, this isn't your town. It's their town. We're simply trying to bring in something that will both increase the value of our current holdings and put more money in the pockets of the residents. Coming together to find common ground on how to make it work isn't something that happens over a conference table. You have to spend time with them. Listen to their concerns. Understand how they're affected."

Silas ignored her, instead choosing to frown out at the future condominium site just beyond the current resort grounds. He took in the lack of significant progress. "Why aren't we further along in construction?"

"It's midwinter in Alaska," Lana said. "How exactly would you suggest I budget in the removal of this much snow or digging foundations in permafrost?"

A snort was his only reply. Silas's phone chirped with a

self-important beep. He held up an imperious finger, indicating he needed to take the call.

With Silas distracted, Killian leaned in, whispering out of the corner of his mouth, "Hey, is it me or does that look like a—"

"An acre-wide snow penis? Yes." Lana shot him an amused look.

As they walked toward Lana's compact SUV, Killian sighed. "Don't you ever get tired of it all? Every day is the same old thing. Jump when the group says jump. Always pick up when Aunt or Uncle call."

"Mother and Father for me, but yes, I agree. It's tiresome."

Killian leaned back against the vehicle, crossing his arms as they listened to Silas snarl at someone in Italian.

"His accent is atrocious," Lana shook her head. "You should be on that project, not Silas."

"I'm not reliable enough." When Lana open her mouth to defend him, Killian gave a shake of his head

"No, they're right. I only do what I have to to keep my parents from mortification or the group from firing me. We all know I'm the rotten apple of this family. I'm a good face at functions or a fun night out on the town."

"You're not the rotten apple, dearest. You're slightly mealy at worst." Hugging him around the waist, Lana shook her head. "You're cutting yourself short, Killian."

"Maybe I should learn to play polo…"

Lana leaned into him companionably. "Please don't. I have enough trouble telling you and polo Killian apart. Can you imagine if you both were the same boring suck-up?"

There. She managed to pull a real grin from him, the kind that reminded her of when they were kids. The real smiles from her favorite cousin—not that she'd *ever* tell him he was her favorite— were few and far between. Killian was an adrenaline junkie, and he ran with a crowd that indulged him in his constant need to push the line between excitement and stupidity. But Lana had never gotten the feeling that Killian was ever truly happy.

"But seriously, how's Zoey? I've been thinking about her."

He also had the worst crush on Zoey, not that Lana had ever encouraged him. She also couldn't ask him to leave Zoey alone. That would have painted a big heart-shaped target on Zoey's forehead. Killian loved a challenge.

"Zoey is fine. She'll be very happy to see you." Lana frowned at Silas's back. "I'll bring her around when *he's* not here."

Killian sighed. "He's been glued to the phone since we took off. I think it makes him feel important."

"He's important enough to cause me problems," Lana said under her breath as Silas ended his call.

Silas turned to them. "The reception here is terrible. Why in the world are you so fixated on this place?" He looked at the stunning vistas around the resort as if they were nothing, visibly unimpressed.

"Moose Springs has a lot to offer," Lana said. "When my condos are done, investors will have the opportunity to experience a small-town lifestyle with all the comforts and amenities of the world-class resort connected to the estate."

"A resort widely overstretching its resources versus income. How can a place this popular fail to turn a profit?"

Lana frowned at the resort. "Bad management, mostly. The

Shaws are great people, but they're ready to retire. They've left too much up to Jackson, who isn't as business savvy as his parents. Each year, the town votes to increase the taxes the resort has to pay to stay in business."

"Don't they realize they're cannibalizing themselves?" Killian asked. "The town's income is based on tourism."

"The locals are actively trying to drive out the resort and the people who visit. So far, they've been unsuccessful, but small things are undercutting the profit margins of the place. Unfortunately, they're spearheaded by a man who is a little too smart for his own good. Graham Barnett's the one who keeps pushing the city council to increase the taxes."

Killian's handsome face soured. "I can't stand that guy. I have no idea what Zoey sees in him."

"Probably all the muscles," Lana said. "You don't like him because he's the only one who's ever beaten you in a tussle."

"He took me by surprise. I'd like to see anyone fight well after getting sucker punched."

"If you two are done gossiping, we have properties to visit." Silas clicked through a series of emails on his phone, finding a document and opening it. "Travis sent me the list of our acquired holdings. I'd like to see them all."

Since Lana was trying stupidly hard to fit in with this town, the absolute worst idea in the world was to take Silas to the bulk of the commercial buildings in Moose Springs and let him unleash his power trip on the unsuspecting locals. They would hate him and hate her even more for subjecting them to him.

"I don't think—" she started to say.

"Never stopped you before, Cousin." Silas smirked at her, then climbed into the passenger seat of her SUV without invitation.

She almost took him to the Tourist Trap then and there. If anyone deserved Graham's sense of humor, it was Silas. However, that would mean dragging Killian along too, and Killian might not have wanted to be in Moose Springs in this capacity...but he would stay until the job was done.

Maybe she would be lucky and everyone would be closed. It was a Harold sighting day after all.

Sighing, Lana put her car in reverse, making a three-point turn in the snow.

"Okay, the first property we should go to is the police station. The building is small, and they rent it from us at a discounted rate—"

If anyone asked, Rick had a favorite car in town.

Some of his friends didn't love that particular car, but Rick always felt his heartbeat start to pick up whenever the sky-blue compact SUV drove past.

Up until that summer, Lana's choice of vehicle had changed depending on if she was going to be in town for a few days or a few months. A car, a truck, a town car from the resort. One summer, she even went everywhere on a sleek black motorcycle, although she made everyone a little nervous when she took her corners too fast.

But the day they'd learned she'd invested in the town, Lana had bought a modest-sized, sky-blue Mercedes SUV. Now, every time he saw sky blue, Rick thought of brown eyes that danced. Of slender fingers and a breezy laugh.

The last couple of days had been confusing but exhilarating. Rick's hopes weren't up—he knew better than that. It was just... well...it was nice getting to talk to her. It was why he'd hurried to the resort that morning when Hannah had called. *She* was why he hadn't minded the extra task.

Thinking about Lana caused Rick's heart to do a skipping thing, making the simple act of breathing a little harder than it should be. Like a band squeezing across his chest and his stomach at the same time.

When the Mercedes SUV pulled up in front of his business instead of continuing down the street, Rick's heart progressed to hammering in his chest. She could be headed to another of the unmarked shops on the row, but Rick hoped not.

It was stupid how his palms began to sweat when he heard her voice outside the door.

He hadn't felt this way about someone since high school. Grown men didn't have crushes. They had relationships. Marriages. Divorces. Still, when Lana stepped through the door, her eyes finding his, it was useless to pretend this was anything but a crush.

Lana came inside, shaking a light brushing of snow from her long, thick, cream wool overcoat. He rarely paid attention to clothes, but she had looked stunning that morning at the resort. There was something about the dark slacks, rose-gold sweater, and expensive-looking boots she wore that made him think she was in work clothes. Lana always looked great, but there was a level of perfectionism in her outfit that reminded him of a movie or maybe a photo in a magazine.

And of course, Jake was glued to her side. It was hard not to be a little jealous of the border collie.

Rick had been playing a game, feeling more cheerful than usual that morning. Harold, the Alaskan Food Safety and Sanitation inspector, had yet to be by, and the town's gossip forum said he was at the resort and would be there for a while. Rick had polished everything in the kitchen until it gleamed, with extra time to spare. He personally detested Harold—the pompous ass had made his ex cry more than once—and he counted it as a personal victory when Harold couldn't find anything wrong to mark on his inspections.

After setting his cue down across the table, he met Lana halfway in between.

"Hello, Rick," Lana greeted him warmly, placing her hand on his arm and going up on her toes to kiss his cheek.

Saying something intelligent would probably help, but instead, all he could do was try not to lean into the contact or look like a complete idiot in front of the other—equally well-dressed—men with her.

"Want me to take your coat?"

Sweaty palms, blue cue chalk, and cream coats that probably cost more than his car were a bad match. But still, he had to ask.

"Thank you," Lana shrugged out of her coat. Dropping her voice, she added softly, "And I'm *so* sorry."

"Why?"

"You'll find out soon enough." Raising her voice to normal levels, Lana turned to introduce the men who had followed her inside. "Rick, these are my cousins. You may remember Killian Montgomery, and this is Silas Thomas."

He had to fight to pull his eyes from Lana toward her companions.

"Silas Ward Thomas the third," Silas cut in, sticking out his hand for a shake, a perfunctory gesture if Rick had ever seen one.

"The *third*," Killian whispered jokingly.

"Gentlemen, this is Rick Harding, one of our tenants and a dear friend."

Gah. The f-word again.

Rick dutifully shook hands with Killian and Silas, wondering what exactly about them was making his back stiffen. Not them... *him*. Silas. The third of his particular kind. Having been introduced, Silas turned away immediately, taking in the pool hall as if Rick had ceased to exist. "Lana, this is ridiculous. Why are we investing in small buildings like this?"

Lana frowned at Silas's back while Killian leaned against the closest pool table.

"Perhaps you can keep your commentary to yourself until after we've finished touring all the properties," she said firmly. "As for the sizes of the properties, I can appreciate a large corporate building as much as the next girl. But you seem to errantly believe quality is directly related to quantity."

"Size isn't everything?" Killian joked.

"On the contrary." Lana gazed around the pool hall as if proud. "If you count all our modest, individual holdings, they're worth more than your skyscrapers. Size is definitely everything."

"Meaning hers is bigger than his," Killian said out of the side of his mouth to Rick.

"Diversified portfolios, Silas. That's what I'm bringing to the table."

Silas snorted. "You're also bringing cheap construction and low-to-no profit margins. The door sticks. He's also behind on rent."

This time, Rick's heart did something much different. It dropped into his stomach, where acid from too many years of stress had gathered, waiting for moments like these. Where it became clear that his dream of his pool hall staying afloat without tourist money was destined to fail. If he opened the doors to strangers, he'd never have a moment of peace. But if Silas had his way, the peace was already gone.

"It's been taken care of." Lana's voice was honey sweet, but her eyes flashed.

The look Silas gave Rick made his jaw tighten reflexively.

"Lana, what's going on?" he asked, keeping his hands safely at his sides and choosing to not get arrested for the day.

She started to answer, but Silas interrupted as if Rick weren't even there.

"Lana, what the hell you were thinking? If you'd bought the resort, then yes, maybe I would understand the impulse buy. But this place? All these places?" Silas shook his head in disgust. "If we put them on the market today, we'd barely break even."

"Silas, again, all things that can and should be discussed in a meeting after this. I've reserved a conference room—"

Once more, he cut her off, either unaware of her growing anger or ignoring it. Rick didn't know how Silas could be this obtuse. Lana's hands were visibly shaking, and her teeth were audibly grinding.

"Do you think I came here without doing some digging? There are half a dozen places on this list behind on rent. It's like this whole town is your little pet project. I'm recommending to the board you be taken off this project and everything sold. We can get the collections department to start recouping the tenants' back rent."

Before Rick could fully process what Silas was threatening him with, Lana slapped Silas over the head with her purse.

This wasn't a light slap. No, Lana smacked her cousin so hard the resulting thump made Rick wince.

He must've had a hard head, because Silas stood there shocked. "What was that for?" he demanded.

Lana stalked into his personal bubble, jabbing a manicured finger toward Silas's throat.

"That man right there is good and hardworking, and if I—as the principal on this account—decide to give him extra time on his rent, then he gets it. That was my decision, Silas. *Mine*. Not the group's, not Killian's, and certainly not yours."

"What did I do?" Killian held up his hands innocently. "I like the place."

Which would have been much more reassuring if the possibility of losing his pool hall wasn't still lingering in the air.

Lana stalked forward, her fingernail digging farther into Silas's Adam's apple, causing him to take an involuntary step back.

"Now here's what you're going to do. You're going to apologize to Rick for this and for every snotty look and snarky comment you've made since coming into town. Because trust me, these people think even less of you than you think of my commercial properties."

"The *group's* properties," Silas started to argue, but another finger jab, this one at an eyeball, made him duck.

"*My* commercial properties," Lana all but growled at him. "And if they'd been managed properly from the onset, then good, hardworking people like Rick wouldn't have to deal with peeled paint or wiggling handrails or goodness forbid, a *sticking door.*"

"Now, wait a second, Lana. Aunt Jessica sent me, and I have a job to do—"

"Silas, think very carefully here. I indulge you plenty, but who do you think will be in charge of whether you keep that job in the near future?"

"Excuse me?" Silas sounded shocked, his face going pale before reddening with anger.

"I normally wouldn't rub that in your face and certainly not in polite company. But I don't give a rat's ass about what upsets you, not when you're acting like a complete cad. Consider me unimpressed, Cousin."

Killian whistled under his breath. "And that's why we don't piss off Lana. Brought it on yourself, buddy."

At which point Silas called Lana something not very pleasant, and all those emotions Rick was feeling toward this stranger solidified into a very strong need to throw the pompous jerk out of his pool hall.

Jake began to growl, sensing the rising tension in the air. Stepping up next to Lana, Rick folded his arms, frowning at Silas.

"I know who you are," Rick said quietly. "And I know who I'm not. But you'll watch your tongue around the lady, or you and I are going to have a conversation you're not going to like."

That was the nice version of what Rick wanted to really say to the little shit giving Lana so much hell.

"Did you just *threaten* me?" Silas's voice came out in an affronted squeak.

"No, Silas. You were simply warned to be a little more polite." She glanced at Rick. "I've seen Rick threaten someone. It's very impressive."

Rick felt his neck heat up at her compliment, but he kept his eyes on Silas.

"And, Silas? We're family, but I'm quickly getting tired of the way you treat people, myself included. I'm not above making sure you spend the next forty years flipping burgers on the night shift."

Silas sputtered, then turned on his heel, stomping out.

"Can you really do that?" Killian asked, sounding cheerful. "Get him fired? Because I would *love* to see him flipping burgers on the night shift."

"It depends. Things get tricky when family is involved. But I can certainly make his life miserable, which I have no problem doing if he insists on dishing out the same to you."

Lana glanced guiltily at Rick as she picked up Jake, hugging him close.

"I'm sorry," she told him, sounding beyond embarrassed. "I won't come back here like this again."

As she started for the door, Rick realized something. He'd rather have her in his pool hall while he took hell from her cousin than not have her in his day at all. Jumping after her, Rick risked a startled nip from Jake to take her elbow.

"Wait. That guy isn't you, Lana. You're always welcome here."

Maybe he sounded like a complete fool saying so, or at least a little desperate, but to earn a smile like the one spreading across her gorgeous face? Rick was more than happy to be a little desperate for Lana any day.

This time when she went up to her toes to kiss his cheek, her lips lingered.

"How about this. I won't let him come back here. But if the offers stands, I'll definitely take you up on it."

Would the offer stand? *Absolutely*.

CHAPTER 6

"ARE YOU SURE THIS IS the proper attire?" Lana glanced down at herself. "I'd hate to embarrass myself."

Dressed from head to toe in her own winter ghillie suit, Zoey gave an emphatic nod, furry strips of white and pale-gray fabric swinging with the motion. "We need to be in camouflage. This moose is a trickster."

Lana had dropped Jake off with Graham and then met with Zoey out in the woods, off a section of road she wasn't familiar with.

They'd come prepared. Thermos filled with hot coffee, zero-degree winter gear beneath their ghillie suits, granola bars in their backpacks. Two large flasks of a very spice-heavy eggnog the Lockett patriarch had brought over for Zoey to try and Easton's livestock tranquilizer gun, complete with moose-sized darts. The rest of Graham's truck bed was filled to bursting with all the garish holiday inflatables, weathered plastic light-up figurines, and used polyvinyl Christmas trees one could obtain on the sly.

Strings of lights and power cords overflowed from piled-up buckets. They had two lawn chairs to sit on while hiding in the shadows of the surrounding trees and heating pouches for their gloves if they got cold. And lastly, one satellite phone to call in their capture (and subsequent victory), borrowed from a very hesitant Ash, who promised hell to pay if they broke it.

If one were to catch a Santa Moose, there was only one way to do it—set a Christmas trap.

At first, they'd started small. After all, most of what attracted the moose was blinking lights. Lana wasn't sure where they were or where the power cords Zoey kept stretching were running to, but they'd divvied up the work. The more decorations they set up, the more focused Lana became on not only setting the scene but telling a story. Theirs was a Christmas town filled with hope, full of cheer, and even perhaps full of romance.

Lana had seen the way Mrs. Claus was making bedroom eyes at Frosty's button nose.

"Lana? Does any of this strike you as a little perverse?"

"Nonsense. It's perfect."

They were crouched out in the woods, doing their best to blend in with their surroundings. Between them, they had recreated Santa's workshop closest to their hiding spot, complete with elves at their toy-making table and all the reindeer happily munching away at brightly lit Christmas light cookie piles.

"This can't be good for the environment. Global warming is a thing, Lana."

"Oh, it's definitely a thing. I make it a priority to actively invest in sustainable businesses. Pass me the tranquilizer gun."

"Why do you get the tranq gun?"

"Because of the two of us, I'm the only one with specialized training."

"Making out with a guy from the Chicago SWAT team does not make you an expert shot, Lana."

"Hiring a professional is a perfectly acceptable way of learning how to defend oneself. His attractiveness doesn't make my training any less lethal. And that was years ago."

A sound in the distance caused them both to tense. "Is that—?" Lana started to ask.

"Not unless moose have started stomping through the woods." She stood, turning toward the direction they'd parked the truck. "Graham, is that you?"

"Sorry, Zoey Bear. I know you have a thing for Easton, but I decided to rescue you this time."

"How did he find us?" Lana asked.

Zoey snorted. "Serves me right for leaving him a note about where we'd be." Hands on her hips, she glared at the man emerging from the woods. "Rescue me from what? Our awesome plan of awesomeness? Don't lie. You got bored and wanted to poke your big fat nose into our plans."

"I got lonely," he practically purred in her ear. Anyone else would have melted at the sheer sexiness of the smoldering look Graham gave her. Not Zoey.

"You'll live. Now go away. We're busy."

"I can't. I caught a ride here. You have my truck, remember?"

"Not my problem. Now scoot." Zoey pushed on his flat stomach. The result was Graham gazing down at her like she was the cutest thing in the world.

It was very cute, but Lana was super-duper single, so she looked away, taking a long drink of eggnog. "If you want to go home, I can stay here," Lana told them.

"Naw, I'd hate to ruin the fun." Graham winked at her before turning back to Zoey. "It's a little mean to set up where I had to say goodbye to Ulysses, don't you think?"

"I think it's the only spot I knew that wasn't in town and was a known moose hangout."

"Why didn't you ask me? I know plenty of places."

"Because that would be asking you for help. And this is a female bonding activity. No men necessary."

Graham opened his mouth, but Zoey scrunched her nose at him. "Female bonding, Graham. So butt out, big guy. There will be no additional bonding from you."

He held his hands up in innocence. "I wouldn't dream of it, darlin'."

"Good." She pointed two fingers at her eyes and then at him. "I'm watching you."

Chuckling, he snuck an arm around her, ghillie suit and all. "You weren't answering your phone," Graham said. "I—wait, is that a gun?"

"This is eggnog," Lana provided helpfully, waggling her thermos at Graham.

"Are you seriously out here with alcohol and guns—?" he started to say.

Zoey cut him off. "A tranq gun. And we're just having eggnog. We're not drinking."

"*Tranquilizer* guns—"

"One. It's a singular gun." At Lana's correction, Graham growled in exasperation, but Lana only grinned. "It's annoying, isn't it? Taste of your own medicine."

"You actually set a trap." He seemed equally horrified and impressed.

"Yes, until you stumbled onto it and ruined everything. Do you know how hard it is to stretch power cords to this part of the woods?"

"If you plugged them into Rick's barn, it's going to blow a fuse any second. I can't believe the power even ran this far."

"It's Rick's barn?"

Zoey blinked innocently. "Oh, did I not mention that?"

Suddenly, a loud crunching sound of a branch being stepped on caused them all to turn. It was dark and very hard to see, but Zoey pointed into the woods, saying in excitement, "It's the moose!"

There was definitely movement through the trees, coming straight for their Christmas trap.

"Umm, Zoey, I don't think—" Graham started to say as Lana lifted the tranquilizer gun to her shoulder.

Now, Lana didn't make a habit of getting sloppy with her moose catching tranquilizer gun safety. But she also had worked hard for this single opportunity, and she wasn't going to waste it by being slow on the draw. Unfortunately, about the time she squeezed the trigger, Lana realized that Rick looked a whole lot like a moose when coming out of the woods on a snowy winter evening.

It wasn't funny. Accidentally shooting someone with a

tranquilizer dart intended for a large animal was a great way to hospitalize someone. Which was never funny. But the dart didn't hit Rick; it just sort of grazed him in the process of flying through the air and thwapping into the tree next to him.

They all stood there in silent horror, listening to that thwap echo through the forest.

"Umm...you just tranquilized Rick."

"I didn't tranquilize him," Lana said, feeling a little light-headed as she hurried across the clearing. She tripped on a Ninja Turtle dressed as a Christmas caroler. "Rick, are you okay?"

"Lana?" He was looking between her and the Christmas town with surprise and confusion on his face. "What are you doing out here?"

"Umm..." She hedged. "It was a moose-catching, female-bonding, trying-to-earn-the-town's-trust...thing."

"Did you *shoot* at me?"

"I promise I did not shoot at you," Lana told him.

"You didn't shoot *at* him." Zoey pointed to the bit of fabric pinned between the dart and the tree trunk.

Rick rolled his shoulder to better see his triceps. Yep. That was one torn jacket. In a very calm voice, he said, "I think you hit me."

She quickly pulled Rick's jacket off his arm and down to expose his shirt underneath. "There's no way. Not with all these layers of clothing."

It was only a tear in his shirt and...oh.

"Well...okay," Lana hedged. "It's maybe a teeny bit of a flesh wound."

Graham groaned. "Of course you shot him."

"I didn't *shoot* him. I nicked him. Nicked isn't shot."

Zoey tilted her head. "I think we may need to get him to the hospital. Nicked or not, that's a powerful combination of—" Lana tuned her out as Zoey began to list the ingredients of the tranquilizer dart.

"Rick, dear. Zoey's right, we need to call for an ambulance."

"Nope, no hospital." Rick shook his head. "I'm fine, I'm…whoa."

"—and it's going to stay in his system for up to thirty days, so no one should eat him." They all turned and looked at Zoey. "What? I'm just saying. I do my research, okay? If you didn't want research, you shouldn't have involved me in this."

"No hospital." Rick's voice was a low growl. "It's only a scratch, and they'll use this against her."

"Rick," Lana said softly, touched by his concern.

"You've been drinking."

"No, I haven't."

"You two are both tanked." Graham poked Zoey's shoulder, and she wobbled. "We can smell it on your breath from here."

Well, that wasn't very attractive.

Zoey wasn't buying it. "But it's only Mr. Lockett's eggnog. It's cinnamon-y. There's no alcohol. I tasted it to check."

"Yes, which is why it's deadly. I would have mentioned that if you'd told me you were bringing it out here."

"Don't call anyone," Rick repeated, then he took a step and stumbled. "Don't call Jonah. He'll cause her problems."

Now, it was possible Lana wasn't at her best, but she certainly wasn't hammered. She definitely knew prioritizing Rick's health was much more important than a little thing like the law.

"Well, it was an honest mistake," Lana said. "It's not like we've never been incarcerated before."

"Lana, do not tell him that," Zoey hissed.

"You're going to have to let Graham in on at least a few of our secrets one of these days. Rick, we need to get you to your house. Graham, would you be willing to help him on the other side?"

"Immookay." Rick's voice was starting to slur. "Graham—"

"Yeah, yeah, no cops." Shaking his head, he said, "You're a loyal SOB, aren't you?"

"What are we going to do?" Zoey asked as they helped him walk back the way he had come.

"About what?"

"*You shot Rick*," Zoey said in a hiss.

"I didn't do it on purpose." Lana tightened her hold on Rick's waist. "There you go. Lean on us."

"And yet he still has dangerous chemicals coursing through his veins," Zoey said. "You can't drink and tranq."

"You gave me the eggnog. I didn't know it was alcoholic."

"Well, I didn't know either," Zoey argued back. "All I could taste was the thousand cups of cinnamon Mr. Lockett poured in there."

"You didn't ask him if it was spiked?"

Zoey drew herself up, indignant. "Lana, that is Easton's *grandmother's* recipe. Of course I didn't ask."

"What else did he put in here? I'm feeling all paranoid."

"You're paranoid because what's left of your collective sobriety has realized one of you just committed a crime." Graham grunted as Rick leaned more of his weight against Graham's shoulder. "Come on, Rick. One foot in front of the other, buddy. We're almost to the porch."

"My nana liked cimmanon." Rick cocked his head and tried again. "Mininmon. Cimmimmim?"

"Close enough," Lana said. "Come on. Let's get you up the steps."

They weren't the quietest in their approach, especially with Rick staggering every step. Now, for the record, if Diego wasn't expecting them to all come stumbling through the door, he certainly covered it well. A single eyebrow rose, followed by a low curse.

"What did you do this time?" he asked, taking Rick's arm away from Lana.

The extra help was a relief, because she might be tall, but Lana wasn't quite in shape for helping carry a 180-pound, muscular adult man through the woods.

"I...There was a dart." Rick paused halfway to the couch, staring blearily at the wall. "Roger's judging me. Roger, stop judging me."

Lana followed Rick's line of sight to where a massive tabby cat perched on a bookshelf, flicking his tail.

"Yeah, he's messed up," Diego said with amusement.

"We're going to call an ambulance for you, okay?" Lana told Rick.

Rick weaved unsteadily on his feet. "Imma...imma good." Good enough to give her the most drunken, happy smile she'd ever seen on his face. "You're cimmomin." He took a strand of her hair, inhaling deeply. "Is my favorite. Cimmonin and apples. You're my favorite."

"This isn't happening." Zoey took Rick by the shoulders,

shaking him. "Don't, okay? Do *not* profess your innermost secrets. Rick, no secrets."

"Imma lay down."

At which point Rick stretched out on the couch, pulling Lana down with him. He put his head in Lana's lap and began to sing. For a man under the influence of dangerous chemicals, Rick had quite a pleasant singing voice. One ambulance, two paramedics, and an IV later, Rick was still lying with his head on her lap, although he'd stopped singing around the time he announced the room had stopped spinning.

Zoey hustled back into the living room. "They said to go to the emergency room if you start feeling heart palpitations. But the dart only scratched you. They think the chemical exposure was minimal compared to what it could have been."

"Go. I'll stay with him." Lana adjusted the blanket around Rick's shoulders. "It's my fault."

"It's our fault," Zoey said stubbornly.

Graham was still outside pleading their cases with Jonah. Apparently, one couldn't accidentally tranquilize one's crush without the cops being called. Zoey glanced at the living room window, through which Lana could see Jonah and Graham in a heated discussion.

"Graham will get Jonah to back off, but don't be surprised if Jonah wants to talk to you." Zoey hesitated. "I should stay and help."

"Rick and I are perfectly fine. Right?" She ran her hand through Rick's hair, earning a grunt of agreement from Rick in her lap.

Jonah walked in, giving Lana a look that she was sure had convinced many a reluctant witness into talking. However, she'd grown up in the Montgomery household, and it would take more than his side-eye to crack her.

The officer sat on the coffee table, elbows on his knees.

"I'm not all that surprised to be getting called out on a hunting accident, but I'm surprised to find you, Ms. Montgomery."

"There was no hunting."

At her calm reply, Jonah cleared his throat, eyeing her ghillie suit. She'd taken the headpiece off, but the rest of her was covered in white and gray strings.

"It was more of a moose-stalking situation."

"So I'm hearing a lot of what could have happened and what probably happened. I'm wondering what actually happened."

"I'll be happy to tell you," she said. "But I'm sorry, it will have to wait until the morning. I'll have to call my lawyers."

"Lawyers? Plural?"

"Yes." Lana readjusted the washcloth on Rick's forehead. "How are you feeling?"

Rick watched them through bleary, reddened eyes. "Like you shouldn't say anything. Jonah, leave her alone."

He had stopped slurring, but he still seemed out of it. When Rick started to push himself up to his elbows, Lana stopped him.

"I don't need you fighting my battles for me," she said gently. "The paramedics said to rest."

The door slammed, making him groan, a low, pained noise. So far, Diego had stayed on the far wall, watching everything but not saying a word. But when Jonah frowned, Diego stepped forward.

"If Uncle Rick says nothing happened, then nothing happened." Diego spat off to the side. Inside the house. On a perfectly nice rug. Eyes fierce, Diego added, "If you're going to keep calling him a liar, maybe we should get our lawyer involved too."

Jonah sighed. "All right, I know when I'm not wanted. But, Ms. Montgomery, I'd like to talk to you again. I have a court appearance to make in Anchorage tomorrow morning, and I'd like to see you afterward."

He was more than overworked. He was *exhausted*. The expression on his face had bypassed stressed and bordered resentment.

"Jonah? Do you have any help? This town is too big for a single officer without any backup. Even Andy of Mayberry had Barney Fife to help him."

"It's occurred to me more than once, ma'am." He looked at her. "But if you're thinking of suggesting something to help, I'd like to remind you that I'm here because of your drunken, disorderly, and dangerous conduct. So if you're about to add bribing a police official on top of that, you may want to think long and hard about what you say next."

That wasn't what she had been intending, but like always, the people here didn't trust her intentions at all.

Lana lifted her chin, holding his eyes. "Go ahead and arrest me. I'm still going to make sure you have the support staff you need to keep Moose Springs safer. It's not a bribe. It's a solid business decision. I have a lot of money invested in this town."

Jonah looked at Rick, then rested a hand on his shoulder. "You sure we can't take you to the hospital?"

"The hospital will make trouble for her."

"Between us, I have the feeling that Ms. Montgomery is more than capable of handling herself."

The officer headed outside to his cruiser, leaving Diego, Rick, and Lana in the living room. Diego watched through the window until Jonah was gone, then he turned back to Rick. A smile almost cracked his face.

"Still stoned?" he joked.

Rick rolled his eyes, flopping a hand at Diego. "Can't you be anywhere else right now?"

"Yeah, I know when I'm not wanted." Smirking, Diego headed down the hall, presumably to his room. Rick shook his head, then groaned as if the motion hurt him.

"Headache?" Lana bit her lower lip, worried.

"I've had worse," he promised. "It'll pass."

Readjusting the blanket higher on his shoulders, Lana said softly, "I'm so sorry for tonight. Are you mad at me?"

"For thinking I was a moose?" Rick reached up to tug the end of the same hair tendril he'd been fixated on all night.

"For trying to capture you."

"You did that a long time ago."

Lana ran her fingers through his much shorter hair. "You're still drugged, dearest," she said. "Try not to say things you'll regret tomorrow."

Or maybe things she wished he meant now.

"I'm not mad at you. Don't think I have it in me."

As she held Rick's head in her lap, it occurred to Lana that he was the only one in Moose Springs who didn't.

"I think it's time I start dating again."

They were halfway through a morning coffee and a cinnamon roll at Frankie's when Rick made the quiet announcement to his friends. Normally, Rick didn't splurge like this, but he'd recently survived a near moose-catching experience, and he was celebrating. Graham blinked at his announcement. Ash stared at him. Easton said nothing, but he did take a sip of his coffee. After this much time single, Rick figured they could have reacted a little more supportively.

"I think I want to ask out Lana," he continued on, because it was the truth. And...well...they were his best friends. They should know he was finally taking this step. All three had expressed their concerns about how long he'd been single after his divorce, so he'd expected a little more enthusiasm than this.

"Are you insane?" Ash finally asked, reaching over the table to squash her hand on his face.

"What are you doing?"

"Feeling for a temperature. Graham, feel him. Is he running a fever?"

Graham dutifully followed suit. "Yep, definitely feeling hot over there, buddy."

Rick tried to duck away from their hands, scooting his chair half an inch closer to Easton. Then he sighed as Easton finished a bite of cinnamon roll and wrapped a large hand across Rick's forehead.

"This isn't very supportive," Rick said grumpily. "And someone has icing on their fingers."

"You were just shot by this woman," Ash reminded him.

"Grazed."

"She travels a lot, buddy." Graham shared a worried look with Ash. "I know you've been sweet on her for a while, but are you sure?"

"He's fine," Easton decided, finally removing his hand from Rick's face. "What about a dating site?"

With an annoyed look at all three of them, Rick grabbed a paper napkin and scrubbed someone's icing off his face. Ash brightened at Easton's suggestion.

"Ooh, a dating app is a great idea."

"Or I could just ask out Lana," Rick countered as Ash stole his phone.

So far, Rick's morning wasn't going the way he planned.

"I'm not going on a dating site," he said to the group, not that anyone was listening.

"How about this one?" Ash ignored him completely, leaning over to show Graham. "It's for rural Alaskan singles looking for a—oh. Well, that's not exactly what I was thinking for him, but it wouldn't *hurt*."

"It could hurt if he doesn't stretch first," Graham replied with a chuckle.

"You're not helping. Here." Easton took Rick's phone, typing in another site before setting the phone on the table in front of Rick. The icing had to be Easton's, because now it was on Rick's phone. He added in a rumble. "Ash is on this. What about you two?"

The suggestion earned a simultaneous shudder from both of them. It was one thing to fall in love with someone he'd known growing up. It was another to consider dating the closest thing to a sister he had.

"I just threw up in my mouth a little." Ash made a face. "It tasted like kissing a first cousin, not removed at all."

"Again, not internet dating," Rick said. "I want to ask—"

The doorbell jingled as another customer walked in, this one impossible not to notice.

Her. Rick very much wanted to go out with her. A real date, not just a vague "hey baby" version…whatever that actually was.

The last time Rick had seen Lana, he'd been stoned out of his mind, sprawled across her lap. Remembering that made him want to groan in embarrassment. It also made him wonder if getting a second dart was possible. When he closed his eyes, Rick could still smell her perfume lingering in his senses.

"Lana," he called, her name slipping from his mouth before he had made the conscious decision. Those glorious eyes met his, and immediately a rosy blush stained her cheeks. And when he rose, offering her his seat, that blush darkened.

"Oh, no need," Lana said, waving him back down. "I don't have very long. Are you… Everything okay?"

"She means are you still high on moose tranqs?" Ash said out of the side of her mouth.

"I'm fine," he told her.

A checkup with his regular physician this morning revealed he was perfectly healthy. Other than his arm being sore and being mortified at singing love ballads to Lana, Rick was no worse for the wear.

Embarrassed but no worse.

While she ordered her drink and a pastry to go, Rick cast

around and found a spare chair, pulling it over to their already crowded table. Returning, Lana offered him a grateful look, sitting next to him. She glanced with mild curiosity at his phone still lying on the table, then politely averted her eyes.

"That's not real…" Rick stuttered, seeing the fake profile his friends had started building for him. "These three are idiots."

Ash and Graham gave her twin waves of matching innocence. Easton hid his guilt behind his beard.

Lana exhaled a soft laugh. "It's a very nice profile. And the picture is almost as good-looking as you are."

Rick flushed at the compliment. He couldn't help but remember the feeling of her leg beneath his head, her fingers in his hair, stroking soothingly. It was that—her touch—which had sent a shot of adrenaline into his recently anaphylactic sex drive. When Lana touched him, Rick knew how ready he was to have human contact again. Someone who wanted his hands on her too.

Lana's eyes lingered, as if making sure he was definitely okay, then she turned to his companions.

"Ash," Lana said. "I was hoping to hire you to take me for a little ride."

"A little ride where, exactly?"

"Oh, you know…out and about."

For some reason, she was being evasive, which only made Rick more curious. He wasn't the only one.

"Do I want to know?" Ash asked, sounding suspicious.

"I'll try to keep my evil machinations at a minimum. Rick? Do you mind if I steal a moment of your time? I was hoping to talk to you for a minute. Privately."

"You're not going to shoot him again, are you?" Easton rumbled, causing Ash to snicker as Rick rose to his feet, following Lana outside.

She looked nervous, fiddling with her coffee cup with slightly shaking fingers. "I'll pay you for the electricity we used the other night."

"Naw, it's no big deal."

"Even though I tranq'd you?"

"It wouldn't be the first time something like that happened around here." Rick shrugged. "Won't be the last either. But since I'd rather spend my time anywhere other than the emergency room, I appreciate your crappy aim."

"My aim is very good when three gallons of Ruby Lockett's eggnog isn't coursing through my veins."

"You and everyone else." He noticed her hands were still trembling. "Are you cold? We can go back inside."

"No, just concerned about you. I wanted to see how you were feeling."

"Now that the moose tranqs are out of my system?" Rick chuckled at the consternation on her face.

"I promise, I had no idea the cinnamon in the eggnog was cinnamon schnapps. I would have been far less indulgent. I also plan on covering all your current medical expenses and any that may occur as a result of my...indiscretion."

"Thinking I was a moose."

She wrinkled her nose when she was upset, and if it weren't so cute, Rick would have tried harder to stop teasing her. Instead, he stepped closer. This time, he didn't mind the hand reaching up to press against his forehead, checking for a fever.

"Lana. It's fine. *I'm* fine. It's actually kind of funny."

Suddenly, she had her arms wrapped around his neck, hugging him. The action was so unexpected, Rick stood there for a moment. Then he tentatively placed his palm on the small of her back. He'd only meant for it to be a chaste hug in return, but Lana leaned into his chest. Rick's arm slipped around her waist of its own accord, drawing her snug to his torso.

It hadn't occurred to him how much she needed a hug until her arms tightened about him.

Man, she felt good. How long had it been since he'd had a woman in his arms? Long enough that he wasn't sure if he was holding on too tight or if she minded his head dipping down. Lana's hair was silky as it brushed against his throat.

"I'm sorry," she said, abruptly pulling away. The loss of her was a shock to his system. "I feel terrible about everything yesterday. I kicked Silas out of Alaska. He's on his way back to Chicago. You won't have to deal with him anymore, not if I have any say in the matter."

"That's a relief. I might have just locked the door if I saw him coming again."

"You and everyone else who's ever met him." Taking a deep breath, Lana plastered her breezy smile in place. "It's never a dull moment with us, is it?"

"You keep me on my toes," Rick said gently. He waited, but she didn't say anything. Instead, she chewed on her lower lip, the same way she had on his couch. In his somewhat stoned state, he'd been mesmerized by the action, but today he understood it for the concern it was.

"Lana?"

"Hmm?"

"Stop worrying about me. You have enough on your plate."

Allowing himself a moment of sheer self-indulgence, Rick held out his hand to her in silent request. When she placed her fingers in his, he stepped closer, wrapping her up in a much better hug. This time, she rested her cheek against his chest.

"You're a really good guy, Rick."

"It's all a lie. I rob banks and seduce billionaires when no one's looking."

This time, her smile was softer but real. "Then I'll have to be on my toes." Pressing a quick kiss to his cheek, Lana said, "Thank you." Then she hurried away, tugging her jacket around her to ward against the cold.

Rick watched her go, then he rejoined his friends inside. Ash and Easton had been having far too much fun setting up Rick's dating profile.

"Delete it," he told them firmly. "I'm going to ask Lana out."

Ash pulled out her phone, typing into it. Her movements were quick and precise, the way they always were when she was pissed. "You're an idiot. East, tell him he's an idiot."

Easton took a drink, smart enough to not get in the middle.

"Graham, please save him from himself."

Graham watched through Frankie's window as Lana headed down the steps to her car. "She's a sweet girl. Just don't know how long it'll last, buddy. She's never here in town. But if you're just looking for a holiday fling..."

"I don't know what I'm looking for," Rick admitted quietly. "But I'd rather figure it out with her."

"Fine." Ash stood up, resigned. "She did shoot you in the arm. Makes sense for you to shoot yourself in the foot. If you'll excuse me, the princess needs a 'lift.'"

As a sky-blue SUV drove toward the resort, Rick knew that he wasn't waiting anymore. Jen had moved on, and it was time to do the same. Time to start living his life while he still had it. A guy could be mistaken for a moose any day.

Rick was going to ask Lana out—for real this time—and pray she said yes.

———

"Is there a reason why I pulled the short straw today?"

The usual acerbic tone in Ashtyn's voice was almost lost beneath the thwapping of helicopter blades cutting through the cold winter air.

Normally, Lana would have met Ash at the hangar on the far side of town, but she had been wrapped up in phone calls, and she needed to be back for a meeting with Hannah about the Christmas party. If she wanted to do this, she needed to go in a very small window of time, meaning it was far more convenient to have Ash pick her up at the resort's private helipad.

"Shuttling people to and from the airport isn't my gig. Tell me why I agreed to this again?"

"Because I asked nicely," Lana said as she climbed into the copilot's seat, pulling a headset over her ears. "And I doubled your normal fee for the convenience."

Through the headphone, Ash's sarcasm came through loud and clear. "There are other pilots, you know."

"I prefer to support female-owned businesses."

Ash snorted. "I'm not buying it."

She might not believe Lana, but it was true. There was no point in trying to argue with someone who couldn't be convinced, so Lana looked out the window instead.

"Besides," Lana said, "the other pilots were too scared to go up here in December."

"Don't do me any favors." Ash's lips had curved into a smug smirk as they lifted off, angling over the mountainside. "Nice penis, by the way."

"I'm growing rather fond of it. Hannah is going to tell on me if I don't get rid of it."

"Good luck with that. Jax thinks it's hysterical."

The familiar way she seemed to know the resort owner's feelings caught Lana by surprise. "Oh. Are you and he…?"

Ash grimaced. "Not if his life depended on it. I grew up with the little brat. There's no way I'd ever get with him. I wasn't aware we came up here to discuss my love life. I should have charged you more."

"Trust me." Lana grinned at her. "You're charging me enough to have proved your point."

Ash snickered before seeming to realize she wasn't supposed to. Slipping her sunglasses on, Lana settled in to appreciate the view as they flew higher into the snowy mountain range. In another place, she and Ashtyn could have been friends. Lana didn't only respect her. She honestly liked the other woman. She'd love to hire someone like Ashtyn Lockett and keep her on the payroll for those tough jobs that needed doing. There was nothing Ash was afraid of, except for maybe the massive mountains her brother was so famous for climbing.

Lana didn't blame her. Freezing to death on the top of Mount Veil wasn't Lana's idea of a fun time either. Ash was far smarter than her twin, as far as Lana was concerned.

"How's your brother?" she asked.

"Preoccupied. He's got this informal thing going with a local newspaper reporter, but she wants more than he does. East doesn't know how to let her down easy. He's dragging it out and causing himself all sorts of problems."

"Easton never seemed like the settling down type. I always guessed he'd stay a bachelor as long as humanly possible," Lana said.

"You and me both. But you never can trust people." At Lana's questioning look, Ash explained. "I don't like change is all. Seems like lately, everything is changing around here. You're not helping things."

"People grow," Lana said. "So do towns. Stilting Moose Spring's potential is like trying to keep a child frozen in time. We all grow up eventually."

"Some versions of adults are far superior to others," Ash said drily. "If my town is unrecognizable in ten years, don't think I'm not blaming you."

There wasn't much Lana could say to that. She already knew.

Overlook Ridge lay high above the town of Moose Springs, right before the tree line gave way to ice and snow. Between the remaining evergreens and the constant gusting of winds off the monstrous Mount Veil in the distance, the ridge was a particularly difficult place to land. A deep blanket of snow was spinning off the ridge in flurries, obscuring the visibility but leaving a small area clear. *If* the pilot was skilled enough to combat the combination of elements fighting to toss a helicopter back off the mountain.

Ash was skilled enough.

They landed much quicker and with less curse words than the last person who had flown Lana up here, which was the point of using Ash's piloting services. She was the best. And while being budget conscious was always important, Lana preferred to save her coupons for when she wasn't on the edge of a thousand-foot drop-off.

Lana waited until the helicopter was settled in place, then she unbuckled her seat belt.

"You're not going out there, are you?" Ash's eyes widened.

"Don't worry. I've been here before."

"If you get blown off the mountain, I'm not jumping after you." Ash killed the propellers and unbuckled her seat belt. The Lockett blood had too much protector built into it to keep her in the aircraft, no matter what Ash liked to say.

They edged along the ridge until they were out of the worst of the flurries. Here, they had the best view of Moose Springs. Several thousand feet below them, the town was a tiny dot against the base of the mountainside.

"Okay, why are we up here?" Ash asked. "If it's because you're buying the whole mountain range, you'll need to hike down. My ass is leaving you up here to reconsider."

Lana didn't answer. She knew her reasonings weren't going to be what her pilot would appreciate.

There were only about six and a half hours of daylight in Moose Springs in December, with the mountains obscuring much of the sun's light. Farther north, that amount of time decreased to much less. Higher up where they were, Lana had a chance to feel more sunshine on her face than the people she cared about would feel down there.

She wasn't oblivious to the privilege of being able to charter a flight to Overlook Ridge just because she needed some time to think and the perspective of distance to do it in.

"Watch out over there," Ash warned, jutting her head to indicate a loose bit of rock beneath Lana's boots.

Nodding gratitude at Ash's warning, she braced her feet wider for stability. Sometimes in business, one had to step back from the minutiae that could bog a project down. Stand back and really see the project as the whole it was supposed to be, not the individual parts.

Moose Springs was Lana's project, and lately, she'd been far too bogged down in the tiny details. Tiny details were important, but Lana had been raised to see the big picture first. Thirty thousand feet worked better when one was in an airplane, but three thousand feet worked too.

"There aren't a lot of roads in and out of town, are there?"

Ash glanced at her. "Not many, but we keep them clear. Why?"

"I'm trying to see this from a different angle," Lana said. "I know what the group wants for Moose Springs, and I know what Moose Springs wants for Moose Springs. I'm trying to see if there's another way to look at it. There's nothing else around here, is there?"

"No," Ash grunted, crossing her arms. "Just us and the rest of the mountains."

"And Moose Springs used to be a mining town?"

"They closed the mines a long time ago. No one's opening them back up, if that's what you're asking."

Lana shook her head. "I'm trying to imagine what would be here if the resort was gone. Why people would be here. How far they'd have to go to find work."

Opening her mouth then shutting it again, Ash must have decided to keep her thoughts to herself. At least initially.

"We'd find something," she finally said. "We're not that easy to take out."

"In the meantime, how many of the town would you lose to Anchorage?"

A crease of concern crossed Ash's brow. "I honestly don't know."

They fell silent, and Lana took in the scenery. Mount Veil remained a formidable monster in the distance. Maybe, somehow, the answer could be there.

Suddenly, Lana's companion cleared her throat. "Hey, do me favor," Ash said. "We'll call this even on fuel and hours flown."

"No special tourist rate?" Lana asked.

"I don't know what you are." Ash shrugged. "But you don't count as a tourist anymore."

She was making progress. Slow progress was still progress.

"You know my buddy Rick? The one you nearly took out with a tranq gun?"

His name brought a warmth that her cold weather gear

couldn't come close to comparing to. "I've had the pleasure of his acquaintance," Lana said.

"If he ever gets up the balls to ask you out, let him down easy, okay? He's had a tough time of it, and at some point, he needs to start putting himself out there again. The idiot has a thing for you, and we haven't been able to talk him out of it. He'll probably say something soon. Just don't laugh in his face. Please."

That "please" was quiet, the appeal of a worried friend.

"I wasn't aware we came up here to discuss *my* love life," Lana said.

"Trust me, it's not high on my to-do list." Ash dropped down into a squat, then folded her arms over her knees. "It's not that I don't like you. I do. I'm not sure why…" Eyeing her, Ash gave a little shrug. "I don't know. Maybe there's a part of me that buys into the whole caring about what happens to all of us. The difference is, I think the town will be better if everyone else on the planet forgets we're here."

"The business owners might disagree."

"Only half of them. The other half will breathe a sigh of relief. The way I see it, you have to adapt to stay alive. That's what some people did. They adapted to adjust to the influx of tourists. It doesn't mean we can't adapt our way back to normal. It might be hard, but we're tough. We can make it."

"Trust me, the last thing I'd ever doubt is how strong this town is." Lana meant it completely. In all her travels, she'd never met a group of people with half as much sheer grit as the townsfolk of Moose Springs.

"We're tough, but we're not bulletproof." Ash took a deep

breath in the thin, cold air, exhaling a puff similar to smoke. "Rick…he's one of the great guys. But I've been watching him since his divorce, and he's just not that adaptable. He won't do well with you."

Suddenly, the town below her wasn't nearly as interesting as what Ash was saying. "What do you mean?"

"You breeze into town, and you breeze back out again. For some reason, he's developed this thing for you, but he's not like you. He takes it seriously. And if he asks you out, he'll mean it. Don't play with him, okay? A regular Friday night for you will be the first date he's been on since Jen. It'll mean more to him, and he'll get hurt."

It took a lot to insult Lana, but in her well-meaning request, Ash had managed it. Hearing Ash's breakdown of who Lana was and how she was no good for Rick went straight through her like a strike of cold air.

She probably shouldn't mention the "hey baby" date. If Lana had known that was his first date since his divorce, she would have let him buy her that drink.

Standing, Ash nodded to herself. "Let him down easy. He'll get over it."

Lana wanted to tell Ash she was wrong. That she didn't know Lana at all. But really, *was* she completely wrong? Her days in Moose Springs were numbered. A week or two a few times a year was the best she could give anyone. And a man like Rick deserved more than that.

Except it was her life too. Her stressful, exhausting, lonely life. And it wasn't as if she was going to break his heart. Rick knew how much Lana had to give—they'd already talked about that. And if he was still interested despite her glaring flaws, Lana was more than interested in him. The man had been in her thoughts constantly, and Lana was done fighting herself over what she wanted. Rick was like Moose Springs. He was worth the risk.

"Did you get what you needed from this?" Ash asked. "The winds are changing. We need to get down."

"Of course," was all Lana could say.

———

Rick had finished vacuuming the tables and replacing the used-up chalks when Lana came through the door like a mini avalanche. Dressed head to toe in white, she was the prettiest—and most intimidating—abominable snowperson he'd ever seen.

"Would you like to have dinner with me?" Lana asked, flushed and breathless, as if she had rushed over there.

Rick's brain stopped working the moment he saw her, every single damn time, but this time, it refused to give him a single response.

"With you?" No. That had been the wrong answer.

"You and me, dinner whenever and wherever you choose. I'm buying, and you're driving."

"I'm driving." It was like he'd turned into a man-shaped single-celled organism.

"If you want to go." Her eyes dropped, her wind-reddened cheeks flushing deeper in color.

His brain finally kick-started again, ungluing his tongue from the back of his teeth. "And here I thought I was shooting too high asking you out for coffee."

Glorious dark eyes blinked. "Did I miss you asking me out for coffee?"

"Only half a dozen times in my head." Rick tried to keep the slow, stupid smile off his face. "How about tomorrow?"

It did wonderful things for his self-esteem when the most gorgeous woman he'd ever seen in his life blushed, saying, "Pick me up at six."

CHAPTER 7

WHEN RICK TOLD LANA HE'D take her out, he hadn't had any certain place in mind. The entire thing was a blur of her waltzing into his place and blowing his mind and some awkward guttural responses on his part assuring him of the impossible. Somehow, because the universe had turned itself inside out and flipped upside down a few times, Rick had a dinner date with Lana Montgomery.

His dream girl. Dream woman. She was definitely his dream woman.

No one in his inner circle seemed to be able to wrap their heads around this change of events either. Ash seemed confused, then kind of put out, although he had no idea why. Graham groaned and told him to gird his loins. Even Easton texted Rick a rare message, albeit a more positive well-wish of "Congrats, have fun."

Out of all of them, other than Rick himself, Diego seemed to be struggling with it the most.

"I can't believe you have a second date with Lana Montgomery."

Rick had listened to the same words repeated from his nephew's mouth for the last twenty-four hours. "You don't have to look so surprised," he grumbled. "We went out once, didn't we?"

"Did you? A glass of water and a hug isn't exactly a real date."

"And sitting off to the side while Quinn hangs out with her other friends is?"

Diego rolled his eyes and offered Rick a dirty look, making Rick chuckle. Apparently, of the two of them, Rick was winning their dating wager. Their "hey baby" evening had felt like the start of something between Rick and Lana. Poor Diego had asked Quinn out, and the girl had thought it was just as friends. Diego had been too embarrassed to correct the misunderstanding.

The f-word. Rick had never been happier to not be in the friend zone. It was much better to be in the should-he-wear-a-tie zone.

Rick adjusted his tie, readjusted it, then took it off and very calmly stuffed it in the trash. Jen had gotten him that tie. He was not bringing her on his date with Lana Montgomery.

"Is it bad that I keep adding her last name to her first when I think about her?" Rick asked.

"It's not good." Diego tilted his head. "Seriously though. Where the hell are you two going to go? It's Lana Montgomery."

"See? You're doing it too."

Rick reached for another tie, this one with snowflakes on it. "Do you think she likes blue?"

"I think you're screwed." Diego's brow furrowed. "Who's running the pool hall? You didn't close, did you? You don't get enough business to piss people off."

Rick wasn't so utterly incompetent as to not get someone to cover for him. He almost said so, but it was nice the kid cared.

"Easton has been there for the last hour." Rick ditched the snowflake tie and lobbed it toward his bed. "I told him to call you when he gets tired of it."

Maybe no tie would work?

"Answer the phone if he calls. I promised him backup."

Diego snorted. "What made you assume I don't have plans too?"

For the same reason it never occurred to anyone that Rick might have plans. They were two bachelor peas in a cereal-eating pod.

"*Do* you have plans?"

When Diego said nothing, Rick walked out into the living room and aimed a kick at the back of the couch.

"Fine, fine," his nephew grouched. "It's not like my ass has anything better to do." He added in a low mutter, "Quinn's out with Grass."

Four words that Diego would never say in front of anyone else. As unrequited crushes went, that one was going on strong. Rick clapped a sympathetic hand to his nephew's shoulder.

"You're not wearing a tie?" Diego asked.

"Should I?"

"How should I know?"

The two stared at each other. Yeah. This was going to go fabulously.

Diego started smirking, earning a light growl from Rick. "Shut up."

The kid was too smart for his own good, his eyes catching on something Rick had accidentally left out. "Dude, what are these?"

Rick grabbed for the stack of index cards he'd left on the coffee table next to his wallet and phone, but Diego was faster than he was.

"Compliment her appearance?" Diego turned over the card and read the other side. "No politics or religion?" He dropped down to the couch, laughing so hard, tears streamed down his face. "This is the most pathetic thing I've ever seen."

A second, somewhat offended growl escaped Rick's throat. "I haven't been on a dinner date in a while."

"You can't walk into a restaurant with a stack of cheat cards."

"It's better than staring at her and saying nothing. And I'm not going to bring them," Rick added, reaching for the cards again. "I'm just studying them."

"Like this is a test? Wow, you're pathetic. Here, try it out on me."

"I'm not using a card on you. You're my nephew."

Diego smirked. "And I'm not dealing with you dragging your sorry ass back in here after you crash and burn. Compliment me."

"No."

"Yes."

Glare for glare, neither one of them backed down. Finally, Rick groaned. The kid had a point.

"Fine, but you can't make fun of me." Rick dropped on the other end of the couch, the notecards in his lap. Diego sat there, waiting. And waiting. And waiting some more.

"Are you seriously not going to say anything to me?"

"This is weird," Rick grumbled.

Diego rolled his eyes from beneath his baseball cap. "Tell me you like my hair or some shit."

"I can't see your hair."

"Fine. Tell me you like my shoes." Diego kicked his dirty tennis shoes up on the coffee table. The part of Rick that appreciated his coffee table not being covered in a day's worth of mud and snow grimaced. Diego waggled his toes pointedly.

"I don't like your shoes. They're disgusting. Buy some new ones. And I'm not practicing lying to her."

"Then find something you do like about me." Diego waited while Rick thought about it. "Really? It's not that hard, asshole."

"It's not that easy." Rick couldn't help but grin at the deeply offended expression on Diego's face.

"Whatever, man. I don't need this. Enjoy blowing it."

Still, Diego sat there while Rick fiddled with the stack of cards.

"You're loyal." Rick didn't look at the kid as he stared out the window. "When Jen left, I thought you would go with her. Real glad that you stayed."

Diego cleared his throat, as uncomfortable receiving a compliment as he was giving them. "Aunt Jen didn't appreciate you the way she should have."

Rick opened his mouth to defend his ex, but Diego grunted sourly, cutting him off.

"You put up with a lot from me when you could have sent me to the state. Every lie I told you, every time I snuck out. All the fights I got into. You never kicked me out, even though I deserved it."

"You were hurting," Rick said quietly. "You'd lost a lot. You didn't need to lose more."

Diego didn't answer, because they never talked about that. The car accident that had taken his family—including Jen's sister, Diego's mother—was a topic permanently off-limits.

Instead, he cleared his throat, and Rick continued to stare out the window until whatever Diego was feeling had been shoved as deep inside as the kid could force it. Rubbing a rough hand over his eyes, like maybe he'd had an itch to scratch, Diego leaned over and took the cards from Rick. He slouched down in the couch a little more as he read the top card.

"What are three topics you shouldn't bring up?" Diego asked.

"Politics, religion, and exes." Rick *had* been studying.

"Three topics you should bring up?"

"Her job, her interests, her future dreams and endeavors."

Making a face, Diego said, "That sounds awful."

Rick stood. "Yeah, but she's awfully pretty. I'm going to have to wing the rest of these. I need to go pick her up."

Diego didn't wish him luck, but Rick didn't expect him to. It was enough to know that if this went bad, there would be a bowl of cereal waiting for him when he limped back home. He'd cleaned his car, filled it with gas, and double-checked the oil and antifreeze. He'd showered, shaved, and done his best not to look like an idiot. The only thing left was not to be late. The rest... well...he didn't know. Rick wasn't good with this kind of thing, and he never had been. Lana Montgomery was about to realize how big of a mistake she'd made asking him out. Climbing into the driver's seat, Rick started the engine and then sat there, hands gripping the steering wheel.

"You can do this. Her name is Lana," Rick repeated to himself. "Just Lana."

———

Lana had learned early the way to hold the power in a room was to know exactly the outfit everyone else would be wearing and then wear something a touch more. In a room where everyone had their hair up, wear her hair down. In a room of two-inch heels, have two-and-a-half-inch heels. Order champagne when everyone else drank wine. Decline the champagne when everyone else was drinking it and sip a scotch on the rocks instead.

In a world of pencils, have a pen.

The problem with her upbringing was the one-upmanship wasn't a rule, it was a way of life. But Lana hadn't been on a date in years with a man she liked anywhere close to as much as she liked Rick. In an effort to make herself perfect for this date, she was second-guessing everything.

"While I understand the need to bring in reinforcements," Zoey said as she applied Lana's eyeliner, "I'm not sure I count."

"Nonsense. I have absolutely no business holding any sort of beauty product. I'm liable to poke my eye out, and then where would I be?"

"The most beautiful woman I know in an eye patch."

Not for the first time, Lana wondered if Zoey had any clue how talented she was as a makeup artist. Tonight was important to Lana, so she'd requested the use of the resort's salon. Under the professional lighting of the beautician's station and with full use of all Lana's beauty supplies, Zoey was putting Lana into passable shape. More than passable if she knew her friend. A rock steady hand with liquid eyeliner was Zoey's superpower.

Really, it was beyond her why Zoey didn't do this for a living instead of giving tours. Probably because tours were what Zoey loved. Makeup was only something she did.

Lana didn't know what that was like. She'd been raised

that what she did was who she was. And who she was was a businesswoman.

"I should have studied marine biology," Lana mused. "I might have liked swimming with dolphins for a living."

Zoey moved onto her lower lids. "Random comment of the night number four. If I didn't know better, I'd think you were nervous."

"I'm going out with a man who I like very much, one who absolutely deserves better than my lifestyle and relationship timetable. One who likes me despite my accidentally grazing him—"

"Shooting him."

"It was definitely a graze. And because a tattooed woman with a helicopter told me I shouldn't ask him out, I marched right up to him and did it anyway. Either tonight will go badly, in which we will both end up disappointed, or tonight will go wonderfully, in which we'll both end up disappointed. I'm scared to death," Lana said under her breath.

"I was wondering what pushed you into saying something. You never could resist a challenge." Lana couldn't open her eyes, but she could hear her friend's amusement. "You know you're going to make that poor man's eyes fall out, right?"

"What do you mean?"

"The dress. The heels."

"Is it too much?" Lana risked Zoey's handiwork by opening her eyes and glancing down at herself in concern. "Honestly, he gave me very little to go on."

"He'll be in jeans. I don't know if he owns anything else."

"Maybe this *is* too much." She glanced down again, brow

furrowing deeply enough that she could feel the lines. "Is the dress too dark for winter?"

"Fret with your eyes closed," Zoey encouraged her. "Or you're not going to be ready in time."

"Wouldn't that be the perfect social faux pas to start the night?"

"Lana, this is Rick. He's a nice, sweet man. I think that's why everyone's so worried about him. He's kind of...a duckling."

"I'm sorry?"

"Ducklings are really good with other ducklings, but when they're alone, anyone with a heart is going to want to protect him."

They had both been very good at ignoring the figure in the corner, but at Zoey's comment, the third wheel in the room snickered. "If Rick heard you describe him as a duckling, he'd never get over the shame."

"Hush, Graham," Zoey said. "No one is listening to you right now. Open your eyes, Lana, and look up."

"Is there a reason you brought him?" Lana asked her friend, dutifully following her directions.

"The brat brought himself. Graham, be useful and tell us what you think of Lana's dress."

Lana couldn't see his face, but she could hear Graham's voice, only half joking when he answered. "I think two more dresses worth of material and she might have something she won't freeze in."

"*Graham.*"

"The dress looks fine. L already knows she looks fine."

"It looks great." Zoey shook her head. "Ignore him."

"What do you think? Is this a terrible decision?" Lana asked Graham.

At Lana's question, Graham rose and crossed the room from the corner Zoey had long since banished him to, sitting on the next station's chair.

Taking Lana's hands, Graham squeezed her fingers. "No. You two like each other. That much is obvious. Just take it easy on him, okay? And take it easy on yourself. I don't want to see either of you get hurt."

Not for the first time since she'd walked into Rick's and asked him out, Lana wondered if she had made a mistake. But would it hurt him more to cancel? Especially when she didn't want to cancel. Lana wanted this night for herself.

A night with a man she was attracted to, one whose kind voice and strong hands she couldn't get out of her mind.

Hating that she'd begun to doubt herself, Lana squeezed Graham's hands once before letting go, resting them in her lap. Having few real friends meant she was overly susceptible to their opinions. It was highly possible that between them, Zoey and Graham could convince her to stay home. It was possible a part of her wanted them to try.

"Well, I'll do my best not to break any unsuspecting hearts," Lana told him, aiming for her normal breeziness, but even she could hear her joke fall flat.

Graham gave her a sympathetic look. "We know you wouldn't do it on purpose, darlin'. I'm just worried about the accidental heartbreak on both sides."

"If I promise to be on my best behavior, will you be able to keep yourself from sneaking around and spying on us tonight?"

"Why would you think I was going to do that?" Graham asked, trying for casual and innocent, but it was clear by the way he wouldn't meet her eyes that Lana had busted him.

"Because it's the middle of the dinnertime rush. You're here, not at the Tourist Trap, meaning you closed. And you wouldn't have closed during nonpeak hours when the locals get to finally show up and eat your food in relative peace. Unless you two have big date plans, you're spying on Rick and me." Silence, then Lana arched an eyebrow. "Unless your big date plans *are* to spy on Rick and me?"

"It's almost as if you know me, darlin'."

"Not my fault if you're predictable," Lana said smoothly.

Chuckling, he leaned back in his chair and turned in a circle. "Okay, fine. Maybe I was. But someone else put me up to it."

Zoey's eyes widened, then her cheeks went bright red. "I can't believe you outed me," she hissed.

"I can't believe you were going to let me take the blame." He stole her fingers and pressed a quick kiss to the inside of her wrist. Zoey smiled up at Graham as if unable to help herself, then she adjusted her glasses higher on her nose. For some reason, that simple action always made Graham look like he was about to drop to one knee and spout love sonnets to her.

"All right, ladies. I'll get out of your way." He dipped his head to press a kiss to Zoey's cheek, then headed for the salon exit. Pausing, Graham looked over his shoulder. "Hey, L? You look gorgeous. Every man deserves a heart attack in heels at least once in his life." Whistling a little Christmas tune, Graham slipped out of the salon.

Zoey watched him go, sighing the sigh of the truly smitten. "Is it me or does he keep getting hotter? Even when he's extra annoying, I want to jump him."

"I think he's perfect for you," Lana replied. She could list his best attributes, but if Graham could be enough of a gentleman not to comment on her dress, Lana supposed she shouldn't tell Zoey that his rear end was fabulous.

"Lana? Are you sure we can't…"

Lana waited until Zoey was finished with the last stroke of color on her lips before shaking her head. "No way. I'm so nervous right now, I can't even imagine having you two sneaking about in the shadows."

"You did it to me the night I met Graham."

"Yes, but that was entirely different." Lana adopted a mock snooty tone. "Montgomerys sneak about. They are not snuck about *on*. We *do* have reputations to maintain, you know." Reputations that preceded her. Worrying wasn't her style, so Lana took a deep steadying breath. "This will be okay."

"This will be great. Be yourself. Rick already likes you or he wouldn't have said yes." Zoey leaned back and studied her handiwork. "And Graham's right about one thing."

"What's that?"

Shooting her a wink, Zoey all but smirked. "You are definitely going to give him a heart attack."

Trying to get somewhere on time in a town full of moose was easier said than done. Sometimes the suckers just wouldn't *move*.

Rick honked his horn again, hoping this time the noise would do more than earn him a long, annoyed look. "Come on, Dude. I have places to be."

The moose remained in the center of the road, staring at him through the windshield.

Since the relocation of Ulysses the previous summer, an opening had been left for the next most annoying town megafauna. Dude was firmly in the running. The juvenile bull moose had never figured out the concept of roads...what they were, why they were, how it was a good idea to stay off them. For some reason, Dude preferred the Moose Springs public roads for his transportation needs. And when one played a game of automobile/moose chicken with Dude, the moose always won.

Rick edged the car toward the far side of the road, trying to skirt around the massive animal.

"Take it easy," he said. "No big deal. Just a—"

Midsentence, Dude's switch flipped, and he attacked the passenger's side of the car without warning. With a curse, Rick hit the gas, one arm coming up instinctively to protect himself as hooves struck faster than he could get away.

The thump was better than shattering glass would have been. As he looked in the rearview window, the moose was already trotting off. Rick drove the necessary distance to put himself safely out of reach of a return moosing, then he pulled off the side of the road. Climbing out of his car, he checked out the damage. Sure enough, a nice, large dent now caved in his quarter panel.

"Really? *Dude*, you *suck*."

The moose always had lived up to his namesake.

He took out his phone, snapped a quick picture, and added it to the town's message board. Keeping track of the local naughty moose sightings was one of their pastimes, and it helped the next person know which areas to avoid.

Only as he started back up the road did it occur to Rick that he'd announced to everyone that he was going to the resort in the evening. For once, Rick didn't care about being the center of the town's gossip. He was proud that he had a date with Lana Mont— just *Lana* tonight. If anyone had a problem with it, they could mind their own business, because he was freaking ecstatic.

It would have been nice not to show up in a dinged car, but Rick was grateful a colossal piano hadn't fallen out of the sky to land on his head. As he pulled up to the front of the resort, Rick saw a figure waiting for him on the bench beside the tall wooden entry doors.

"Hey there, Rickie boy." A friendly shoulder pat was not nearly good enough to compensate for Graham's unexpected and unwelcome presence.

Rick frowned. "Please tell me you didn't scare off my date."

"Naw, L has nerves of steel. I showed her every baby picture of you that I could find, and she still insisted on going through with tonight. I think the lady has designs on you." When Rick looked at him, Graham sighed. "Why is everyone so serious tonight?"

Rick reached up to adjust the tie he wasn't wearing, then groaned. "Don't know, and I don't care. If you don't mind, I have to be in there."

"It's weird, right? Picking someone up from a hotel? It's like the biggest front porch in Alaska."

"Graham..."

"Do you think Hannah will flick the lights on and off on you two if she catches you kissing later?"

"This is me leaving," Rick said, taking a step.

The valets were ready to open the doors, which always made Rick uncomfortable. They swung open with a creak.

"Reminds me of *Jurassic Park*," Graham said. "You don't know what bloodthirsty creatures are in there, waiting to be unleashed on us."

"I'm assuming you're not including my date in that description." Rick was about to tell Graham that he wouldn't mind a velociraptor taking his friend down, then he stopped dead in his tracks.

Rick nearly swallowed his tongue when he lifted his head and saw his date.

Conceding to the temperatures by wearing a cowl neck, long-sleeved sweater dress and thigh-high leather boots, Lana must have failed to consider what that absolutely devastating inch of bared skin between the tops of her boots and the hem of that curve-hugging dress would do to him. The jacket over her shoulders did nothing but accentuate what was beneath, and Rick couldn't breathe, let alone move toward her or say hello.

A heavy hand smacked him on the back hard enough to force the air out of his lungs.

"Now, since Lana has no one else to watch out for her—" Graham started to say, but Lana breezed right past him. She linked her arm in Rick's.

"I'm perfectly capable of doing so myself. Now please, scurry off."

"I really think you two should talk about what a big step this is. Has either one of you signed an abstinence pledge?"

Rick was going to kill him. Slowly but surely, he would strangle every last breath from his friend.

Ignoring their third wheel, Lana turned to Rick, her liquid dark eyes raising to his. It felt like getting punched in the stomach but in the best of ways. He didn't know what she'd done with her eye makeup, but he couldn't stop staring at her.

"Are you ready to leave? I'm famished."

Hungry. She was hungry. Rick could fix hungry.

"You might want to say something to her at some point tonight, buddy," Graham supplied helpfully. "Zoey and I have the night free. We can double-date this thing if you need some wingpersons."

Lana leaned in and whispered conspiratorially. "If we get in the car, Graham stops being a part of our evening. But it's your choice, Rick. I'm flexible."

Did she have to use that word? What was left of his brain officially gave up, lying down in the gutter and rolling around like a happy dog scratching its back.

Rick swallowed again, trying to make his mouth work properly. "Let's save the torture for another night."

Lana beamed at him. "Perfect. Now, if you'll excuse us..."

Walking was something he was still capable of. Rick led her to his car, where a valet had stolen notecard number fourteen: "Open the door for her." The valet probably had no idea why their politeness earned a frustrated look from him. Out of the corner of his eye, he saw a slender woman in glasses peering through the expansive windows of the resort lobby. Zoey gave him two thumbs-up in encouragement.

"Is it me or are these two extra invasive tonight?" Rick grumbled. "They're worse than parents on prom night."

Lana shot him an amused look before noticing the damage to his car.

"Oh, what happened?" She stopped before getting in. "This wasn't here earlier. Did you get in an accident?"

"Just an angry Dude," Rick said. "Moose kicks in car doors are a fact of life around here. I'll pop it out when I get home."

"You know how to do that?"

"If it's only the metal and nothing structural underneath... yeah. It's a few screws and a plunger." Not really a big deal, but she seemed impressed. And Rick *really* wanted to impress her.

He probably should have worn that tie.

"If kicking cars is a moose thing, do you think a sleigh would lure it?"

"The Santa Moose? I sure hope not. It's going to be an awfully scary Christmas Eve parade if that's true. Let's not give it any ideas."

Lana shuddered. "Oh dear. Yes, let's not."

When Rick had gotten ready for tonight, he'd figured he'd wing it with the restaurant. It wasn't that he wasn't willing to plan for a nice night on the town. But the only really nice places to go were in the resort. Considering she lived in the resort, taking her to dinner there seemed far too akin to taking her to her own kitchen on a date. There weren't many restaurants in Moose Springs, but Rick was willing to take her to her favorite.

"Does anything sound good?" he asked her as they pulled away from the curb.

"I'm guessing the Tourist Trap is off the menu now since Graham is here and not there."

Rick nodded, trying not to notice how her dress slipped up a few inches as she crossed her legs. "If you're cold, I can turn up the heater."

He started fumbling with the dials, somehow having forgotten how to operate his own vehicle.

A slender hand touched his. "You look very nice tonight, Rick. I'm perfectly comfortable. And pick whatever restaurant you'd like. I'm just happy to be spending the evening with you."

He'd never been at such a loss for words. She was just so damn beautiful.

"You're gorgeous, Lana," Rick said, finally going for honest and pathetic instead of suave and capable. "I'm still trying to figure out what to say."

And wouldn't you know it? Lana slipped her fingers through his, the prettiest blush on her face.

Maybe he wasn't so bad at this after all.

———

Every place seemed worse than the last.

Rick kept driving, his left hand gripping the steering wheel harder with each mile that passed. His right had stayed loosely holding Lana's slender fingers in his own. Nothing seemed good enough for her, each choice of sandwich shop or dive bar subpar and unappealing.

He almost turned into a biker bar just outside town out of sheer lack of anything left, but as much as he liked the people who frequented the bar, he wasn't taking Lana in there. At least not in that dress.

The dress that cost him a little more of his sanity every time she shifted, knowing he needed to keep his eyes on the road instead of on her.

When they finally reached the one-stop market outside town, Rick knew he'd passed the point of no return.

"Oh, are we going somewhere new?" Lana perked up, her fingers squeezing his in excitement.

"Umm...yeah."

Apparently, they were going someplace new to both of them.

A light flurry of snow started to fall as they left Moose Springs and all its dining options behind. Dining options that seemed glorious and completely date appropriate now that Rick had lost the possibility of turning around and driving back to any of them.

"If I didn't know better, I'd think you were taking me into the middle of nowhere."

"It sure feels like it, huh?" He inwardly cringed.

Think, Rick. Think of some place. Any place. Why hadn't he turned the other way? It would have been a long drive, but Anchorage was eventually that direction. This way, there was nothing. Absolutely nothing.

"So tell me about you." Lana turned in her seat toward him,

making herself comfortable. "None of this usual date stuff. Tell me something good."

"I finally remembered to bring home Diego's milk for once."

"Is forgetting the milk a thing?"

"Yep. And it pisses the kid off like nothing else." Rick grinned at the thought. "I might be doing it subconsciously. You should see the face he makes when he has to eat his Raisin Bran dry."

Her laugh was a much-needed balm to his nerves. "I like Diego. He always seems very serious though. It's good he has you to tease him."

"He's good for me too. Diego's been living with me for a while now."

"How long is a while?"

Rick hesitated, because no one liked to talk about the accident. Glancing at her, Rick's mouth opened of its own accord. "Since he was a teenager. His family passed away. Drunk driving accident."

Lana's voice softened with sympathy. "That's terrible."

"Yeah." Even now, memories of getting that call still gave Rick a cold shiver. Having to tell Jen her nephew was being airlifted to the hospital and the rest of the family was gone was one of the worst things he'd ever had to do.

"None of us are fond of tourists driving drunk in town. Diego's got the scars to back up his feelings on the matter. He lost his parents and his little sister that day. Jen...my ex. Her sister was his mom."

"Does Diego have any other family besides you two?"

Rick shook his head. "Not locally."

"It's really good of you to have taken him in."

"If you'd seen him sitting there in the hospital, stitches in his forehead, totally lost, you wouldn't have been able to leave him there either." Rick couldn't help the pride in his voice as he added, "The kid's rough around the edges, but he's a good one. First person I'd want in my corner."

"He had your back with Jonah. I was impressed."

Not many people were impressed with Diego, which only made him like her more. Which was why it was unfortunate that at any moment, Lana was going to decide he'd lured her into the middle of nowhere to ax murder her.

"Oh," Lana said, looking up with excitement. "Are we here?"

They'd reached the end of the road. As sheer freaking luck would have it, the end of the road coincided with a particularly nice view of the surrounding mountains. Without that view, the modest, two-story log cabin bed-and-breakfast in front of them wouldn't be there. Or at least it wouldn't have had an "Open" sign in the window.

Somehow, Rick had found a B and B with an actual restaurant attached.

This was it. Literally. If he turned left, they would end up on a gravel drive leading into a national forest, and if he turned right, they would end up headed for Canada. It was the end of the road, so whatever Molly's Bed-and-Breakfast was, this was it.

Molly sounded like a normal name. This could work. He was saved. It was a Christmas freaking miracle.

"A B and B, huh?" Lana aimed a flirtatious look at him. "Are we at the overnight stage already?"

Rick winced. "I didn't even think of that. We can go back if you aren't comfortable." Back because forward wasn't much of an option. Forward would take them so far into the bush, he'd need four-wheel drive.

"I'm sure this place is absolutely lovely." She squeezed his hand once more before releasing it to unbuckle her seat belt.

Lana's heels were not meant for this kind of drive, but she never wobbled as she joined him at the front of the vehicle. Crap, he hadn't opened the door for her. Apparently, he was determined to blow all his chances to use card number fourteen. He'd jumped out and stared at the restaurant as if he could warp it into a four-star steakhouse out of sheer willpower.

"Are you all right?" A sculpted eyebrow rose, those gorgeous eyes sweeping over him in concern.

"Yep. All good."

Nope. Nope nope nope.

Lana threaded her arm through Rick's. "I'm starving. It's always exciting to try someplace new."

Yes. Exciting. This was exciting, and he could really luck out here. Some places were hidden gems, and just because he'd never known about this place didn't mean it wasn't one of those unexpectedly amazing restaurants that would make tonight worth the drive.

Letting himself hope for a kinder, gentler universe, Rick opened the door at the top of the stairs, offering a shy smile to the woman with him. She was so beautiful, he couldn't get over it. And when she returned that smile, his heart paused in his chest, took its own breath, and finally started to beat again.

This time, Rick moved fast enough to hold the door open for her before following her into the restaurant. She stopped so quickly, he bumped into Lana's back, quickly placing a hand on her hip to steady them both.

"Sorry—" he started to say, then Rick trailed off, finally seeing what had caused his date to hit the brakes.

Rick had lived in Alaska his entire life. Many people he knew were avid hunters, and some relied on hunting and fishing to feed their families throughout the winter. Even though it had always struck him as macabre to mount a trophy animal on a wall, he was used to it. Growing up in Alaska meant one wasn't a stranger to that sort of thing.

But even he had never seen this much taxidermy in a single room.

"Are they—?" Lana started, sounding startled more than horrified.

"Squirrels." Rick kept his hand on her hip out of sheer protective instinct. One did not expect to step into a room with taxidermy squirrels everywhere.

"And are they—?"

Rick shuddered. "They're dressed for the holiday season."

Looking around, Rick had no idea what to do. Everywhere he looked was another squirrel. One dressed as an early 1900s St. Nick. Others working as elves in Santa's workshop or loading his sleigh. A Rudolph squirrel stood impatiently with the other reindeer squirrels while excited squirrel children waited by fireplaces in little squirrel pajamas. There were squirrels reenacting the ending of *It's a Wonderful Life* and others ice skating beneath a Christmas tree in Rockefeller Center.

Someone had put a Ghost of Christmas Future outfit on a particularly grim squirrel, complete with chains and a sickle.

A tall, thin woman in thick-rimmed glasses appeared from the back, blinking in surprise when she saw them. "Oh, I didn't hear you come in. Two for dinner?"

If Lana had run screaming, Rick would have understood. But instead of cringing, his date turned sweetly to the hostess.

"Yes, thank you."

"Sit wherever you want. We're empty tonight."

The hostess handed Rick two menus and promptly disappeared into the back once more. "Carl, we have a two-top," the hostess yelled, loud enough that they both started.

"Well, I prefer to sit by the window," Lana said cheerfully as they headed to a table on the far side of the empty dining room.

Rick raised an eyebrow. "Next to Santa's sleigh?"

"It seems festive." Festive was one way of putting it. "Have you eaten here before?"

"Do you think I would have dragged you all the way here if I had?" Rick pulled her seat out for her as per card twelve's recommendation.

"I might question your sense of humor," she said with a teasing smile.

If she was horrified, she was hiding it well. Now was the time to own up to his mistake or to flat out lie. Rick wasn't a liar, even when his pride was on the line, so he groaned softly.

"Hey, Lana? You know when you take a beautiful woman out to dinner and you keep driving past all the places because they don't seem good enough and end up in the worst possible place by accident? It's something like that."

The grin she flashed him was full of mischief. "You mean you don't normally go full squirrel on your first dates?"

"I keep wishing I was back in the resort buying you a steak, but it just isn't happening."

"Don't worry," Lana reassured him. "I've been to every kind of dining experience under the sun. You get points for being original."

Rick chuckled, resting his arms on the table. "I bet double-dating with Zoey and Graham is sounding better by the minute."

Lana exhaled a soft laugh. "Trust me, unless they *serve* squirrel, this is far superior."

A man appeared from the back, stumping up to their table with two glasses of water in his hands. Early thirties, partially balding, with a pockmarked face and a lingering scent of something sketchy clinging to his clothes, their server did not inspire Rick's faith that this experience was about to get better.

"I'm Carl," he grunted at them. "Ma's in the back. We're down a cook tonight." Carl pulled a piece of paper out of his pocket, then he read off of it in a bored voice. "Our special is the sausage plate, and we have a stroganoff."

"What kind of stroganoff?" Rick asked. In this place, he wasn't taking any chances.

"I don't know. It's stroganoff."

Carl stared at Rick. Rick stared at Carl. Lana raised her glass of water to her lips in an attempt to hide her mirth.

"I'll ask." Carl stumped away.

"Do you think it's squirrel?" Rick asked her, earning another mischievous look from Lana.

"If it is, I'm going to pass. I prefer my adorable chittering creatures happily running around in tree limbs."

"Not recreating the nativity while you enjoy your meal?"

Lana snickered as she took another drink of her water. "I was trying not to look directly at that one. Or the squirrels in holiday-themed steampunk kissing beneath a mechanical mistletoe."

A noise had been bothering Rick, familiar but quiet enough that he couldn't quite figure out what it was. Then the sound grew louder, followed by a toy whistle.

"I was wondering what that was," Lana said. "I love model trains—*oh*. Oh dear."

The model train track had been neatly hidden among the other decor, so Rick had missed it until the train came out from a hole in the wall leading to an adjacent room and into the dining room. It wrapped around the outside of the room, passing by them beneath the window.

The train had a conductor. With conductor clothes.

And furry ears.

"If we leave now, it's only a two-hour drive to McDonald's," he said, quietly enough that Carl and his mother wouldn't hear.

"Yes, but think of the stories we'll have to tell." Lana glanced surreptitiously at the room. "How do you think they manage to avoid Harold?"

"Taxidermy isn't banned in restaurants."

"True, but nondisclosed meat in ambiguous stroganoff has to be."

They shared a grin over the table. The menu was—surprising to Rick—mostly Italian-themed dishes and fairly standard options, although many items seemed "house sausage" based. There was literally nothing that would have identified this place as an Italian restaurant, but technically, Italian food was considered a more sensual dining experience.

Squirrels aside, maybe he hadn't entirely struck out with this one.

When Carl returned, Lana ordered the pasta arrabbiata, the same dish Rick had been eyeballing. Their server looked at them, sighed heavily, and stumped away. In the kitchen, his voice could be heard growling.

"Ma, they got the spicy sauce. I don't know. Yeah, I *told* them about the specials."

"Do you get the feeling that we didn't order what they wanted?" Lana asked.

Rick didn't get a chance to answer because Carl stomped his way back to the table. "Ma wants to know if you want the house sausage in your sauce."

Absolutely not. No way. Hard pass on that.

"No thank you," Rick said, trying for polite.

"Are you sure?" Carl didn't seem convinced.

"Pretty sure."

The train came around a second time, blowing its whistle right next to their table as Carl stared at Rick, eyes unblinking, as if trying to mentally force Rick into caving.

There was no way he was giving in on this, so Rick upped his staring game until Carl grunted and stomped away again.

Lana managed to hide her giggles until Carl disappeared in the back. On a whim, Rick offered his palm to her on top of the table. Bless the woman, she placed her hand in his as if it belonged there.

"You wanted to know something about me," Rick said. "I was wondering the same thing about you."

"Oh, haven't you heard? I'm the pure evil scourge of the town's existence. I chase deranged moose in my free time, and I'm absolutely in love with anything baked at Frankie's. Her food is criminal."

"Any evil exes I should know about?" The cards said not to mention exes, but the words had come from his mouth before Rick could stop them.

"No one worth mentioning." She shrugged. "I didn't date much in my twenties. It was hard to get close to anyone because I never knew if they were interested in me or interested in getting a foot in the door at the Montgomery Group. And since taking on a bigger role in the company, I simply travel too much." Lana flushed a cute shade of pink. "I suppose you think that I'm wasting your time."

"Actually, I was thinking that I was pretty lucky. If it helps, I'm not interested in taking over your company. I gave up my desires for economic domination years ago."

Lana leaned in. "That's an interesting take for a business owner," she said with an arch look.

"One business. Imagining owning a hundred businesses like you guys raises my blood pressure."

A funny expression crossed her face.

"Did I guess too low?" Rick asked.

"A bit."

Pulling a number out of the air, Rick figuring he was highballing it. "Five hundred?" When she shook her head, he was impressed. "A thousand?"

"After the recent Moose Springs acquisition, the Montgomery Group owns over a quarter of a million properties currently being subleased to commercial and private business owners. Such as yourself."

Rick choked on his water, then tried to cover by coughing. "Sorry. And what part do you manage?"

"The parts that like to cause problems," Lana said jokingly. "So aside from Diego, do you have any other family around here?"

"Nope, it's just me." Rick held Lana's eyes. "And you changed the subject. Don't like talking about work?"

"Talking about work is dangerously close to talking about my family. And trust me, we're going to need something stronger than water to dip into that mess."

"Would you like something stronger?"

She smiled at him. "I'm not above a glass of wine with my meal. Maybe once we return to town though. You might need backup with Carl."

"He doesn't seem to like me much, does he?"

"Not at all." Lana laughed. "So any kids with your ex?"

Oh no. They were back in forbidden territory, a hard right turn with tires squealing.

"Oh...umm...well..."

"We don't have to talk about that if you aren't comfortable," she said immediately. But an awkward silence fell between them, the first since they'd reached the restaurant.

Rick grimaced. "Can I have a do-over? What I meant to say was no, we didn't have any kids. I'm sorry, Lana. I'm not very good at this. I haven't dated since I was in high school, and I read this article...there were cards...I shouldn't have brought up exes."

Could he be any more embarrassed? Thankfully, she reached across the table, resting her hand on his.

Lana's eyes were bright with curiosity and some amusement. "Let me guess. The article said no politics, religion, or past experiences that could cause discomfort or awkward pauses."

"Pretty much."

She leaned back in her seat. "You would not believe how many of polite society's 'rules' I've had stuffed down my throat since I was born. And you know what? Two drinks and a cigarette and all that crap goes by the wayside. Just know that I'm open to talking about whatever you'd like. I want to know more about you, Rick. That's why I lured you to the middle of nowhere and surrounded you with holiday-themed taxidermy."

How could a woman who made his mouth go dry every time he looked at her somehow make him feel so at ease?

The tension in his shoulders relaxed as he said, "No kids, but we both wanted them. It never worked for us. That's not why we split up, but it was hard to swallow never having a family. We're divorced now, but it wasn't Jen's fault. When her sister died, a lot changed for her, and I was one of the things that changed. I don't blame her. Life is hard. I don't hate my ex, and I never could."

"You're a really good guy, aren't you?"

"Not according to Diego," Rick told her jokingly. "He called me an asshole tonight, and I probably deserved it."

They shared another moment, this one equally silent but not awkward at all.

"You know what, Rick? I think you and I are going to get along fabulously." Lana held out her water, and they clinked glasses.

That was exactly what Rick was thinking too.

CHAPTER 8

NEVER IN A MILLION YEARS would Lana admit to hating the restaurant.

The last thing she wanted to do was make Rick feel bad. If sparing his feelings meant sitting in a room full of increasingly disturbing holiday-themed taxidermy, then that was what she would do. That being said, the place had made her flesh crawl from the moment she stepped inside.

Funny how all it took was looking at Rick's horrified expression and none of it seemed so bad. Not when she got to spend an evening with him.

The meal was far more appetizing than she had expected, and now that Rick was starting to relax around her, Lana was starting to relax around him too. The longer she looked at him, the more handsome she found him. Rick cleaned up even better than good, and he was an utter dear to talk to. Except for Carl standing in the corner, gloomily staring out the window, the entire thing might have been perfect.

For a blessed ten minutes, Carl disappeared into the back, then he stumped his way to the table, dropping their check on the edge.

"The snow's getting bad." Carl pointed out the window. "Ma says you might want to stay the night."

"We're fine." Rick reached for the check, but Lana snagged it first.

"I asked you out," she told her date, handing both the check and her debit card to Carl. For once, their waiter headed across the room with a more jovial step, as if perked up at the idea of getting rid of them.

Hazel eyes amused, he said, "So if I ask you out for a second date, I get to pay?"

"Hmm, that's to be decided." She flushed, then added quickly, "The paying, not the second date. I mean, not that I expect you to ask me out again. Or a first time, since I asked you out this time. I'm babbling, aren't I?"

"It's cute. And if my choice in restaurants didn't scare you off, I'd love to ask you out for a second date."

He'd called her cute. Which was much better than if he'd called her beautiful. Lana was used to being judged for her surface, and cute was more than skin deep. Cute felt like maybe he saw her for her.

"Rick, at the risk of ruining this, I feel like we need to talk about the elephant in the room."

"They dressed one up like an elephant?" He shuddered, twisting around to look at the decor.

Laughing softly, Lana shook her head. "No, although I wouldn't be surprised if one is hiding somewhere. I just...I feel like I should be clear about my intentions here."

Rick's eyes sparkled in the low restaurant lighting. "Is this where you promise those intentions are honorable?"

"Oh goodness no. Where would be the fun in that?"

They shared a grin. When hers started to slip, Rick squeezed her fingers gently.

"You travel. A lot." He sounded resigned.

"It's part of the job. I want a home...I always have. I want that home to be in Moose Springs. But right now, a suitcase is the closest to that as I'll get. And right now..."

"Could last a long time?"

"Pretty much."

Lana chewed her lower lip, knowing it was probably messing up her lipstick but unable to stop herself.

"So my options are a short-term fling or—?"

"We could always be friends."

He visibly flinched at her suggestion, and despite herself, Lana giggled. "I'm guessing that's not your first choice."

"Sweetheart, I'm not used to having a choice, first or last or in between. But if I did get to choose..." Rick drifted off, glancing out the window next to them, dark as it was outside. "I think that I've had more fun with you these last few days than I've had in years. So if I can get a little more of that, I'm willing to accept this is just for now."

"A holiday fling?"

"Fling?" Rick grimaced at the wording. "That sounds... temporary. And kind of cliché."

"We can't do much about the longevity, but I love a good cliché." They shared a smile before Lana added, "So I'm thinking you really should ask me out again. At the risk of not playing coy, you'll probably get a yes."

The man had no idea how sexy he was when he leaned in like that, his voice lowering a little. "Probably or definitely?"

"Definitely," Lana heard herself murmur, a thrill of anticipation running up her spine as he took her hand.

"Good to know."

She leaned in too because he had this look on his face as if he were about to ask her. Only the expected request never came. When she realized he was teasing her by making her wait, Lana said, "Or I could remind you that I'm perfectly capable of asking you out a second time, which is becoming less likely by the moment."

Rick's lips curved. "Changing your mind about me so fast?"

"Never. I know a good thing when I see one."

He blinked as if surprised at the compliment. Then his hazel eyes grew greener, the way he was looking at her making Lana's pulse race. Carl brought back the bill, and after Lana had waved off Rick's offer to leave the tip, she signed the check and stood. The combination of Rick's manners and appreciation of her capabilities was sexy beyond belief. She'd spent an evening in his company and had not felt like she had to prove herself, defend herself, or keep her defenses up once.

Taxidermy aside, it might have been the best dinner date she'd ever had.

"What are you doing tonight?" Rick asked her huskily. "Because I'd love to take you out again, someplace better. Dessert and drinks at the resort? I can call ahead, see if Hannah would score us one of those outdoor fireplaces on the balcony, the ones with the couches."

"Are we talking ice cream and Kahlúa?"

"I was thinking red wine and chocolate cake."

Sighing contentedly, Lana all but purred at the thought of snuggling next to this man by a warm winter fire. "You're reading my mind."

Rick's eyes sparkled with amusement. "And this time, I'll be lucid enough to enjoy a couch with you."

"I was wondering if I was going to manage to get through tonight without that being brought up. You tranquilize a guy one time..."

Chuckling, Rick moved behind Lana as she started to put on her jacket, holding it for her so slipping her arms inside the sleeves was easier. Even though she was more than capable of putting on a jacket all by herself, Lana appreciated the gesture. It was as if every small kindness was innate to his personality, subconsciously done.

One meal together and Lana was ready to kiss Rick senseless. Unfortunately, a twitchy Carl was determined to ruin the mood.

"Hey, guys, it's actually coming down really bad," he said at them. "You two shouldn't try to drive anywhere in this."

The darkness outside the windows made it hard to see what Carl was talking about, so they went out to the parking lot. Sure enough, the light flurry they'd driven through on the way to dinner—the kind of snow so often encountered in this area—had turned into a heavy fall. The wind had picked up, making the visibility dangerously lowered.

"I didn't think it was supposed to be this bad." Lana frowned out at where the road should have been.

Rick scratched the back of his neck awkwardly. "Well, back

home, it's probably not as thick. We're in a bit of a bad area, weather wise."

"It will let up eventually though. Right?"

Hope tinged her tone, but Rick gave her a pained look. "Maybe. I'd hate to start out and get stuck in this. I don't think freezing to death would be a great way to spend the evening."

"You don't mean…?"

"I wish I didn't. Lana, I'm so sorry."

"Nonsense. You're not any more in control of the weather than I am." Lana tried for breezy, but inside, her brain was screaming.

The idea of spending the night made her shudder.

There was no choice though. Lana could see the road they'd taken had become impassable, and the weather was only getting worse. The wind had made visibility half what it was getting there, and even as she stood outside the restaurant, Lana could see less and less of their vehicle parked in the parking lot.

As much as she wanted to escape this place, doing so would be downright dangerous.

Rick went back inside to talk to the staff while Lana stayed where she was, growing colder by the moment. She stared at the sky as if she could turn off the snow by sheer force of will. Rick returned, standing at her side with a piece of paper in his hand.

"They have rooms." Twisting her head to look back at him, she could see the pained expression on his face. "One for each of us. I guess the third is permanently occupied."

"Permanently occupied?" Lana's eyebrow rose of its own volition. "Who lives here? It has to be one of the family or the staff."

Rick shot her a wry look. "That's the same question I asked.

Apparently, the answer is none of the above. They also said the bathroom is shared."

The bathroom was shared. With someone who liked this place enough to stay there permanently.

Montgomerys didn't run away screaming into snowstorms.

"We're in rooms right next to each other. You can have whichever one is better." Rick sounded embarrassed.

"I live out of hotels, dearest." On a whim, Lana pressed a kiss to his jaw. "Stop worrying. This will be fine."

Hazel eyes gazed down at her as warm, strong hands found her hips. "You're trying really hard to make me feel better. It's almost working."

Lana looped her arm around his waist. She tugged him closer as she stepped back, her shoulders bumping into the exterior wall behind her.

Snowflakes dusted his shoulders and clung to his hair as Rick dipped his head. Then he stopped.

He *stopped*.

"We should get inside," he said, his lips almost brushing her own.

"You're kidding." Lana puffed out a breath of disappointment when Rick pulled back.

"You're shivering," Rick said in explanation, wrapping an arm around her shoulders. Okay, so maybe the manners thing wasn't quite as good as it was cracked up to be.

As they went back into the bed-and-breakfast, Lana wondered what he would do if she ignored Carl and his mom and everything else, dragged Rick back outside, and forced a do-over. That wouldn't be bad, right?

"Are you okay?" Rick asked as he handed her the keys to the rooms.

"Right as rain," Lana said, because *I'm thinking about jumping you* might scare him off.

The old wooden stairs creaked as they climbed up to the second floor, where a hallway of rooms sat over the restaurant. And maybe in the daytime, it could have been cute. The hall had lots of pictures of Alaskan scenery, of wild animals, and old black-and-white photos of what might have been the owner's family. But the lights flickered, and the floors were suspiciously stained beneath their coat of varnish.

"If we see twin girls at the end of this hallway, I'm using you as a human shield," Rick said, bringing a quick laugh to Lana's lips.

"I'll beat you down the stairs." Her feet sounded way too loud, as if every step echoed in the restaurant below.

They passed the shared bathroom. While Lana was as appreciative of an antique claw-foot tub as the next person, the floor-to-ceiling dark wood paneling and the spotted glass mirror above the pedestal sink only added to the dubious ambience. The next door over was their first assigned room.

"The door's stuck." Rick tried to twist the doorknob and pull at the same time, but it wouldn't go anywhere. "It's an old place," he said as he jerked harder. "Or it opens to the inside." A cute little look of concentration stole across his features as he pushed the door in. It continued to stay locked in the doorframe, unwilling to give way. "Huh."

"It's a door to nowhere. It's a sign we shouldn't go in."

Rick grunted as he put his weight behind the door. "Would you rather stay in this hall?"

"It's a nice hall. Cozy and less pit of doom-y."

"It's almost as if something's pushing against the other side," Rick said, then he blinked, realizing what he'd said. "Let's try the next room."

"You're a wise man." Lana patted his shoulder. "Did I ever tell you I spent a week at the Stanley in Estes Park? The elk were rutting, which was very interesting to behold. Also, it wasn't nearly as haunted as people think. Only a little haunted. Medium haunted at most."

"You're not making me feel better."

"All I'm saying is just because someplace seems creepy doesn't mean that it is. Sometimes it's..." Lana opened the room, then paused midsentence.

"Filled with dead squirrels with doll's clothes?"

"Who are these people?" Lana asked, horrified.

"Who stays here permanently?" Rick countered.

"Let's go back to room number one." Lana shut the door and hurried back to the first room, putting distance between herself and the dolls. "Or we could be airlifted out of here. I can have a helicopter come get us."

Even as she said it, Rick shook his head. Before he could respond, Lana sighed. "And probably get the pilot killed in this zero visibility. Fine. Push harder."

"I am pushing."

"With your muscles?"

"The ones I've got anyway."

"Here, let me push."

"I'm pretty sure I can—*omph*."

The door abruptly gave way, banging open so hard, they stumbled into the room. Instinctively reaching out to steady him, Lana realized that Rick had done the same for her. His muscled arm had wrapped around her waist, holding her tight.

Lana had a very powerful family, but she couldn't remember ever having someone reach out to help every time she stumbled. In her family, you either caught yourself, or you went down and learned from the fall. Reading too much into it wasn't going to help her with this utterly relentless crush she'd developed for Rick. Still, his arm felt warm and solid around her, and Lana had to take a moment and a breath, letting herself remember that yes, she was human, and yes, she liked having a man's touch.

She definitely should have kissed him outside, temperature be darned.

"You don't have to hold me up," Lana said.

"I was returning the favor."

Only then did she realize that yes, his arm was around her, but both of hers were locked around him.

Rick didn't seem uncomfortable with her death grip on him, but his lips had quirked up at the corners.

"You know those books and movies where the girl is clumsy and keeps falling and the guy has to rescue her from her lack of coordination?"

"We tend to watch things about time-traveling killer robots or driving cars into skyscrapers in our house," Rick said. "But there was a point in my life when Diego wasn't in complete control of the television. I'm vaguely familiar."

"I'm not that girl. I might slip, but I always catch myself."

"It's highly probable that I'm that guy." Rick winked at her roguishly before turning to investigate their surroundings.

The theme of wood-paneled walls continued throughout the room, making it darker than she would have preferred, especially with a single lamp on the dresser to provide light. The fireplace looked like it hadn't been used in years, and the space heater on the floor was the kind that tipped over by accident, then promptly burned one's house down.

There was no television, no radio, no phone. Just Rick, Lana, a bed, and a squirrel.

A single squirrel that was perched on the windowsill wearing a white cotton nightgown, dark hair flowing down its squirrel back in perfect curls as it stared longingly out the window. For some reason, that one bothered Lana most of all. Breaking the time-honored convention of not rearranging hotel decorations, Rick put the squirrel in the top drawer of an antique dresser, the only furniture in the room besides the bed.

Lana gave Rick a breezy laugh to cover the fact that she was *sure* she could hear something moving in that dresser drawer. She patted the mattress beneath her.

"So...which side do you prefer to sleep?" she asked, although to be honest, it wasn't going to matter.

Lana was taking whichever side was farthest away from the squirrel.

She sat on the edge of the bed.

"Are you going to be okay in here?" Rick wasn't the most observant of men, but despite her cheerfulness, Lana looked a little peaked around the edges. "I can leave you alone or stay—"

A door slammed downstairs, followed by a heavy thump. The kind of thump that involved a large object being dropped on a table. Then the kind of rhythmic, horrific chopping that came with butchering something with large kitchen weaponry. With every chop, she flinched, until the sound was replaced by a loud, high-pitched squealing noise. Midsqueal, it turned into a grinding noise that would haunt Rick to the end of his days.

"What is that?" Lana asked, eyes wide.

"I think they're making sausage."

"The house sausage?"

Rick nodded, sitting on the bed next to her.

"That's it. I'm out." Grabbing her jacket, Lana shrugged into it and hopped up. "There are plenty of ways to go, and I'm not letting this hotel of horrors be the thing that takes me down."

She eyed the fireplace, then grabbed a nearby fire poker. Lana hefted it a couple times, took one iffy practice swing, then turned to the door.

"Get behind me, Rick. Let's do this thing."

She looked so cute, all ready to fight her way out of the hotel, even though it was clear Lana was completely freaked out. Which was why Rick decided then and there, if he was ever going to get married again (which he wasn't) or found himself falling in love again (which he shouldn't), he was going to pick a woman like her.

"While I appreciate the sentiment," he told her, "I don't think freezing to death is better than being made into sausage."

"Oh, it is. Trust me, the only casing I'm going into is the Spanx in my closet." She turned back to the door. "Freezing is the far superior option."

"Or—and hear me out on this one—we could put down the poker and play poker instead. I saw a deck of cards in the lobby."

"Lobby is too generous." With a sigh, she sat next to him, still holding the fire poker.

Rick straightened because it was hard to pretend to be relaxed when her hip was mere inches from his own.

The door banged open, revealing Carl in all his glory with an armful of towels, and Rick had the absolute wonder of finding himself with Lana jumping three feet in the air like a startled cat, landing on his lap. A frightened Lana didn't scream, and her hair was in his face so he couldn't see hers, but Rick had the feeling she had placed herself in between the threat and him for the second time that night.

A warm feeling of amusement filled him. Still, he wanted to show Lana that he didn't need her protection. Not from Carl anyway. Silas...possibly. The solid weight of her on his lap? Definitely. But not from Carl and his towels.

Rick wrapped his arm tight around her waist, then shifted her over enough so he could see.

"That was unexpected," he said. "Maybe try knocking next time?"

"These are towels." Carl stared at them, not blinking.

Yes. Yes, they were.

"Ma said we turn the lights out at nine. I put the other set in the other room."

"There were dolls," Rick told him. "We only need this one."

If Carl cared, he certainly didn't show it. Instead, he grumbled all the way back to the door, then slammed it shut.

"How did he walk so quiet on the floor out there, but now he's making so much noise?" Lana asked in a whisper.

"You probably couldn't hear him because of the sausage grinder."

Lana shuddered. "Rick, I think we should leave."

"In the snowstorm?"

"We're going to be made into sausage. I'd make a terrible sausage. Do you know how much body fat percentage I have? Because sausages are supposed to be twenty-five percent, and I have at least twenty-eight percent. Maybe more. I'm probably closer to thirty, because these things are not pure muscle."

When she stuffed a thumb into her breast and poked it a few times for emphasis, Rick's brain tried very hard not to notice.

"How do you know the fat content of sausage?"

"Everyone knows that, Rick. *Everyone knows.*" Her voice was taking a panicked tone, which would have been more alarming if her thumb had changed places. But nope. Still poking, giving her a somewhat squashy lopsided appearance on that side.

He'd never been aroused by a squashed breast before, especially not when the owner of said breast was frightened, but Rick was only human, and she was...well...in that dress. On his lap. And it had been a long time since his lap had entertained anything other than a cereal bowl or his cat's abject disapproval.

"You'd make an even worse sausage," she continued, "Because let's be honest, you don't have an ounce of fat on your body. Which would be sexier if I didn't think it was because you don't eat enough. That's probably my fault. I'm charging you way too much rent, and you can't afford to eat, and now they won't make you into sausage, and you'll probably end up strips of Rick jerky covered with too much pepper or not enough teriyaki and—"

Okeydokey. Watching her have a mild coronary event was not in the plan for this date. Rick took her hands so she stopped poking a hole in one of the most appealing breasts he'd ever seen.

"Lana, breathe."

The sausage grinder's choice to make several loud squealing noises at the time did not help his case. Her eyes widened, so Rick pulled her in closer.

"I can afford to feed myself," Rick said. "Rent's high because rent's always high in Alaska. No one is making jerky out of me, and they're definitely not going to make sausage out of you."

"How do you know?"

"Because even I don't have bad enough luck for that to happen on the first date I've been on in years." Rick wondered if it was too much to ask that she keep leaning into him like that. "But... on the off chance that we are actually in a slasher movie, what's the plan here?"

"That's not funny," Lana said with a cute pout.

"I wasn't joking."

Yes, he was totally joking, but it took her a moment to realize it. Then she grinned. Not the breezy smile he hated—the one covering what she really thought and felt—but her real smile. The one that made his blood sing in his veins.

Slender fingers reached up to touch his cheek, and Rick found himself leaning into the contact. "The plan is we'll take over the dining room and set up our defensive perimeter," Lana said conspiratorially. "With a squirrel army at our backs, we'll definitely last until morning."

"As long as one of us knows what they're doing." Rick winked at her.

Silence fell between them, a silence where Rick desperately wanted to say the right thing, but all he could focus on was how good her hair smelled and how soft it felt brushing along his arm.

"I haven't really done this whole dating thing in a while," he admitted in a rough voice. "It's like being benched for forever and abruptly finding yourself up to bat with bases loaded."

"If you're going to make sports analogies, I much prefer football. And trust me, as far as my dates go, this is much better than most."

"Are we still calling this a date?"

"Huddled together for safety in a hotel of horrors?" Lana asked, her bright eyes full of mischief. "Absolutely."

Her lashes were long enough to brush her cheeks. How had he never noticed before?

"My last actual date was with a masseuse last July," she said. "It wasn't much to speak of."

"I haven't kissed a woman since my ex. I probably don't even remember how."

"Twelve months." When he raised an eyebrow, Lana clarified. "It's been twelve months since I kissed someone. Last New Year's."

"You're kidding me."

"It wasn't even one of the good kisses. Too much teeth, not enough...*not* teeth."

"Not teeth is important when kissing."

"And yet someone never told him." Sighing with playful dramatics, she rested her palm against his stomach. "If I had known it would be so long, I might have tried to enjoy it more."

A comfortable silence fell between them, but that silence was punctuated by the metal of the roof creaking as it contracted in the freezing temperatures.

"The rest of me is fine, but my fingers simply refuse to warm up."

"Body heat is better than thin blankets," he said.

"And evil sausage grinders?"

"You're the one who thought this would make a great story." Rick chuckled.

"Story, yes. For grandchildren and the like. Not to be on the local news. I can see it now. Two new lovers found ground to death in squirrel mausoleum. Try the stroganoff. The mystery meat is delicious."

Rick gently squeezed her waist. "Will it help if I promise I won't let anyone chop us up to bits?"

"It won't hurt." She sighed, then snuggled into his shoulder. "Rick?"

"Hmm?"

"This was the best date I've ever been on."

"You can't be serious."

"I'm completely serious." Brown eyes gazed up at him. "Do you want to know why?"

"Why?"

"Because you cared enough to keep driving."

Beauty was more than skin deep. Beauty was a kind heart and hands willing to help, no matter how dirty they got. Beauty was a quick grin and eyes that noticed everyone in a room. Noticed and cared about everyone, no matter who they were.

Eyes that saw him, when he'd been sitting in the background of his life for far too long.

"Can I—" Pausing midquestion, Rick cleared his throat. Bless the woman for not making him finish his sentence. Lana nodded in encouragement.

Heart hammering in his chest, breath caught in his lungs, Rick leaned in. He wasn't sure what he expected...maybe a slap to the face, despite her arm wrapped around the back of his neck. Instead, he found soft lips, warm despite the cool air. Just the slightest of pressure, his mouth to hers. Pulling away, Rick glanced at her.

"See? I promised I wouldn't bite."

"Not yet anyway. I'm sorry." Lana nodded, kind enough not to mock him for his trembling hands. "Guess I need some more practice."

"Or more time?" she asked gently.

"No. I've had more than enough of time."

It had been too long since Rick had taken a woman in his arms, holding her close. And he never would have expected this woman to be the one. He felt outclassed, outmatched, and beyond overwhelmed. But when he slid his palm up her back, Lana leaned against him, melting into his touch. When his fingers threaded into her hair, the silky strands clinging to his wrist, this time, she kissed him.

Deepening the kiss, Rick relaxed back against the bedding, drawing her with him. The scent of her subtle perfume was almost as intoxicating as the warmth of her body beneath his hands. He could have stayed like this forever, her ankle hooked around his, her arm hugging his rib cage, as if she needed to hold him as much as he needed to hold her. Each touch of her lips against his was even better than the last.

Abruptly, Lana started to giggle.

"Should I ask?" Rick's murmured question earned another—even better—giggle from her.

"I just think it's funny that I got you into bed so fast. You give off a certain 'hard to catch' vibe."

"Says the date who wouldn't let me walk her to her elevator."

"I'm hard to catch too." Lana flashed him a pretty grin. "Takes an impressive person to pull it off. Besides, the 'hey baby' rules are different."

For a guy who had spent an inordinate amount of his life feeling like he wasn't quite enough, this woman could make him feel pretty damn great.

"I didn't 'hey baby' you," Rick reminded her, earning a peal of laughter as he rolled over onto his side, tickling her ribs as he pulled her close. "I'm much too debonair for that."

"You totally hey baby'd me."

"Can you blame me?"

She was still giggling when he kissed her neck, then her earlobe, then her lips one more time. Then Rick relaxed into the bedding, because she was right. Rick wasn't hard to catch, but he also didn't jump into something this fast. Not even with a woman he wanted this much. Rick didn't want either one of them to regret anything tomorrow.

At some point, they'd have to get ready for bed. He'd probably have to go find Carl and see if they could get some toothpaste at least. Or maybe a pack of gum. Someone at some point would have to pee.

But right now? Rick wasn't going to move a muscle, not if he could help it.

He loved the way her fingers felt threaded through his fingers. Better still was her nose pressing against his bicep. Did his armpit smell? Had he put on too little deodorant? Too much? Rick had more than his share of getting shit wrong, but it was impossible to miss the way she snuggled in.

Damn, how much he wanted to be just right, just this once.

"Rick?"

"Yeah?" The single word came out rougher, quieter. Whatever she said, he'd be okay with it. She'd already given him more than he could have hoped for, and the rock his heart had become was already softening.

If this was over, it would be enough.

"I have to pee."

Yep. Someone always had to pee.

"You want me to guard the door, don't you?" he asked in

amusement as he sat up, already missing the pressure of her skin to his.

"Would you mind?" Lana asked. "This is the hotel of horrors after all."

"As long as you lead the way." He winked at her, earning a rosy blush to her cheeks.

Waiting for her to use the shared bathroom wasn't a big deal. When the lights went out and they returned from the bathroom to find the squirrel in her nightdress back on the windowsill, that was fine too. They ended up spending the night in his car, doors locked and their blankets wrapped around them as she kept a hand on the fireplace poker, ready to protect them both. Up until Lana fell asleep and dropped the poker. She drooled on his shoulder, the snow falling across the windshield like her hair across his chest, their fingers intertwined against his stomach.

It was the best date of Rick's life too.

CHAPTER 9

THE TRICK TO KEEPING WARM in a car out in the snow without dying of carbon monoxide poisoning was to roll down the windows a tiny bit and only run the engine for a few minutes intermittently.

Which meant Rick hadn't slept very much. Lana was curled into Rick's shoulder, a deep enough sleeper that once she was out, turning the car on never bothered her. And if he kept it on a little longer than he should have, well, he didn't want her to get cold.

Rick had been dozing when Lana shifted, her nose pressing into his bicep. Then she raised her head, woken by the sound of the snowplow going past on the road next to the parking lot. It wasn't the first plow to come through, but Rick hadn't wanted to wake her.

Having her cuddled into his side was far too pleasant for such mundane things as getting safely home.

"Good morning," she said, blinking sleepily. Eyelashes long enough to brush her cheeks left his brain utterly incapable of coherent thought. "Hmm, that was very unfair of me to pass out while you were stuck turning the key on the hour."

"Do I look like I mind?" Rick asked her in an amused voice.

"I suppose we didn't get made into sausage after all."

"Speaking of which, do you want to get some breakfast?" Rick nodded toward the B-and-B, a little grin on his face.

"Oh goodness, *no.*" Lana shuddered at the very idea. "Although I should probably return their poker."

She picked her weapon of choice off the floor. Even as Lana started to tug her clothes to tidiness, Rick took the fire poker away and opened the door.

"Give me a moment. I'll be back," he told her.

When Rick returned a few minutes later, Lana looked far more awake than the sleepy version he'd left.

"How did it go?" she asked as he got into the car.

"I think they're mad at us for leaving. There were lots of angry sighs."

"Did you tell them about the squirrel?"

"I told them."

"The nightmarish squirrel with the nightgown that moves of its own volition?"

"Yep, that squirrel."

When he handed over a small takeout container, Lana brightened. "Ooh, muffins."

"They're squirrel muffins."

"They are not." Inhaling the scent of blueberries, she took a bite of one of the muffins. "Oh yeah, come to momma."

"Don't say I didn't warn you if you find a little squirrel ear in there."

Sighing blissfully, she leaned back in her seat, holding out a piece for him to take. "You can't ruin this for me, Rick," she said. "But you're welcome to try."

And try he did. For the next fifteen minutes, they drove down freshly cleared roads, still slick with ice, while Lana handed him bites of muffin and Rick thought up every gross thing imaginable that Carl could have put in said muffin.

"So are we doing this?" Lana asked around her last bit of muffin. "The holiday fling with a yet to be determined termination clause?"

"You know how to make a guy's heart swoon," Rick said teasingly. "Termination clause?"

"I just like knowing the terms and conditions of my business arrangements. Especially the ones as handsome as you when you're snoring."

She gave him an arch look. Damn, it felt good to laugh.

"I'm not the only one who snores, sweetheart." It was dangerous to pull her in and kiss her while driving, but Rick was feeling risky. "There are worse things than letting yourself have fun on the holidays."

Lana beamed at him, and this time, she was the one to make the car bobble on the icy roads, her mouth on his.

When his phone rang, Rick was planning on ignoring it, then he saw who was calling on his dashboard. Hitting the Accept Call button, Rick regretfully kept both hands and eyes on the road.

"Hey, Jonah," he said, hoping this was another Santa Moose call, even though his gut said it wasn't.

"Rick, I need you to come down to the station."

The standard self-indulgent tiredness was gone from Jonah's tone, replaced by a professional seriousness. Instantly, Rick's chest tightened down.

"What is it?" he asked.

"I've got Diego here," Jonah said. "You all are going to need to call a lawyer. If you can't afford one, he'll get one appointed by the state."

"What happened?"

"We'll talk about it when you get here."

Jonah had a habit of not actually booking the unruly locals who ended up in some sort of skirmish or another. It took something bad to have him officially take someone into custody.

The roads were still slick, but Rick drove faster than he should have. Halfway back to town, Lana placed her hand on his leg, a silent show of support.

"Is there anything I can do?" she asked him.

Covering her hand with his own, Rick shook his head. "I don't even know what the kid did this time."

"Has he been arrested before?"

Hesitating, Rick finally answered, "Not in a while. And not without reason."

By the time they arrived at the tiny Moose Springs police station, the sun had started to rise in the sky. After listing the charges, Jonah led them back to the small holding cell serving as the town's drunk tank. Sitting alone on the single bench along the back wall, Diego was shaking, he was so upset.

"You brought her here?"

The baleful glare Diego was sending Lana's way was beyond the kid's normal sourness.

"We were together when Jonah called." Rick shifted in front of Lana to force Diego's attention to him instead. "What happened?"

"It doesn't matter."

Rick rested his arm on the cell bars, leaning in toward his nephew. "You're being charged with assault and destruction of public property. *Something* happened."

Diego didn't reply, but Rick wasn't going anywhere. He opened his mouth but stopped when Lana put her hand on his shoulder.

"I'll wait outside. Let me know if you need me."

Even now, it was hard not to watch her walk away, the touch of her fingertips lingering like expensive perfume. But family in trouble was the most important thing, even more than a gorgeous woman who seemed to know exactly when to give them space. As she reached the doorway, Lana paused, looking back.

"I hope hitting that is worth it."

The venom in Diego's voice was only matched by his disgust. Diego had timed his comment well, managing to bring a flash of hurt to Lana's face. A low growl pulled from Rick's throat before he clamped down on the instinctive reaction to come to her defense. She disappeared out of the room, the damage already done.

The fact that Diego had tried to hurt her in the first place said a lot about the emotional state the kid was in. Some people chose flight, but Diego would always stand and fight. He didn't know any other way.

"Was that necessary?" Rick asked.

"She's going to screw things up for you."

Rick could have shut him down. He could have said Lana Montgomery was the best thing that had happened to him in a long time. Waxing poetic about how perfect she was could have occupied every breath Rick took for the next few weeks.

Instead, Rick nodded. "She could. I suppose that's the hard part about letting someone in. They can do all sorts of damage." A flush of color reached Diego's face, and Rick knew his suspicions were right. "You're in here because of Quinn." When Diego didn't reply, Rick said, "Staring at the floor isn't going to help you, kid."

"This guy's been giving her a hard time at the resort."

"And you stopped him?"

A muscle in Diego's jaw rippled from the sheer force of his gritted teeth. Before Rick could pry anything else out of his nephew, a curly-haired whirlwind came through the door. Quinn's pale cheeks were stained red from the cold, her already large eyes widening even more when she took in Diego sitting behind bars.

Diego groaned. "Shit, Q, why are you here?"

"Because you're an *idiot*," she declared hotly, speaking so fast, Rick could barely understand her. "And I spent the last *hour* arguing with Hannah to let you keep your job, but you have no idea how much of a fuss Mr. Bayard is causing, which is why I said that I'd cause a fuss about him, and there's absolutely no way I'm letting you sit in here for doing nothing wrong but defending me, which was completely *stupid* by the way."

Quinn paused to inhale, which was good. Rick was starting to worry the young woman would pass out midsentence.

Diego might not have wanted to care about anyone, but his feelings were clear as day as he stared at the floor between his feet. "He had his hands on you."

Quinn bit her lower lip, worrying at it as she put her hand on the door and gave it a little tug. "Jonah locked it."

"Were you planning on breaking me out?" Amusement tinged Diego's tone.

With a huff, Quinn put her hands on her hips. "Of course, you're not taking this seriously. Why would you? Well, I'm going to fix this. Stay right there, and don't hit anyone else while I'm gone."

Quinn hustled back out with the same force of energy she'd come in with.

With a sigh, Diego leaned his head back against the wall. "Where the hell does she think I'm going to go?"

He wasn't wrong. When Diego was formally charged, it would take every bit of rent money Rick had to post bail. Rent money he desperately needed to keep his business afloat, but Diego was family, and family came first. No matter what. No matter why.

"This will be okay, kid," Rick said in a rough voice, even though they both knew it was a lie.

"No, it won't be." Diego just stared at his feet.

There was nothing Rick could do but brace his elbows against the cell bars and wait for a judge to decide both their fates.

———

Silas was at it again. He'd called an emergency meeting with the board of directors and somehow had managed to do so when she was out of contact last night. No one had called her phone, which meant that Killian had probably been left out of the meeting as well. She'd only been notified by email, and Lana hadn't checked her email while out with Rick.

Which meant she'd missed a vote to liquidate the Moose Springs properties.

Thankfully, according to the minutes, her mother had postponed the vote until a full board could be in attendance, but Lana knew that was only a temporary roadblock.

As she scrolled through her emails, Lana tried to ignore the churning in her stomach, hearing Diego's words reverberate in her head. Allowing herself to be frustrated with Silas was much easier than processing how much Rick's closest family didn't like her being involved with him.

Lana was used to the glares, but for some reason, having those glares aimed at Rick bothered her so much more.

Quinn had been in such a rush when she'd pulled up, Lana had only noticed her as the younger woman passed by Rick's vehicle. This time, when she emerged from the police station, she stopped in the middle of the icy sidewalk and burst into tears.

Lana only had to approach her for Quinn to turn those tears Lana's way, throwing her arms around Lana's neck.

"Diego is just so *stupid*," she sobbed. "That guy was a jerk, but you know what he'll do. They can't afford a lawyer, and Diego will go to jail."

It didn't take much coaxing for Lana to get the story out of Quinn. How she was trying to work, but a chatty guest kept bothering her. She'd tried to be nice, but he hadn't left her alone. And when the guest had put his hand on her backside in front of Diego, Rick's nephew had taken exception.

"Sometimes I think *being nice* is something women need to stop doing." Lana kept an arm around the crying Quinn. "What's his name?"

"Mr. Bayard."

"Lee Bayard? The one with the short dark hair? Stands too close to everyone?"

Quinn nodded, wiping her eyes.

Yes, Lana knew who Lee Bayard was. And she was well acquainted with Lee's father, Jefferson Bayard. The apple didn't fall far from that particularly misogynistic tree.

"I'll take care of it," Lana told Quinn. "And you made sure Hannah knew what happened?"

"Yes, and Mr. Shaw too."

Frankly, Lana couldn't believe Jax hadn't handled the situation with his knuckles already. Neither he nor Hannah took well to their employees being mistreated.

Then again, right now would be a terrible time for a lawsuit. The Shaws were on a tight enough financial rope as it was.

Lana didn't know if Quinn was okay to drive, so after helping her get home, she texted Rick that she needed to do something and took a ride share from Quinn's house to the resort.

Lana found the new hotel manager in her office. Hannah always looked like she should have been on a runway or at a photoshoot instead of running a hotel, and she was great at her job. Much better than the previous manager had been. At some point that week, Hannah had traded her usual shoulder length braids for a super short curly pixie cut. One hand pressed to her forehead as she argued on the phone, Hannah looked like she hadn't slept in a solid week, her eyes reddened from too many shifts for too long a time.

Yes, Jax definitely needed to hire a full-time night manager. With the resort this busy, she was far too overworked and understaffed. Lana waited until Hannah ended her call, then lightly tapped her knuckles on the open doorjamb of her office.

"Come in, Lana." Hannah waved her over. "Quinn texted me that you were headed my way."

"I saw her at the police station," Lana said, setting a hip to the doorframe. "She's pretty upset."

"She's not the only one," Hannah replied in a growl. "I want to take a tire iron to Bayard's crotch for getting handsy with one of my employees. He'd be kicked out of here already if it weren't for Diego."

"Diego reacted, and now you're playing damage control?"

"My hands are tied." Hannah sounded beyond upset. "Bayard already called his lawyers. I told Quinn to press charges, but I don't know if she will. She's scared of him."

"And Diego?"

"Diego should have stayed out of it and let me handle Bayard. The Shaws had me terminate him, effective immediately."

"And you don't think that's a little harsh?" Lana asked.

"Talk to Jax if you can find him. So far, all my calls to him have gone unanswered. His parents are the ones who decided to terminate Diego and lawyer up."

Lana frowned. If Quinn was scared of Bayard, then no, she probably wouldn't press charges. Like too many women in a long line of employees sexually harassed by that family. It made Lana's blood boil. It made her want to get in a semitruck and run Lee Bayard over, then back up a few times for good measure.

"Jax isn't here to help?" she confirmed.

Hannah snorted. "He's currently off the premises cooling

down, on his parent's orders. Jax's temper only made things worse. Bayard is threatening to call his lawyers on *us*."

That was completely on brand with the resort owner's son. Of course Hannah was stuck dealing with this alone.

Lana had seen Bayard in the hotel bar more than once in the last couple of days. So far, Lana had managed to avoid him and all the business talk that would come along with even the briefest of encounters. The Bayards were powerful but smarmy. And—apparently—this one was a complete ass.

Still…if Hannah couldn't do anything about it and the Shaws wouldn't do anything about it, maybe it was time someone else did. The look on Rick's face when he'd walked in to see his nephew in the holding cell was burned into Lana's memory. As if the two men had been there before, and Rick was powerless to help the family member he loved.

Lana couldn't stop Silas's power play, but she could step in the ring for Quinn and Rick.

She took her time changing before coming back downstairs in search of her quarry. Bayard had spent the bulk of his time at Moose Springs in a "retreat" with some other colleagues. Meaning they'd been playing high stakes poker and getting roaring drunk the last several days. Finding him was easy…all Lana had to do was follow the sounds of raucous laughter and the telltale fragrance of male fragility.

Sometimes the best armor for war was a low-cut dress and Prada stilettos. Crossing her legs and meeting his gaze across the bar was all it took to have him abandon the group he was with, heading her way. Tall with expensively cut dark hair and deep blue eyes, Lee wasn't bad looking, but the bruise on his jaw was already darkening. Diego must have just clipped him.

Too bad the kid hadn't crushed Lee's aristocratic nose into a pulp.

"Can I buy you a drink?" Lana asked, letting her eyes linger, knowing he'd take it as interest.

Sure enough, Lee leaned on the bar next to her, already standing too close. "That's usually my line. You're Lana Montgomery, aren't you?"

"Depends on who's asking."

Lee placed his hand on the back of her chair, boxing her in. "You know who I am," he said smugly. "Your mother brokered a deal with my father last August."

"We broker a lot of deals," Lana said. "That's a nice little bruise. Have you been having too much fun while you're visiting?"

He tossed back a swig of his scotch. "Local trash, you know how it is. I'll own him and the next three generations of his trash family by the time I'm done with him."

Little did this idiot know that Lana had just had the best date of her life with Diego's "trash family."

"So when he hit you, was that before or after you sexually assaulted his girlfriend?"

Lee blinked, startled. "I'm sorry, what?"

"Oh, it's not that complicated. A big strong man like you, you probably prefer the smaller women. Ones you can lean over, crowd into small spaces, make them know how you have the control."

"I don't know what you're talking about."

"Sure you do. It's why you already have your lawyers on their way here. But you're not going to sue him." Lana calmly took a sip of her drink. "And you're not suing the Shaws either."

She paused to let that sink in, then said, "You know that big deal your father brokered with my mother? It was for an overseas shipping company, right? With the majority of the contracts between Europe and the Eastern Seaboard? You've spent quite a lot of money in obtaining those ships. One would almost think that you'd stretched a bit too far. Unfortunately, those ships are going to need to use shipyards, which happen to be owned by a subsidiary of the Montgomery Group. It would be awfully inconvenient if you were to suddenly...I don't know...find yourself without a place to dock and repair your ships."

Horror slowly dawned on his face. "You can't."

"Oh, I promise you, I most certainly can. And I absolutely would." Lana let that register before continuing. "Trust me, there will be no need to own the next three generations of *your* family when I'm done having your balls removed. Metaphorically speaking, of course. I'm not a complete monster." One more sip, then she added, "Probably."

"What do you want?" Lee asked in a low, controlled voice.

"Drop the charges against Diego. Plead no contest if Quinn presses charges against you. And do be a dear and drop the lawsuit against the resort as well. We can't have you ruining a nice place with your disgusting behavior, can we? You should also get your hand off my chair. I'm finding you rather repulsive at the moment."

"I'm not pleading no contest because some girl got the—"

"Got the *right* idea that you are in no uncertain terms *not* allowed to put your hands on her? That woman now *owns* you.

She's too sweet to come talk to you, so I'm her proxy. Tell me, would you like to continue doing business with me, Lee?"

A snarl was his answer, but she could see in his eyes that Lee knew she had him cornered.

"Good. I feel the same way," Lana added sweetly. "Now, are you sure you don't want that drink?"

———

Lana should have spent her evening in a more productive way, like going back out on the Santa Moose search, but instead she decided to err on the side of better phone reception. She had texted an offer of a lawyer for Diego, but Rick had only replied that things were "happening" and he'd contact her with an update soon.

She even took her phone into the dry sauna with her, even though the heat was as bad for the technology as it was good for her sore muscles. Sleeping in a car with Rick might have been a pleasant way to wake up, but it sure wasn't great for the neck. After melting away some of her tension, Lana went back to her room, idly sketching out a new plan of attack on catching her moose.

When the knock came on her door, Lana wasn't sure she really wanted to answer. After all, she'd meddled. And meddling—even with the best of intentions—always had consequences.

Still, Lana had never been afraid to meet the hard conversations head-on, so she opened her door for the man standing on the other side.

Even though they'd woken up together that morning, it felt like a lifetime had passed.

"What did you do?" Rick asked quietly. "The charges were dropped but no one is saying why."

Lana was tempted not to answer, to breezily pass it off as good luck. Instead, she leaned her shoulder against the doorframe.

"Are you sure you want to know?" Tilting her head, she looked up at him, biting her lower lip.

"Would I be here if I didn't?" The heat from his body warmed the air between them. "Diego was nearly sick from relief when I drove him home. I'd like to know why we're not both still sitting over there with Jonah or headed to Anchorage."

Sighing, Lana said softly, "Because I made it go away. That's what we do. We make things go away when they don't suit us."

Lana could hear the slightly self-derogatory tone in her voice, matching the way she felt about that aspect of her family...and herself.

"I threatened Lee, and he backed down. Bullies always back down." Embarrassed, Lana pushed on. "It's not something I'm proud of—"

Midexplanation, Rick closed the distance between them, taking her face in his hands as he kissed her. Like before, the instant his skin touched hers, a fire flared inside her, leaving Lana a mess, plastered to him in the open doorway of her hotel suite.

"In his whole life, that kid has never caught one single break." Rick's voice was husky with emotion. "Never apologize to me for protecting my family. Can I come in?"

The polite request was overwhelmed by the way his hands wrapped around her waist, drawing her in closer.

"Rick, you never have to ask," Lana said.

Rick took one step inside, and to her surprise, he lifted her up off her feet with the strength of one arm. Turning, he pushed the door closed with his other, pressing Lana's shoulders into the door. Her knees tightened into his waist, her arm wrapping around his neck for balance as hungry hands slid up her sides.

"Is this your version of a thank-you?" Lana bit her lip as he nipped at the sensitive skin behind her earlobe.

"I could write you a letter instead, but I'm not too good with words."

Maybe, but he was absolutely amazing at what he was doing. Closing her eyes, Lana relaxed into his hold, running her fingers through his hair.

"How far do you want this to go?" he asked her in a low, hungry voice.

"Hmm. The couch seems like a good distance."

Rick chuckled. "That's not exactly an answer."

They ended up on the couch in a mess of limbs, with Lana pulling his face to hers. Lana wasn't sure how far she wanted things to go, but his arms felt wonderful wrapped around her, the solid weight of his form leaning against her.

After a night spent so comfortably sleeping against his side, Lana expected that same comfort in this second kiss. Except... well...it wasn't. The soft, peaceful glow of the twinkling holiday lights didn't match the heat between them.

Damn, this man could kiss. He could hold her just right, anchoring her to his muscled form as he deepened the kiss. Like a shiver going over her skin, a pressure that could only be assuaged by gripping his forearms and pulling him in tighter.

Lana hadn't been ready for this. Kissing him, yes. But coming up for air, plastered all over him? Either she had climbed on his lap or Rick had pulled her there, Lana honestly couldn't remember which. Panting to catch her breath, she hoped her nails hadn't cut the skin of his shoulders where they had dug in for purchase.

His hands wrapped around her waist, sliding up and down her sides in a way that made her melt like chocolate beneath his touch.

"Maybe we should slow this down." Rick inhaled deep to regain his own wind.

"I'm perfectly happy with the opposite."

She'd been teasing him, but the way he looked down at her said he took this seriously. "I like you, Lana."

The admittance must have cost him, because he wasn't meeting her eyes now. Voice rougher and quiet, Rick added, "You're worth slowing down for. Doing this right."

"Even on a short-term basis?"

She tilted her head to catch his attention, drawing his gaze back up to her. What she saw there made her nervous, made her lick her lips and almost drop her own gaze, because it was hard looking into a mirror.

"Lately, I've been thinking it's better to risk the heartache than to be lonely all the time," Rick said gruffly.

Loneliness had become Lana's way of life. Whatever this was, it was going to mess up her status quo. Honestly, there was a really small, really lonely part of Lana that was ready to have her status quo ripped to shreds already.

"Then you're right. I think we should definitely slow down." Lana pressed her mouth to his. Rick's hand slid up her back, palm cupping the back of her head and fingers in her hair. He had always said a lot without saying much.

"This isn't slowing down," he said. A sweet smile curved his lips, eyes brightening with humor.

"I'm getting there," Lana promised as she reached for him all over again.

He should feel guilty for enjoying this so much. Heck, he did feel guilty. Rick wasn't even sure why he felt that way when there was no one who cared what he did...and didn't...allow himself anymore.

She was napalm, setting him on fire every place she touched. The kind of burning that turned reasonable men completely idiotic and left them with broken hearts. The last thing in the world he should be doing was entertaining the idea that this could ever be anything more than two lonely people trying to get through the holidays.

Except...well...lonely wasn't so lonely with her hands pulling his face back down to hers again.

She was all soft curves and silky hair, warm breath and cool fingertips. Manicured fingernails dug into his skin, those soft curves crushed to his chest. He knew he should pull away, give them both a chance to think...or rethink...what they were doing here. Then a small noise of breathy pleasure escaped her lips, and he was done. Done thinking, done waiting. Done wanting.

He wanted her, and by the way she was pulling him closer, he could tell she felt the same. So of course, his phone had to ring with the only name he'd pick up for right now.

"Sorry, it's Diego. I have to take this."

Lana nodded, scooting back to give him room. Rick waited until she rose to her feet before wrapping his arm around her hips, squeezing her in a brief hug.

"Hey, I'm kind of busy with Lana right now."

"The barn was on fire," Diego said so tonelessly, he might as well have told Rick that he was eating Cheerios.

"What?"

"It's not on fire now."

"What do you mean it's not now?"

Diego snorted. "Exactly what I said. It's. Not. Now. Have you been drinking?"

"No, kid, but I'm seriously considering starting. Did you call the fire department?"

"Nope. I used a hose."

"How big was this fire?"

"About hose-sized."

Setting the phone down on his leg, Rick pressed his forehead to Lana's stomach, inhaling the scent of her and allowing himself to enjoy the way the silk slid over their skin.

"I'm going to kill him."

"Maybe it's a good time for a scotch." She ran her fingernails through his hair in a soothing action that seemed utterly in character for her. Then the woman of his dreams sashayed her way across the hotel room. He didn't need scotch. He just needed to watch her walk back across the room again. Maybe in slow motion for the part of his brain still trying to keep up. She was gorgeous. He was a lucky bastard. His barn was on fire.

"Do you know what started the fire?" Rick finally said into the phone.

"It probably has to do with the Christmas lights that were trampled into the snow. You should probably come home before Jonah gets here to take his report. I'm not sticking around to do it."

"You mean...?"

Diego took a long, serious breath. "The Santa Moose just cockblocked you." Then Diego hung up on him.

CHAPTER 10

LANA HAD GOTTEN OUT OF bed when a light knock came to her door. She wasn't expecting anyone, and honestly, those who would have come to see her would have texted or called first.

Except maybe Zoey. Zoey had free rein on intruding unexpectedly anytime she wanted. As Lana's best friend, she'd earned that right.

But it wasn't Zoey—it was Rick. And she was not anywhere close to her normal state of affairs for him to be seeing her.

"Rick?" Lana called through the door. "What are you doing here?"

"I brought you a surprise. I know it's early, but I wanted to catch you before you got tied up working today."

She peered through the eye hole but could only see Rick standing there, not whatever he had in his arms. That was squashed to the side, deliberately held out of sight. "No peeking, gorgeous," he added.

Glancing at her reflection in the entry mirror, Lana cringed. Why hadn't he shown up thirty minutes later, when she'd at least put herself into some semblance of respectability? Her hesitation must have given him the wrong impression of his welcome, because he coughed, sounding uncomfortable.

"I can leave this outside the door if you're busy. Sorry, I didn't think."

Pulling open the door, Lana decided it was better for him to see her at less than her best than to think she was doing the kind of entertaining he wouldn't be invited for.

"It sounds like you're insinuating that I'm hosting another date the morning after spending an evening with you. I'm tempted to take offense."

"I wouldn't dream of it."

Opening the door all the way, Lana stepped aside, allowing him to carry his offering inside. And what an offering it was. Rick was carrying a fake tree so real she could almost smell the pine needles. A beautiful blue spruce with the limbs lightly touched with the most realistic snow she'd ever seen.

"Rick, it's perfect."

"I checked, and it's recyclable. Nothing died in the preparation of this holiday celebration."

"I'm a mess." Lana touched a hand to her headscarf self-consciously. "You're welcome to wait while I tidy up. I could call down for some breakfast."

She started to turn, but Rick caught her hand, not an easy task when his arm was still full of counterfeit Christmas tree.

"You're perfect." This time when he cleared his throat, his eyes dropped to their entwined fingers. "Don't change. I can leave. I just wanted you to have this."

He set it down, then helped her set it up in the corner near the window and her thinking chair. Then he left to get something out of his car. Rick returned with two large shopping bags in his arms.

"Ornaments are kind of a personal thing." He handed her one of the bags. "But it seemed wrong to give you a tree with nothing to put on it. If you don't like these, the resort probably has more. I can get Quinn's number from Diego. She probably knows."

"These are lovely." When Rick started for the door, she added impulsively, "Rick? Would you like to decorate this with me?"

Which was how Lana ended up in her nightgown on the couch, stringing popcorn on a piece of thread from one end while he worked on the other.

"Did you expect to spend your morning poking a needle through popcorn?" she asked him, bumping Rick's shoulder companionably.

"I like popcorn." He scooped up a handful and dropped it in his mouth, somehow managing not to choke to death. "It's my go-to when I'm sick of cereal."

It was hard not to like popcorn when she was sharing it with him, even if she had stuck her thumb so many times, she'd been forced to put a Scooby-Doo Band-Aid on.

"I like your Scooby."

"Healing is always faster with crime fighters and mystery solvers." Lana added another piece of popcorn to her side of the string. "Thank you for this. It was very sweet."

"Hey, I was wondering if you wanted to come over for dinner tonight. I close the pool hall early on Sundays." He glanced down at his hands, then looked back up earnestly. "I'm not the best cook, but I'd like to try for you. I'd like to treat you to a real date."

Rick was killing her in the slowest, sweetest, best way.

"No taxidermy?" she asked, having a hard time keeping her hands off of him.

"Minimal taxidermy." Rick's voice lowered sexily. "Probably only moderate taxidermy."

Right then and there, Lana decided she might have met the most perfect man she'd never get to keep forever. "I'd love to."

When Lana pulled into his drive for their date night, Rick was waiting for her on the front steps. He'd prepped the sauce he was making that morning, and Diego had pitched in on cleaning the place. It was possible he'd overprepared a smidge, but Rick would rather that than get caught unawares again. Of course, in all his planning, he hadn't expected her to hop out of her vehicle with a small plastic animal carrier in her hands.

"Okay, before you say anything, this is not what it looks like."

Rick met her in front of her vehicle, peering inside the carrier. Two bright eyes blinked back, followed by the tiniest little mew he'd ever heard.

"You didn't bring me a cat?" Rick raised an eyebrow.

"Of course not. I merely invited my newest feline companion to join us for dinner." Lana hugged the plastic carrier as if the action could impress upon the kitten inside how much she loved it already. "The poor thing started crying when I went to leave the room."

"You didn't have a kitten this morning." At least not that he'd noticed.

Lana gave him a hug too, not unlike the hug she'd given the cat carrier. Rick didn't know why his brain made the comparison, but he knew he'd never in a million years own up to wondering if a kitten was his competition.

"One of the cats at the hotel had kittens," Lana explained as they walked to the porch. "Hannah was giving them away, and she was down to the last one. It seemed awful to be the only kitten without a home, so I decided to increase the search radius."

"Does that include me?" he asked, opening the front door for her. "Come on in."

"Not unless you're in the market for a kitten. I know you have your hands full already." Her smile warmed him, and Rick found himself following her through his house to the dining room table.

"Now, we'll have to ask Roger if he minds that the kitten is here," Lana said. "It's very important for him to have a say in the matter. No cat wants an unwelcome dinner guest."

For the record, Rick always listened when Lana talked. Always. But the woman was so damn pretty, he sometimes had a hard time focusing one hundred percent on what she was saying. When she was around, it was like his senses were on overload. The sound of her voice, the playful crinkle in her eyes, the curve of her hips, or the way she nibbled her lip. He only managed to refocus when he heard another plaintive mew from the carrier in her arms.

"Okay, let's look at this kitten."

Lana set down the carrier, taking out a tiny black-and-white furball. "Isn't he precious? They had names already. This is Peyton."

Rick dropped into a chair. Wrapping an arm around her waist, he pulled her close. To his immense pleasure, Lana sat on his leg, leaning into his shoulder as she cradled the kitten. The part of Rick he tried to keep hidden deep down had shied away from the animal the instant he'd laid eyes on it. This was what Jen had done. She'd find something to take care of, and he'd be the sucker that ended up taking care of it.

How many fights had they had over "one more kitten" or "it's just a fainting goat"? And here Rick was again, caught between wanting to make the woman in his life happy and not wanting to be a schmuck.

Maybe the expression on his face gave him away, because Lana touched his stubbly cheek with slender fingertips.

"You don't have to look so worried, Rick. I promise this isn't me pushing him on you. I'm planning on taking him to the Lockett place tomorrow. Or Graham might want a friend for Jake." Lana adjusted the kitten in her arms. "I wish I could keep him with me, but traveling all over the place is no life for a kitten. What if it's too cold or too hot, or there's some sort of kitty disease that no one had discovered?"

"You love animals." Rick deeply enjoyed how happy holding Peyton seemed to make her. Even if he really didn't want the kitten himself.

"I do. I never had a pet growing up. We were encouraged to think of the horses as working partners instead of pets. Everyone had their jobs to do, even if that was to jump an oxer. You wouldn't believe how many deals Killian has brokered covered in horse sweat and bits of mud."

"Polo Killian?"

"Yes, race car Killian is half-useless on anything with four legs," she joked. "Do try to keep up."

Keeping up with her was almost impossible, but damn if he didn't love trying. Careful not to squish the kitten, Rick threaded a hand through her hair.

"It feels different." His fingers slid through the dark strands, softer and slicker than the last time they had been together.

"I got a Brazilian blowout."

"I have no idea what that means."

Lana had Peyton in her arms, so she was unable to touch her hair self-consciously, but her hand started the motion. "Just a smoothing treatment. No ponytails for the next few days."

"You wouldn't be caught dead in a ponytail," Rick said teasingly. "Not in *polite* company."

She laughed. "You are keeping up, aren't you?"

He didn't need to close the distance between them because Lana had already done so. Her lips were soft against his, those silky strands falling over his face.

"Want to meet the other woman in my life?" he asked, earning himself one sculpted eyebrow lifting. "Be warned. Darla's the jealous type."

"Your hedgehog." Lana's eyes brightened in instant pleasure. "Yes, of *course*. I can't believe I haven't said hello yet. My manners are slipping."

They tucked Peyton back in his carrier before Rick led her to the study, turning on the lights so Lana could see better. Would she notice the handcrafted hedgehog furniture? Or the tiny Christmas tree? He kind of hoped she'd notice the tree. Rick had spent an embarrassingly long time gluing miniature presents beneath it, arranged just right.

"Oh, she's *perfect*."

"This is Darla," Rick told her, opening the cage and handing Lana the little ball of quills. True to form, Darla wiggled her tiny snout, staring up at her with soulful eyes. "She likes her belly rubbed."

"Don't we all," Lana cooed. "Hello, Darla. Oh, you are precious, aren't you?"

"She's my ex-wife's." Why? Why did he say that? Other than the truth. "She got Darla right before she left. Jen liked animals."

"Did that stop?"

"No, but she couldn't take them all with her." Rick winced at his own statement. "We had a dog, Sam. Roger would have done better in a smaller apartment than the dog, but I think she was scared to live alone. Sam made her feel safer."

"What makes you feel safe?" There was a softness in her tone that made Rick wonder if maybe she understood him a little better than he realized.

"A roof over my head," he said, wrapping an arm around her waist. Deciding to be honest, Rick added, "A job that pays the bills and having people I care about close to me. I'm a pretty simple guy."

"Not simple, Rick. Steady. Strong. Dependable. Those things aren't simple at all. In fact, they're complex and absolutely rare in this world."

The compliment, given in a quiet voice as Lana cuddled his hedgehog, made Rick's whole world tilt on its axis. It had been a long time since he felt *good* about himself as opposed to simply accepting of who he was. But Lana had this way of building him up without even trying.

As if he needed a reason to become even more infatuated with her.

"I promised you dinner," he said in her ear, unable to verbalize how much her kindness meant to him.

"Mmm. I'll take you up on that. Darla, it was lovely to meet you. Your tree is beautiful."

Dinner was on top of the stove, the covered pot set on low to warm it. Lana peeked her nose in.

"You made stroganoff." Lana looked delighted.

Rick gave her a little squeeze. "I won't tell you what the meat is if you don't ask."

"Oh, I already know it's squirrel. All our meals together are destined to be squirrel."

They ate at the table, a rarity for Rick, playing with Peyton in between bites. Roger stared at the intruder from the farthest chair until Lana managed to coax him into grudgingly meeting the little furball. With a grunt of annoyance, Roger rolled over on his back, staring at the kitten from upside down.

"That might be the best you're going to get from him," Rick said.

"Well, it's Roger's home. He'll feel better when we're gone."

Rick chuckled. "Roger will never forgive or forget the intrusion. Which is the part I like the most. Peyton will be a good distraction for him when I'm at work."

Her features lit up with pleasure. "You want the kitten?"

A some point in the middle of his plate of stroganoff, Rick had already started figuring out how to accommodate Peyton into his life. A bigger litter pan for starters. Some actual cute little cat toys, because Roger's taste in toys trended toward the extreme.

In response, Rick simply shrugged. "Cat needs a home. I've got one to share. It's not a big deal."

Lana was quiet for a moment before she reached out, touching his arm. "Rick? You know you can say no, right? You don't have to fix this for me. I'm sure there are plenty of people who would give him a home too. You don't have to do everything for everyone. What you want...or don't want...matters."

Rick hesitated. Too many years of a tough marriage had wired him this way. So Rick stabbed a piece of beef onto his fork, put it in his mouth, and chewed while he thought about what he wanted. Not what he had to do but what he—Rick Harding—actually wanted.

"You're probably leaving after New Year's," he finally said.

Lana nodded, eyes downcast. "Yes. I have some accounts in Europe I need to check in on."

"Then it might be nice to have something to remember you by. Something that annoys Roger. Feels like a win-win."

The sweetest smile spread on her face, and the look she gave him made Rick take a drink of water to wet his instantly dried mouth. Yep, that was a good look. That was a "maybe he should have double-checked his current deodorant situation" kind of look.

"So..." Lana said, her voice a low purr. Damn, how did she manage to give him chills just from breaking off a piece of bread with her fingertips? "I have a proposition for you."

Yes. Done. Absolutely. If it involved whipped cream, even better.

Yeah, his sex drive—only last week drawing in tiny squeaky gasps of breath—had risen full force. Another bite of bread from her fingertips, and he was officially out of his mind, he wanted her so badly. Thank goodness she hadn't brought over a camel or some shit. Who knew what he'd agree to adopt at this point?

"Would you like to watch a movie?" she asked.

"What kind of movie?"

"The boring kind that no one actually pays attention to."

Yes. *Absolutely.*

Abruptly, the door opened, with three twentysomethings piling into the house, headed straight for the couch. A cheerful hello from Quinn and Grass, followed by a grunt from Diego, was the final nail in the coffin.

So close. He'd been so close.

"Our date just got crashed," Rick told her, shaking his head. "Sorry about that. I can't kick the kid off the couch. It's his safe space."

"I don't mind." Lana lowered her voice to not be heard in the next room over. "How is he? I haven't seen him since the day he was in jail."

"Frustrated. He's going to help me out at the pool hall until he finds work. Hannah won't hire him back while Bayard is still staying at the resort. I talked to Jax, but his hands are tied."

"I'll see if there's anything I can do to grease the wheels." Lana aimed a sympathetic glance toward the living room, where the three had turned on a movie. "He was protecting her. I hate that he's being punished for it."

Yeah. Rick hated it too.

In the living room, Diego had turned on a movie. On one side of the couch was a young man the same age as Diego, nice-looking and well-dressed. Grass always seemed put together. On the other side was Rick's rumpled housemate, surly glare ramped up about ten notches. Between them, the reason for that glare was perched with her legs crossed beneath her.

When everyone knew everyone in a small town, it was impossible to miss the girl with the largest eyes ever. And when Quinn turned those eyes Diego's way, Rick could see the reaction she had on him. With every single part of him, Diego was clearly trying to pretend he wasn't head over heels in love with the girl.

A grunted, "Want some pizza bagels?" was Diego's version of an epic 80s power ballad.

"*Yes.*" She thumped Diego's arm with excitement. "Oh my gosh, I *love* those." Quinn immediately started chattering about how much she loved them and why she loved them and how she could eat all of them. And the kid listened to her too, every single word, before rolling to his feet.

"Thanks, man," Grass said. "Those sound good."

If Grass had only seen the look that passed over Diego's face, he would have left Rick's couch and house and pizza bagels far behind. But Grass was too busy watching Quinn's face instead.

The poor girl was oblivious to the fact that both were in love with her.

"Maybe we should give them some space," Lana said as they cleared the table.

"It's cold outside," Rick reminded her.

She bumped her shoulder into his companionably. "I won't turn into a popsicle."

They tucked Peyton back into his carrier before heading out to the porch. The swing had acquired a nice thick layer of snow in the time since he'd left that morning.

"Why don't you have any Christmas lights on?"

"The Santa Moose destroyed what I still had up. Plus, someone blew the main breaker in my barn. I haven't had a chance to get to the hardware store to replace it yet."

Guilt flashed over her features. "Wow, I bet that sucks. Who would do something like that?"

"Someone who decided to shoot me full of moose tranquilizer and take advantage of my inebriated state to pry all my deepest and darkest secrets out of me."

This time, Lana's eyes widened with indignation.

"I did *not*. I would never." Rick waited, then she giggled. "Not on purpose anyway. What you chose to say was entirely on you."

Like a surly kid on one side of the couch, Rick couldn't help looking over at her. Lana's lashes kept brushing her cheeks as she glanced down at the snowflakes on her knees. Maybe they were all the same. Dumb guys without a clue how to cover the distance between their part of the seat and hers.

But Rick wasn't a kid. He was willing to try.

Lana's eyebrow rose. "Did you just yawn and put your arm around me?"

"Technically, I yawned and draped my arm on the back of the swing. If you so happened to be in front of it..."

She leaned into his shoulder. "It was very smooth. I was very impressed."

"I thought you would be."

Since she was snuggling in, Rick figured he might be allowed to snuggle a little too. Wrapping his arm around her, he shifted to make a more comfortable space for her to lean. And when a soft sigh escaped her lips, he rested his chin on the top of her head, inhaling the scent of her hair.

"Thank you for dinner. I had fun tonight. And last night. And pretty much every moment I've spent with you."

Diego showed his loyalty and affection through mini bagels covered in cheese and pepperoni. Rick showed his by closing his eyes and ignoring the mitten-covered fingers sneaking a bit of snow into his shirt. When she slipped her leg over to straddle his lap, Rick took a moment to remember this. The way her hips felt beneath his hands as he steadied her. The softness of her lips as she pressed her mouth to his. Her hair sliding through his fingers as he cradled the back of her neck, drawing her into a deeper, more heated kiss.

When they pulled away, Rick wondered if Lana could see the hunger in his eyes. Every muscle in his body felt shaky, he wanted her so much. Instead, he said quietly, "I'd be lying if I said I didn't keep hoping you'd do that again."

"Depends if you were a good boy this year," she said coyly.

"You're teasing me." He'd never admit how much he loved it.

"You're a really cute target." Lana winked at him.

"Are you ever not pretty?" His question was soft, his thumb lightly brushing the sleeve of her jacket.

"You should see me after half a bottle of tequila and a phone call with my tax attorney."

"Nah, pretty sure you'd still be a knockout."

More snow found its way beneath his collar, and this time, he flinched as it slipped down to stick between his shoulder blades.

Rick broke the kiss, reaching back to try to free himself from the iciness. "That was mean."

"I'm pure evil. Haven't you heard?"

"They don't know you." Rick held her gaze, thinking no one had ever had eyes as beautiful as hers. "I'd make you pizza bagels."

Her smile took his breath away.

"Considering the context, that might be the nicest thing anyone has ever said to me."

"I get the feeling that people don't say nice things to you very much." Rick held her eyes, because he wanted her to know that whatever else did—or didn't—happen, he saw her. "Which is a shame. I'm tempted to say nice things to you every second of every day."

"Really?" Her voice was always sexy as hell. But when it softened, her body leaning into his a little as if her defenses were softening too, Rick had never heard anything sexier.

"Yep." This time, he pulled his gloves off, not caring about the cold as he wrapped her up in his arms, squeezing tightly. "I'd make you chicken wings too."

"Spicy ones?" Lana asked as he pressed a kiss to the side of her slender neck.

"The spiciest. And carrot sticks with ranch."

"Love, one must only eat their wings with celery and blue cheese. Really, what kind of heathen are you?"

Love, huh? That was a first. And man, if Rick didn't like the word on her lips. He kissed her there, tasting the lingering endearment before it slipped away from him. The chill in his knuckles was worth it to feel those silky strands beneath his hands, tilting her face down to his again.

"I'd even make you breakfast."

"Trout and toast?"

"Good lord, woman, your taste is terrible."

"On the contrary, my taste is *fabulous*." A deeper kiss this time, passionate enough that Rick didn't care if it was fifty below... there was no cooling the fire burning through him. "One expects nothing less from a Montgomery."

There, that slight tone to her words, as if self-mocking. And yeah, he wanted to pick her up, carry her inside, and throw everyone else out of there. Diego and his friends could sleep in the barn for all he cared at the moment. Or they could stay right here, doing exactly this, until they both turned into ice cubes.

But he wanted that slight tone to go away even more.

Their breath misted in between them as Rick chose his words carefully. This was the kind of shit he'd always gotten wrong, no matter how badly he'd wanted to get it right.

"Lana? I don't expect anything from you. Just being next to you is enough."

When she leaned her forehead into his shoulder, he realized how wrong he'd been. The woman he'd thought was softened in his arms was nothing compared to the one he was holding now.

Right or wrong, he was glad he'd said it.

CHAPTER 11

THIS TIME WHEN LANA WENT out in the woods with a tranquil-izer gun, she went alone. She also wore the accidentally sexually explicit Christmas sweater Graham's mother had made her. Maybe it would give her some much-needed moose-catching luck.

Alas, all Lana found was a cold nose and too many emails from her family. She'd wanted to take the day off and focus on her quest, but by the time Rick called on his lunch break, Lana was back at the resort, locked in a conference room and eyeballs deep in a nightmare of a meeting.

As much as Lana wanted to take Rick's call, she couldn't. Instead, she was stuck in her seat, trying not to let her reactions show on her face. A private video conference with her mother, Silas, and Killian to determine the fate of Moose Springs was one of the few things more important than her deepening relationship with Rick or her desire to catch the Santa Moose.

"I think the best thing we can do is halt construction on the condominiums," Silas was saying.

"There's no way we can recoup what we've put in this," Lana argued. "The condominiums will sell for a range of $1.5 million to $4 million per unit. The purpose of investing in the town was to force through the project. If we back out now, not only do we eat the cost of those properties, but we lose $250 million in potential sales."

"So?"

"I'm sorry, Silas, at what point have you become so disconnected with reality that a quarter of a billion dollars is negligible to you?"

"I'm with Lana," Killian said. "Liquidation makes less sense."

"Silas, why is this so personal to you?" Lana demanded.

Silas snorted. "I was going to ask you the same question, but considering your reaction to that flannel-wearing moron at the pool hall, it's clear. The Montgomery Group coffers don't exist for your warped version of a dinner date."

"Would someone explain that please?" Jessica arched an eyebrow.

Silas wasn't as good at hiding his own facial expressions. He thought he had won. "It's become clear that she's only pursuing this project because she's emotionally invested in Moose Springs."

"Yes, okay?" Lana said. "I'm emotionally invested in Moose Springs, but not because of Rick Harding and not because of anyone else there. We have all seen what happens when a tourism-driven town loses their main source of income. The day the Shaws close their doors, that town will die. If I have personal reasons for not wanting that to happen, then at least I've balanced those reasons with financially profitable alternatives."

"Dear lord, Auntie, your daughter wants to be a small-town queen." Silas groaned dramatically. "Will someone cut off her access to the corporate accounts, *please*?"

"Silas, trust me," Lana snapped, her cool officially destroyed. "Your attempts at undermining me are even more thinly veiled than you think. You're not getting control of this company because yours is the loudest voice in the room. The Montgomery Group is my mother's, and then it will be mine. No amount of showboating and grandstanding and acting like a complete jackass will put it in your utterly incompetent hands."

"That right there is exactly what I'm talking about," Silas said, narrowing his eyes at her. "Lana needs to be pulled from the Moose Springs account. She has no concept of self-control when it comes to these people. Sorry, Cousin. You're too emotional."

"And I suppose your penis makes you just emotional enough?" Lana glowered back.

"Before this descends into whose genitals are the most impressive, can I say something?" Killian asked dryly.

"Please do," Jessica said. "They're giving me a headache."

"Silas, give us one good reason that we should liquidate the Moose Springs account and halt construction. Beyond your concern that it's taking Lana away from bigger accounts. Because she's right. A quarter of a billion dollars isn't something to ignore."

"I've run the numbers, and the tax rate the town imposes on out-of-state ownership is insane. That alone makes every single property we've acquired in Moose Springs a loss, and that's *if* the tenants pay their rent. Which many aren't. Rents need to be raised to barely break even. And while we're fronting the tax money for improvements, there's no guarantee the condos will sell. Without the additional income, the Shaws' property will go into bankruptcy within five years."

There was a look in his eyes and an eagerness to his voice that made Lana's blood run cold. This was Silas's ultimate plan. "You *want* to let them go under, then buy the resort for pennies on the dollar."

"Exactly. The Shaws cater to an upscale clientele, and they've been hemorrhaging money because of it. Let them go under, then remarket the town as the poor man's Aspen. We bring in chain restaurants, big box stores, a waterslide or two for the kids. Maybe even reach out to Disney. If we put Mickey Mouse or a Stormtrooper on skis, you know people will flock to the place."

"And in the process of letting the current Moose Springs die, then what?" Lana challenged. "What happens to the townspeople?"

"It's Darwinism. Survival of the fittest. Or in this case, those with the most business savvy."

"Mother, you can't possibly be considering this." Jessica remained quiet, as did Killian. Trying to cover her rapidly beating heart, Lana shifted her appeal. "Killian, you've been here. You know these people."

"I think...Silas's idea isn't unsound. It's cruel, but it isn't unsound."

"And when did we get in the business of being nice?" Silas leaned back in his chair, arm outstretched as he relaxed. A relaxed Silas was a Silas who thought he'd won.

Lana was beside herself, barely able to focus on the screen in front of her. She was seeing red. "I can't believe any of you are considering this. You're talking about letting people get hurt, letting them lose their livelihoods for a profit we don't even need."

"You're the one who made the investment, Lana," Silas said. "Without consult from the rest of us. We're trying to make the best of the mess you made."

"I need to think on this," Jessica finally decided. "Lana, Silas, put your positions on this in writing and send them to me by the end of the day."

For the first time, Lana ended a conference call without the normal pleasantries. When her mother called back, she didn't answer. Instead, Lana sat in an overly plush chair, the backdrop of the Chugach Mountains behind her.

If Silas had his way, too many people in this town would never make it. People like Rick would lose everything. And it was all her fault. There wasn't much she could do. The Montgomery Group wasn't *hers* to control. However...

Picking up her phone, Lana dialed the number of a man who really didn't want to talk to her.

"Hey, Jonah? It's Lana. I need a favor."

She was sitting alone at the bar when a voice behind her said, "Can I buy you a drink?"

A lot of men had tried to buy Lana a drink over the years. In her world, it was a power play, a game she wasn't interested in participating in. So Lana bought drinks for others and always for herself. But when she twisted around and saw Rick standing there, his work boots and button-up shirt not quite fitting the cocktail bar, Lana found her first smile all day.

"That would be lovely. How's Peyton?"

"He's already convinced Roger that he's evil and Diego that he's perfect. Although Quinn is so in love with that kitten, he might end up with her."

That thought made Lana perk up. At least finding Peyton a good home had been something she'd done right. He settled into the chair next to her, his broad shoulders softening as he slouched a little in his seat. Rick was looking right at her, never wavering in his attention. For some reason, that gave her hope this day could end better than it had started.

"What would you like?" he asked.

"Double martini on the rocks," Lana said honestly. "But I probably should have a coffee. I called a town hall tonight and need my full wits about me."

"You called a town hall?" Rick raised an eyebrow. "Can you do that?"

"Technically, Jonah called it. I promised him it would be worth his while to indulge me this one time. I figured you would already know."

"Are we okay?" The way he said it was quiet, those hazel eyes more brown than normal. If greener meant passion, what did brown mean? He sounded worried, hesitant and uncertain of what he was trying to say.

"Of course. Why wouldn't we be?"

"I know last night, things went further than I'd expected. I tried to call you. I didn't want you to think..." Rick trailed off uncomfortably. "But when you didn't reply, I didn't know if I was bothering you."

Reaching over to hug him was as instinctive as it was badly

needed. "I would never think that. I couldn't imagine you ever ignoring me after—"

This time, Lana hesitated, a slight heat in her cheeks.

"Swing-time activities?" Rick offered with a wry smile.

"Porch swing-time activities," Lana replied, flashing him a quick grin. "And I wanted to pick up, but I was busy ruining lives."

He shook his head as if he didn't believe that for one second. Lana wanted to tell him how badly she had screwed up, but the bartender came over. Rick ordered them both coffees, then twisted in his seat.

"Lana? What's wrong?"

"Am I so easy for you to read?" she asked softly.

He picked up her hand, frowning down at her fingers. "These are like a little window into your head. You can be smiling and cheerful, like everything is okay. But your hands always give you away."

She didn't reply, because she refused to let everyone in this bar know she was rattled.

"Do you want to take a walk?" Rick's voice was quiet so no one could overhear.

Yes. Lana desperately wanted to get out of this bar. And for the first time in a long time, she wanted to get out of this town. Guilt pressed in on her, making it hard for her to breathe.

Getting their coffees in to-go cups, they found a quiet hallway no one was using. It wasn't scenic, but it was private. Decorative stone facing on the walls was punctuated by hand-formed metal artwork. Fish jumping in a stream. Elk grazing in a meadow. A solitary, majestic moose.

What would happen to the wildlife in Moose Springs if Silas got his way?

"I know this is just a holiday fling," Rick said in a low, gruff voice. "But you can talk to me. If you're upset, you can always talk to me."

Realizing she had been abnormally silent, Lana paused by an unmarked door. Probably a supply closet, if the light scent of bleach reaching her nostrils was a tell. She took a deep, steadying breath. They were so close, the thick, scratchy fabric of his faded Carhartt jacket brushed the butter-soft leather of her own coat. Slowly, almost as if he was unsure of his reception, Rick slipped his free hand around hers, their fingers entwining.

Wrapping her arm around his neck, Lana made sure not to spill coffee on the back of Rick's coat as she went up on her toes, kissing him. His reaction was immediate. Deepening the kiss, he released her hand, pulling her flush against his body.

"I had some bad news at work. I think I messed up."

Rick leaned back against the wall, drawing her with him. "Everyone makes mistakes, sweetheart."

"It was a big mistake." Lana inhaled the scent of him. "The kind that wrecks people's lives. It came out of left field, and now I've got to fight with the board of directors to make a case not to let it happen."

"Is it a fight you can win?"

"It's a fight I'm going to win," she said determinedly. When people like Rick would get caught in the middle, it was a fight she absolutely had to win.

"Is there anything I can do to help?" Rick asked with a quiet sincerity far rarer than he knew.

This sweet man had no idea how much his kindness meant to her. Lana wasn't sure of how to verbalize it, so she tried to show him instead. The coffee cups kept getting in the way until they abandoned them on the floor. It was much better having two free hands. One to slide through his hair, boyishly messy, and another to press against his muscled torso, hard and strong beneath his shirt.

"Rick?" Lana whispered. "You know those porch swing activities? I could use some distracting."

He took her hand, murmuring in her ear in a low, husky voice. "That's definitely something I can do."

Rick was a grown-ass man. He was not a teenager on prom night with a borrowed credit card.

There was no reason why walking into a hotel room should make him uncomfortable, not when he'd been there twice before.

Her suite had been decorated for the holidays with subtle touches of red and green in the bedspread and the blanket on her couch. The hand towel by the microwave was festive, as were the holly berries and frosted evergreen branches atop the mantel. The tree they had decorated together looked perfect next to the fireplace.

"Would you like a water or—" Lana began to say, but Rick caught her hands.

He lifted them, pressing a kiss to the inside of her left wrist first, then her right. The low tremor was something he'd noticed more often. When she was agitated, it seemed to be worse. The fact that her hands were shaking this badly meant that she was trying very hard to hide how upset she was.

Beneath the breezy exterior was a woman who could be hurt. Then and there, Rick vowed to never, ever forget it. Sitting on the couch, he continued to hold her hands as she stood in front of him.

"Lana."

"Holiday flings are supposed to be lighthearted and fun, not me word vomiting my bad day all over you."

"Maybe I like a little vomit." The words were out of his mouth before Rick could reconsider. Her nose wrinkled, then she giggled.

Lana sat on the coffee table across from him. "I guess I'm not used to having someone who wants my vomit."

"Maybe we should change metaphors," he said, chuckling. Rick ran a thumb across her skin, an invitation. "You're too far away."

Lana scooted forward an inch on the coffee table. "Better?"

He wanted to reach over and scoop her up, haul her into his arms, and kiss her senseless. But Lana wasn't a woman to be hauled around. She was fine wine. A woman to be appreciated and waited for. Rick had as much patience as she needed.

"You can trust me," he said quietly. "I know trust is earned, but I'm hoping you give me a chance to prove you can."

She slipped over to the couch. This was what he needed, having her resting against him, her curves pressed to his chest.

"I do trust you, Rick. It's just...this is new for me. I've been running solo for a long time."

"I know the feeling." Rick ran a soothing hand down her back.

"I think I was promised porch swing activities."

Rick had always been a man of his word.

When she leaned in and pressed her mouth to his, Rick felt the tension inside him settle. With Jen, even when things were good, the tension never truly settled... No. He didn't want to think about the things he'd done wrong or the things he'd tried to do right. Rick wanted to be here, with Lana. Appreciating every moment of whatever this was between them.

Wrapping an arm around her waist, Rick lifted her up and turned, laying her back on the couch gently. Bracing his weight on his knee and his elbow, he waited for her to wriggle into the cushions to make herself comfortable.

"You're still too far away." She gave him a cute, hopeful look. He let the slender arms wrapping around his waist pull him closer. Wanting more but in the best way, not the desperate, painful way.

Rick settled against her, drinking in how good it felt to finally not be alone.

Lana could have stayed in his arms forever.

As the sun set in the early afternoon sky, the soft glow of holiday lights outside the window and inside the hotel room set the kind of ambience completely perfect for being with Rick.

Whatever this was, it was happening slowly, as if he wanted to memorize each touch, each sound she made when he held her just right. She'd never had slow leave her feeling so hungry for more.

They hadn't even taken anything off, and Lana was close to losing her mind beneath his skilled hands.

"You're killing me," he groaned as she broke first, fisting his shirt and pulling it up to his ribs.

"You're wearing too much. I may die from sheer curiosity." Another sound escaped her throat unbidden. He was far too good at far too many things.

Lana's phone beeped. If it had been for anything else, she would have ignored it, but Moose Springs was too important.

"I'm sorry," she said, still rucking his shirt up higher. "I have to check this."

If he minded, he didn't let her know. Instead, Rick rolled onto his back, drawing her across his chest and giving her the perfect spot to reach for her phone on the coffee table, where she'd abandoned it forever ago.

"If it's an evil moose attacking my Christmas decorations, ignore it. We're busy." Rick inhaled deeply to catch his breath. Lana knew the feeling. She wasn't much of an exercise girl, and she was definitely winded.

"I'm going to have to start doing more cardio to keep up with you," she said.

The pleased look on his face was so endearing, Lana made a mental note to repeat it as often as possible. He deserved to feel good. Rick certainly made her feel more than good and more than once. Had she ever had a hand stroke lazily down her back like this, finding the perfect places on her spine to make her toes curl? Lana could barely read the words in front of her face.

"Be less attractive for a minute."

Rick's hand settled on her hip. "You're ruining me, gorgeous. Absolutely ruining me."

"If I'm killing you and ruining you, then I had better make amends. But right after I send this text."

Hazel eyes watched her, distracting her even as she read the message.

Pleased, Lana patted Rick's chest. "Good news. Something very positive just happened. Unfortunately, I'm going to have to cut this short because we have someplace to be. The emergency town hall meeting I asked for was just officially called."

"I have it on good authority that town hall meetings have terrible cookies and mediocre coffee."

"Yes, but this one will have something very important I need." She headed to the hallway mirror. "Oh dear. You've mussed me good, and there's no time to fix it."

"You look great." Coming up behind her, Rick wrapped an arm around her, pressing a soft kiss to her neck before looking at their reflection in the mirror.

Lana wasn't at her best by far. Her makeup was smudged, and her hair was in desperate need of a combing. But Rick had never looked so relaxed. Lana turned, then kissed him, unable to help herself. A sound of masculine approval met her action, and Rick in turn pressed her back into the wall, hands roaming.

"I wish otherwise, but I really do have to get to the town hall. It's for the good of the town."

"The town is perfectly good," he said even as he stepped back. "The town has never been better."

Lana patted his muscled arm. "The town is fabulous. But trust me, this is one meeting I absolutely cannot reschedule."

Lana did her best to fix what two hours with Rick had mussed up, then she gave up and called it as it was. She had make-out face. There was no getting past it.

"I'll call for my car," she told him as Rick drew on his jacket.

Rick pulled his keys out of his pocket, jangling them. "No need."

"You're coming with me?" When he tilted his head as if confused, Lana clarified. "I'm not...popular at the moment. I don't want to cause you problems."

Understanding dawned, followed by a frown. "You think I'd mess around with you but pretend we're not together?"

Lana's voice was soft. "I don't want you to lose any friends because of me."

"If I lose a friend because of who I love, then they weren't a friend to begin with."

Who he *loved*?

The words must have slipped out, because Rick's face went all kinds of shades of red. "I didn't..." Immediately, Rick clamped his mouth shut. Of course he didn't. Who fell in love with someone so quickly? Especially when this was just a holiday fling, meant to help two people get through Christmas. This wasn't a love story to last.

This wasn't a love story at all. Just a holiday-themed coping mechanism.

So why was she so crushed?

"Lana." Rick's tone softened. Nope. She knew what was coming next, and this had been a rough enough day. She didn't need to hear him explain that his blunder was just that: a mistake.

"It's okay, dearest. We all slip up."

She hustled around, finishing getting ready and not meeting his eye. Of course he didn't love her. Rick was a smart man, too smart for that. It was the season of cheer, not the season of bad choices. Then she steeled her spine, because she would not let this hurt her. Turning, Lana smiled breezily at Rick.

"Okay, how do I look?"

"Lana." Rick's voice was quiet. "Just because there's an elephant in the room doesn't mean we have to pretend it isn't there. I don't know how I feel. But when I do, you'll be the first to know. If I'm slipping up, it's because I do care about you."

Lana's phone beeped again, and if a beep could sound more urgent, this one managed to pull it off. They really did have to go.

Resting her palm on his cheek, Lana said softly, "It never occurred to me otherwise."

She'd let him off the hook far easier than she should have. Telling someone you loved them and then retracting it was the kind of screwup that should have resulted in a yelling match or at least some well-deserved tears. Instead, Lana had stood straighter, plastered that smile he was starting to hate on her face, and promised him everything was okay.

Everything wasn't okay, not by a long shot, but Rick was determined to make it up to her. Lana was too used to having to stuff her feelings down deep, to ignore when she wasn't being treated well, to the point that she was oblivious to what she deserved from a partner. Honestly, up until today, it hadn't occurred to Rick that she'd never had a partner she could trust to have her back.

She hadn't even thought he'd want to go with her to the meeting.

They'd driven all the way to the town hall when Rick realized he hadn't said two words to her, so lost in thought as he was.

"I'm not ashamed of you."

Lana had been scrolling through her phone, frowning at what she read in her email. Before she could respond, Rick added tightly, "If anyone has a problem with you, they have a problem with me too."

"I can handle this," she said softly, resting her hand on his arm. Then she shook her head. "We're late, and I'm going to be in trouble if we don't get in there."

As they got out of the car and headed across the parking lot, Rick wondered at this feeling in his chest. Tightness, the kind he wasn't used to. Not quite anger...more like he was ready to fight. Rick didn't like the feeling, and it bothered him to think that Lana must feel this way all the time.

"Lana, you're late for your own meeting," Jonah said as they entered the barn.

"Unfortunately, this afternoon has been a little more packed than I expected," she said cheerfully to the room full of eyes watching her warily. "However, I appreciate—"

Midsentence, Rick stole her hand, causing her to pause and turn. "Rick?" She tilted her head in question.

He knew he'd hurt her, and the absolute last thing Rick wanted Lana to feel was rejected by him. This was her decision; the ball was in Lana's court. But dammit, Rick was playing too. And he wanted the win.

"You're standing under mistletoe," he told her, not caring if the whole town heard the husky tone in his voice.

Lana looked up. Sure enough, she was just beneath a sprig of mistletoe that had been suspended from the barn rafters. Her eyes flickered to the crowded room, then back to him. When she tugged on his hand, Rick came willingly, stepping in close. Close enough that everyone would know exactly who Rick had come here with.

"Now you are too." Lana flashed him a little grin, going up on her toes and kissing him.

When she wrapped her arm around his neck, pulling his head down to hers, Rick laughed, taking the opportunity to dip her dramatically. Someone catcalled, and he was pretty sure Ash started gagging. He couldn't have cared less.

"I wanted to do this the last time you were under mistletoe, but I thought I might get in trouble."

"You still might," Lana said archly, but her cheeks had a rosy tint, and her eyes sparkled.

Instead of taking a seat with the rest of the group, Rick leaned against the refreshment table, arms crossed, watching Lana take the stage next to Jonah.

"Thank you all for coming out here."

"We didn't think we had any choice," Graham spoke up teasingly. "Word gets around that you're a dangerous shot, L."

"Only for those who annoy me, Graham." Lana smiled sweetly at her longtime friend before continuing. "It's not lost to me that there has been a lot of concern and unrest in town, most of which is centered on the Montgomery Group's investments.

I think everyone would feel better if they had a strong political figure to champion their concerns. As for myself, it would be easier to streamline those concerns through a focused entity with whom we can do business."

Lana's smile widened. "Therefore, I nominate Graham Barnett as mayor of Moose Springs. For a full term, not a couple of days until he can pass it off on someone else."

The look of sheer astonishment on Graham's face was only matched by the expression of glee on Ash's. Easton's beard twitched in what might have been a smirk.

"I second the nomination," Ash said, hopping up.

"Wait, this isn't how mayors are elected," Graham protested. "I can't be elected against my will."

"Everyone in favor?" Easton rumbled, earning a resounding "aye" from the gathered townsfolk. Horror dawned on Graham's features.

"Did you know about this?" Graham demanded of Rick and Zoey.

"Why would I know about it?" Zoey asked.

"Because you two have been in cahoots with her."

Rick flashed Lana a grin, even though he hadn't known a thing about her plans. "I like being in cahoots with her," he told Graham.

Glaring back and forth suspiciously, Graham narrowed his eyes at Zoey. "Zoey Bear?"

"Yes?" She sounded perfectly innocent, but her eyes flickering to Lana gave her away.

Lana brushed a piece of imaginary lint from her leg. "Zoey

had nothing to do with it. If you're going to be upset, be upset with me."

"Oh, trust me, L," he said. "I am."

Jonah looked around the room. "Anyone object to Graham Barnett as mayor?" No one raised a hand except for one.

"I object!" Graham said. "Lana, you can't be serious."

"Actually, you would make the perfect mayor, Graham. You pretty much do it anyway, and at least this way, you'll get paid for the trouble."

"I don't want more money; I want to be left alone."

"Then maybe you should have thought about that before you decided to take care of every single person in town." Zoey said cheerfully, "I love you, by the way."

"I love you too, traitor." He turned puppy dog eyes to Lana. "L, this is the meanest thing you could do to me."

Lana flashed him a sweet smile. "The way I see it, you care about Moose Springs, and you're willing to do anything necessary to protect it. I want to work with the best person I can to keep Moose Springs' interests at the forefront of any changes the Montgomery Group makes to their properties.

That's you. Sorry, Graham. You care too much."

Groaning overdramatically, Graham slunk out of the barn, Zoey following. She gave Lana a double thumbs-up behind Graham's back.

Everyone was watching her, and for once, the eyes pointed her way weren't filled with distrust. Well, maybe some distrust. But definitely not the normal animosity.

"This town is the most important thing to Graham," she

told them. "And he's not afraid to go head-to-head with me. He's going to make the best mayor, no matter how much he whines about it."

"Why would you give Graham the power to shut you down?" Ash wondered. "You know he's going to try."

Ash may have asked the question, but curiosity was on more than only her face. Everyone stayed quiet, waiting for Lana's answer.

"Because the town matters to me too. I know you don't believe that, but it's true."

"Well, thank goodness that's been arranged." Jonah sounded relieved. "Town halls are now up to the mayor to hold. Show up to the Tourist Trap on the second Monday of every month from now on. If he tries to leave, I'll block the door."

The crowd started to disperse, the townsfolk energized at the new change in their local government. Rick joined her, wrapping his arm around her waist. A buzz of conversation followed everyone out the door, leaving Lana and Rick in the relative privacy of the emptying barn.

Rick pulled her in for the biggest, best hug she had been given in years. "This was a good call. You're brilliant."

Flushing at the compliment, Lana said, "Graham being in a position of power will actually make doing business in Moose Springs easier. It's better to deal with a figurehead than an angry group of people. The town needed a strong protector now more than ever."

She started to say more, but Lana grew distracted when Rick took her face in his hands, pressing a kiss to her left cheek, then another to her nose. A third to her lips, leaving his own tingling, like cayenne pepper in chocolate. Sweet and rich but fiery. He couldn't get enough of her.

"I promise I'm not the enemy," Lana whispered, breathless.

He tilted his head down so that his forehead rested against hers. "I know. I've always known. One day, they'll know it too. From now on, I'm going to help you prove it to them."

"You'll help me catch a moose?"

"Only if you aren't holding the tranquilizer gun."

"I shoot you one time by accident, and you just won't let it go—" Lana huffed, then she could only laugh as he pulled her close, kissing her all over again.

CHAPTER 12

IT WAS USUALLY A BAD sign when someone showed up first thing in the morning without an invitation. But considering this someone was carrying an armful of Frankie's bear claws while wearing the sexiest ugly Christmas sweater in existence, Rick was willing to let it slide.

Besides, Lana was welcome on his porch any day of the week, pastries or no.

"I tried to call you, but I was having reception issues," Lana said as a way of saying hello when he opened the door. "It occurred to me that maybe I'm overstepping my welcome here."

Drawing her in for a long, slow kiss, Rick allowed himself the luxury of resting his cheek against her hair as he held her. "You're always welcome with me." His voice was still low from sleep. He'd been up for a bit but was not nearly the level of awake Lana was.

The look she gave him was better than caffeine, and the second kiss left him far more alert than the first.

"Where did you find a sweater with Jake on it?" He flicked the jingle bell attached to Sweater Jake's snout.

"A girl has her secrets," Lana said. "Especially one who flies too much and always reads *SkyMall*."

"So to what do I owe the surprise?" Rick led her inside, out of the brisk cold. He set them both a seat at the kitchen table, speaking quietly because Diego was still asleep.

"I figured you had a busy day ahead of you with the tournament, and I have a busy day ahead of me with the Christmas party. Since I'm not the one who has to stay up all night, I thought I'd bring you some breakfast." She shot him a cute look. "A healthy breakfast, of course."

"Naturally."

"And...maybe I didn't want to wait until tonight to see you," Lana said. The flirty statement came out more shy than normal for her. Rick had the feeling whatever had happened at her job yesterday was still on her mind. She seemed distracted and uncertain. That was okay. He was happy to eat another bear claw and prove to her that she was right where she belonged.

"You didn't think I would show up to your party?"

Lana shrugged, focusing on a forkful of pastry. "I think you have a business to run. The last thing I would do is divide your attentions from where they need to be."

This time, her lips tasted like sugar and cinnamon.

"I wouldn't miss it, gorgeous."

"Well, in that case..." Her speculative glance made him immediately shift in his seat. "Are you still not opening the pool hall until tonight?"

Rick nodded. "That's the plan."

"Do you need today to get set up for it?"

Hmm. He had the feeling he was about to get propositioned. Some fairly enjoyable imagery came to his mind on that one, but Rick could tell Lana was shifting into work mode.

"I know tonight is a busy night for you," she said. "But I was wondering if I could borrow you for an hour later this morning. An hour and a half, tops."

One look at Lana's hopeful expression and he knew he was going to do whatever came out of her mouth. "What do you need?"

"I'm sort of out a Santa Claus."

Rick blinked. He knew he was blinking, because all he could see was her pretty face, the snow behind her shoulders, and fresh flakes on her shiny hair. Then eyelid. Lots of eyelid.

It was never too late to start making boundaries for oneself.

"I'd be Santa," she explained as if instinctively knowing he was ready to back out. "But I'm already an elf, and the suit really wouldn't fit me. I'd arranged for someone from the resort to be my Santa, but he's come down with a rather nasty cold. He said he'd still do it, but it seems cruel to ask him to have a townful of children asking for toys while he's sick."

"But it's not too cruel to ask me to do it?" Mouth curving despite himself, Rick shook his head. "I'm not really the Santa type."

"Not jolly enough?" Her eyes danced. "I promise to get you out as soon as possible, and I'm happy to help you tonight at the tournament as a thank-you."

He liked the idea of having her there tonight, but he didn't want her to feel obligated. "You should come, but I don't need the help unless you're bored. I'll have Diego working."

"And if I show up anyway?"

"Then the terrible rosé is on me."

Lana grinned. "It isn't *that* bad."

"It isn't that good either." Rick took a swipe of icing on his fork, then shook his head in bemusement. "Santa huh?"

"If it helps, I'll have a pitcher of special 'no children allowed' eggnog to coax the cheeriness out of you. I certainly plan to partake. Are you all right? You look a little pale around the edges."

"I've seen the damage you can do with special eggnogs." Rick's hand found her knee, his body oriented in her direction. Was the physical pull between them as overwhelming to her as it was to him? The inches between them felt way too far. "What would I have to do?"

"Oh, the normal Santa things. Lots of ho ho hoing, I'd imagine. Sit on a chair and let people take pictures with you. I'll be right there with you." Lana flashed him a quick grin. "Don't worry. I won't let any of the women sit on your lap and pull your beard."

"I thought you were trying to convince me I should do this." He gave her a teasing look as they stood before taking their plates to the sink.

"I can promise you all the cookies and milk you want, plus a very grateful Grass. He's the next in line. Hannah said she'd twist his arm to make him if I couldn't come up with an alternative. You don't have to though. No pressure."

If she'd stayed her smiling, cheerful self, maybe Rick would have had a chance. But the moment her smile slipped, so did his self-respect, his self-awareness of what was best for him, and any generally intelligent decisions he was capable of making.

"I'll do it."

As her face lit up, Rick tried not to think about how good happiness looked on her. "Thank you, Rick. You're going to make this party absolutely perfect."

When she kissed him, Rick was more than happy to lean against the sink and do that for a while. Breathless, they pulled apart. "Do you have plans before the party?" he asked, voice lowered with desire.

Lana's cheeks were flushed, her eyes half-closed as he pressed soft kisses along her neck.

"I have a remote conference scheduled with the company's board of directors," she said. "Then, Zoey and I are meeting for a quick Santa Moose catching planning session before I have to start setting up the party."

The things this woman did on a daily basis made his flesh crawl. Rick didn't even like video calls on his cellphone.

"Zoey told me to bring my A game," Lana added.

Rick wasn't sure this woman had any other default setting than A game.

"How do you bring your A game to catch a moose?"

"I'd tell you, but it would be breaking the super secret code of moose catching between women. Sorry, Rick. You aren't allowed in our tree house." As she headed for the door, Lana winked at him. "See you later, Santa."

Everything was perfect. The resort's massive river rock fireplace had been turned into a winter wonderland.

Hannah stood in the middle of the room, pursing her lips as she oversaw the final details. She checked her watch, then glanced over at Lana.

"Well, everything's ready on our end. This is a lot of food."

"And I promise to pay for every crumb," Lana told the other woman. "I know you don't think anyone's going to show up, but I refuse to invite a town full of people to a Christmas party and not have a town's worth of refreshments for them."

Lana was proud of the decorating table. It was loaded with cookies ready to be iced and covered with all kinds of sprinkles. But the best part was the gingerbread town. If anything was going to win her points with Moose Springs, it would be the miniature gingerbread town.

A soft, uncomfortable cough pulled her attention to the man standing in the doorway of the room. Rick always looked good, but he was bringing it today. His long-sleeve shirt hung on his broad shoulders just right, and he'd put on a pair of jeans so new, Lana could see the faint outline of where he'd peeled the sizing sticker off the leg.

Too bad she was about to ruin him with a Santa suit.

Rick was staring at her from across the room, jaw slightly slack.

"Oh dear," Lana sighed. "I was hoping no one but Hannah would see me with my elf hair."

Her teasing seemed lost on him, then Lana realized that her hair wasn't why he wasn't speaking.

"I had to improvise," she told him. "The costumes came a bit snug."

"Thank goodness for that," he replied.

Sharing a look of mutual amusement with Hannah, Lana crossed the distance between them. She slipped her arm through Rick's companionably.

"Now, don't be nervous. This is your workshop. What you say goes. You are Santa, after all."

He didn't look convinced. "Are you sure you don't need a cookie decorator? Or a present passer outer?"

"Nope. Santa it is. Come with me. I left your outfit in my room."

Lana had chosen a pair of festive green pumps to complete her outfit, and the height of her heels had her at eye level with him. Rick kept glancing at her then quickly glancing away, as if guilty for having looked in the first place. It was more than a little adorable, especially considering he'd had his hands all over her that morning.

Rick followed her to her suite, then stepped inside, the door partially closing behind him but not latching shut.

"Don't worry. You won't accidentally see anything embarrassing. No frilly underthings to send you running screaming."

Shoulders loosening at her joke, Rick leaned back against the door, arms folded over his chest. "I was enjoying the frilly underthings last night," he said, voice husky with remembrance.

The door snapped shut on him, making him fall back that critical inch between cool and adorably awkward.

For the second time since he'd arrived, Lana had to bite her lip to cover her mirth. She waved him into the suite's bedroom, taking down a garment bag from where it hung waiting on the closet door. "As much as I'd love a repeat, the guests are due to arrive in ten minutes."

He cringed as she pressed the outfit into his arms.

Lana waited outside the bathroom door while Rick changed, using the moment to double-check her makeup and hair.

"I'm not sure this will fit," he said, sounding dubious.

"You're approximately the same build as my last human Santa sacrifice."

"Ha ha."

Unable to resist teasing him a little more, Lana added, "I'd recommend wearing your underthings, frilly or otherwise. They promise they dry-clean these in between uses, but you never really know what's happening in a Santa suit."

"You're trying to make this worse, aren't you?"

"Of course not. Now, let me see."

"I don't want to."

"It can't be too bad. Santa is iconic. If you're dressed in velvet with a fluffy beard, you're fine."

"That could be any number of things." Grumbling audibly, Rick stepped out of the bathroom. Face turning nearly as red as his outfit, he stood in front of Lana for her inspection.

"I can't wear this."

Lana stepped closer. "Actually, I think you wear it rather well."

Her compliment was met with an audible curse. The Santa suit wasn't just snug. It was skintight. This was no round-bellied Santa, no jolly old Saint Nick. This was rippling-muscles-beneath-crushed-red-velvet Santa. Broad shoulders and a flat stomach that would not shake when he laughed like a bowl full of jelly.

Maybe a bowl full of rocks or a washboard or two.

"Turn around," she encouraged him. "I want to see what we're working with."

Giving her a distrustful look, Rick did as she asked. Not only was the Santa suit snug in the top, it was equally snug in the rear.

"Mrs. Claus is a very lucky woman."

"I'm changing." Rick stomped toward the bathroom.

Lana pulled him back. "I'm teasing you, dearest. It's fine. Despite the sweets provided, I think a fit, healthy Santa is a good example for the town's youth."

It took some coaxing to get him down to the party room where the staff milled around. Their entrance pulled more than a few glances.

"Oh my." Hannah eyed him in appreciation.

"That's what I said," Lana told Hannah, lowering her voice conspiratorially. "I think I accidentally ordered the stripper Santa."

Rick groaned. "Please stop saying that. You're making this worse."

She turned to him and straightened his beard as if it were a crooked bow tie.

"Trust me, Rick. With you here, this party will be *perfect*."

No one showed up.

Not only did the party flop, there wasn't even a party to begin with.

Rick hadn't expected many people, knowing what he knew about the town's feelings on her construction plans. But even he wouldn't have expected *everyone* to boycott the event. For the first time in his life, Rick found himself ashamed of the town he came from and the people in it. People he loved but who he could have throttled with every passing hour.

They passed the time rearranging tables and decorating their own cookies, although with every failure of a body to come through the door, Lana's disappointment grew harder for her to hide. On one table, a gingerbread recreation of the town stretched out, bowls of candy and little miniaturized marzipan figures waiting for tiny hands to decorate it.

"I bet the staff went cross-eyed trying to make those," Rick rumbled, watching her straighten a small container of crystalized candy moose.

"Special ordered from Sweden." Plucking two of the moose out with her festively manicured fingertips, she popped one in her mouth and offered him the second. "In hindsight, I probably could have spared myself the shipping charges."

"Do you want to open it to the hotel guests?"

"No, this was for the town. It was supposed to be something special just for them."

Another woman might have been in tears at the obvious slight from so many. Lana kept her head high. The door opened, but instead of the rush of townsfolk that Rick kept hoping would show up, it was only one person—Zoey.

"Lana, I'm so sorry we're late. Graham and Easton are parking the truck. I kept telling Graham we needed to get a move on, but you know how he gets when he's carving—"

Zoey dropped off midsentence when she saw Lana sitting there. "No one came."

"It's fine." With a dismissive wave of her fingers, Lana added, "More cookies for us, right?"

Settling in next to her friend, Zoey put her arm around Lana's waist, leaning her head on Lana's shoulder. "I'm so sorry," she said, hugging Lana tight.

Graham strode into the room, a silent Easton at his heels. "Hey, L, sorry we're late. I'm sure Zo blamed it on me, but it was totally her fault." Pausing, he glanced around in confusion, then his eyes softened in sympathy. "Damn."

"It really is fine," she said.

Easton's frown was directed at the room, then to Rick's surprise, he went to Lana and hugged her. "Sorry, people suck sometimes. Ash is working right now, or she'd be here too."

"What's happening?" Lana asked from behind the bulk of Easton's shoulders, voice muffled.

"You're getting an Easton hug," Zoey told her. "It's kind of like being hugged by Jason Momoa, isn't it?"

Now, Rick didn't mind for one second that his friends were giving Lana the support she needed. But the Jason Momoa part was a little rough, especially considering his current attire. Rick tugged at his snowy white beard, wondering if he was at least half-Momoa-esque. Red was his color after all.

When Easton stepped away, Lana had the funniest expression on her face.

"This is where she dumps me, isn't it?" Rick said to no one in particular, earning a giggle from Lana. Which was worth the smirks aimed his way by the other males in the room.

On the plus side, Easton could eat a lot of cookies. Zoey was a hard second, and Rick had to admit he wasn't above face planting in some iced deliciousness. In support of Lana, of course. Between the group of them, they made a fair-sized dent in the treats table.

Eventually, Graham and Zoey left to do some last-minute Christmas shopping before tonight's tournament, while Easton left to do those things that Easton did (like wander in the woods in all his overly masculine glory).

It was possible that Rick was starting to get a complex.

He wasn't sure if he should stay or leave Lana in peace, staring out the window down the snow-covered mountainside below.

"We're going to start cleaning up now," Hannah told Lana quietly.

"Hmm? Oh. Yes, that's fine. Would you be willing to gather up the food we didn't use and see if any of the staff wants to take it home? If we have extra, please arrange to have it taken to a shelter in Anchorage. There are plenty of children who don't have enough Christmas joy in their lives and could use a little more right now."

Rick joined Lana at the window. "I know it's early, but do you want to get a drink?"

Her glance down the mountain gave her away. "Why not?" Lana steeled her shoulders bravely.

"There's a perfectly good bar several feet that way." Rick tilted his head toward the restaurant on the far side of the lobby. "Let's stay here for now. I don't want to beat up every single person I meet for bailing on you today."

He wasn't lying. Maybe he sounded calm, but he really wasn't. They found a place at the nearly empty bar. Apparently hiding in bars and drinking away their woes was something they liked to do together.

"So. That was a disaster." Lana dropped her face in her hands.

He wrapped his arm around her green-velvet clad shoulders. "If it helps, I think they missed out. I took a picture of the gingerbread town. Never seen something like it."

"We could go eat it if you want," she offered.

"Nah, I've had my body weight in sugar cookies today."

"You and me both. I'm sorry, Rick. You wasted a lot of time today for nothing."

"I wouldn't call it nothing," Rick said.

He ordered her scotch and a beer for himself. The bartender raised an eyebrow at their outfits but otherwise stayed silent.

"You'd think he'd never seen a sexy Santa before," Lana said.

Groaning, Rick unfastened the top button of his suit, a massive white shiny button that matched the fluffy white trim on the cuffs of his skintight sleeves.

"This is not sexy."

Now, her elf number...that was sexy. Maybe it was her mile-long legs, but even the garishly bright red-and-green-striped tights and a pointy green hat with a bell on the end of it couldn't hide how gorgeous she was.

He flicked the bell on her head to hear it jingle.

"That has been driving me nuts all day," Lana said. "Is Christmas over yet?"

"No, but we're making good progress."

"Are you sure?" Lana tugged the fluffy white Santa beard he'd forgotten was still on his face.

Rick pulled off his beard, dropping it on the bar next to him. "That thing should be burned. It itched like crazy."

"And yet you couldn't take it off." A sparkle in her eye as she teased him. "Beards look good on you."

His own facial hair was a short stubble, and there wasn't anything to pull when she reached over and touched his jaw with gentle fingertips. He didn't know how to tell her that elf suits were an amazing look on her without sounding like a complete idiot. Instead, Rick allowed himself the pleasure of leaning into that smallest of touches.

The bartender returned with their drinks.

"We promise not to tip you in candy canes," Lana told the bartender cheerfully. She twisted on her barstool and held up her glass in a toast. "To nice men who buy you a drink after an absolutely abysmal party."

"To perverted women who make you wear spandex Santa suits against your will."

Lana burst out laughing, a real one that made her eyes sparkle. There, that was worth whatever her scotch had cost and then some. He clinked his beer bottle to her scotch, then they took a drink in solidarity.

"I know you have the tournament to get ready for," Lana told him. "I'll help you set up."

She was sweet to offer, especially when she'd had a tough day so far. Rick kissed her, a long slow kiss. "Relax. Take the rest of the afternoon off. If you don't want to show later, I understand, but I hope you do."

She leaned into him, nodding. "If you want me to be there, I will."

"Always, sweetheart." An idea suddenly occurred to him. "Hey. Do me a favor?"

"Since I did make you wear an indecent Santa suit all afternoon for only my own enjoyment, I suppose I owe you."

"There are always kids at the pool tournament. Do you mind if I take the gingerbread town with me?"

"I'd rather someone get some use out of it than it ending up in the trash."

So they loaded up the town as best they could in his car. The gingerbread town was large enough that he had to put half of it in his trunk. Then Rick turned to the Christmas elf at his side, drawing her into his arms.

"Lana?"

"Hmm?" She'd all but buried herself in the hug, so Rick made sure to squeeze her a little tighter.

"They'll warm up to you." Leaning in, he murmured into her ear, "You're worth warming up for."

For the first time that afternoon, her composure slipped. A brave, watery smile was the closest to tears she was going to let him see.

"Maybe not yet. But I will be."

The Christmas party at Moose Springs Resort had been a flop. Rick's pool tournament was anything but that.

"Wow, this place is packed." From her shorter height, Zoey had to go up on her tiptoes, craning her head as she looked for Graham. "His truck's outside, but I don't see him."

"He's talking with Rick by the bar."

Linking her arm through Lana's, Zoey adjusted the glasses on her nose and led the way through the crowd. Warm greetings met her, including many chin nods and cheerful hellos. Even though Zoey had only been living there since July, she was already one of them.

Not for the first time, Lana checked the rising smudge of jealousy she felt for her friend. Zoey was able to fit into her environment in a relaxed, easy way Lana never could. Her time in Moose Springs had only made Zoey shine.

Today, Lana was feeling the lack of polish on herself keenly.

"Hey." Rick's solemn expression shifted into a small smile when he saw her. "Look."

When he nodded his head to the side, Lana followed Rick's gaze to a single pool table that wasn't being used for the tournament. Instead, a large piece of plywood had been laid on top of the table, draped in a piece of white cloth, with her gingerbread town set in the middle. He'd put a miniature train track around the town, complete with the most adorable miniature train chugging along.

Children gathered on benches set around the table, leaning over the track and giggling when the train bumped their arms as they decorated the parts they could easily reach. One father held his son over the table so he could add a candy cane to the front of the gingerbread police building.

"You did good," Rick told her quietly, coming up behind her. "They might not have realized it earlier, but they know who did this for their kids."

Moved beyond the ability to speak, Lana nodded. A warm hand rested on her shoulder, squeezing it gently.

"Are you playing?" she asked him, turning.

"Naw. It's too much to run the bar and run the tables."

"Do you want some help?"

Rick had all the help he needed in Diego, but Lana decided to keep him company at the bar. Designating herself the pizza mistress, Lana contentedly kept the oven full and the slices coming for those who needed a snack as they played. More than once, Rick stole a moment he didn't have to snug an arm around her, pressing a kiss to her neck.

Lana didn't know the person who ended up winning the tournament, but she bet Rick could have beaten them. Then, because a gingerbread town was meant to be eaten, she helped Diego put the different buildings on paper plates to send them home with anyone interested, wrapped carefully in plastic wrap.

A few appreciative smiles were sent her way and even a murmured thank you or two.

"See? We're not so bad," Rick told her as the last of the people left.

"Just half-bad?" Lana said as she helped clean up. She and Diego had already closed the kitchen and wiped down the bar, freeing Rick to get the floors swept and mopped.

She'd never noticed Diego leaving, but she did notice that once Rick's nephew was gone, Rick's attention had turned a lot more to her than to the floor he was mopping.

Never had Lana wanted to grab someone by the collar and push them onto a pool table this badly. But it had been a long day, and she knew Rick had to be exhausted.

"I should probably take off," she told him.

Rick nodded, dipping his head to press a soft kiss to her cheek. "You okay to drive in this?"

"A little snow never hurt me," Lana said. "See you tomorrow?"

"Definitely."

So she took her raging sex drive and tucked it into her back pocket, heading for the door, her hotel room, and a very cold shower.

"Lana, wait."

She turned around. Even though he was leaning back like he was relaxed, Rick's hands were gripping the edges of the pool table, his gaze locked on her as the muscles of his arms flexed beneath his waffle shirt.

"You want to stay awhile?" His voice was quiet, huskier than normal. "Play a game?"

"Absolutely," Lana told him. She didn't try to hide the way her eyes were drinking him in. "But no games."

He tilted his head. "You think I've been playing with you?"

"I hope not, because this is feeling dangerously real on my side of things."

Abruptly, he pushed off from the table, straightening and striding right for her, hazel eyes flashing with desire. Instinct had her taking a step back, not from fear but to give them both more room for whatever was coming. But Rick must not have wanted room. Another step had her chest-to-chest with him. He wrapped his hands around her waist, pulling her tight to his body.

"I figured you knew by now," Rick said. "Whatever this is... definitely isn't a game to me."

"Most holiday flings end with the holidays." And then she

would leave town and he would stay. Who knew when she'd be able to return? Lana ran her fingers down the side of his face, his stubble tickling her palm.

"Then maybe we're defining this wrong," he said in a low rumbling voice.

"Rick, I want you." Those words were the easiest thing to admit and the absolute hardest to feel. Wanting him was killing her.

Hazel eyes grew greener in the low light of the pool hall. "The feeling is definitely mutual."

"Yeah?" Her words came out soft, her breath a cloud of mist in the space between them. A strong hand rested carefully on her hip.

A shudder rolled through him, his hands sliding down to squeeze her backside, pulling her tight to his body.

This time, his breath tickled along Lana's throat, warm in her ear.

"Trust me, sweetheart, I want you so much, it's making my head spin."

Unable to wait anymore, she pulled his face down to hers.

The moment his lips were against hers, it was like inhaling oxygen for the first time. But like oxygen rushing toward too much heat, it burst into flame. Her very skin burned beneath his hands.

This was what she'd never felt before, this instant all-consuming desire. All she could do was swallow the flames, letting them burn her from the inside out.

"Damn." Rick's voice was raw, almost savage. His whole body trembled with restraint, muscles tight and eyes hot with desire as his hands threaded into her hair, biceps flexing beneath that scratchy work shirt.

"I don't like your shirt," she said against his lips. "It can't be comfortable."

"It's not," Rick agreed, eyes drifting down.

"We could take it off."

Groaning audibly, he closed his eyes. "Lana, are you sure—?"

Her answer was to all but climb up into his arms, crushing her mouth to his as he picked her up. The wood paneling on the wall thumped into her back, but Lana was too busy pulling at his shirt to care. Without warning, the door slammed open, smacking Rick so hard that he cursed and dropped her.

Mid sexiest make-out of her life, Rick *dropped* her.

Lana stared up at him from the floor. "Are you okay?" she asked as if he hadn't tossed her like a bag of grain.

The look of horror on Rick's face was priceless. Lana startled to giggle as the door tried to open again, which was not going to help this any. With a snarl of frustration, Rick shoved the door back closed, earning a curse on the other side.

"Hold on," he said with a growl as she tried to get her shirt back in place.

This time, the door hit him so hard, Rick must have seen stars, opening enough that a person squeezed through. A really big person.

"Something's wrong with your door," Easton told him as Rick helped Lana off the ground. He raised an eyebrow at them. "Did I interrupt?"

"It's all right, Easton, we don't mind." Giggling at the consternation on Rick's face, she hugged Easton. Apparently, they were on hugging terms now. "We missed you at the tournament tonight."

"I had a private climbing lesson I couldn't get out of."

Rick rubbed his head with a rueful look. "Your timing could use some work," he told Easton, who raised an eyebrow.

"I saw the light on and figured you might need some help cleaning up."

"Pretty sure I was doing fine on my own."

Lana winked at Rick to assure him he was *definitely* doing fine all on his own.

"I don't suppose you caught that moose yet?" Easton asked.

Lana sighed playfully. "I think I might need to bring in more serious backup. I'd hate to have the town lose another display."

"Too late. It already took out that big spotlight above the resort, the one that puts a sleigh on the mountainside. Hannah asked me to check why the sleigh wasn't lighting up last night. Something smashed the light to pieces and dragged it around for a while. I tracked it as far as I could, but the moose is smart. It takes the roads, so I always lose the tracks."

"Are we sure this isn't a person?" Lana raised an eyebrow. "I feel like this level of Christmas-themed disgruntlement is overboard for an animal."

"Have you met my cat?" Rick asked drolly, earning a small chuckle from Easton.

"We're doing a thing tomorrow out on the lake," he told them. "Ash feels bad about missing your cookie thing and wanted to make sure you knew you were invited. So...you two want to come?"

"Together?" Lana asked, wondering if they were at this point. The point of no return, where she wasn't hanging out with him in a pool hall, lost in his arms when no one was looking. The town didn't like her, and a single gingerbread municipality wasn't going to change that. She'd understand if he wasn't ready for that step yet in a town that never missed a thing.

Lana would never tell him how much it meant to her when Rick wrapped his arm around her waist, never hesitating. "Absolutely."

CHAPTER 13

IT TOOK A BRAVE GROUP of people to build a bonfire on a frozen lake.

"I may be showing my out-of-townness here, but isn't this a dangerous idea?"

Rick got out of her SUV, heading around to the back to grab the folding chairs they had brought along.

"Naw, it's fine." He tucked the chairs beneath one arm and hooked a cooler with the other. "The ice is more than thick enough to handle this."

"Even with people parking on it?" she asked, gathering up the few items Rick hadn't already taken. A heavy knit blanket big enough for two people in lawn chairs to share if they sat close enough together. Enough paper plates and bowls to feed the mass of people out on the lake.

"That's a bad idea." Rick followed her line of sight. "The ice is thick enough to handle the weight, as long as they stay close to the shore. Kids get reckless sometimes. Don't worry. We'll make them move. Just stay away from the area past those orange cones. That's where the ice gets thin."

Lana threaded her arm through Rick's as they headed across the ice. "I wasn't worried at all. Not about your ability to handle an unruly teen. I should have brought something to eat though. It seems wrong to go to a potluck and not bring something in a pot."

She'd been fretting about that all morning. She'd fretted her way through fifteen outfits, four different hats, and far too many websites about proper potluck offerings. The result had been cute jeans and a fluffy cream sweater, a lime-green naughty reindeer sock hat, and Rick promising her no one was going to care if all they brought were paper products. There would be chilis and cheese dips to spare.

"Next time, we'll figure out what to bring," Rick told her.

Next time. A flush of warmth filled her chest. He'd said it so easily, as if it was assumed there would be parties after this, and they'd be attending those parties together too. Her fingers gripped his arm tighter, because she knew it wasn't that easy. A holiday fling was one thing. But at some point, Lana would have to go to her other jobs, attend to other accounts, and put out other fires.

Would it be enough, knowing she would be back eventually? Was it wrong to ask him to wait?

Long distance never lasted. Walking away from her family wasn't even on the table and not because of the money. Montgomerys were loyal if nothing else, and loyal to a fault to their own. No. Leaving the company, her career, and everything she'd worked for wasn't an option.

"You okay?" Kind hazel eyes gazed down at her. "No one will give you a hard time. I promise."

The man was sweeter than he realized, and the way he was looking at her made Lana's heart twist in her chest.

"I'm better than perfect." Lana leaned her cheek into his shoulder. Rick flicked the fuzzy ball on the end of her hat.

He'd been in a great mood all day. Apparently, if everyone was out on the water, no one would be interested in playing a game of pool. Besides, the tournament had been a huge—and lucrative— success. By default, he was getting a day off. They'd spent a lovely morning together, in which Rick tried and failed to convince her that trout and toast was a terrible excuse for a breakfast. They'd taken snowmobiles—*snow machines*, if she wanted to be a local— out in a half-hearted attempt to locate the Santa Moose, but they'd spent more time making out and playing in the snow than actually trying to find the animal. Rosy cheeked from the cold and from sheer happiness, Lana succeeded in convincing him that sneaking into the dry sauna was a perfect way to hide from her growing email inbox.

She'd been tempted to steal Rick away for an entire day of only the two of them, but Lana wasn't the type to admit defeat. Instead, she was soldiering on, hoping that a new day might bring new results.

Besides, it was hard to stay discouraged with her hand in Rick's, especially when he kept catching her eye, shooting her smoldering looks. They were lucky the ice was thick on this lake. The growing heat between them was liable to leave them both sloshy messes as they melted right through the ice beneath their feet.

True to his promise, Rick and Ash forced those parking too far out on the ice to move their trucks back to the shore where she'd left her helicopter. When most people arrived in regular vehicles, Ash was going to fly.

Yep, Lana definitely wanted to grow up to be her.

There was something about knowing they were on a giant ice cube that made the party even more fun. She was still getting worried looks, but the hostility had gone down a few noticeable notches, especially when everyone was focused on enjoying themselves.

Zoey and Graham were in their own world...or at least they were attempting to be. Their newly elected mayor was trying very hard not to be in charge, despite constantly having people come up to him, asking for help or advice. In their moments left alone, the couple kept sharing inside jokes and little touches that meant nothing to the people next to them and everything to each other. Easton had settled off to the side, quietly chewing on a sandwich and participating in the activities only when forced. Jake had abandoned them all for Rick, draped in Rick's arm and his tail thumping relentlessly against Rick's shoulder.

"I think the dog in the fedora stole my date," Lana told Ash, watching the pair playing together.

"I think your date doesn't mind." Ash's gaze lingered on Lana, then flickered to Rick. "So you ignored me completely. How's that working out for you?"

"So far, pretty well."

Ash sighed. "You know, when these big lugs get their hearts broken, I always have to drag their drunk sorry asses into a snowbank to sober them up."

"What if I end up the drunk one with the broken heart?" Lana asked wryly.

With a chuckle, Ash pulled a pack of cigarettes out of her pocket. "I suppose snowbanks work for all of us." Catching the look Lana gave the cigarettes, Ash rolled her eyes. "I don't need another person telling me what's bad for me."

"If I call you a hypocrite, you'll probably beat me up, huh?"

This time, Ash laughed. "Touché. And I suppose there are worse things than a holiday fling," Ash said.

"You should see him in a skintight Santa suit."

Ash shuddered. "Rick's like my brother. I really shouldn't." Her expression suddenly turned serious. "Lana? Is that—?"

Lana followed Ash's gaze, then her heart dropped somewhere in the vicinity of her knees. "Get help," she said.

Without thinking, Lana began to run.

Rick didn't know what was happening—only that someone had started to shout, followed by people rushing past the bonfire.

"What's going on?" he demanded of Zoey, the one person going the opposite direction.

"I'm calling for an ambulance," she yelled back over her shoulder. "Someone fell through the ice."

Meaning if they got them out in time, the swimmer would need to go immediately to the hospital. *If.* The water temperature was only slightly above freezing beneath the surface of the lake. Running fast on ice wasn't easy, and people were slipping and falling as they converged toward the east side of the lake, the side everyone knew not to go onto.

The ice was too thin for everyone to go farther, leaving only a few of them reckless enough to head for the figures in the distance.

"Who is it?" he yelled to Easton, then Rick's heart sank to his stomach as he saw a shock of multicolored hair and a figure kneeling where the ice had broken.

"Ash, get away from there!" Easton yelled. The ice creaked under Easton's feet as he started to cross to his sister.

"Stay back," Ash called back. "Graham, get my rope. They're in the water!"

They.

They.

Rick's heart knew it before his eyes found her in the broken circle where ice gave way to slushy water. That lime-green Christmas knit hat soaked and slipping sideways.

"Lana!" Before he knew what he was doing, Rick had cried out her name, ripping his arm free of whoever held him back.

Ash was dangerously close to tumbling in herself, stretching as far as she could to try to reach Lana's hand. And within the water, fighting against the bobbing ice chucks, was the woman he loved. He didn't know if she was a strong swimmer, but with one arm clinging to an ice chunk and another trying to hold a sobbing eight-year-old above the water, Lana wasn't going to last long.

"Someone call Jonah," Rick yelled to the crowd behind him. "It's Daniel."

Daniel was Jonah's second-youngest son, and he must have snuck away from the watchful eyes of his mother. Jonah's wife, Kelly, cried out in terror. She pushed her infant daughter into

Frankie's arms, darting out across the ice, but Diego caught her, pulling her back.

"Take him," Lana said through chattering teeth, trying to push Daniel close enough for Ash to reach.

Lana was already turning blue, and the ice beneath Ash's knees was pooling with water, about to break. The cracking of ice beneath them was a bad, bad sign. She shoved Daniel closer, just enough for Ash's fingers to hook his jacket hood, then the ice beneath Ash gave way. Rick grabbed for Ash, and Easton grabbed for him, a human chain managing to pull the child out of the water and onto the dubious safety of the ice.

Pushing the duo into Easton's hands, Rick abandoned them for the woman still in the water. Lana was holding onto an ice chunk, but her grip was slipping.

"Rick, don't," Easton snapped, but he wasn't going to wait. Shrugging out of his jacket and kicking off his shoes, Rick dove into the water.

He'd only have a short chance to help her before the ice water stole his strength too. But he knew Graham was going for a rope, and Ash always kept one in her helicopter.

The water was like a punch to the stomach, so cold he cursed. Four seconds to swim to her, two to lock his arm around her, getting a hold on the slipped ice chunk and hauling them both higher out of the water.

"I've got you," Rick promised.

"Who's got you?" Lana asked, breathless and chattering.

"Easton has us both. Look at me, sweetheart. Don't be scared."

He was terrified, but when those liquid pools turned his way,

Rick knew he would jump every single damn time. His arms shook as the cold stole his strength, along with his breath.

"Rick, grab the rope!"

Easton's yell was barely audible over the rushing of blood in his ears. Then the rope splashed into the water next to him, giving him something to grab onto as Easton and Graham hauled them out of the water.

The entire group slipped and slid on the ice, scrambling to get back to the safer, thicker surface of the lake.

Lana was a shivery, blue-tinged version of herself, but adrenaline must have kept her moving as she reached for him. Shaking, icy hands pushed at him frantically.

"Are you okay?" she demanded, her eyes wide in concern.

"I'm fine," Rick said with a grunt. "Your clothes are soaking wet. Socks, shoes, pants. You need to get them off before you get even colder." She blinked at him, uncomprehending. "Lana, you're freezing and in wet clothes. You have to get them off."

They herded her across the ice and toward the shore where someone had already started a car, the heater on blast. Lana protested when Rick all but shoved her inside.

"You're going to freeze standing out there," she said through chattering teeth, trying to tug him inside with her. But Rick was more concerned with taking the spare clothes from Ash's arms.

"I had some extras behind the seat," Ash said, jutting her head toward the helicopter. "But they won't fit her well."

"Is the child okay?"

Rick glanced over to where Graham had taken charge, ordering everyone to stay back and give Daniel and his mother room. A natural leader, he might not have been sworn in yet as mayor—that was supposed to happen after the holidays— but Graham was exactly the person to keep everyone calm in a crisis.

He'd been the perfect choice to take care of the town.

The sound of sirens in the distance answered Lana's question, which was good, because Rick wasn't leaving her to go find out more information. "The ambulance is almost here. I don't know how long Daniel was in the water, but I can see that he's crying, which is a good sign. You saved his life."

"Ash saved him." Lana's words were hard to understand, she was shaking so badly. "She's the one who saw him."

When it was clear her hands weren't working well enough to manage her shoelaces, Rick helped her. Peeling half-frozen slacks off her mile-long legs was not nearly as sexy as his daydreams, but she gave him a tight, appreciative smile when he helped her pull on a pair of Ash's snow pants.

"What about you?" Lana asked.

"I wasn't in the water as long," he told her as he shrugged out of his own wet clothes, taking whatever was pushed at him.

Lana was an ice cube by the time the ambulance got there. Kelly was sobbing in relief, cradling Daniel close in the warmth of her own car.

"Don't fall asleep," he warned as Lana leaned her head against the window.

She didn't answer him, and she wouldn't look at him, but at least her eyes were open.

"Lana, the ambulance is here. You need to go with them."

When he reached for her to help her from the car, Lana pulled out of Rick's hands.

"I'm fine." She tried for her trademark breezy tone, but it fell flat between her chattering teeth. "No hospitals. Can you take me to the resort?"

"Bullshit," Ash said, returning to the car. She watched as Lana scooted across the seat toward the door. "You need to go get checked."

Yes, that was exactly what Lana needed to do. But instead of agreeing, she shook her head in a tight jerking motion, once more refusing Rick's help as she decided to get out of the car instead. He didn't know how she was still standing, but her back was straight and her chin high, every inch the woman who made boardrooms sit up and take notice.

"Jonah was helping Fish and Game with a problem moose near Girdwood, but he's on his way. Garcia and his partner are headed here to help." Ash turned to Lana. "Jonah's pretty upset, but he radioed Easton and told him to tell you he's grateful to you for saving his little boy."

She didn't say anything, instead just standing there, shivering. The paramedics were still focused on Daniel, but Graham was pointing to the car Lana and Rick were next to. Ash frowned.

"She might be able to ignore them, but Jonah isn't going to take no for an answer. He'll make her go to the hospital."

"Lana, let us help you," Rick said softly. When she opened her mouth to protest through blue-tinged lips, he added, "I get it, okay? If you show one ounce of weakness, the town jumps on you. But after today, no one is going to treat you that way."

She watched Kelly press Daniel into the paramedic's arms. "Thank you for jumping in with me." Lana finally added in a whisper, "I've never been that cold in my life."

His instincts told him she needed a place to hide before she'd consent to a checkup, so Rick slipped his arm around her waist. Kelly shot Lana a quick, desperately grateful look before climbing into the front seat of the ambulance. Rick didn't know if Lana saw it.

More and more people gathered in as those on the lake came to see what they could do to help.

"Hey," Ash told Rick, watching Lana shift away from the growing crowd. "Are you good to drive?"

"Yeah."

"Then get her out of here. She looks ready to bolt."

"She can barely stand." Rick growled in frustration. Ash wasn't wrong. Far from wanting to celebrate her bravery, Lana looked like a cornered animal.

"Come on," Rick said in her ear. "You at least need a hot bath to warm you up."

Lana allowed him to herd her back to her SUV where he turned the heater on full blast. It would take more than a few minutes in a car to take away the chill. He drove off, wondering if he should ignore her request and drive her to the hospital anyway. She didn't seem to be suffering from hypothermia, but Rick didn't want to be wrong and have Lana pay the price.

Her fingers shook as she pulled out her phone. "I have a conference call scheduled. I need to cancel...the reception here isn't good enough...*dammit*."

Of course the reception sucked. No one's phone would work on this road, and if that made her miss a work call, then so be it. Rick would feel guilty about that tomorrow, but he didn't care now. Lana wasn't the only one with shaking hands.

"Lana. I'm the last person in the world with the right to tell you what to do. But I am the guy with his guts in his throat because I almost lost you today. I need a minute, baby. Thirty seconds, even, just to breathe. Fifteen where I don't have to share you." Rick inhaled a rough breath. "Hell, I'd take five seconds of hugging you and telling you everything's okay."

"If I let you hug me, I'm going to fall apart. I can't, Rick."

"Is that why you won't go to the hospital? You don't want anyone to see you upset?" When she didn't answer, staring out the window, a growl of sheer protectiveness escaped his lips. "You think I'd let anyone say shit to you? You think they would after you saved that little boy? Lana, you don't know us at all. You don't know me at all."

"I know I don't belong."

She belonged with him. Rick almost said it, but the words caught on his tongue. Memories of her—eyes wide with fear but arms bravely holding Daniel out of the water—made his heart hurt in his chest.

"Give us a chance, Lana." Give him a chance. Except there was no way. Even now, when she slipped her fingers inside his, Rick knew he didn't have a chance to keep her forever.

The truth didn't make him want her one single bit less.

"I don't know," she said. "I don't know what I'm doing anymore. It's all so jumbled."

Everything wasn't jumbled for Rick. For him, it was all crystal freaking clear. He'd fallen for a woman he couldn't have forever. But he had her right now. So Rick didn't hug her, but he did hold her hand, those perfect fingers icy cold in his larger, rough ones. He got it. He knew what it was like to do everything in his power not to fall apart when a moment of kindness was all it took to bring the paper-thin walls of outer strength crashing down.

By the time they reached his place, Rick was barely looking at the road, so focused on watching her pale skin still a worrying tinge of blue.

"This isn't the hotel," she said through chattering teeth.

"You need a real bed, under a real roof," he grunted as he parked under the carport. "But I'll charge you too much for a cup of tea if you want."

Rick hovered behind her shoulder as she got out and headed wearily up the porch, her movements slow, as if the water had stolen her strength.

A slight exhalation of relief left her lips as Rick held the door open for her, letting her inside.

He and Diego hadn't expected company, so the ever-present cereal box was still on the table, and he hadn't taken out the trash. A rinsed stack of bowls and spoons had yet to be cleaned.

"Would you mind if I made some tea?" Lana's voice was strained. "I'm not feeling all that well."

Halfway between the front door and the kitchen, her legs quit working. Rick was ready for it, having watched what little color was left in her face drain away the last couple of miles of the drive.

He caught her, his arm around her waist keeping her on her

feet even as she sagged. Lana was a proud woman, and she tried to pull away. "I'm really fine, love. I promise."

"You promise, huh?" he said gruffly. This time, he didn't ask. Instead, he scooped her up into his arms, cradling her protectively to his chest. "No offense, but I'm not buying it."

She'd get her tea, but he'd be getting it for her. First, he needed to warm her up. The fireplace in the living room didn't work half as well as the woodburning stove in the bedroom. Setting her down on the oversize chair he liked to read in on cold winter nights, Rick stripped the bed of its coverings and brought them to her, wrapping Lana up as tightly as he could. Then he worked on getting the stove going, feeding it small sticks of kindling until it started to roar with heat.

At her murmured thanks, Rick headed into the kitchen and fixed her the tea she'd asked for. By the time he returned, she'd snuggled into his blankets so deeply, only her eyes and nose were visible.

Since Lana's toes were tucked beneath her, Rick sat on the ottoman, arms resting on his knees as he faced her. She was still wearing his jacket, and only now did he realize he was pretty cold himself. Nothing worth mentioning, but still. The heat from the fire felt good on his shoulder. And when his hands had warmed enough, he took her still ice-cold ones in his own, helping her steady the shaking as she drank her tea.

"Do you want another cup?" he asked, watching her drain the mug like it wasn't burning hot on her tongue.

"Thank you. Are you mad?" At his raised eyebrow, Lana said, "You seem mad at me."

"I'm not. I'm mad at me."

This time, she was the one to raise an eyebrow.

"I promised I wouldn't let anything bad happen to you today," he said tightly. "Instead, I wasn't by your side when you needed me."

"I'm pretty sure I remember you jumping in the water too."

"Only because my incredibly brave date jumped first." Holding her hands and her gaze, Rick told her in a quiet voice, "You saved someone today, Lana. I am so incredibly proud of you, I can't see straight. But I'm ready to drag you to the hospital at the first sign of a sneeze."

"Don't worry, dearest. Montgomerys never sneeze." She offered him a sweet, tired smile. "Now where are we on that second cup of tea?"

She was roasting alive.

At some time in the night, cold had turned to comfy and comfy to warm. They were way past the point of warm, and Lana could feel sweat beading down between her shoulder blades, along her spine, and behind her knees.

"I'm stuck." That came out far more plaintive than she'd intended.

Rick had been dozing next to her chair, his voice husky with sleep as he woke and helped her pull away the top blanket. "I had to make sure you didn't go back to work."

"I'm a person lasagna. Too many layers."

"I don't know," he rumbled. "I've always kind of liked lasagna."

"Even when lasagna was being stubborn?"

"Especially when lasagna was being stubborn." His strong hands slid into her hair, now damp from sweat. "It's my favorite part about lasagna."

Oh. Well, that was nice.

"Thank you again for saving me," Lana said softly. "You jumped in the water for me."

"You jumped in the water for us," he reminded her gently. She could see him hesitate, but the words he always kept inside for the first time came to his tongue. "I thought I was going to lose you. It would take a hell of a lot more than a cold swim to stop me."

"She had no idea what she left, did she? Your ex was insane."

His jaw rippled, and then he brushed his thumb down the side of her cheek in wordless question. Lana leaned in, because she didn't think she could find it in herself to stay strong anymore.

Whatever this was, it had always burned hotter than a stove and too many blankets. But the heat was more than what she could handle right then. Somehow, he understood, and when Rick lifted her into his arms, carrying her to the blanket-stripped bed, the look in his eyes tempered that fire.

It had been so long, and it had been for him too. Lana didn't know what she'd expected, but when he reached for her, she had already reached for him. In the darkness of a room lit only by the stove's glowing embers, Lana closed her eyes and finally found peace.

CHAPTER 14

FOR THE FIRST TIME IN a long time, Rick didn't wake up in his bed alone.

Half of the bed wasn't cold. His arms weren't empty. A knee was dangerously close to his groin. He wasn't sure what had roused him, but the clock on the nightstand said it was only five in the morning. Memories of the night before swirled through Rick's head, leaving him wondering if he was in some sort of waking dream. Maybe if he opened his eyes, he'd wake up and realize he couldn't possibly be this lucky. Maybe if he held still, the weight of her head pressed to his bicep wouldn't suddenly disappear.

But the reality was, somehow, he'd gotten his dream girl. And he was a fool if he didn't at least take a little peek through one eye to commit this to memory.

"Morning." Lana's voice was thick with sleep, her own eyes still closed.

"It's still early." Rick shifted as she snuggled in, his body instinctively making a place for her to burrow. "You can go back to sleep."

She hummed in distinctive feminine appreciation, her cold

fingers finding a nice warm spot along his side to tuck into. And yes, maybe that was somewhat hard to ignore, but he'd take cold Lana fingers versus no cold Lana fingers any day of the week.

Even as she fell back into a light snooze, Rick tried to think of anything he could do to make this happen again. Nope. Not a thing. He'd literally botched them up from the very beginning, from the atrocious first date to not being by her side yesterday when she'd jumped into the lake. Rick was on overload, overwhelmed by everything about her. Respect and desire and sheer freaking relief. That was what she made him feel. Like he was drowning, and she was that first desperate gasp of air. An invisible weight he hadn't realized he'd been carrying on his shoulders was tossed aside somewhere between the chair and his bed.

Rick never wanted to pick that weight back up again.

"You're not sleeping," Lana said into his chest. "Do you want me to leave?"

Her question took him off guard. "Do you want to leave?"

"I don't know. Depends on how upset you look when I open my eyes."

Running his hand down her side, Rick found himself smiling. "Is that why you won't look at me?"

"No."

"Really?"

"Maybe."

Cradling her close, Rick kissed her, a long, slow kiss. "Sweetheart, I don't want you going *anywhere*."

A single eye opened as if to secretly check. It had made sense when he was afraid of this not being real. But in what universe would she need to worry? Rick rolled over onto his back, drawing her across his chest, her hair falling across his neck and jaw.

"Trust me, the last thing I am right now is upset."

He wasn't used to insecurity from her, but he could guess where it was coming from. It wasn't as if he'd made his bedroom welcoming for anyone new to walk in there.

Heck, his ex's clothes were still in the drawers, and the bedding was still lavender and gray, her choices.

"What was she like?" Lana asked quietly, as if reading his mind.

Rick's eyebrow rose. "You really want to talk about my ex?"

"She was a big part of you. Besides, you've got that same expression on your face you always get when you're thinking about her."

That was bad. Extra bad. He was the absolute worst. Which was why he had no idea why Lana was grinning at him.

"I'm trained to read facial expressions," Lana reassured him. "It's a boardroom game I learned as a child. And I'm not jealous. This was new for you, and if you want to talk about her, I'm okay with that. I don't expect you not to have feelings."

Sighing, Rick closed his eyes, allowing himself to take a long, steadying breath.

"I have feelings," he said. "A little guilt, even though it's ridiculous. Jen's remarried and living in Seattle. I have nothing to feel guilty for."

"Divorce isn't something people get over easily." Lana's hand rubbed a soothing circle over his chest. "It takes time."

"I think if she'd been awful, it wouldn't have hurt the way

it did. She was good, and she was kind, but she didn't love me the way I loved her. Moose Springs wasn't right for her anymore, so she let me go the nicest way she knew how. No dragged-out divorce, no fighting over what we had. All she wanted was to be free."

His voice quieted on the last word, so much that he'd be surprised if Lana could hear him.

"I'd loved her a long time. Tried my best to make things work, even when they weren't. It wasn't until we were standing there with the attorneys that I realized after her sister died, she just needed to get out."

"Did you ever tell her that?"

Rick sighed, rolling back to rest on the pillow, staring up at the ceiling. "She wanted to be left alone. I couldn't make her happy, but at least I could give her that."

His arm was still looped around her waist, so Lana wriggled until she could rest her chin on his broad chest. "Were you happy?"

It took him a long time to answer. Then Rick sighed again, deeper this time. He threaded his fingers into her hair, sitting up enough that he could kiss her. A long, slow kiss that had her arm tightening around his waist.

"I thought I was," he said. "But that was before a woman in a dead sexy dress looked me in the eyes and told me to put on a Santa suit two sizes too small."

"It was a really good look on you." She sighed at the memory.

"That remains to be seen, gorgeous."

Lana snugged in closer. "Does it bother you? Lying in her bed with me?"

"It stopped being her bed a long time ago. It's mine. And no, it doesn't. Does it bother you?"

"That you're divorced? Only that you think you did something wrong. I didn't know you then, but the man I know now...I can't imagine it."

Rick ran a hand over her hair. "We grew apart. I didn't want to see it."

"And now?"

"Now I want to be happy." Taking her in, Rick added softly, "And I'm happiest when you're happy."

Lana sat up, eyes sparkling in the low glow of the woodburning stove. "I want you to be happy too," she said. "So what do you want to do today that will make you happy?"

Rick stretched out, wiggling into the bedding to make himself more comfortable. "Pretty sure this is about as good as it gets for me, gorgeous," he told her. He ran a thumb down her side. "Besides, you need to stay warm and dry today. You had a dunking yesterday. We really should have gone to the doctor."

"I'm right as rain." Lana dipped her head and kissed him. "Not a sniffle in sight."

"If I catch wind of a single sniff, you and I are heading straight for the hospital. This is not going to be a pneumonia Christmas."

She made the cutest face at him, causing Rick to chuckle and pull her back down to join him. Slow, luxurious kisses in the morning were something he could get used to.

"You know...it *is* two days before Christmas," she mulled, just as he was thinking of staying right where they were forever.

"And?"

"And I have a Santa Moose still on the loose."

Well...in that case...

———————

They could have been in bed. They could have been cuddled up in front of the living room fire, eating cinnamon rolls at Frankie's, or drinking hot chocolate at Dirty Joe's. But no. Rick had to be dressed head to toe in a skintight Santa costume for the second time that week.

"I don't see how this is going to help," he told her, grimacing down at himself.

"My initial plans fell through, and now I have to think outside the box. Besides, you look darling."

"Really? *Darling?*"

She laughed at the expression on his face. "Handsome. Very masculine and sexy. They'll make a movie about Santas like you one day."

He stole her hand, pressing a kiss to her wrist.

"You do realize that I'm a complete sucker for you, right? I would never in a hundred years do this of my own accord."

"I know," Lana said, voice softening as she leaned into him. "The feeling is mutual, dearest."

It felt a little wrong to be making out like this dressed as he was, especially when his snowy Santa beard kept tickling her chin and making her giggle.

So Rick settled in to lure a moose, trying not to be nervous about the fact that Lana had a tranquilizer gun in her hands once again, hiding out in the bushes, waiting.

He tried to stay patient, but there was only so long he could sit out on a stump, trying to look festive.

"This isn't working," he told her.

"Sing a Christmas carol." Her whispered suggestion only horrified him a little. It was possible Rick was starting to get used to all this.

It was even more possible that he liked it.

"What do you want for Christmas?" he asked her instead, taking out his phone and turning on his downloaded holiday-themed music.

"A present isn't necessary, love." She hummed from her hiding spot behind a large clump of blackberry bushes. "I appreciate the classics, but this moose seems more of a contemporary creature."

He dutifully switched over from Bing Crosby to Mariah Carey. "Is the beard really necessary?" Rick asked, tugging on the scratchy thing.

"I doubt the moose will be fooled without it," Lana piped up. "This seems to be an above-average-intelligence animal."

"I'm getting you something for Christmas," he said. "If you don't give me any ideas, I'll have to wing it, and no one wants that." Hearing a giggle from the bushes warmed his heart, even if his hands were cold. "How do you feel about hedgehog-themed ugly Christmas sweaters?"

"If you're trying to turn me on, it's working," she said.

If only. Memories of the previous night curled through his mind, leaving him warm all over, even his hands. She had felt so perfect against him, sleeping with her nose pressed into his bicep. And yes, the sex had been great, but waking up like that?

With Lana in his arms? That feeling blew everything else out of the water.

"I care about you," Rick said to the woods, because it was true. Because she needed to hear it more than in the middle of the night, when he was reaching for her.

Vulnerability wasn't his thing, but neither was luring moose in Santa suits. He'd do more than this to make her know she was cared for, that the things that mattered to her mattered to him too.

The only reason she was out there was to try to make people happy.

"I'll stay out here until New Year's," he added calmly. "Just know that you don't have to do this. People can think whatever they want to. I know you. I know you care about us. There's nothing you have to be forgiven for."

Silence, then he heard a rustling in the bushes, followed by his absolutely perfect snowlady in her winter camouflage ghillie suit emerging from the woods.

Lana joined him on the stump, her hip pressed to his. "Do you really think so?" Lana asked softly.

"I know so." Finding her within the ghillie suit's fronds wasn't easy. But it was kind of fun.

"I care about you too, Rick. So very much." Those liquid dark eyes pooled with sincerity. There was a time he'd never have believed it. But he believed it now.

Life had never felt this good.

His phone beeped with a text message. "Sorry, Lana. Your quarry hit the Lockett property."

"Is everyone okay?"

"Graham says its pandemonium. Whatever that means."
Standing from his stump, Rick stretched. "We probably should
get over there."

————————

"I didn't know what was happening." Ash sounded a little dazed.
"I was out on the porch, checking my email, and then boom.
Something was attacking the lights."

On the front yard of the Lockett family home, several tall,
very attractive people were gathered, gazing up at the destruction
done to the porch in front of them.

In the midst of them was tiny little Zoey, her pocket notebook
out as she took charge of the situation, rapidly scribbling down
notes. "Something attacked lights. Can you be more specific?"

"Specific?" Ash tilted her head in confusion, vibrant hair
catching the low sunlight.

Yep, these were definitely some attractive people all squished
together in front of a backdrop of pristine snowdrifts beneath rich
evergreens. If Lana were to make a flyer for Moose Springs to
entice people to come look at her condos, this was the picture
she'd use.

"Were they blinking lights or nonblinking lights? What color
coordination?"

Ash looked over at Easton for help, where the massive man
was nudging a broken porch rail with his gloved fist. "Umm...
blinking? I think?"

"They were blinking," Easton grunted. "Red, green, blue,
white pattern, small outdoor bulbs."

"Small...outdoor...bulbs." Zoey finished scribbling in her notebook and turned to Lana. "What do you think it means?"

"What do *you* think it means?" Graham asked Zoey, sounding amused.

"I think it means the Santa Moose is establishing a pattern. It seems to be triggered by the brightest light combinations, high-pitched Christmas carols, and life-size decorations. The moose definitely has a thing against the larger holiday decor."

"Like Rick over there?" Easton wondered.

"I was wondering if anyone was going to mention that," Graham said to Ash.

Lana shifted in front of him. "We were moose luring. When one tries to capture a sadistic holiday scrooge, one must use the tools at one's disposal."

"One can also admit when one looks stupid, sweetheart," Rick said in her ear, looping an arm around Lana's waist. He pressed a kiss to her cheek. "Can I take the beard off yet?"

"If the moose is close, you may be our best chance at finally nabbing it."

Graham jutted his head at the porch, then at Lana. "What's your plan?"

Zoey actually growled. "Graham, it's not her responsibility. If she wants to find the moose, she'll find it. But don't you put pressure on her."

Instead of teasing her in reply, Graham grinned. "Yes, ma'am."

"Besides, you're the mayor now. Isn't it your job to do something about the Santa Moose?"

Graham blinked. "Me?"

"Lana and I have nothing to prove to you or everyone else in this town. We are perfectly fine how we are."

"Zo—"

"Not finished." She continued to scribble in her notebook. "But just because we don't *need* to catch this moose doesn't mean we aren't one hundred percent capable of doing so. This is for us, not you. So hush. I'm sure you have all these witty things to say, but I'm working."

Everyone suddenly grew very quiet, startled and staring behind Zoey.

"Here's what we're going to do." Zoey held up the game plan she'd drawn. "Lana, we're going to need some spaghetti. No, hear me out on this."

Lana's breath caught, not hearing a word her friend was saying.

"Hey, Zo?" Graham said gently. "I know you're busy, but I can't wait anymore, darlin'."

Zoey turned around and saw what the rest of them were seeing. Graham had knelt on one knee in the snow, a ring box in his hand.

"I wanted to ask you on Christmas Eve," Graham told her. "Jake has a special outfit. It was supposed to be a thing. But I can't..."

He cleared his throat, and for the first time since they'd met as children, Lana saw Graham at a loss for words.

"Zo, you're just...and I can't..."

The poor man was completely overcome. Lana reached for Rick's hand, unconscious of the action until his fingers tightened around hers.

"Need some help there, buddy?" Easton asked kindly.

Graham shook his head. "I can do this," he said. "I want to do this."

He wanted to, but it was clear he was fighting back tears. Graham was not the kind of person to let people see him cry, and keeping those tears away was causing his shoulders to shake with the effort of containing his emotions.

Zoey knelt in front of him, taking Graham's hands in hers. "Graham Barnett. You have made me so happy from the moment I walked into the Tourist Trap," she told him with a watery smile.

"That was my line," Graham told her, voice cracking despite his curving lips.

"And every day since has only been better."

"My line too."

"I love you, and I can't imagine spending a day without you at my side. You and me and Jake. Our family."

"You're really good at this," Graham said in a low, rough voice.

"So if you're going to ask me, it's okay. You already know what I'm going to say." Zoey pressed a kiss to his rough knuckles. "Also, it's really cold down here."

"Dammit," he groaned. "I love you."

Wrapping her up in his arms, Graham whispered something into her ear, something Lana couldn't hear. Immediate tears filled Zoey's eyes, but she was smiling too as she nodded. Another whisper, more words that were for them and them alone. This time, Zoey was bawling as she choked out a yes.

Then Graham put the ring box in her hand. Zoey gasped as she opened it and saw what was inside. A sparkling diamond set in a hand-carved cedar band, decorated with delicate images of the forest and mountains of Moose Springs.

"Did you carve this?" Zoey asked, eyes huge.

Graham nodded, wiping at her tears and keeping her tucked close. "Do you like it?"

"This is *perfect*."

The couple finally seemed to realize they had witnesses to their engagement, and they turned. Lana had managed to keep herself contained until the moment Zoey looked at her, holding up the ring box.

"Lana, we're engaged!" Zoey said, as if she couldn't believe it herself. With a squeal of delight, Lana closed the distance between them and flung her arms around Zoey.

The others gathered in to congratulate the couple.

"You can put it on," Graham said into Zoey's ear. "I did make it for you."

"I'm afraid I'll drop it. What if it falls off my finger? What if I ruin our happily ever after? I have really slim fingers. No, it's staying in the box."

"What if you lose the box?" Graham countered.

At her worried look, Graham took the box from her hands and carefully slid the engagement ring onto Zoey's finger.

"It won't slip off." He glanced over at Lana. "L helped me size it right."

"You knew?"

"Dearest, everyone knew the night he met you." Lana was feeling a bit misty-eyed herself. "I told him your ring size the day you decided to stay in Moose Springs."

Lana turned to Graham, and to her pleasure, he squeezed her in a hug so tight, he lifted her off her feet. Setting her down, Graham kept an arm around Lana's shoulders.

"Thank you for bringing her up here," Graham told her. "I met the love of my life because of you."

"Zoey brought herself here," Lana assured him. "She would have found this place eventually. I was lucky enough to be here when she did."

"Yeah, me too." He squeezed her shoulders. "How are you? You took a dip in an ice bucket yesterday."

"I'm fine. Not even a sniffle. Rick's been taking good care of me."

Graham followed her line of sight to where Rick was standing with Easton.

"He's a good guy. Being around you has made him a lot happier than I've seen him in years. Let me know if he causes you any trouble. I'm happy to play protective big brother anytime you want."

They shared a grin.

"Thank you, but I can't imagine him doing a thing wrong," Lana told him. "Actually, since I have your ear, I was wondering if I could talk to you. Not now, obviously."

Sighing dramatically, he leaned into her. "You're going to make me do actual mayor things, aren't you? On my engagement day. You're so mean to me. They haven't even sworn me in yet."

"Oh, no one will care if a few formalities are skipped. I only want a little meeting to talk about some things we can both do for Moose Springs. I'm thinking Jonah desperately needs a day off and some help."

Chuckling, he pressed a swift kiss to her temple. "All right, darlin'. Only because I love you."

He ambled away to rejoin his friends, steal a kiss from his fiancée, and wrap Zoey up in his arms. Knowing those two, they wouldn't be letting go of each other anytime soon. Standing off to the side, Lana watched them celebrate. Four friends…five now that Zoey was officially one of them.

Rick came up to her, his Santa beard now tucked into his coat pocket.

"You belong here," Rick said in her ear. "With them. You're part of their family too."

She wanted to believe him. Large, fat snowflakes were falling, dusting his shoulders, and he looked so cute in the Santa costume, Lana wrapped her arms around his waist.

"This is the best Christmas I've ever had," Lana told him. "I know it's two days away, but still…"

Those hazel eyes had lightened to a shade of green she'd only seen last night.

Taking her face in his hands, Rick kissed her, a long, slow kiss that made Ash start gagging in the background. He kissed her again, mouth lingering. "You're gorgeous."

Lana started to reply she had nothing on his Santa-ed self, but he added, "You are, inside and out, and braver than anyone I've ever met. You've taken on the Santa Moose."

"The Santa Moose isn't that scary. Elusive but not scary. I've completely failed at catching it so far."

"The Santa Moose is terrifying." He pressed the softest of kisses behind her ear. "And I know you'll catch it."

Lips curving, he drew her deeper into his arms. Lana really didn't care when her phone started to chirp in her back pocket, but when it went to voicemail, she checked the caller ID.

"It's my parents' home," she told him. "My mother's office line. They have to be the only people still living with more than one landline."

Lana answered when her phone started to ring again. "This is about the worst time possible," she said as Rick pressed another kiss to her neck, then her collarbone. "I promise to call you tomorrow on Christmas Eve, Mom. But I decided to stay in Moose Springs for Christmas this year."

"Lana, you need to come home." Jessica's voice was sharp with the kind of tension she never let anyone see. "It's Killian. There's been an accident."

CHAPTER 15

FLYING WASN'T NEW TO RICK. He'd travelled plenty in his semipro days and more than a couple of trips to see his parents. Flying in a chartered jet from Anchorage to Chicago on a moment's notice? That was definitely new.

Rick had packed a bag without even asking if she wanted him to go with her. He knew how much she loved her cousin, and from what Rick could tell, Killian was in bad shape.

Like…really bad.

He'd gone through this before, and Rick's heart was breaking for Lana. He didn't want her to lose someone she loved. But if she did, she wasn't going to go through the trauma alone. So he had boarded the plane with her, holding her hand as they flew directly to O'Hare. He kept her hand on the ride to the hospital.

Only when they stepped into the lobby did she let go, shifting the slightest bit away from his shoulder.

Lana kept her head held high as they walked through the hospital, her face a mask of dispassionate professionalism that didn't match the caring, passionate woman he knew at all. The clicking of her heels on the floor seemed louder than normal, grating on

Rick's senses if only for the fact that she had changed into them on the plane. As if Lana felt she *had* to wear heels to the hospital.

"Are you sure you want to come in?" Lana asked him as they reached the elevators. "My aunt says that Killian's hard to look at."

"I'm not going anywhere," Rick said, respecting the extra inch she'd put between them. The instant she needed him, he'd close that distance faster than she could blink. "Are you sure we're allowed in ICU? I thought only one family member at a time."

At least that was how it had been after Diego barely survived his own family's car crash as a teenager.

"The Montgomery name is on the side of the building. They've been letting us back in pairs."

Two people were in the hall outside the hospital room, a man and a woman familiar to Rick from the pool hall, but he didn't know them personally.

"Those are Killian's best friends. My mother said they were there when he crashed," Lana explained before stepping up to the pair. "Enzo, Haleigh. How is he?"

"Killian woke up finally." Haleigh's eyes were red rimmed, and her mascara had smeared from tears. "He's upset."

"What do you expect?" Enzo snapped at her. "He's paralyzed."

"They don't know that. And at least he's not dead."

The two began to argue about whether or not Killian would survive his crash, their voices rising and falling, pulling glares from the nurse's station.

"I don't know what he sees in either of you," Lana said with unusual sharpness. "If you're intent on making a scene, please do so somewhere else."

Ignoring their offended expressions, Lana brushed past them and entered the room. Rick didn't know where he would be most helpful—tossing these two out of the hospital for her or following her.

He chose to follow her.

The astringent scent of chemicals hit his nostrils, combined with sweat and urine. Rick tried to ignore all the wires and the IV running from the machines behind him into Killian's arms and torso, and the plastic tube leading to a catheter bag hanging on the edge of the bed. If the substantial bruising and lacerations on Killian's face and arms didn't clue him in to how hurt Lana's cousin was, the blood in his urine was a bad sign.

Rick had known Killian was badly hurt. It wasn't until that moment that it occurred to Rick that Killian might die.

One eye was swollen closed, the other opened a slit. Killian's voice was so hoarse, Rick wouldn't have recognized him. "I know. I look great, don't I? A real Harrison Ford."

"Nonsense," Lana said calmly, sitting at his side. "Harrison Ford never had anything on you."

His right eye opened a little more at Lana's voice. "I was hoping I would get to see you."

"Nothing could have stopped me." Lana took his hand. "What happened?"

"It's a long story." Killian shifted, an expression of pain creasing his features. "The morphine isn't doing much anymore. They won't give me more."

"I'll talk to them." Lana started to rise, but Killian grasped her hand tighter, holding on.

"Don't leave. Please."

Sinking back into her seat, Lana nodded, her eyes watery. "I'm not going anywhere. Is your mother here?"

"They sedated her. She's very upset."

"We're all upset, dearest," Lana said. "But stay positive. You're too strong for some silly car crash to take you down."

Killian tried to smile, but it wasn't easy. Not when so much of him had been injured. "The doctors are politely saying I'm dying. Something about internal bleeding. I've never done it before, but I *think* this is what it feels like. Dying has to be better than listening to those two out there."

Haleigh and Enzo had started screaming at each other out in the hall, causing Lana to turn and frown.

"Rick? Would you mind?" she asked.

"Gladly." Rick turned on his heel and strode to the door.

His intervention wasn't necessary, however much he wanted to grab the two by the scruffs of their necks and toss them both into the elevator. Security had already been called. Rick waited until a protesting Enzo and a crying Haleigh were escorted out of ICU.

When Rick slipped back in, Killian's eyes were closed. Lana still held his hand tightly in her own.

"He fell back asleep." Her voice cracked. "I promised him I would stay."

"Then we'll stay," Rick said quietly.

"Last night, everything seemed so perfect. Was it only twenty-four hours ago?"

"Seems like a lifetime, doesn't it?" There wasn't another chair, but Rick was fine settling down on his heels at her side, holding Lana's hand as she held Killian's.

For thirty-six minutes, they listened to him breathe. Then they watched him stop.

Of all the things Lana had witnessed in her life, watching her cousin have shock paddles pressed to his chest had been among the worst. Even now, she could hear the monitors flatlining.

The skilled doctors and nurses had revived him, but they'd insisted family leave the room. Donors or not, they would have to wait in the waiting room like everyone else.

Lana's aunt Rebecca was a mess, but for once, Silas was being helpful. He'd let her lean on him, keeping an arm tight around the sobbing woman as they waited for her husband's transcontinental flight to land.

Attempting to console her aunt was futile, not that Lana blamed Rebecca for being so upset. In the end, all Lana could do was hold Rebecca's hand. Every so often, a heavy palm rested on her shoulder, squeezing gently, reminding Lana that Rick was there with her. No matter what happened, she wasn't alone.

Lana appreciated it more than he could possibly know.

They plied Rebecca with enough sedatives that she fell into a state of quiet weeping, then finally sleep. Only then did Lana slip outside the private waiting room they'd been given.

"This could be a while," she warned him. "You might want to take a rideshare back to a hotel."

"I'd rather stay with you," Rick said kindly. "Can I get you a coffee or some tea? Your hands are shaking, sweetheart."

Before Lana could accept his offer, her phone rang. A brief phone call later, she ended the call and frowned at her cell.

"My mother wants us to come by the house."

"Is that what you want to do?"

She wavered, watching a well-dressed man stride toward the waiting room. "My uncle is here for my aunt and Killian. I'm not sure what we can do waiting here. At least we could freshen up."

In the end, Lana erred on the side of taking Rick back to her parents' house in a suburb of Chicago. Their home looked like every other home on the street. Old but well maintained. Three stories, brick exterior, a nice door, and neatly trimmed evergreens out front. As home bases for the ultrawealthy, it wasn't what most would expect.

As the car pulled into the drive and through a discrete gated entry, it seemed far less intimidating than what people thought they'd be walking into.

Lana glanced at Rick, staring out the window.

"Not what you expected?"

"I was trying to think of a nice way of saying that," Rick said ruefully.

"Old money is old for a reason. We save."

As they got out of the car, Rick held his arm out for Lana. "As much as I enjoy ending up in a pile of gummy bears with you, there's ice."

He could make her laugh, even in the hardest of times. Grateful for his presence and his supportive arm, Lana tucked her fingers into his bicep.

Lana's heels clicked on cobblestone pavers, then on gleaming marble as they entered the home through an unobtrusive back door. The marble mudroom was their warning sign things were about to get a whole lot more expensive, if subtly so. Rare paintings from the 1800s graced the foyer. Antique chairs once used by French royalty sat in the study. The garage outside held a 1930s Rolls-Royce that had set her father back almost $2 million, not that he'd ever be gauche enough to drive it.

Speaking of Langston, he was headed down the hall, having been alerted by the security system of her arrival.

"Lana."

Her name on her father's lips was enough to almost break through the composure Lana had fought so hard for since getting the call about Killian's accident. She hugged him in greeting, holding on just a touch too long before stepping back and saying, "Dad, this is Rick Harding. Rick, this is my father, Langston Montgomery."

"I've heard good things about you from my wife," Langston said, shaking Rick's hand. "It was kind of you to come with Lana. This is a trying time for our family. A friendly face is appreciated."

Meeting the parents wasn't the easiest on the best of terms, but Rick held any discomfort he might have felt close to the chest.

"It's nice to meet you, sir," Rick simply said, then shifted back to let Lana have her father's full attention. He didn't often hug her a second time, but this was a double hugging occasion if ever there was one.

Releasing her, Lana's father sighed. "Your mother should be down in her office by now. I know she wants to talk to you before we leave."

Only then did it occur to Lana that her father was in his best tuxedo, a fashionable Italian number tailored to fit him perfectly.

"Leave for where?" she asked, frowning.

Langston didn't answer, merely glancing at Rick before heading toward the library that had served as her mother's "office" for the last several decades.

One day, Lana wanted to have a library that was used for curling up and reading, not for holding meetings or entertaining important guests. Two stories of gleaming bookcases, a curved massive fireplace, and rustic wood beams drawing the eye up to irreplaceable antique stained glass window artwork. In the middle of it, her mother leaned one hand on a leather cigar chair. Dressed in a cocktail dress Lana had never seen before, Jessica pulled on a pair of heels, balancing her phone between her shoulder and her head. "Yes, thank you, Silas. I know. I'll tell her."

Ending the call, Jessica tossed her cell on the chair, addressing them without turning. "Langston, your sister-in-law is going to need her own room soon. They're taking Killian into surgery to cauterize a bleed next to his kidney, and she's falling apart."

"Her son is in intensive care."

"Yes, and this is the time she needs to be strong for him." Turning, Jessica realized Lana and Rick were with her husband.

"Lana, you're just in time," Jessica said, sounding relieved. Hustling over, she hugged Lana tightly, then did the same to a surprised Rick. "Rick, you're a dear for coming too. I'm Jessica. It's so nice to meet you."

Rick mumbled a reply, thrown by the hug and—Lana assumed—how much cleavage her mother had squashed into his chest. Jessica was a stunningly beautiful woman, and Rick wouldn't be the first one of her dates to drop a jaw when her mother walked by. In a different situation, she would have teased him mercilessly.

"Your cousin is going into surgery," Jessica continued. "Silas is keeping me updated, but Langston and I are headed over to the hospital after the ball."

"The *ball*?" Lana had no idea what her mother was talking about.

"I had a few things brought over for Rick. I'm sorry. There's obviously no time to have anything tailored for him, but I doubt anyone will notice."

"I'm sorry. I'm here for Killian, not a holiday party."

"A holiday party being hosted by Forester and Dunning. We have too much at stake to offend the Foresters by not showing up. I know you've been focused on your Moose Springs project, but the rest of us have been up to our ears in this. We can't afford any mistakes now, and not having the majority of the board of directors attend is the kind of insult they won't forget."

"My cousin is dying."

Jessica sighed. "Unfortunately, F and D couldn't care less. What they do care about is the show of power for their major shareholders, all of whom will be there tonight. Rebecca, your uncle, and Killian were all supposed to be there. You and Rick will be their stand-ins."

Lana's composure finally slipped, shock filling her voice. "This is *absurd*—"

"Your mother and I don't like it either, Lana," Langston said. "Unfortunately, fulfilling our obligations to the group doesn't stop because we're in the middle of a family crisis. You know that better than anyone."

"And you don't believe that's a little harsh? Killian—"

"Killian wrapped a quarter-million-dollar sports car around a brick wall because he never put the family first," her father said firmly. "I am brokenhearted at his prognosis and sick to my stomach at how much this is hurting the family, but we all know this call was coming. The boozing, the women, the fast cars."

"We kept hoping he'd settle down," Jessica added sadly. "Apparently, he took too long to grow up."

Lana didn't know how her parents managed to say those things and still sound compassionate.

"Go to your party," she said, bristling. "We're going back to the hospital."

Lana's mother sighed. "Silas said you might feel this way. We'll manage without you if we have to. Silas can stand in for you if he must. He's been the family's rock throughout all this."

The fact that those words were spoken without a hint of sarcasm made Lana's blood run cold. Of course. Of course Silas would take advantage of a tragedy to ingratiate himself with her parents. He couldn't have been less subtle about his intentions.

Langston caught her eye, and Lana knew without saying a word that she wasn't the only one aware of Silas's machinations.

And with Moose Springs on the line, the less power Silas had, the better. Langston patted her shoulder.

"It's only an evening," he promised. "A Montgomery can withstand anything for an evening."

———

"One of these days, I'm going to figure out how to not look like an idiot in a tie," Rick told Lana as they dressed in their borrowed finery. This time, Rick was fighting with a bow tie, one of the most complicated objects he'd been forced to deal with in his adult life.

He missed his simple snowflake tie dearly.

"Did this have to be a tie-on? They make clip-on bow ties."

"Yes," Lana said from inside the largest closet Rick had ever seen. It was almost the size of his living room. "Montgomerys never clip on."

"Hardings *always* clip on. Black works, right? I tried on the white one, and it looked stupid."

"The black will be perfect. Stop fretting; you look good in anything." Lana stepped out of the closet, and Rick's ability to breathe simply stopped. He stood there, staring, knowing he should say something and unable to force his tongue to move, let alone make a coherent sentence.

She was wearing the kind of gown he'd only seen in movies.

"I've missed this dress," Lana said to herself, running a hand down her hip. "It was always one of my favorites."

"You should wear that all the time." Running through his memory, Rick couldn't remember ever seeing a woman look as beautiful as Lana did right now.

She flashed him a quick grin. "Even when moose catching?"

"Especially when moose catching."

Her parents had already left for the party, so Lana and Rick took a separate car. At least that saved Rick from the distressingly low-cut gown Lana's mother was wearing. Few first impressions were as bad as checking out his date's mother...even if accidentally done.

The drive through Chicago was surreal. Rick had toured the lower forty-eight while playing billiards, but it had been a long time since he'd been surrounded by skyscrapers. Where Anchorage felt crowded, this city was overwhelming.

Lana wasn't the only one nervous about tonight, but Rick tried his best not to let it show. He didn't want her to have to help him or worry about him. She had enough to worry about.

He could tell by her reaction to her cousin's name that Lana wasn't happy with Silas...not that anyone could be happy around the noxious man. But Rick didn't understand how Silas's presence was enough to make Lana leave her cousin for the evening. There was more to her worries than she would tell him, and Rick was having a hard time not asking.

He wanted her to be open with him, but he wasn't going to push. But damn, it bothered him that she was pulled between her job and her family, and it made him wish there was something more he could do.

Maybe Lana didn't need his comfort and support, but he was going to make sure she had it. And if he needed to help her deal with Silas, then Rick was all in. He'd dump the twerp in a punch bowl if she wanted him to.

They pulled up to the mansion where the party was being held, a four-story midcentury modern monstrosity that could have held the entirety of his town within the sleek concrete walls. When Rick stepped into the mansion, Lana on his arm, he had a brief feeling of being in someone else's life. This certainly wasn't *his*. His life was a pool hall that was always too cold in the winter and too warm in the summer. A mortgage that wouldn't go away, even when he wished it would. A grumpy kid on the couch, lamenting both their love lives.

Rick's life wasn't crystal glasses of champagne, ball gowns, or chic tuxes, surrounded by professionally designed wintery floral arrangements and diamond-crusted ornaments on Christmas trees suspended on nearly invisible wires from the ceiling. The white tuxedo, black bow tie, and black shirt she'd given him for the occasion left Rick feeling like an inverted penguin. But with Lana in the deepest, richest red gown next to him, Rick knew it didn't matter one bit what he wore. No one was going to be looking at him.

All eyes were on her.

"I'm going to have to mingle," Lana warned him. "If you get sick of it, squeeze my hand twice, and I'll ask you to get me a mixed drink."

"I'll be fine," Rick told her. Boy, was he wrong. On the twenty-second repeat of the same conversation, Rick conceded defeat and went to get her a drink. With each reiteration of "how was her poor dear cousin, what a shame, would she want to set up a meeting with them to talk business?" Rick had to keep biting his tongue harder. Silas kept interjecting himself into the conversation, reminding Rick of a toy-sized dog jumping up and down to be noticed.

Lana introduced him to each newcomer, and initially Rick worried maybe Lana's colleagues would think he wasn't good enough for her. But the reality was, to them, he wasn't even there. Even Silas was ignoring him. Lana handled everything like the professional she was, deflecting requests with compliments and somehow remembering everyone's name.

Only Rick knew how uncomfortable she was with it all and only because her thumb never stopped drumming against her hip.

"Scotch, neat," Rick told the bartender, grateful to be away from the masses. "And a second for me."

He almost laughed at the absurdity of it all. Waitstaff were passing around caviar on actual silver platters, but this was a cash bar. Of course the fancy fish eggs were free when all Rick wanted was a stiff drink.

One wouldn't hurt. Not on a day like this.

"My daughter is beautiful, isn't she?" Jessica's voice pulled Rick's attention. He'd been so focused on Lana, he hadn't noticed her mother leaning against a table near the bar. Like Lana, Jessica had picked a rich red for her gown, although with a plunging neckline Rick was trying very hard to avoid glancing at.

"Lana's stunning," Rick agreed.

"She's the heir to one of the most powerful real estate conglomerates in the world. She could be cross-eyed in a burlap sack and everyone would tell her how amazing she looks." Lana's mother took a sip of her scotch, breaking from the rest of the room's choice of champagne. "But you're right. She's stunning. You'd have to be blind not to notice her."

He didn't know what to say, so he paid for a third scotch instead, nodding to the bartender to give it to Lana's mother.

Jessica's eyebrow arched as she accepted the new drink. "My daughter lets you pay for her?"

"When I'm lucky enough," he said. "It took some convincing."

"I'm sure. Are you in love with her?" Jessica smiled slightly. When Rick blinked at the question, she added, "I know the answer. I was just wondering if you do."

Rick didn't know this woman, and to be honest, she radiated a sort of intimidation that made part of him want to find anywhere else to be right then. But she was Lana's mother, and that meant something. So Rick set his glass, untouched, to the side.

"Yes. I'm in love with her."

Acknowledging that out loud to Jessica and to himself wasn't easy...but it was freeing. He was in love with Lana. How could he not be? Saying it to Lana's family instead of her first felt wrong, but Rick wasn't going to pretend he was something he wasn't, no matter how many bow ties the Montgomerys tied around his neck.

Jessica swirled her scotch in the glass, eyeing him. "Why?"

Frowning, Rick wasn't sure how to answer. "Why do I care about her?"

"If you loved her for her money, then she never would have brought you here to meet us." Jessica licked a drop of amber from her lips. "So I'm curious as to why you love my daughter."

The challenge in her eyes was clear. There was nothing Rick could say that would justify his place at Lana's side, and he knew trying would only leave him a crushed ant beneath this woman's thumb. And because she loved Lana too, Rick didn't blame her.

He didn't think he was good enough for her either.

Straightening, Jessica turned and looked out at the ballroom.

"There are men in here who would marry her in a heartbeat if she agreed to it. She's rich and she's powerful and she's beautiful. And one day, she will own more than anyone else in this room ever will."

With an indelicate snort, Jessica took a sip of her scotch. "Lana knows that's what they see when they look at her, so I've never worried about her falling for the wrong person. My daughter has never been the type to let her feelings blind her to reality. Usually."

When Jessica let that hang between them, Rick inhaled slowly, then exhaled a long breath.

"You think I'm bad for her." Just because he wasn't surprised at the information didn't mean Rick liked hearing it.

"You? I'm not sure yet. Moose Springs? Absolutely."

Rick's frown deepened. "I don't understand."

"Lana has been running away to your little town since she was old enough to drive herself. She'd idolized it as this perfect place where she can be happy. And in her attempts to carve out a place there, she's making choices that will cost her. If the board of directors doesn't have faith in her ability to dissociate her emotions from her financial decisions, she's going to lose her spot at the head of the company."

"Isn't the board her family?"

Jessica nodded.

"And you still don't trust her?"

"I trust my daughter with my life. I'm still deciding if I trust her with my money." Jessica finished her drink. "I usually let people make their own mistakes, but I appreciate you being here for Lana. I'll give you a word of advice, Rick. The more ties Lana has to Moose Springs, the worse off she's going to look. Buying a town because of a schoolgirl's crush isn't what CEOs are made of, no matter how savvy my daughter is."

Rick stood there, watching Lana move about the ballroom, unable to go more than a few feet without someone new wanting her attention. She might not want to be the center of attention, but damn, she was good at it. She deserved a lot more than he—or Moose Springs—would ever be able to give her.

And she still found his eyes despite the crowd, checking on him. Smiling at him in a way that would always bring Rick to his knees.

"You asked me why I'm in love with her," Rick said quietly. "It's because she tries to catch moose so people keep their Christmas lights. She finds kittens homes and helps grumpy kids when they make mistakes. She makes completely accurate gingerbread towns for people who don't even like her and dives into freezing cold water after strangers."

Rick drained his scotch and picked up his date's drink, the anger he was feeling at Lana's family undisguised in his tone.

"Because she's not like the rest of us. What Lana's 'made of' is more than we could hope to be. And what she does with that is her choice. If you'll excuse me."

Leaving Jessica to watch him walk away, Rick met Lana in the middle of the ballroom, where she was still surrounded by an increasingly growing group of people. Her smile was genuine, and the strain in her eyes was so slight, no one would be able to notice it. But he'd done nothing but stare at Lana since the day she'd walked into his life. He knew every expression, even the ones she was so good at hiding.

"Dance with me?" he asked, ignoring everyone else.

"I thought you'd never ask."

Leading her onto the dance floor, Rick ignored the fact that he didn't know how to dance very well, concentrating on Lana instead. When he pulled her into his arms, she came willingly, even though others were moving around the floor with far more skill than Rick would ever possess.

"This is my new favorite song," Lana told him when it shifted to a softer, slower melody.

Rick winced. "Did I sing this to you when you tranquilized me?"

"If you did, I'll never tell." Eyes sparkling with mischief, she rested her head on his shoulder.

Allowing himself a moment of sheer indulgence, Rick closed the last inch remaining between them. Let people stare. He didn't care about them or what they thought. He didn't care if they all wanted something from Lana. When she was wrapped up in his arms, none of them could get to her. Speaking of which...

"Do you mind if I cut in?" A man he didn't recognize had approached their party of two, standing there as if he had every right to interrupt.

"I mind." Okay, maybe that came out too much of a growl, but Rick wasn't interested in letting anything or anyone come between them tonight.

Lana giggled at Rick's flat refusal. "I'll dance with you the next song, Alex," she said.

"Not if I can convince her to dance with me again, *Alex*." Rick turned so his back was between Lana and the stranger.

Lana lightly smacked his arm. "That was rude."

"And yet you look happier than you have all night. Random stranger Alex doesn't get to steal you away until that smile stays at least another dance longer."

"I never said I minded rude." Lana winked at him. "I'm just saying it was."

Fine. If everyone thought he wasn't good enough for her, he might as well reinforce the idea and have some fun with it. Rick turned her in a quick, unexpected circle and then dipped her. Lana was still giggling at his antics when he straightened, curling a hand behind her neck and drawing her in for a long, deep kiss.

"There was mistletoe," he said, because technically, it was true. In a place like this, there had to be mistletoe *somewhere*.

"Do you want to get out of here?" Lana asked. "We've made our presence known, and considering the gossip about Killian is spreading like wildfire, no one will question why we're leaving."

"I'm still questioning why we're even here." Rick shook his head.

As Lana looked around the ballroom, he could hear her whisper, "Because money makes people prioritize the wrong things. I'm so tired of playing by these rules."

Rick had only been in her world a couple of hours, and he was tired of it too. He could only imagine a lifetime of having to "save face." Not being broke would be nice, but Rick would pick his life—including his grumpy cat and empty pool hall—over this any day of the week.

He'd pick standing by Lana's side every day of the week.

They tried to slip away unnoticed, but the collective attendees at the party had other ideas. Even with her hand in his, person after person stepped in their way as they tried to make it to the door. Yes, Lana would have her people call their people. No, she wasn't in town long enough to meet for dinner. Sorry, Alex, there would be no dance.

They reached the valet parking in record time: the longest two people had ever taken to get out of a house and to the sidewalk out front.

"Do I need to ask you to get me another drink?" Lana asked him as if he had said something funny.

"Why do you say that?"

"Because you're glaring at everything but me."

"If I'm glaring at everything, it's because everyone is determined to keep me away from you."

"And Killian," Lana said with a sigh. "I'd like to check on him to see if he's stabilized. No one is giving me any updates, and I'm worried."

Rick was worried too. He kept an arm around Lana's shoulders on the drive back to hospital, resting his cheek against the top of her head. Even now, with only the two of them, her defenses were still up, her body tense as she leaned on him.

"He's going to be okay," Rick promised, even though he knew he might be lying. Killian was in bad shape.

Her weak smile was worth that possible lie. "He will. Killian's strong."

Rick just hoped Lana's cousin was strong enough.

The hospital shouldn't have allowed them after visiting hours, but more rules than one were getting broken for the hospital donors. They were halfway out of the elevator when a crash from down the hall pulled their attention. They rushed to Killian's room, the source of the commotion.

"I said, get me the damn doctor," Killian yelled at whomever would listen.

"Killian, stop it." Lana's sharp order was enough to stay

his hand. The remains of all the flower vases within his reach lay shattered on the floor, expensive flowers crushed and water pooling beneath their feet. "What's wrong?"

The look he gave her was wild, and he was panting. "I need the doctor. I need more pain meds."

Ignoring his heaving chest and clenched fists, Lana sat on the edge of his bed and placed a hand on his forehead. "You're burning up from fever. Where's the nurse?"

"I threw her out."

Leaning his head back on the pillow, Killian's fists clenched into the bedding. Rick positioned himself close enough to interfere if he turned on her. This wasn't the cousin she knew. This was a man in terrible pain, and Rick doubted he truly understood what he was doing right now.

"I'm here." The doctor strode into the room. "Mr. Montgomery, I understand you're in a significant amount of discomfort, but it's dangerous to up your medications. Your kidneys have been severely damaged—"

"You think I don't know? You think I don't know that I did this to myself?" Killian bellowed. He swung his arm at what was left on the side tray, a plastic pitcher of water. Rick didn't have time to stop him, so he grabbed Lana and twisted, taking the force of the flying object to his shoulder.

"Killian, *stop it*."

This time, Lana sounded near tears.

When Killian didn't stop, Lana stumbled out of the room, her near-constant composure finally shot. Leaning against the wall outside the door, Lana turned to Rick, clearly shaken. They could both hear Killian yelling at the doctor, the laid-back cousin replaced by someone neither of them could recognize.

"I don't know what to do," Lana said in a whisper. "I don't know how to help him."

"Let's take a drive. Staying here staring at the floor isn't going to help."

Wordlessly, she handed him her car keys. Her hands were shaking far too badly to hope to drive safely right now.

————————

When they hit the edge of the city, they kept driving. Empty corn and soybean fields stretched all around them, blanketed in snow.

"Here. Pull over here."

At her request, Rick exited the highway, turning in to an all-night truck stop. It was late enough that a few truckers had parked for the night, everything dark but the undercarriage lights glowing on their rumbling semis. A restaurant took up the bulk of the truck stop, filled with more people than Rick would have expected this late in the evening.

"The Mudgeton truck stop is always busy, no matter how late at night," Lana explained as they slid into in a booth in their finery.

"Mudgeton?"

"This place was the start of the Zoey-Lana ladymance. Like a bromance but far more productive and long-lasting."

After waiting a few minutes, a cheerful—if tired—waiter came over and took their order. They ordered strawberry milkshakes because Lana promised they were the best on the planet. The kitchen was quick, and within a couple of minutes, their server placed a massive glass in front of Rick overloaded with whipped cream and fresh strawberries on top. For the first time that evening, Rick found himself looking at something he actually wanted to eat.

"You might have been underselling this milkshake." Rick slurped a sip, not caring that the straw made a loud sucking noise. "This is ridiculously good."

"Right? I told you! You should try the apple pie. It's to die for."

It was the most animated she'd been in hours. Milkshake forgotten, Rick took Lana's hand. "Are you okay?"

She glanced down at the table, swallowing hard. "It's difficult seeing him like that. He's never raised his voice or mistreated someone in his life. That wasn't Killian in there."

"Pain can make us become people we aren't. Make us do things we would never consider doing."

Lana nodded, falling silent. Deciding not to push the issue, Rick looked around instead.

Even though they were in the lower forty-eight, it wasn't all that different from home. The land was flat, true, but the heavy Carhartt jackets were the same. Cold hands wrapped around hot cups of coffee as truck drivers ate slices of pie. Waiters and waitresses on sore feet spoke tired greetings to their customers, and the smell of French fries permeated the air.

"So this is where you met Zoey?" Rick took in the restaurant, trying to imagine Lana and Zoey here without him.

"Yes. She always worked the night shift, usually those tables over there, and I stopped in one night on my way to see some friends."

"Real friends or people who wanted something from you?"

Lana smiled wryly. "You picked up on that tonight, huh? You know, love, it's possible you're starting to understand me a little *too* well."

Love. Did she mean it the way Rick meant it earlier that night? Or was it just an affectation of speech? He didn't know her nearly well enough.

She pointed at the far corner of the restaurant. "That table is where I technically met Zoey," Lana told him. "Right over there. She was serving a table of truck drivers, and they were teasing her about being short. I watched her tell six men to go screw themselves and then pour a glass of water on the closest one's lap. She was so fearless. I wanted to be her when I grew up."

"And now?"

"Now I'm still very inspired by her, but I wouldn't want to have to be married to Graham. I'm content being me."

Rick chuckled, scraping the sides of his milkshake glass to get the last drops. "So this is where it all began. The Thelma to your Louise?"

"Absolutely. I could have lived here," she told him. "I tried to. Zoey rode a bicycle home after her shifts, and I offered to give her a ride. She introduced me to her grandmother, and I fell in absolute love. I don't think I left Mudgeton for a month."

"Does her grandmother still live here?"

"Grandma Madge? Yes, she's here." Lana hesitated, then she bit her lower lip. "Would you like to meet her?"

Rick would. It was nearly eleven at night, but according to

Lana, Madge was a night owl. She also informed him that she would be in big trouble if Madge found out Lana had been in town and hadn't said hello. Calling up Madge was easy. Procuring her the last piece of apple pie from the greedy hands of the other diners was harder, but Lana managed it.

They drove down the street to a small single-family home, decorated with an eclectic collection of windchimes and ceramic gnomes in Harley clothes.

"Is Madge a biker granny?"

"Totally. Brace yourself," she told Rick as they knocked on Zoey's grandmother's door. "And just agree with her. Madge won't take no for an answer."

An absolutely delighted elderly woman opened the door as if it were noon and they were completely expected. Zoey's grandmother was as tiny as Zoey was and then some. Head to toe in Hogwarts-themed pajamas, Madge Caldwell hustled them inside, telling Rick he was handsome so vigorously that his cheeks burned by the time he was told to sit down at the kitchen table. She made a fuss over Lana like she was a long-lost granddaughter.

"Sweetie, just look at you," Madge kept saying. "You're so thin. I bet you haven't eaten all year. Sit down, no no, sit. I'll get you something to eat."

Unlike Zoey, Madge wasn't shy in the least.

"So tell me about my granddaughter. Zoey keeps sending me pictures of that man she met, and he's certainly good-looking enough. But I worry about her up there all alone."

"Zoey's happy." Lana took Madge's age-spotted hand. "I've never seen her so happy. She and Graham are perfect for each other. And I promise, he's not leaving her alone for a second. He's smitten."

"I looked him up online, you know. These fingers might be old, but they're more than capable of finding dirt on a man who's stolen my only granddaughter away from me."

"Are you doing okay? Zoey worries about you too."

"Nonsense. That child has lived with me for years, and it's about time she went off and took something good for herself. I have plenty of company, and you know the local boys are always over here helping me out. If they knew *you* were here, the tires would already be squealing."

Seeing Lana grin was even better than the thick slices of banana bread Madge kept putting on their plates. They ate until Madge was satisfied…long past the point of being stuffed. Lana told Madge about Killian and her family and about the party they'd abandoned. She told her about Moose Springs and the group's investments and how she wasn't getting along as well as she'd hoped.

"You've always been a loner, child, and not by choice. Sometimes the more you want to have a connection with someone, the harder it is to make it happen. The best thing to do is sit back and let the world bring your people to you. Isn't it better to have one or two of the right ones instead of a hundred wrong ones?"

Lana glanced at Rick, worrying at her lower lip. Madge looked knowingly between them. "I think we are who we are, not who we planned on being."

Then they were told that they absolutely must stay the night. There would be plenty of time to go back to Chicago in the morning.

"I made up Zoey's bed for you, child." Madge said. "Young man, you can have the couch."

"I'd rather sleep on the couch if you don't mind," Lana said. "I have a lot of fond memories of that couch."

"That couch has some questionable memories of you." Madge patted her head. "I'll get your quilt."

"You have a quilt?" Rick asked Lana, chuckling.

"And a pillow. I've spent a lot of time in this house over the years."

"Come on. You too," Madge said to Rick, grabbing his arm and dragging him through the house. "I'll get you some night clothes."

Lana had learned early that there was never a shortage of sleepwear in the Caldwell household.

The options were endless and endlessly amusing. Holiday socks with jingling bells, pumpkin and scaredy-cat pajama bottoms, more soft flannel and fluffy fleece in bright colors, none of which had any hope of matching.

Rick, quiet and reserved as he was, had settled on a pair of men's pajama pants that said "BootyTastic."

"Are you okay in the bedroom?" Lana asked him after Madge went to bed. She kept pinching his bootytastic rear end, which Rick seemed to be taking in stoic stride.

"Feels a long way from you," he said. "Are you sure—?"

"Madge will come out in fifteen minutes to check on us." Lana giggled. "Do you want to risk her wrath if she finds me with you?"

"Hmm...good point. You should sneak in after twenty minutes."

After such a long day and night, Lana was exhausted. Fully intending to go meet up with Rick after Madge was asleep, Lana laid her head down on her pillow. She must have passed out instantly, because the next thing she knew, it was the middle of the night and more than a little chilly. Soft footsteps woke her.

Rick was in the hallway just off the living room, peering at the fuse box.

"Rick?" she called softly. "Is everything okay?"

"The furnace went out," he told her quietly. "I checked the fuse box, and it blew a fuse. Do you know if Madge has any extra fuses?"

"Her workshop is in the garage. She keeps her tools behind the Harley. I can show you."

"I'll find it." Rick added kindly, "Go back to sleep. I'll get it going again."

Knowing he was fixing the heat wasn't only nice. It was also incredibly sexy. Sexy enough that Lana didn't go back to sleep. Instead, she snuggled up in her quilt, watching a small light through the mudroom door, showing him moving about in the garage. He returned a couple of minutes later with a small package of multisized fuses.

"That used to be Zoey's job. When the fuses blew, she would change them out for Madge. It's hard on her fingers to grasp things that small."

"My dad has arthritis too," Rick said absently.

"Does he live in Moose Springs?"

For some reason, it bothered her that she hadn't met Rick's father.

As he looked for the right size fuse, Rick glanced over at her, looking amused. "Don't give me the lip, gorgeous. I would have introduced you if my parents weren't busy playing golf in Florida right now."

"There wasn't a lip," she protested, but maybe there was. And when he shut the fuse box, the furnace once more humming, Rick walked over to her.

He sank down to a knee next to the couch, brushing her hair out of her eyes. Chuckling, he tapped her lip with his thumb. "No?"

"Definitely not. Montgomerys don't pout." She poked a finger into his pajama pants. "You really are bootytastic." She waggled her eyebrows at him.

"I try." His palm slid over her hip where the hem of her own pants had dipped to reveal her hipbone. He squeezed her gently, as if tempted. Then Rick shook his head. "You've had a long day. You need to get some rest."

Okay, this time, there might have been the tiniest hint of a lip.

"Or I can get you some more banana bread," Rick added.

Tempting as that was, Lana slipped her hand behind his neck, pulling Rick in for a long, slow kiss. "I like it when you talk banana bread," she said to him, scooting tight to the back pillows of the couch to make room for him. A low, warm chuckle accompanied his equally warm arm wrapping around her waist, drawing her into his warm, flannel-y form.

"Lana? Tonight at the party...your mom told me some stuff. About you and the company."

"Yeah? Did she scare you away?" Snuggling in, Lana looked at him. "Mom loves to give everyone a thorough interrogation if they're interested in me."

"I'm not scared," Rick told her. "I just didn't realize how important to them you are. It's really huge. Your job...your place in that room tonight. You matter."

"It's the family business. We're all worker bees doing our parts."

"Are you? Because what it looked like to me was everyone was circling you like the heir apparent."

Lana didn't answer immediately. "It's not for certain. Silas is trying to make a move for the company by discrediting me. Killian was my strongest supporter."

"And now?"

"Now I have to watch my back. Especially if I don't want anything bad to happen to Moose Springs."

Rick tilted his head. "What do you mean?"

"Work is the last thing I want to think about now." When he simply waited, Lana closed her eyes. "If I tell you, you'll hate me."

"Or you could let me decide," Rick replied quietly. He threaded her fingers inside his, as if knowing instinctively they were starting to shake. "Lana, I'm your person. I have you, sweetheart."

Opening her eyes, Lana nodded. "Okay. Silas is gathering votes to liquidate the Moose Springs properties and halt construction on the condos. He wants to wait until the Shaws go bankrupt."

Rick went still.

Swallowing hard, Lana said quickly, "I'll fix this. I won't let it happen."

"Sounds like it's already happening."

"Rick, I promise I won't let it go through. Whatever I have to do, I'll do it. Please trust me."

Lana braced herself, waiting for him to get angry. To tell her she was the worst thing to happen to his town. That good intentions had resulted in terrible consequences, and now, even if she helped the town, it was because she had broken it in the first place.

Taking her face in his hands, Rick kissed her instead. A long, slow kiss, his body strong and solid against her. "I trust you, Lana. I *love* you. How could I not?"

His words were so soft, his touch gentle as he drew her in closer.

"You love me?" she asked in a whisper.

A sweet smile curved his lips. "I was a goner by the time you walked out the door of my pool hall."

"I love you too." She'd never said that, taken that risk or that leap before. "We made a mess of this Christmas fling, didn't we?"

Rick didn't answer, instead pressing the softest of kisses to her temple.

In hindsight, when he lingered, gazing down into her eyes as if trying to memorize this moment...she should have asked him why he was saying these things now. Instead, Lana reached for him, letting Rick's strong hands take her problems away.

Rick's intentions had been aiming toward the seductive, but trying to be quiet so that they didn't disturb Madge resulted in far more giggles from her than other noises.

As they lay there, Lana and her fuzzy pajamas tucked into his form, Rick realized something very important. It wasn't that he loved her. Rick had loved Lana Montgomery for a very long time. He had always understood that Lana was made for bigger things than a guy and a worn-down pool hall in a tiny corner of the world. It had just been nice to pretend for a while that what they had would last. But she had places to go, very important things to do. While he could never resent that—because he was so proud of her, he couldn't see straight—he also couldn't be a part of it.

Every interaction he'd had so far with her family, in her world, had shown him that whatever this was, it was destined to be short. At least it had been sweet.

He'd kept Jen tied to him, thinking love would be enough to make her accept a small-town life. For her to be happy. But Jen had never been happy, because it wasn't enough to love someone. You had to have your dreams too. The Montgomery Group was Lana's future, and she was going to do such amazing things for the world. But she couldn't do those things in Moose Springs, and not with him pulling her down.

Loving her had been the absolutely best thing that had ever—and would ever—happen to Rick. But he knew what he needed to do. This holiday romance was destined to run its course. Rick wasn't taking her down, dragging this out, or hurting a woman he desperately loved. No, it was time.

He had to let Lana go.

The roads were icy that morning. Since they were both used to the slick conditions but only one of them kept getting work emails and updates about Killian on their phone, Rick drove.

Zoey's grandmother had filled them to the stuffing point before allowing them to leave, causing Lana to feel pleasantly sleepy.

"The only thing better than the milkshakes are Madge's biscuits and gravy," she decided contentedly.

"Lana, we need to talk."

Those words were never good. Lana turned to make a joke, then she saw the way Rick's hand gripped the steering wheel.

"Ah."

Two letters, one word. Neither of which did justice to the feeling of utter dread ripping through her right now.

"I need to go back to Moose Springs. Diego's responsible, but he's never had to handle a delivery shipment or pay the bills. My landlady's not going to appreciate it if rent doesn't get paid. Plus, I don't want him to be alone on Christmas."

Rick's voice was quiet, his eyes locked on the road. Every single muscle in his arm was tensed.

"You're breaking up with me." She didn't even need to phrase it as a question. Lana hadn't said the words accusingly, but Rick still flinched.

"It's not because I want to," he told her, voice lowering to a rough whisper.

"And yet, here we are, full of too many carbohydrates, and you're about to end things."

Finally, he looked at her.

"Is there a reason why? Or should we call an end to a good thing and say we'll still be friends?"

Trying for breezy and light only fell flat. Rick pulled off the road, hitting the hazard lights. "Lana, we both know the reason."

"It's because of Silas's power play, isn't it? Rick, I swear I'm going to fix—"

He cut her off with a shake of his head. "That's not why. Am I worried about what might happen? Yeah. But I've been worried every day for years about whether my business will keep afloat. If I'm screwing up by not taking tourists' money. If I'm screwing up with Diego after all. I worry all the damn time, Lana. What's happening with the group is just more of the same."

Rick's hands gripped the steering wheel too tight as he sat there staring out at the expanse of snowy crop fields. "That's how it's always been. When you live in Moose Springs, you never have control of what happens to you. You just have to survive what's constantly being thrown at you."

"Like me."

Hazel eyes found hers, despite her attempts not to look at him. "You are the best thing to happen to me. You're amazing, Lana. Which is why this isn't going to work and why I'm not going to hurt both of us by dragging it out."

"I don't understand," she said softly. "You told me you loved me last night. I refuse to believe that wasn't what you truly feel. So how does 'I love you' turn into 'let's break up' by the next morning?"

"Your shoes click."

She had no idea what that meant.

"I never noticed it before." Rick pressed on in a gruff voice. "I mean, I did. But when you were with your family, every woman's shoes clicked on the floor. Every man was wearing slacks."

"You're ending this because of my shoes?"

"No. I am just starting to realize that we live in different worlds. Your world is a lot bigger and a lot more important than mine. Being with me…your loyalty to my town…it's costing you."

"Whatever my mother said—"

"What she said was you might lose control of the Montgomery Group. A multibillion-dollar company. Lana, this is just a holiday fling. I didn't realize what the stakes were at play. I can't cost you that."

"The choices I make in my professional life are my own, Rick." Lana's voice caught on his name.

"I know. And I have the choice to make things harder for you or to walk away."

He made a soft, soothing noise in his throat, as if she were a deer about to shy away. Lana didn't feel like a deer; she felt like a lion, digging its claws in, desperate not to let something good slip out of her hands.

She didn't want to lose him.

"We don't have anything in common, Lana. And this has been so good…" Rick's voice choked, and he stopped talking. He cleared his throat roughly before continuing. "I've loved every minute with you. You make me laugh, and you make everything so much better. But one day, you're going to wake up and realize the guy at the pool hall in some nowhere town doesn't wear slacks on a Tuesday."

"You're being amazingly insulting to both of us."

"Sweetheart, we don't fit. And when you realize it, I don't want to be a decade in and too far gone to survive watching you walk away. The first time gutted me, but you…I don't think I'd get over it. You don't know the damage you could do without even trying."

Anger flared inside her. "Don't you think I'm scared too?

Rick, I've never told a man I loved him in my life. I don't do flings, because I don't *want* temporary. I want real. I want permanent. I want a home and a family and a life with someone. And I thought…"

She stopped midsentence because it wasn't fair to tell him she'd wanted that with him. Not when she was the one destined to walk away.

"I don't know what this could have been, but I'm not making another woman miserable by tying her to my side. I won't go through that again, Lana."

Lana would not cry. She would not. "It's not my job to fix what your ex-wife broke. It's not my responsibility to prove myself because she couldn't."

"I know. But it's my choice to walk away before I get hurt. Before we both do."

He was doing this with the quiet acceptance of a man who had decided he was beat.

Unable to stop the silent tears from leaking down her cheeks, Lana said in a hurt voice, "You're not going to fight for us at all, are you?"

That flash of heat filled his eyes, that determination, that fire she only saw when he was holding her in his arms. "This isn't what I want, gorgeous. But it's the right thing to do. I can't give you what you need. I can't be what you need."

"I never asked you for anything. I never wanted you to *be* anything or anyone other than who you are. I refuse to fight for a man who won't do the same for me. Either you're in or you're out, Rick."

He didn't answer, but that was all the answer she needed.

Lana wanted to scream. She wanted to kick him in the leg for being an idiot. She wanted to cry, because he was breaking her heart into a million pieces, and she didn't think she'd ever be able to glue them back together again in the right places.

But Montgomerys didn't make scenes. They accepted tough news with decorum and grace. Sometimes the only thing to do was keep her head held up high.

"I'll arrange for a flight home for you, dearest," Lana said, because she didn't know if he had the money saved up to get himself back. Chicago was beautiful during the holidays, but broken up or not, Rick was the best man she'd ever met. The last thing she would do was strand him at Christmas.

Not with someone he was done with.

CHAPTER 16

THE HOSPITAL ROOM WAS SILENT except for the steady beeping of the vital signs monitor. Lana sat in the plush chair placed next to the side of Killian's bed, careful to be as quiet as possible. His eyes were closed.

"The surgery to stop the bleeding worked. I guess I'm not dying after all."

Killian's Adam's apple moved as he swallowed hard.

"You almost sound disappointed." Lana poured him a glass of water from the pitcher at his bedside.

Gone were his impeccable manners, replaced by a hand nearly crushing the thin plastic cup as it shook. He knew he'd badly injured his spine. Reminding him of that wasn't going to help. Not when unshed tears glistened in his eyes.

"I can't do this. I can't watch them come in here and look at me like I'm…"

"Damaged?"

"Yeah. That." He exhaled heavily. "You're the only one brave enough to say it. The rest give me platitudes. They tell me I'll heal, when they have no idea if I will or not. I see it in their eyes. They think I deserve this."

"No one deserves this," Lana told him softly. "Especially not you. But you're the one going through it. No one can tell you how to feel, least of all the rest of our family. Focus on what you need, not what they say."

"Is that how you've survived them so long? Tuning them out?"

Lana didn't answer. Killian craned his neck around as much as the brace would allow. "Where's Rick?"

"He left."

"Left Chicago or left you?"

Her expression, so carefully schooled into calmness, still gave her away.

"So that's it? You're going to sit there with that fake-ass pleasant smile pasted on your face and let him go? That idiot's in love with you. Whatever his reasoning, he's not leaving because he wants to."

"Would you suggest I make a grand gesture? Beg him to take me back?"

Killian snorted. "Well, what grand gesture could Rick possibly make? Here, surrounded by them? We *all* feel like we aren't enough. Even Aunt Jessica and Uncle Langston. None of us are good enough to run this place. None of us are as skilled as we need to be. The only one close is you. You're the prodigal child, succeeding when the rest of us are silently screaming at the top of our lungs."

"That's not true," Lana protested.

"Please, Cousin. I'm the court jester at best. The fool who is rolled out whenever strangers need entertainment." Killian ran a hand over his face, scrubbing bruised skin roughly. "Do you think they'll stick me in an office so I can pretend to have a job? Or set me up with a caretaker and forget about me except for the holidays?"

Her heart broke at the certainty in his voice.

"Don't give up, Killian. You're strong enough to get through this."

"You're the only one of us worth anything. If you're giving up, what's the point?"

Killian rested his head back on his pillow, staring up at the ceiling. Lana sat in her chair silently for a very long time. Then she rose to her feet, moved to the edge of his bed, and leaned over.

"If you hate it here, then heal." When he wouldn't look at her, Lana ignored his bruises and took his chin in her hand, forcing him to. "Heal enough to get out of here. I don't know what happens next, but I know you *don't* have to stay here. When it's safe to travel, I have a whole town where you can go, where you won't have to deal with them."

There was enough of Killian left to pull his face out of her hand before holding her eyes challengingly. "I thought Moose Springs wasn't your town."

"Places don't belong to us because of money. They belong to us because we love them. My heart is in Moose Springs. It's my home, and I'm going home. When you're ready, come home with me too."

Pressing a kiss to his bruised forehead, Lana left Killian to decide for himself what he needed to do.

Her mother was leaning against the wall outside Killian's room, within easy earshot of their conversation.

"I'm going back to Alaska," Lana told Jessica. "I'll be working out of the office I set up in Moose Springs for the foreseeable future."

Jessica took her hands. "Lana, are you sure this is the right choice for you? Rick seems like a good man, but will this be enough?"

"This isn't about him. It's about me. I stood on a mountain, and I looked down at the problem. Do you know what I found? *We're* the problem. I'm selling the Moose Springs properties to the business owners. Any of them who want to buy, I'll negotiate with them myself. I'm putting control back in their hands."

"And if I put in a vote to stop you?"

"It's not your company," Lana said. "It belongs to all of us. I'll do what I have to and get the votes I need to push it through. I'm not sacrificing the town to Silas's greed. He's welcome to live his life as a pawn of the Montgomery Group's revenue, but I'm more than that. Moose Springs is worth more than that. And if you're smart, you'll realize that the Montgomery Group is worth more than his greed too."

For too many decades, the fate of Moose Springs had been in the hands of the wrong people. The Shaws, sitting in their gilded tower of a resort. The commercial property companies, sitting in Anchorage, counting their dollars. Her own hands and the hands of her family. People who simply didn't understand.

It was time for Moose Springs to be in the right hands again: their own.

"You're playing a dangerous game with your future, Lana. Are you sure he's worth it?"

There wasn't cruelty in her mother's voice, just an honest question.

"I don't know," Lana said honestly. "But I know I am."

"The town will shut your condos down, Lana," her mother told her as Lana walked away. "All your work will have been for nothing."

On the contrary. This might be the first business deal in her life that would be worth it.

The next time Lana offered to fly him first class, Rick was taking her up on it.

After a miserable trip back home in coach—in which his longest flight had been spent wedged in between two people his own size in the row closest to the rear bathroom—all Rick wanted to do was go home. Every single minute since leaving her in Chicago, Rick had questioned whether he'd done the right thing. Shouldn't doing the right thing feel better? Because this felt like he'd been shredded from the inside out. He'd left her there to deal with her family alone. He'd left her there to deal with her hurt cousin alone. Instead of standing by her side, he'd bailed the first chance things looked like they could be tough.

What the hell was he thinking? What the hell was he *doing*? He should be on a plane back to Chicago right that minute.

But his choice had been made. Going back now would only make things worse, because nothing had changed. She still deserved better than having him and his town come between her and her family. No, Rick had to stay this course, no matter how terrible it made him feel.

After his flight finally landed in Anchorage, Rick got his snow-covered car out of the airport's short term parking and drove back to Moose Springs, barely seeing the road.

He only started to notice his surroundings when he reached town. The Santa Moose had made it to the center of Moose Springs, where up to this point, the best decorations had remained safe. Now, the town's Christmas tree was tipped over, its ornaments crushed and scattered. Plastic snowflakes lay broken and battered.

Only one poor inflatable elf remained standing, staring at the carnage with haunted eyes.

If Diego had been home, Rick would have kept driving instead of turning off at Graham's driveway. But Diego had his own plans, having not expected Rick to be back so soon. Since Diego was at some holiday party with a group his own age, Rick figured he might as well do the same. He wasn't ready to spend Christmas Eve alone.

When he arrived, Graham's house was stuffed full of people, so at first, Rick was able to slip in the door and blend in without anyone noticing. He hadn't told anyone what had happened in Chicago, and he'd hoped to avoid talking about it tonight. Losing Lana was causing a slow bleed in his heart that he couldn't stanch, and he wasn't ready to discuss this with anyone yet.

So of course a sloshy little person stumbled his way, her voice slurring with the effects of the Lockett family eggnog.

"I talked to Lana," Zoey said, eyes flashing. Rick could smell the alcohol on Zoey's breath from three feet away.

"How is she?" He couldn't help but ask. Ending their fling... relationship...whatever it was with Lana's cousin still in intensive care had been terrible timing. He'd felt like the biggest jerk alive since leaving Chicago.

Zoey actually growled, which would have been cute under other circumstances. "She got dumped on Christmas."

"Christmas Eve, darlin'," Graham murmured helpfully, coming up behind his fiancée.

"*Christmas Eve.* You big...big...*meanie.*"

"Zo's pulling out the big guns," Graham said jokingly, giving Rick an apologetic look. "Pretty sure there are two sides to every breakup, honey."

"Lana deserves better than I can give her," Rick said quietly. "It's wrong to keep pretending otherwise."

Rick really wished he didn't have to deal with an angry protective friend right now. He felt terrible enough.

No one had ever rolled their eyes harder than Zoey at his statement. "Gimme a break. Chicken. You're a big...chickenman. One look at her family and boom. You bailed. Cluck cluck. Like your family is sooooo easy to get along with. Hi, Imma Diego. I grunt 'nstead of speaking."

Graham draped an arm over Zoey's shoulders, steadying her. "Sorry, she's a little bit drunk, buddy, and it brings out her protective side. Zo, maybe we should leave Rick here to consider his life choices without our running dialogue."

Zoey shoved Graham's arm off her, giving Rick her mightiest death glare. Her slurring grew worse with every word. "You'restupid. S'stupid, chickenman."

When she stumbled in his direction, Rick reached out to steady her. He ended up with Zoey's nose mere inches from his own, the alcohol on her breath making his eyes sting. Sloppy drunk had never been his style, so he couldn't imagine why Graham looked so amused. Graham sat on the arm of the couch, grinning as Rick tried to avoid the finger waggling in his face or her clucking at him. Drunken burps *weren't* cute.

"Lana's smarter than you. No chickenmen for her. Imma sit down."

Zoey stepped back, flopping down to Graham's knee, and promptly fell asleep.

"Well, that's one way of putting it." Graham wrapped a secure arm around Zoey's waist. "The other way is 'Hello, Rick. How was Chicago?'"

"It could have been better," he said shortly.

Graham gave him a concerned look. "What's the real story? Because you two were pretty solid when you left here."

Rick really didn't want to talk about it, and not in the middle of a party.

"Lana deserves someone who won't trap her in the middle of nowhere," Rick said, dropping his voice as quiet as he could.

Graham gave him a sideways glance. "She's a woman who hides out in Moose Springs every chance she gets. I'm not sure you and she are on the same page here, buddy."

There were too many curious eyes and perked ears in that crowd. Heading outside to the porch for some space, Rick sat down. He looked up at the mountain, the warm glow of the resort lights making it appear like an ornament against the evergreens. Somewhere behind all the tree cover was the last remainder of a snow penis, with everything but the jingle bells filled in with snow.

She'd never taken it down, as if she understood that the town needed to get their frustrations out somehow.

Had it only been two weeks since the town hall meeting? It felt like a lifetime.

The door opened again, and two bodies joined him on the porch steps. They'd spent a lot of time sitting on porches, him and Easton and Graham. Sometimes, in a town like theirs, there wasn't a lot else to do. In Moose Springs, momentous decisions were made on porch steps. Drunken ridiculousness happened on porch steps, first teenage kisses and marriage proposals, grieving the loss of a family member, falling in love, or losing someone you loved.

This was where lives happened. Where *his* life had happened. And apparently where his friends would help him pick up the pieces.

"You want to talk about her?" Easton asked in a low rumble.

Rick shook his head. There was nothing to say. He'd lost the woman he loved, again. Only this time? This time, Rick wasn't sure he was coming back from it.

"Someone needs to check on Lana," Rick finally said. "I hurt her."

"You're not looking too hot yourself," Graham replied, clapping a hand to his shoulder.

Easton took a drink of his beer. "We'll check on her. We're just checking on you too."

Rick continued to stare up at the soft glow coming off the mountain. Following his line of sight, Graham frowned up at the resort too.

"You know anything about that place I don't?" Graham asked.

Rick turned his eyes away from the mountains, where he no longer knew if the resort would last. Getting rid of the resort was something they'd always wanted. If he asked Lana to stand back and do nothing, to let Silas have his way, they might finally have their wish. But at what cost?

"Graham, if I told you that the Shaws aren't going to stay in business much longer, what would you say? If this place could be a ghost town in a couple of years, us included?"

Graham was quiet for a long time. "I'd say that Zo wants kids. Not soon but someday."

"Lot harder to have kids when we're all out of work."

With a sigh, Graham nodded. "Yeah."

"Lana's trying, but she's going to have to make some big decisions soon. My place is proof a business can barely stay open here serving locals only. I have to open it to the tourists, or I'll have to shut the doors by the end of January."

Easton and Graham grimaced. "I didn't know things were that bad."

"Without the tourism dollars, a lot of us just can't keep afloat. We've tried." Rick scuffed his shoe on the wooden porch step. "I still don't like it. I still hate what they did to Jen and Diego, but it's hard to watch everyone else fill their wallets, knowing mine is empty and will stay that way."

"I'll call Lana. See what we can work out."

Rick tried. He tried to sit there and shut off what he felt. He tried to believe what he'd told himself over and over again since he'd walked away. But really, when it came down to it, Rick had been wrong.

"Guys...I think...I think I really screwed up. Someone needs to check on her. She's going to need a friend."

"More than you do?" Easton asked quietly.

Maybe...maybe not. But for right now, within their small friend group, Rick was going to make sure Lana had dibs.

―――――――――――

Lana spent the last hours of Christmas Eve on a red-eye flight from Chicago to Anchorage. There was no point in chartering a private jet to get her there faster.

At thirty thousand feet, draining a glass of champagne as she looked down at the darkness outside her window, Lana wondered at what point she'd lost all her perspective. Probably the day she'd walked into the town hall meeting and Rick Harding had smiled at her. Close or far, it didn't matter. There was no perspective, not when all she could see was him.

It would be easy to simply let him go. Painful, but easy. He wasn't wrong—she would always feel a pull back to him when she was working abroad. The difference was Lana wanted that pull. She wanted a place and a person to come home to. Someone and someplace that wanted her there too.

A layover in Seattle gave Lana an hour to kill. She didn't bother to check the time before calling her mother. No matter what else their failings, Montgomerys always answered at any hour. Jessica picked up on the third ring.

"It's a long flight alone, isn't it?" Jessica said sympathetically, skipping a greeting. "How are you holding up?"

"Longer than usual." Lana was grateful for her mother's

voice. "Mom, how do you do it? You and Dad? How do you make it work when you're always gone? Don't you resent each other?"

Jessica was quiet for a very long time. Then she said simply, "We love each other. That's always been enough."

Closing her eyes, Lana asked softly, "And you don't regret it?"

"Not for one second of one day. He gave me you, Lana."

The love her mother felt for her came through so strong and so certain, Lana couldn't help but feel hope welling through her. Of course, her parents had married for love instead of business.

Lana knew what she was picking, if the choice was still on the table. She'd never know until she tried.

When the plane landed in Anchorage early on Christmas morning, Lana switched to a smaller aircraft to fly her to Moose Springs. For once, she didn't feel guilty about splurging. Lana drove straight to Rick's house before she lost her nerve. She didn't want to waste one more second without telling Rick the things she should have told him when he left. If he still didn't want to be together, then...well...Lana would simply deal with that when it happened.

It took every ounce of her courage to drive to Rick's place. So of course, he wasn't there. All Diego could tell her was that Rick had gotten home from a Christmas party and gone out into the woods. He invited her to wait inside, but Lana stayed out on the porch instead. Since Rick's car was parked in its spot, he'd be back eventually.

Feeling chilly and ridiculous, Lana was still waiting on the front porch steps half an hour later when Rick emerged from the woods behind his barn. He seemed lost in thought as he trudged through the snow, head down, so he didn't notice her car until he was almost to the house. When he realized her vehicle was in the drive, he stopped in his tracks, head snapping around. Lana's heart stopped too, at least for the moment it took for him to offer her that quiet smile of his. It was worn but real. Like him.

They had only been apart a few hours, but Lana had missed him so much.

Rick crossed the drive and approached the steps, looking at her with a confused expression.

"I took a red-eye," she said, feeling as if she should explain. "I wanted to be back here for Christmas. Diego said I could wait inside, but I didn't know if you wanted me here. Showing up after a breakup is kind of a stalker move."

"You're always welcome here," Rick said in a rough voice. "I'll never make you leave."

Rick winced at his own words. Lana didn't have the heart to throw them back at him, not when pain was etched across his face.

So instead, she gently said, "You just couldn't stay."

"Ever since I got on that damn airplane, I keep telling myself that it was the right thing. That you deserved better. But breaking your heart sure didn't feel like treating you better. It felt like being a scared idiot who lost the best woman he'd ever had." When Lana didn't reply, Rick stood there, fist clenching and unclenching helplessly at his side. "I don't know how to make it up to you. I left you when you needed me. I've been on the bad end of that, and I swore I'd never do it to someone. But I did it to you."

Lana didn't even try to stop the tears welling up in her eyes.

Rick had always gotten to her, and she wasn't afraid to let him see her upset. Not anymore.

He took a step, instinctively moving toward her when she was crying. Then he stopped, giving her space like he had the first night at the town hall, as if not sure of his welcome.

"My personal bubble is less inflated than most," Lana reminded him, because he would always be welcome with her too. Welcome, wanted, desperately needed…all of it. Everything.

"Mine's destroyed," Rick whispered. "Being with you ripped that shit in half and threw it away."

Lana's hands were shaking worse than ever before. She didn't know if she had the courage to tell him what she needed to say.

"I'm so sorry, Lana. I don't know how to make this up to you. I tried all night to find that damn moose. I knew I'd hurt you, and I didn't know what I could do to make up for it. I thought maybe this time…"

When Rick trailed off, Lana rose to her feet and met him at the bottom of the steps. "Maybe life would cut you a break?"

Rick just shook his head, pushing on. "I'll try again tomorrow. I'll keep trying until I find it. I know how important this is to you, so I won't quit on this. I give you my word."

And when a man like Rick gave his word, he kept it. Too bad the moose was the last thing Lana cared about.

"A moose isn't what I need from you."

His expression turned bleak, but Rick just nodded. "Yeah, I understand."

"Actually, I don't think you do." Lana looked up at Rick, her heart pounding in her chest. "I came back because it's Christmas.

And I didn't want it to be Christmas without telling you how much I—" She stopped, the things she wanted to say sticking in her throat. "I know being with me is complicated for you."

"Lana, I love you. I've loved you since you almost killed me with a tranquilizer dart. It's not complicated. It's simple." His words were quiet, exhausted, as if loving her was a weight he was carrying. Or maybe loving her and not having her.

Loving him and not having him was slowly killing her.

"You deserve everything," Rick continued. "The best I can give you is not being dragged down by me."

"No."

"No?" He quirked up an eyebrow.

"I'm refusing your explanation. The terms are unacceptable."

"Love isn't a contract," Rick said, shaking his head.

"What if it was? My shoes will always click. I can't change that. I don't want to. But who you are, everything you are, is everything I need. So if that's the only thing keeping us apart, then I'm calling bullshit. You need to do better."

"You're not going to let me break up with you?" He sounded astonished. And her heart was crashing in her chest, because in his eyes was hope.

"I'm countering your offer of a breakup with a happily ever after."

"Your company—"

"It's my decision. It's my life. I have the right to be happy, Rick. So here are the best terms I have. I love you," she said simply. "You're the first, really. And I'm hoping you'll be the last. Because if this is what love is like, it's..."

She hesitated, voice catching.

Warm, strong hands took her face in them, broad shoulders blocking away the rest of the world. "It's what, Lana?"

"It's scary. Terrifying. I want to throw up a lot of the time, and Montgomerys do *not* throw up."

Lana found herself blinking away the tears in her eyes, his fingers wiping away the ones she missed.

"I don't know how to keep being me without you. I can figure it out, but I really don't want to. Because you're the best man I've ever known. The terms I'm proposing are these: me and you. No termination clause, because no matter what, I know what we have is real. I know we can make each other happy because we already do. These last two weeks have been the best of my life, and that's not because of my job. It's because of *you*."

She had more; she could do this better. Lana knew she could.

"I also promise you get the side of the bed you like the most, killer sex every time I get back from a business trip, and the remote at least twenty percent of the time."

"Forty-five," Rick countered.

"Twenty-five," she said. "Not a moment more."

Rick took her hands, folding them inside larger, rougher fingers.

"Lana, are you sure? Leaving you once is all I've got in me. I don't have the strength to do it again. If you really want this, if I'm enough for you, then I'm not going anywhere. Not for the rest of my life."

Rick's heart was on his sleeve, his eyes locked onto her. A man who loved her. A man who needed to know he was safe with her too.

"You're all I need," she said softly. "I'll carve it in snow on the mountainside if that's what you need to believe me."

Rick closed his eyes, took a deep steadying breath—as if the air in his lungs had been missing for far too long—and then he nodded. "Terms accepted."

And just like that, Lana had closed the most important deal of her life. Rick pulled her in close, kissing her the way she'd desperately missed in the short time they'd been apart.

"Should I have my lawyers draw this up?" she asked, breathless.

"It's a verbal agreement. Our happily ever after is legally binding." His lips curved against her ear. "Come on, gorgeous. It's Christmas. Let's go home."

Home was three steps up to a worn porch swing and a door that had seen better days.

Diego had a bowl of cereal waiting for each of them.

EPILOGUE

WHEN THE YEAR ENDED IN Moose Springs, it ended in style. Fireworks, festivities, a "who can last longest buck naked on a block of ice" contest, more fireworks. The whole nine yards. Food and alcohol were consumed in copious amounts. Someone always ended up drunk on top of the Locketts' roof.

Considering how heavily Jonah was drinking when Lana and Rick had snuck away, the officer was the most likely to earn that distinction, although Lana didn't blame him. Graham had been sworn in the day after Christmas, and the first thing Graham had done as mayor—with a bit of funding from Lana—was hire a deputy policewoman. Jonah deserved a night off.

Lana and Graham worked together well. Too well, honestly, which meant at some point, Graham was going to have to admit he was right for the job. Maybe on his deathbed, he'd get around to it. Which freed up Lana to continue waging her war against Silas. It had taken calling in every favor she had accumulated with her family members and promising future support on other projects to push them into agreeing to sell the Moose Springs commercial properties back into the hands of the people who deserved them:

the town. Nearly everyone wanted to buy, but not all could secure funding, so Lana had started pulling strings with the Anchorage banks to force those loan applications through.

She'd flexed more muscle, called in more favors, and strong-armed more people than she ever had in her life, and that had just been in the past week. But it looked like the private businesses were going back to their owners. Even Rick was getting his place, despite his limited capital. The effort invested had been more than worth it.

Lana didn't know what was going to happen to her condominiums. It was possible the town would use their increased voting power to push her out. But maybe not. In the meantime, Lana had tried to do her part to help by suggesting to Jax that the resort might benefit from a private investor, one whose money was built on her own portfolio instead of her family's prowess. So far, Jax hadn't gotten back to her on that one. He was too busy celebrating the New Year in style.

The last she'd seen him, Jax had been one of the brave ones still sitting naked on an ice block in the Locketts' front yard.

Lana had been to a lot of New Year's parties in her life, but nothing had been anywhere close to the party she and Rick had together after leaving, cuddled in front of the fire on Rick's couch. He must have figured out her preference for sleeping on them, because they'd stayed right there all night long, without a bottle of wine or a glass of champagne in sight.

There was a hedgehog in a Christmas sweater, a grumpy cat in an uglier Christmas sweater, and a kitten that liked to chew on them, but Lana was willing to share. Rick had a big enough heart to love them all.

She didn't know exactly what this relationship would end up looking like. She was still going to have to travel, even though she was setting up her own office in Moose Springs (as close to Frankie's bakery as humanly possible). But they'd agreed that for every week they spent apart, they'd make sure to spend three together.

And if the Montgomery Group didn't like that? Too bad. Lana finally had a home and a place she belonged. She wasn't going to waste that precious gift for one single second.

As the fire died down, the clock on her phone clicking over to six in the morning, Lana slipped out from beneath the blanket she and Rick had shared on his couch, padding to the door. She had always greeted every new year, every new beginning. Even as things changed, who Lana was would always stay the same.

Rick opened his eyes when she slipped on his jacket and tucked her feet into his boots. Then his lips curved as he closed them again, rolling over into the space she'd left next to him. Trust took time, and it would be a long time before the scar tissue in his heart completely softened, giving way to the belief that she wasn't going anywhere. That he was more than enough for her. But clomping her way outside in Rick's oversize boots was a start.

The world was at its darkest this early in the morning, and the thick blanket of snow had muted the forest into the kind of silence that one experienced only a few times in their lives. For Lana, with the silence came peace. As she leaned against the railing of Rick's porch, the moon slowly drifting across the sky, a moose stepped out of the forest.

At first, she didn't understand what she was seeing, not until it moved fully into the yard.

Never had she seen a female moose so delicate, so tall and perfectly proportioned, her sleek coat gleaming beneath the moonlight in a white so pure, it took Lana's breath away. An albino moose.

Then that perfect moose destroyed the carefully constructed Christmas display in front of Rick's porch, as if the lights were a cobra and she was determined to save them all. The Santa Moose stepped back, snorting a breath into the air.

Yep. One more job well done.

Lana knew exactly what that was like: hurting something in the hopes of fixing the problem. The only difference was the businesses of Moose Springs were far more resilient than a string of holiday lights. They'd given her a second chance, and she was determined to make the most of that chance. Unlike this incredible moose, Lana had good people willing to stand by her, even when she screwed up. People to help show her the error of her ways. Moose Springs had never needed Lana to save them. There was only one thing they had ever needed from her.

"Rick?" she called into the house, eyes never leaving the ghost slipping off into the forest.

"Yeah?" He already sounded resigned. The man loved her... and he knew her too well. Lana never had been able to resist a challenge, and Moose Springs was her home. She was determined to prove she was worthy of it. She just needed a good lure.

"I'm going to need you to put that Santa suit back on."

ACKNOWLEDGMENTS

IT'S FUNNY WHAT STARTS THE idea for a book. In the case of *Mistletoe and Mr. Right*, it all started with a penis on a mountainside. And a moose gone rogue. Then it just sort of took off from there.

I'm a sucker for a love story between two lonely people, and I have a special place in my heart for Lana and Rick. One bigger than life, one quiet and shy, both ready to just find each other already. The holidays are a special time, but they can also be especially lonely. It makes my heart happy that these two never have to spend another holiday apart.

As always, this book wouldn't be here without a lot of people's hard work, dedication, and support. Publishing is absolutely a team sport, and I'm so grateful for my teammates!

The biggest thanks will always be to my husband, Kenney. You bring so much light to my life. Thank you to my family for your amazing support every single day, and as always, thank you to God for this life that I love so much.

Thank you to my editors, Mary Altman and Christa Désir, for your patience, insight, and guidance on this manuscript. Your brilliance made *Mistletoe* come to life! Thank you to Stefani Sloma, Sarah Otterness, and the entire Sourcebooks team for all your hard work, each and every day. You are all amazing!

As always, thank you to my agent, Sara Megibow, for being the best agent I could ask for. You make being a published author so much less scary.

Thank you to my GH sisters for being there through this publishing journey, every step of the way. Thank you to all my talented critique partners for your help making this book come together. Special thanks to C.R. Grissom, Laurel Kerr, and Leigh Sullivan. C.R., thank you for always being so generous with your time and for your attention to detail. Laurel, thank you for all the plot hunting and advice on this story. Talking destructive moose and plastic elves with you is a blast! Leigh, you always save my tail with your eagle eyes.

Most of all, thank you to my readers. I hope this book brings you a little slice of Christmas joy.

ABOUT THE AUTHOR

GEOLOGIST AND LIFELONG SCIENCE NERD Sarah Morgenthaler is a passionate supporter of chocolate chip cookies, geeking out over rocks, and playing with her rescue pit bull, Sam. When not writing contemporary romance and romantic comedy, Sarah can be found traveling with her husband, hiking national parks, and enjoying her own happily ever after. Sarah is the author of the Moose Springs, Alaska series, including *Publishers Weekly* starred novel *The Tourist Attraction*.

ROMANTIC COMEDY AT SOURCEBOOKS CASABLANCA

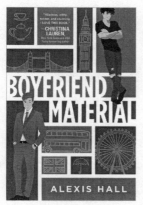

Boyfriend Material

Wanted: One (fake) boyfriend.
Practically perfect
in every way.

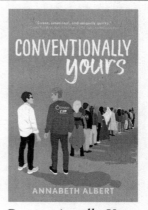

Conventionally Yours

Two infamous rivals.
One epic road trip.
And a journey neither will ever forget.

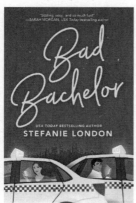

Bad Bachelor

Everybody's talking about the hot
new app reviewing New York's
most eligible bachelors. But why
focus on prince charming when
you can read the latest dirt on
NYC's most notorious bad boys?

The Tourist Attraction

Welcome to Moose Springs,
Alaska: a small town with a big
heart, and the only world-class
resort where black bears hang out
to look at you!

Mistletoe and Mr. Right
The holidays are happier when
you find a place to belong.
Especially if it's with your true
love…and a Scrooge-like moose.

Enjoy the View
A grouchy mountaineer, a Hollywood
starlet, and miles of untamed
wilderness…
What could possibly go wrong?
**Coming to Sourcebooks Casablanca
January 2021!**